A KISS FOR CATHERINE

"Why did you come after me?"

"Because I could not help it," said Jonathan. "I knew I ought not to follow you here, but when I saw that fellow making sheep's eyes at you—well, it was more than I could take. You don't care for him, do you, Catherine?"

"You know I do not. There is only one man I care for."

"Don't speak like that! I don't want you to love anyone else."

"If I did love anyone else, it certainly wouldn't be Mr. Poole."

She meant it as a joke, but Jonathan was past joking. With an oath, he gathered her into his arms. "I won't let you love anyone else," he whispered. "I won't!" Lowering his lips to hers, he kissed her, a hard, possessive kiss that seemed intent as much on subduing as seducing. . . .

Dear Readers,

Desire, dreams, and destiny—with a healthy dose of betrayal, villainy, and adventure—are the very things songs have been written about for centuries. And Ballad Romances is our love song to you: a brand-new line featuring the most gifted authors in historical romance telling the kinds of stories you love best.

This month, we launch the line with four new series. Each month after that, we'll present both new and continuing stories—and we'll let you know each month when you can find subsequent books in the series that have captured your heart.

Joy Reed takes us back to Regency England with the first book in *The Wishing Well* trilogy, **Catherine's Wish.** In this enchanting series, legend has it that, when a maiden looks into the Honeywell House wishing well, she sees the face of her future betrothed—with decidedly romantic results. Next, celebrated author Cynthia Sterling whisks us off to the American West with **Nobility Ranch,** the first in an uproariously funny—and sweetly tender—series of *Titled Texans* who have invaded America with their British nobility intact, and their hearts destined for life-changing love.

An ancient psychic gift is the key to the *Irish Blessing* series—and a maddening, tantalizing harbinger of love for the Reillys of the mid-nineteenth century. New author Elizabeth Keys weaves a passionate tale of the family's middle son in the first book, **Reilly's Law.** Finally, Cherie Claire invites us into the world of *The Acadians* in the 1750s, as **Emilie**—the first of three daughters of an Acadian exile—travels to the lush and sultry Louisiana Territory—where desire and danger go hand in hand. Enjoy!

Kate Duffy
Editorial Director

THE WISHING WELL
CATHERINE'S WISH

JOY REED

Zebra Books
Kensington Publishing Corp.
http://www.zebrabooks.com

ZEBRA BOOKS are published by

Kensington Publishing Corp.
850 Third Avenue
New York, NY 10022

Copyright © 2000 by Joy Reed

Zebra and the Z logo Reg. U.S. Pat. & TM Off.

First Printing: July, 2000
10 9 8 7 6 5 4 3 2 1

Printed in the United States of America

*Dedicated with gratitude to
Dr. Nancy L. Brooker,
beloved sister and invaluable authority on
all things botanical and gemological*

CHAPTER I

"Catherine dear, are you going out?"

Catherine turned around reluctantly. Her Aunt Rose was coming down the stairs, the heels of her little slippers tapping as she descended. Rose Payne was a diminutive woman in her mid-fifties, slight and fragile-looking, with a crown of softly waving white hair and a complexion as smooth and unlined as a girl's. At the moment, however, her face was drawn into an expression of deepest anxiety.

Seeing the anxiety on her aunt's face, some of Catherine's irritation melted away. She smiled at her aunt. "Yes, Auntie, I thought I'd walk over to Honeywell House," she said. "I finished the first volume of that novel Lady Laura loaned me and thought I'd get the next one if she was done with it."

She spoke with reassuring heartiness, but the anxiety on Aunt Rose's face did not lessen. "But surely you do not mean to go to Lady Laura's alone?" she said nervously. "Do take one of the maids with you, Catherine. It's been such a dark day that night is sure to fall early—and I am always nervous when you are out after dark. Besides, you must think of your reputation."

It was on the tip of Catherine's tongue to retort, "Am I ever allowed to forget it?" But instead she forced herself to smile again at her aunt. "It's all right, Auntie," she said. "I appreciate your concern, but you know it's only a step across the common to Honeywell House. It would be foolish to rout out one of the maids for such a short trip as that."

Aunt Rose looked more anxious than ever. "Yes, but I really think you ought not to go out alone, Catherine," she said. "In my day, a young lady never set foot outdoors without a maid or footman to bear her company."

Catherine sighed impatiently. "Things are different nowadays, Auntie," she said. "If we lived in a city like London, there might be some point in taking a maid or footman with me when I went out. But here in a little village like Langton Abbots, it cannot be thought at all necessary."

"Oh but I can never think it entirely safe for a young girl to go out alone. Not even in a village like Langton Abbots." Aunt Rose lowered her voice to a discreet murmur. "Remember what happened to that poor girl down at the Crown."

"I'm not a barmaid. I don't anticipate being attacked by a drunken lout." Catherine spoke curtly and then was sorry, as her aunt's face crumpled into a look of distress.

"Oh, no, of course not, Catherine dear. I did not mean to imply that you were at all in the same category as a barmaid, God forbid! But they do say she was quite badly injured, poor girl, and until the man responsible has been found and arrested, I cannot like to see you going out alone. I heard just yesterday that young Jackie Webb has now been proved beyond question to have nothing to do with it."

"That may be, but I don't see that it affects me one way or another, Auntie. I haven't noticed the other village girls had scrupled to go about alone in the weeks since it happened."

"Yes, but you are not quite like the other village girls, Catherine." Aunt Rose's voice was timid, but her blue eyes met Catherine's bravely. "I don't mean to be throwing up your past to you continually, but you know that in your position, you are obliged to be much more careful of your reputation than the other village girls.''

"It's of no use, Auntie." Catherine spoke with decision. "You've done a great deal for me, but no matter how much I cling to the conventionalities, I'll never be thought an entirely respectable person. Much better I should cultivate the reputation for eccentricity. It excuses so many things in people's minds.'' Catherine's mouth curved into a bitter smile.

"I was only concerned for your safety,'' protested Aunt Rose. in a not very convincing voice. Catherine shook her head.

"I'll be back in an hour or so, Auntie. Don't fret,'' she said, and escaped from the house before her aunt could say anything more.

Once outside the house, Catherine walked rapidly down the flagstone path that led to the gate. A fine display of late tulips blossomed on either side of the path, and several lilacs in full bloom cast their perfume recklessly on the air. Catherine walked with her head down, however, oblivious to the beauty around her. Only when she reached the gate did she pause to look back at the house she had just left.

Willowdale Cottage was a highly picturesque structure to which the term *cottage* could only be loosely applied. It was a cottage in the same sense that Westminster Abbey is a church, or the Palace of Versailles a little place in the country. Built by some long-ago nobleman as a country bower for his lady-love, it had served as home to the Payne family for several hundred years now. It had been Catherine's home for the last twelve.

As always, the sight of the house, with its hectically gabled roofline and crazy assemblage of chimneys, made Catherine smile. It was a smile of fondness, not of derision. In the twelve years she had lived there, Catherine had come to love Willowdale Cottage, and she had no wish to leave it now, as she assured herself, turning away from the garden gate. But her life there would have been much happier if her aunt had been less conscientiously tactful about alluding to Catherine's past.

By her very tact, she only seemed to throw into greater prominence that whole painful subject.

Catherine had been born the only child of a retired military officer, Major John Summerfield, and of his wife, the former Miss Lily Payne, who had been the younger sister of Catherine's Aunt Rose. For the first dozen or so years, Catherine's life had proceeded auspiciously enough. At the age of thirteen, however, she had had the misfortune to lose both her parents to an epidemic of influenza, and it was then that the real difficulties of her existence had begun.

Major Summerfield had been a well-to-do man, and his wife had possessed a private fortune of her own. The orphaned Catherine had faced no difficulties in the financial sense, at least. Neither had she seemed, at first glance, to lack the prospects of a loving and comfortable home. Under the terms of her father's will, she had been left jointly to the care of her two maternal aunts, Miss Rose Payne and Miss Violet Payne, who were residing in their own family home, Willowdale Cottage, in the county of Devonshire.

As soon as Rose and Violet Payne were informed of Catherine's orphaned state, they had instantly declared themselves willing to take charge of her. So the thirteen-year-old Catherine had gone to live at Willowdale Cottage, and the result had been tragedy, the effects of which had had quite as lasting an effect on her subsequent life as the death of her parents.

Rose Payne was a sweet, gentle, kindhearted lady who had done her best to make her niece happy in her new home. The worst that could be said of her was that she had a tendency to fuss, and this small failing Catherine was easily able to excuse, for she could see and appreciate the love that lay behind her aunt's anxious concern.

Her other aunt, however, had proved to be made of very different stuff.

Violet Payne had been the eldest of the three sisters, and perhaps it was that circumstance as much as any other that had encouraged her to see herself as a person of authority. She was a grim, rigid, humorless woman, priding herself on the strength of her principles but never seeing that something more than principle might be desirable in her dealings with other people.

With such a personality, she naturally tyrannized over her gentler, soft-spoken younger sister. And when Catherine had come to Willowdale Cottage, Aunt Violet had promptly begun to tyrannize over her, too. Catherine had found her days as rigidly ordered as any prisoner's. Her clothes, her friends, and her pastimes were all chosen for her, and her smallest transgression was subject to a punishment as stern as it was inflexible.

Understandably, Catherine had been unhappy under this regimen. Yet she had found it bearable so long as she had Aunt Rose to sympathize and soften the harshness of Aunt Violet's despotic rule. Aunt Rose never dared to openly flout her sister's authority, but she had nevertheless managed in small ways to ease Catherine's plight, smuggling food to her when she had been sent to bed supperless and consoling her when the rigid discipline of her existence seemed too much to bear.

Things might have gone on in this way for some time if Aunt Violet had been content to tyrannize over Catherine first-hand. When Catherine had reached the age of fifteen, however, she had decided her niece needed more both of discipline and instruction than she alone could provide. A friend of hers ran a young ladies' seminary in Cheltenham, and Aunt Violet was persuaded by this lady to send Catherine there, so that her formal education might be finished and her niece prepared for the position in society which her birth and fortune entitled her to take.

Miss Saddler's Academy for Young Ladies was advertised as "a select school, where attention is given to the acquisition of Christian principles as well as those accomplishments necessary to young ladies of gentle birth." In practice, it was a peculiar institution wherein Miss Saddler's own brand of Low Church theology rubbed shoulders uneasily with such fashionable accomplishments as music, dancing, and deportment. There were some four dozen pupils and half-a-dozen assorted

masters in the school, and over all these ruled the supreme
authority, Miss Saddler herself.

Catherine had not been at Miss Saddler's a week before
she found herself longing to be once again under her aunt's
domination. It was not so much that Miss Saddler's rules were
stricter than Aunt Violet's; that would have hardly been possible. What made Miss Saddler's so intolerable was the absolute
want of human interest or sympathy that Catherine encountered
during her stay there.

The other girls at Miss Saddler's had all, without exception,
attended the school from a much earlier age. This made Catherine an outsider whose presence was at best merely tolerated
and at worst openly reviled. The masters were either indifferent
or so ground down by the demands made on them by Miss
Saddler that they had no interest or sympathy left to give to
their pupils. Miss Saddler herself equated sympathy with softness and would have thought it as contrary to her principles to
show one as the other.

Six months of this existence was enough to drive Catherine
to the brink of despair. There was no one on earth she could
appeal to, no human soul who could rescue her from her plight.
Writing to her aunts would have been worse than useless. It
was common knowledge that Miss Saddler censored her pupils'
letters, and even if Catherine could have somehow smuggled
a letter through to Aunt Rose, she knew Aunt Violet would
veto any attempt on her sister's part to bring her home. Every
night, as she lay in her narrow bed in the dormitory shared by
forty-eight other girls, Catherine wished she was dead, or back
at Willowdale Cottage, or anything but who and where she
was.

Things had gone on in this way for nearly a term when the
school's elderly dancing master fell lame. All the male masters
at the school were elderly and verging upon decrepitude: Miss
Saddler distrusted the opposite sex and judged it unwise to
bring virile members of that sex into contact with forty-nine
young and all too susceptible schoolgirls. In a situation of such

extremity, however, she was reluctantly brought to set aside her prejudices. For the rest of that term, the dancing master was assisted during the active part of his instruction by his nephew Angelo, a young gentleman of nineteen years who had recently emigrated from his native Italy.

Catherine, performing cotillions and country dances under Angelo's professional guidance, had been as much impressed by the young man's gentle, unassuming manners as by his spectacular good looks. He was handsome to a degree that only Italian men attain, with expressive dark eyes, waving dark hair, and a glowing olive complexion. He was not particularly tall, but was in every other respect as physically perfect a specimen of manhood as one was likely to see. It was no wonder that the young ladies at Miss Saddler's united in declaring him "perfectly charming."

Catherine, for her part, felt a strong sympathy for the young Italian. Like her, he was an outsider at Miss Saddler's, and like her, he was clearly unhappy in his position. During dancing classes his uncle ordered him about like a slave and freely abused him in Italian whenever he was guilty of a misstep. Miss Saddler treated him as though he was merely admitted to the school on sufferance, as indeed he was. She would frequently come into the room while lessons were going on and stand surveying Angelo with her cold blue gaze as though to make sure he was taking no illicit liberties with her pupils.

Catherine had observed that, if anything, the reverse was true. Some of the older girls were quite forward in their behavior toward Angelo. Any number of provocative looks were cast at him when Miss Saddler's back was turned; any number of smiles and flirtatious remarks addressed to him while he was partnering first one young lady and then another about the floor.

Yet these stratagems were singularly ineffective. Angelo's behavior was always polite, but he had obviously been admonished by both his uncle and Miss Saddler not to speak more than absolutely necessary to the students. He never by look or word betrayed the slightest interest in the allurements cast so

Joy Reed

generously his way. Catherine was thus the more surprised when one day he addressed her spontaneously when they were practicing a boulanger together.

"You have been crying," he stated in a matter-of-fact voice.

This speech had so surprised Catherine that she had lost track of the steps she was counting and stumbled over Angelo's feet. Angelo had helped her right herself, then addressed her once more. "You have been crying," he said again, looking down at her with liquid dark eyes reminiscent of a Raphael Madonna's. "It is so, yes?"

"Yes," admitted Catherine cautiously. Out of instinct she kept her voice low, so as to avoid the notice of the dancing master in the corner. "Yes, I have been crying. But I had hoped—I had hoped it was not so noticeable that people would remark on it."

Angelo had scrutinized her gravely. "It would not be notice-able to most people, I think. But me, I have noticed. I have been watching you, you see."

"Have you?" said Catherine, again regarding him with sur-prise. Angelo had nodded, his expression solemn.

"Yes, and I do not wonder that you cry. You do not belong here, any more than I do." Lowering his voice to a whisper, he had added, "You are different, anyone can see that. You are different from these others." He glanced around the room with an expression of contempt.

"Yes," said Catherine fervently. No more could be said just then, for the dancing master was looking their way. Angelo had squeezed her hand and smiled warmly, and though they had exchanged no more words throughout the rest of the dance, Catherine went away from her lesson feeling a degree less downhearted than when she had come.

It was amazing what a difference it made to feel there was one person on the premises who sympathized with her plight. The slights and gibes of the other girls became a mere annoy-ance rather than a soul-destroying torment. For the first time since coming to the school Catherine was able to apply herself to her lessons and actually received a stiff encomium from Miss Saddler on the improvement in her scholarship.

It was not possible that Catherine should see Angelo very often, of course. Communication between them was limited to the few words they could exchange when the dancing master's back was turned, and later, when they began to grow frustrated with this very restricted intercourse, to an occasional note that Angelo slipped into Catherine's hand while they were dancing. Catherine felt this to be very romantic, though in fact there was nothing particularly romantic in her feelings toward Angelo. He was merely a friend and a fellow sufferer, but as such he was all she had at Miss Saddler's. As time went on, she came more and more to depend upon the prospect of seeing and speaking to him during their daily lessons.

Things had been going on in this manner for some time when disaster finally struck. Angelo had been very discreet at the beginning of his and Catherine's relationship, but he had become increasingly less so as time went on. On several occasions he had betrayed a slight but unmistakable partiality for Catherine during the course of the lessons. One of the other girls, made jealous by this partiality, had watched closely and detected a note being passed from Angelo's hand to Catherine's. She had immediately informed Miss Saddler of what she had seen. With no warning, Catherine had found herself called to Miss Saddler's private parlor to deliver a full accounting of the incident.

Catherine, most fortunately, had already secreted the note with its fellows in a hiding place she had devised beneath a loose floorboard. Miss Saddler was unable to find any evidence to prove a note had been written, but her suspicions were awakened, and she resolved to investigate the matter from the other end.

Catherine, knowing what fate awaited her unsuspecting comrade, sought desperately for a way to warn him. Miss Saddler saw to it that she had no opportunity to do so, however, and all that night she lay sick in bed, dreading the exposure she was certain the morrow must bring. Surely enough, when Angelo arrived at the school the next day, he was detained in Miss Saddler's parlor and a search made of his person. A note to Catherine was found—a note so innocent in its professions that it must have touched any heart with pretensions to human softness. But there was no softness in Miss Saddler's heart. Angelo was summarily discharged; the school plunged into an uproar; and Catherine, as Miss Saddler coldly informed her, forever disgraced.

It seemed to Catherine that her plight was black indeed. The best she could hope for now was to be sent home to Willowdale Cottage. This fate she could almost have welcomed, for whatever Aunt Violet's reaction, she knew Aunt Rose would be glad to see her return home. But she soon learned she would not escape so easily. Miss Saddler had decided, after due deliberation, to retain Catherine as a pupil, but under terms that amounted to virtual imprisonment. Outings were to be curtailed; her meals and lessons would be taken alone; and instead of sleeping in the dormitory with the other girls, she was to have a small room of her own up under the eaves, into which she would be locked each night by one of the housemaids.

"For you see," Miss Saddler had said, looking at Catherine coldly over her spectacles, "if we cannot *trust* you to behave properly, we must take steps to see that you have no opportunity to do anything else."

When this sentence was read to her, Catherine managed to preserve a semblance of calm. She was determined not to give way to her emotions under Miss Saddler's unsympathetic eye. In this endeavor she was successful, but her composure gave way that evening when the housemaid Annie appeared to lead her away to her cell. Annie shook her head at Catherine's tears, however, and advised her not to take on so.

"Never you mind, miss. It's not so bad as all that," she whispered. "Just you wait till we get upstairs. I've something for you in my pocket that'll make you feel a deal better if I'm not mistook."

Puzzled but intrigued, Catherine obediently dried her tears and followed Annie up the three flights of narrow stairs that led to the garret. Once there, Annie made a great show of closing and locking the door, then drew from her pocket a closely folded note, which she pressed into Catherine's hand.

"From Master Angelo," she whispered. "He came round this afternoon wild to see you, miss. I told him the business'd be a deal better managed by writing, and that if he wrote you a letter I'd see you got it and wait for a reply. Go on, read it, miss. The time's short, and we'd best work quick if old vinegar downstairs isn't to get wind of the business."

Wondering, Catherine had unfolded the note. In a dozen ungrammatical but passionate sentences, Angelo had railed against the cruelty of Miss Saddler, bewailed the loss of his position, and declared his intention of seeking his fortune in the greener pastures of London. He went on to declare it his fondest hope and desire that Catherine should accompany him to London. If she was willing to trust to the industry and perseverance of her Angelo, he would see that she never had cause to regret it. A carriage would be brought around to the side gate just at midnight; if Catherine planned to accept Angelo's proposition, she should collect what luggage she could and put herself in the hands of the maidservant Annie, who had declared herself willing to assist the lovers to the utmost of her ability. Angelo closed his letter by signing himself Catherine's most loving and respectful servant and—he trusted in time—her most devoted husband.

There was much food for thought in this letter. Catherine could have spent a fortnight pondering the decision Angelo was asking her to make, but in fact she had only a few hours until the carriage would be at the gate. Annie was impatiently awaiting her response, obviously supposing that Catherine would be as eager to be reunited with Angelo as he was with her. Her future at Miss Saddler's looked bleak—so bleak that any alternative appeared welcome. And Angelo himself had sacrificed so much on her account. He had lost his position because of her, and now here he was, offering her proof of his love and devotion in a manner that would have touched any girl's heart. What could she do but accept?

Even at sixteen, even with a complete lack of previous experience with love and lovers, Catherine was aware that she was not truly in love with Angelo. But if she was not in love, she did at least feel something like love for him; and she reasoned that this was enough. Besides, the situation was such a romantic one, and her prospects, as viewed from her present position, so uniformly grim and uninviting. She really had nothing to lose by casting respectability to the winds. No matter what she might regret by eloping with Angelo, she was sure she must be happier than if she remained at Miss Saddler's.

The escape itself was easily managed with Annie's help. Shortly before midnight, Catherine and her baggage were smuggled down the backstairs and out to the carriage that was waiting at the gate. Angelo was there, looking dashing and romantic, with his hat pulled low over his eyes and the collar of his coat turned up. He would have taken Catherine in his arms as soon as she appeared, but Catherine found herself shy all at once in the company of her future bridegroom. She turned instead to Annie, who was regarding her and Angelo with the satisfied expression of one who has single-handedly brought a difficult affair to a successful conclusion.

"I do hope you don't lose your place over this business, Annie. Even if Miss Saddler doesn't realize you helped me escape, I am sure she will blame you when she finds me missing. Perhaps it would be better if you came to London with Angelo and me."

This Annie declined to do, however. She said cheerfully that there were other and better places in Cheltenham than Miss Saddler's, and that she had been minded to take one of them for some time now. She then urged the eloping couple to be off before Miss Saddler should wake and discover what they were about. Angelo heartily concurred with this advice, and

Catherine was bundled into the chaise and whisked away to begin a new life in London.

The two weeks that followed had assumed a dreamlike quality in Catherine's memory. She had trouble now remembering the separate events of that time. It was merely a blur of unwonted activity and color; of dirt and discomfort and guilty excitement, flavored with a growing sense of disillusionment.

True to his promise, Angelo had made an effort to marry Catherine as soon as they arrived in London. But it had proved unexpectedly difficult to find a clergyman willing to marry two minors, neither of whom belonged to a local parish, neither of whom had parents to give their consent, and neither of whom had funds for a special license. So it had been necessary to dispense with a marriage certificate for the time being. When this fact was explained to Catherine, she had accepted it without a murmur, for by this time it hardly seemed to matter. She was already committed to her course, and a degree more or less of irregularity only added to the piquancy of it all.

Angelo had found lodgings with a cousin of his, who owned a rooming house in a seedy part of the East End. The single room his cousin grudgingly allotted them was shabby, cramped, and not very clean, but Angelo had assured Catherine that it was only a temporary refuge. Soon he would find work, and then they would find somewhere better to live.

This statement. too, Catherine had accepted without a murmur. Like the absence of a marriage certificate, a touch of dirt and shabbiness seemed hardly to matter. Indeed, the tiny attic room with its battered bed and bolster, tattered linsey-woolsey curtains, and glaring lithographs had at first possessed a certain squalid charm for Catherine. If it was none of it very new, it was at least new to her, and she found enjoyment in contrasting it with the cold austerity of Miss Saddler's establishment.

The new life had been rather fun at first. There was a *vie bohème* gaiety to it all that caught Catherine's imagination and made up for a great many trifling inconveniences.

Angelo took her out at night to public dances and concerts

and on one occasion to Vauxhall Gardens, where they ate ham and chicken, drank arrack punch, and watched a balloon ascension. They had cheap seats at the theater and went by hackney cab to visit Astley's Amphitheater. It all seemed at first much better than Catherine had dared hope.

To be sure, relations on the personal level between her and Angelo were not quite what she had hoped for. Being a nicely brought-up girl, Catherine had up till this time had only the vaguest ideas about physical relations between men and women. What ideas she did have were mostly gleaned from novels, which were wont to leave the mechanics of lovemaking hazy and concentrate instead on the soaring emotions that both parties invariably experienced.

Catherine experienced no soaring emotions. She gave herself to Angelo because he seemed to desire it and because, in the circumstances, she could think of no good reason to refuse him. Had she not already ruined her reputation by running away with him? And were they not to be married someday, after all?

At first the business of making love seemed to her both uncomfortable and curiously inefficient. After the first few times, the discomfort lessened, but still there were none of the passionate outpourings of feeling she had been led to expect. Only once had she felt the beginnings of a sensation that seemed to portend something more promising. But it had come to nothing, and Catherine was never sure afterwards if she had imagined it or not.

The absence of rapture in her and Angelo's physical relationship might be said to mark Catherine's first disillusionment with her paramour. It was not destined to be her last, by any means.

For one thing, work proved much harder to find than Angelo had predicted. He would go out confidently at the beginning of the day, only to return in the evening tired and dejected. After a few such disappointments, he became disinclined to risk rejection and preferred to spend the day sitting in his and Catherine's room, complaining about the injustice of his position.

Catherine had been sympathetic to such complaints before, when there had been Miss Saddler to blame for both their difficulties. Here, however, she could see nothing to blame but Angelo's own want of initiative. She tried to remain cheerful and encouraging for his sake, but it was gradually borne in upon her that the man she had looked to for support was a weak prop indeed. Angelo took to drinking; became surly; snapped at her, then wept with repentance, and in general behaved in a manner calculated to lose what little respect Catherine still entertained for him.

Now and then he still talked hopefully of some future happy time when he and Catherine would be married. But it was clear from his remarks that he was looking forward to it more because he anticipated living off Catherine's money than because he desired the joys of the union itself. This came as a shock to Catherine, who had not realized that Angelo knew of her personal fortune. When he talked maudlinly of forcing her aunts to make her an allowance, she resolved silently that he should never obtain so much as a penny of her inheritance.

In the meantime, of course, money was growing very short. Angelo had spent his small savings freely at first, supposing he would soon obtain work and that there was no need to economize. Now he continued to spend, while refusing to even look for employment. His cousin began to look darkly upon them and to drop hints that he could not spare the use of his room indefinitely. Catherine was thinking seriously of going out to find work for herself when her aunts finally succeeded in tracking her down and arrived at Angelo's cousin's house to take her home.

Catherine had welcomed them with open arms. Even Aunt Violet had seemed rather touched by her niece's evident relief and gratitude at being rescued. She had spoken no word of reproach to Catherine while they remained in the house, but had rather turned the full force of her wrath on Angelo, his cousin, and everyone else who happened to be within range. Angelo was given to understand that no marriage would ever take place between him and her niece; that he was never to communicate in any way with Catherine in the future, or to presume upon what had happened between them in the past. It was intimated that, if he knew what was best for him, he would go back to Italy and forget the entire episode.

Catherine had quietly submitted to this enforced separation from her lover. She was too chastened in mind and spirit to do other than submit, but on this occasion she happened to be in full agreement with her stern aunt. She never wanted to see Angelo again, and if she could only have been assured she would not be sent back to Miss Saddler's, she felt she could have cheerfully endured any lesser punishment her aunt might have assigned to her.

Aunt Rose had seen to repacking her bags, and she had left Angelo and the shabby rooming house without a backward glance. Her aunts had taken her to a respectable hotel in a quiet quarter of London, and there had begun the great debate as to what her future life must be.

Aunt Violet was adamant that Catherine should henceforth live a life of exile as punishment for her sins. A location abroad was suggested or, more moderately, lodgings in Wales or Scotland. But Aunt Rose, with a spirit she had never shown before, insisted that Catherine should be allowed to return to Willowdale Cottage and live there as if her elopement with Angelo had never taken place.

So resolutely did Aunt Rose stand her ground on this issue that Aunt Violet was unable to make any headway. When, as a last resort, she had said that she would never consent to let Catherine set foot in Willowdale Cottage again, Aunt Rose had countered by saying that, in that case, she would sell her own share in the cottage, buy a smaller house nearby, and live there with Catherine herself.

This threat of breaking up the family property had moved Aunt Violet as nothing else could have. In a final burst of rancor, she had washed her hands of both Catherine and Aunt Rose, ceded her own share of the cottage to her sister, and gone off to make life difficult for some unfortunate cousins of hers living in Plymouth.

From that time on, Catherine and Aunt Rose had lived quietly together in Willowdale Cottage. Catherine had often thought how ironic it was that her misdeeds should have brought her a happier and more comfortable home than any she had known since her parents' deaths. She loved Aunt Rose, and for the most part they got on very well together. It was only now and then that Catherine found herself chafing at the restrictions of her position.

It was not that she was ungrateful, Catherine told herself now, as she walked across the village common. She knew, none better, how much she owed to her aunt and what would have been her plight without her.

Willowdale Cottage was located in the village of Langton Abbots, not far from the Cornish border. Despite its remote location, news of Catherine's misadventure had reached the ears of its residents long before Catherine herself had reappeared to take up residence in her aunt's cottage. Stares and whispers greeted her whenever she went out; and Catherine, still in her chastened mood, wanted nothing so much as to bury herself in that seclusion Aunt Violet had recommended. It was Aunt Rose who insisted that she conduct herself exactly as before; Aunt Rose who, with head held high, had forced her niece to enter the drawing rooms of Langton Abbots society once more; and Aunt Rose who, by her own assured behavior, had put to flight the more lurid of the rumors that had been buzzing about concerning Catherine.

It was amazing how complete had been Aunt Rose's success. There were still one or two high sticklers in the village who refused to entertain Catherine in their homes, but these were definitely in the minority. Some breath of scandal must always attach itself to the name of a girl who had eloped, of course, but the scandal had faded a good deal, and after so many years of irreproachable behavior Catherine was generally accepted by Langton Abbots society, if not precisely embraced. Indeed, there were a few people in the village who stoutly refused to see her as anything more than an injured innocent.

Chief among these was Lady Laura Lindsay.

Lady Laura was the daughter of the Earl of Lindsay, a wealthy and well-connected nobleman who had recently taken a house in the neighborhood of Langton Abbots. Lady Laura was beautiful, accomplished, and accustomed to moving in the highest circles of society. Notwithstanding these attributes, she was also the nicest girl Catherine had ever known. A light of warmth and understanding seemed to shine perpetually in her clear blue eyes. Her smile was as sunny as her golden curls, and she had never been heard to say a harsh word against anyone.

Catherine had first made the acquaintance of Lady Laura at one of the monthly Langton Abbots assemblies. Catherine was pretty sure that the local busybodies had already informed Lady Laura of the scandal attached to Catherine's past, but in spite of this fact, or perhaps even because of it, Lady Laura had immediately claimed Catherine as a friend.

There was no doubt that Catherine, in her position, could use friends. And Lady Laura's friendship had the additional advantage of silencing those few who were still apt to criticize her for going into society. Where an earl's daughter could find no wrong, it seemed presumptuous to suppose anybody else could. Thanks to Lady Laura, Catherine's stock of late had risen to a high unmatched since her chastened return to Langton Abbots.

Catherine was grateful to Lady Laura, but she could have wished sometimes that her friend was not so innately good and virtuous, so uniformly loving and generous in her words, thoughts, and actions. Catherine was all too aware of the difference between Lady Laura and herself, and it seemed to her that this difference prevented anything like a real friendship between them. How could Lady Laura ever understand the feelings and motivations of a girl like her, who did on occasion commit a selfish or thoughtless act—a girl who had blotted her copybook so early in life in such a spectacular manner and had ever since hotly resented the slights and snubs that had been cast her way? And if Lady Laura could be made to understand, was it not probable that her affection for Catherine would turn to horror and loathing?

To Catherine, it seemed only too probable. As she trod the well-worn path across the common, she hoped fervently for her friend's sake as well as her own that Lady Laura would never suffer such a painful disillusionment.

CHAPTER II

True to Aunt Rose's prediction, daylight was already beginning to fade by the time Catherine reached the great oak that marked the halfway point between Willowdale Cottage and Honeywell House. She continued doggedly on, however, leaving the well-traveled path across the Common to take a narrower footpath that went straggling off in a southwesterly direction. This path led Catherine, in succession, through a small spinney containing a cluster of workmen's huts; past the woods of the Abbey, the most important estate in the neighborhood, and past the disused quarry that had provided the stone to build it and several other local great houses. Here the path was bordered by an expanse of open heath, but it soon plunged into a small wooded valley. At the foot of the valley began the woods of Honeywell House, and only a little more walking brought Catherine to the gravel drive that led to the house's main entrance.

Honeywell House was a handsome Elizabethan manor built of gray Devonshire slate and set amid extensive formal gardens. A much older house of the same name had once stood on the same site, and in fact the ruins of this ancient house were still to be seen in the woods beyond the gardens. The property belonged to a certain Lord Westland, of whom almost nothing was known except that he possessed a large fortune and an eccentric reputation. The residents of Langton Abbots generally agreed that it must have been this last characteristic rather than the first one that accounted for his leasing Honeywell House to the Earl of Lindsay the previous autumn.

Catherine mounted the front steps of Honeywell House and knocked briskly at the front door. A footman in livery with powdered head admitted her to the house's entrance hall. It was typical of the Lindsays to cling to such niceties as hair powder for their servants, even when most of their neighbors were abandoning them. Catherine was shown to a small parlor off the entrance hall while the footman went off to inform Lady Laura of her arrival.

Lady Laura herself appeared a moment later, a beaming smile on her face. "Oh, Catherine, I am so glad you are here," she said, embracing Catherine, then taking her arm and leading her across the hall. "Why ever did James put you in this stuffy little parlor? You must come into the drawing room with the rest of us."

Catherine, who had already heard the sound of voices and laughter issuing from the room across the hall, tried unavailingly to resist as Lady Laura pulled her toward the drawing room. "But you have a party, Laura," she said. "I did not mean to intrude, upon my word. I only came to return your book and get the next volume if you were done with it."

"But I don't have a party. It's only Mary Edwards and Isabel Wrexford. And certainly you may have the book, but you must come in and sit with us for at least a few minutes before you start back. Sit down right here, Catherine. I'll order more tea and see about fetching the book for you." Pressing Catherine into an upholstered armchair, Lady Laura gave her a warmly reassuring smile, then glided off to see about book and refreshment.

Catherine was left sitting with the other two girls, both of whom had looked up as she came in. They were neither of them strangers to her. Mary Edwards was the daughter of the local doctor and a plump, dark-haired girl a few years younger than Catherine. Catherine knew no harm of her save that she was inordinately fond of gossip. Isabel Wrexford was a different kettle of fish, however. The Wrexfords had been among those families most outspokenly critical of Catherine after her return to Langton Abbots, and even now they maintained their policy of disapproval, never inviting Catherine to any of their parties and vouchsafing her no more than the coldest of greetings when they encountered her in public.

True to form, Isabel gave Catherine a frigid nod, then folded her hands in her lap and lapsed into disapproving silence. She was a pale girl with frizzy curls, a narrow, sharp-featured face, and an angular figure. This last she generally sought to disguise beneath a mass of lace, ruffles, and ruching, and her dress today was no exception. The skirt of her bronze-colored pelisse was trimmed with several flounces and a profusion of velvet bows, and an abundance of puffs, epaulets, and ruffles on the bodice made the top half of her figure as obtrusive as the bottom. Mary, too, was elaborately dressed, her hair a mass of plaits and carefully curled ringlets. Catherine surmised they had come together to call upon Lady Laura and had dressed in their best out of deference to their hostess's rank.

The thought made Catherine smile, in spite of her irritation at Isabel's behavior. Her own toilette was a plain pelisse and matching round dress of green alpaca trimmed with black braid, while her chestnut hair was smoothly drawn back and pinned in a simple knot beneath her black felt toque. No greater contrast could have presented itself than her slim, upright figure when viewed against the frilled and furbelowed costumes of her two companions.

Mary, who shared none of Isabel's disinclination to talk, greeted Catherine in a friendly manner. "So you have come to visit dear Lady Laura, too? Isabel and I just dropped by on our way back from the Mabberlys'. A charming visit we had there, did we not, Isabel?''

"Charming," agreed Isabel in a bored drawl. Turning her eyes to Catherine, she added with significance, "I wonder we did not see you there, Miss Summerfield. As your aunt's cottage lies so near Mabberly Manor, I would think you would always be visiting back and forth.''

Since everybody knew that the Mabberleys, like the Wrexfords, refused to entertain Catherine in their home, this was hardly a tactful speech. Before Catherine could frame an adequate reply, she was saved by the reappearance of Lady Laura, who came bustling into the room with an apologetic smile. carrying the requested book in one hand.

"Here it is, Catherine. I'm sorry I was such a time finding it. One of the servants had put it in Mama's room by mistake. Ah, and here is the tea. Thank you, Mason.'' She smiled warmly upon the elderly maid who had just entered the room bearing a teapot and a plate of scones on a tray. The maid returned the smile as she deposited the tray on the table in front of Lady Laura. Catherine, accepting a cup of tea from her friend, reflected that there was a quality about Lady Laura that seemed to inspire nearly universal devotion. Mary also accepted a cup of tea, then resumed her attack on the subject that had apparently been under discussion when Catherine had arrived.

"I am sure you could tell us more if you wanted to, Laura dear. I have it on good authority that Lord Meredith has been seen not once but three times coming away from Honeywell House during the past week. And though I have the highest opinion of your papa, I cannot think it is Lord Lindsay that brings our wandering hero here so often!''

Lady Laura laughed, blushed, and shook her head. "You make too much of it, Mary. Lord Meredith has called here several times, but I am persuaded he only wished to consult with Papa about business.''

"And I am persuaded it is something else entirely.'' Mary regarded Lady Laura with an arch smile. "Do you mean to say

Lord Meredith has said no word to *you* during any of these visits?''

The flush on Lady Laura's cheeks grew deeper. ''Lord Meredith has been very kind,'' she said, a conscious smile hovering about her lips. ''He has told us all such interesting stories about India.''

''I am sure he has. I am sure he would like nothing better than to sit with you and tell you about his Indian adventures by the hour altogether. Upon my word, this looks serious, Laura. I believe the poor man has lost his heart to you.''

Catherine observed that Lady Laura did not deny it. Instead, she only laughed again and said, ''Well, you will have an opportunity to judge if you come to my party next Friday, Mary. I hope you will come, too, Isabel,'' she added, addressing Mary's companion, who had once more lapsed into silence. ''And you, too, of course, Catherine. I quite depend on you and your aunt being there. Do you know Lord Meredith?''

''I knew him a little, years ago,'' said Catherine cautiously. ''But our acquaintance was of the slightest. I doubt I would know him to see him now. Is he really back at the Abbey after all these years?''

The question was addressed to Lady Laura, but it was Mary who answered it. She turned to Catherine with the zest of a performer delighted to find a new audience.

''Oh, yes, had you not heard, Catherine? Lord Meredith returned to the Abbey two weeks ago, and they say he means to stay and put the property in order. Isn't it too exciting? First Laura and her family coming here to Honeywell House, and now Lord Meredith at the Abbey. I declare, our local society is becoming quite exalted all at once!''

Isabel gave a thin-lipped smile. ''For my part, I should not consider Lord Meredith any great asset to our local society,'' she said acidly. ''It's scandalous the way he has allowed the Abbey to run down. My papa says he ought to have sold it years ago if he did not mean to live in it.''

Mary protested this statement, and Catherine thought Lady

Laura, too, looked less than pleased by it. "It was very bad of him to neglect his property, no doubt," she said in her gentle voice. "But after hearing him talk, I am sure I cannot blame him for spending so many years abroad. India sounds a fascinating place. And you know he has also traveled in China and Japan and a great many other interesting countries."

"I am sure Lord Meredith had the best of reasons to spend so many years abroad, my dear Laura. You were not here when he lived in Langton Abbots before, but I assure you that his doings then were the talk of the neighborhood. It was quite scandalous how he went on. Why, by all accounts he was little more than a boy when he took up with the Widow Cooper. And later on there was that business with that dreadful Radner woman, the one he fought the duel over—"

"All that was years ago," said Lady Laura, cutting short Isabel's exposition with a warmth unusual to her. "And I expect most of what was said about Lord Meredith then was as greatly exaggerated as it is now." With the hint of another blush, she continued, "You must know that I have talked with Lord Meredith several times since he has returned. I am persuaded that, whatever he may have done wrong in the past, he means to turn over a new leaf now and live as a nobleman of his station should."

Although her blush had grown deeper, she spoke these last words with a finality that seemed to forbid any further discussion of the subject. Isabel made no effort to take it up, but instead turned to Mary. "We have been so busy talking of Lord Meredith that every lesser subject has been neglected," she said. "I am sure I have heard nothing new for over a week about this business of that wretched girl down at the Crown. Is it true that the creature is going to live after all? Your papa is the doctor, Mary, and you know we all depend on you to keep us up-to-date."

"Oh, yes, it's quite certain now that she will live," Mary assured Isabel. "Her injuries were not so serious as Papa feared at first."

"But it's true that she was assaulted, isn't it? Not just beaten, but *personally assaulted?*"

Isabel spoke the question in an avid whisper. Both Catherine and Lady Laura regarded her with disgust. Mary, however, replied quite readily, "Oh yes, there can be no doubt that she was molested. Papa wouldn't give me any of the details, but I know he was quite upset about it. He said he couldn't imagine what kind of a monster would treat a woman in such a way."

"She was only a barmaid," said Isabel contemptuously. "And it's common knowledge that she was perfectly depraved where men were concerned. I'm sure no one ought to be surprised if a girl of that class gets herself beaten and assaulted. It would only be justice if they were all so treated, in my opinion."

Catherine thought this might be a barb sent in her direction. But it seemed to anger Lady Laura more than anyone, for she exclaimed, "You cannot mean that, Isabel! I'm sure no one could wish such a terrible fate on any of one's fellow creatures. Whatever this poor girl's failings may have been, she can have done nothing to deserve such a horrible experience."

"No, and it's so frightening to think that her attacker is still loose," said Mary with a shudder. "I declare that I am quite afraid to walk out alone nowadays, even just across the street. I wonder that *you* dare to go about alone as much as you do, Catherine."

This remark, spoken in a curious tone, reminded Catherine that her aunt was awaiting her return. She rose to her feet.

"I'm afraid my aunt shares your scruples, Mary. I must be getting back before she grows worried. It is a pleasure to see you again, and you, too, Miss Wrexford. Laura, I must take leave of you now. Thank you for the tea and the book."

Lady Laura also rose to her feet and accompanied Catherine to the door. "I wish you need not go so soon," she said, looking at Catherine wistfully. "It seems you only just got here. And what with one thing and another, we have had no chance to talk at all." She was too polite to speak against Mary and

Isabel, though Catherine could see she had been irritated by
the other girls' presence. "Could you not stay and dine with
us?" she continued, looking at Catherine beseechingly. "I
know Mama and Papa and Oswald would be very happy to
have you. And there would be no difficulty sending you home
in the carriage, if your aunt dislikes you to walk after dark."

"No, thank you, Laura. You are very kind to invite me, but
I am expected for dinner at the Cottage. I am sure my aunt is
already waiting for me."

Lady Laura graciously swallowed her disappointment and
agreed that Catherine must not keep her aunt waiting. "But
you will come to my party for Lord Meredith next week?"
she urged, as Catherine turned to go. "I do wish you would,
Catherine. It would mean a great deal to me to have you there.
And I daresay Lord Meredith would like to renew his acquaintance with you."

So genuinely anxious did she seem to secure Catherine's
presence at her party that Catherine could not find it in her
heart to refuse her. "Perhaps, Laura. You know I must speak
with my aunt before giving a definite acceptance. But if she is
agreeable, I see no reason why we may not come to your party.
Thank you very much for inviting us." With a warm smile and
a last wave at her friend, Catherine set off again through the
woods toward home.

The sky was getting darker now, and the path through the
woods was fast being swallowed up by shadow. The clumps
of trees on either hand loomed dark and menacing in the fading
light, and every bush might have been the proverbial bear, or
something even more sinister.

Catherine walked quickly, trying not to think of Mary and
Isabel's conversation about the unfortunate barmaid and her
assailant. It was, she reminded herself, only a step through the
woods and another slightly longer step across the common.
And there was no reason to suppose that the assault of the
barmaid had anything to do with Langton Abbots in any case.

The Crown. near which the incident had taken place, lay on the outskirts of a neighboring village some miles away.

To divert her mind from the menaces with which her imagination insisted on peopling the landscape, Catherine reflected instead upon the things Lady Laura had said during her visit. Most particularly did she reflect on her conversation regarding Lord Meredith.

In common with most residents of Langton Abbots, Catherine was acquainted with Lord Meredith. During the time she had known him, prior to her departure to Miss Saddler's, he had not yet attained to his present title and dignities, but had been merely a dark-haired boy some years older than herself who had the reputation of never declining a wager or a dare. Catherine could remember seeing him in the village now and then, and she fancied she had even spoken to him on occasion, but her memories on the subject were exceedingly dim. On the whole they were favorable memories, however. She preserved a recollection of a laughing dark face coupled with a lively charm that was very attractive.

Of course, even back then there had been whispers about his behavior. Isabel had not exaggerated in saying that his youthful affair with the Widow Cooper had been a local scandal, and that had not been the only scandal that had tarnished his name during his residence at Langton Abbots. His crowning indiscretion had come at the age of twenty-one, when he had fought a duel with the husband of the lady who had allegedly been his current mistress.

Catherine was away at school by the time this episode had taken place, but she could still remember the furor it had caused. Her aunts' letters had spoken of little else for weeks, and even the Cheltenham newspapers had carried a reserved but disapproving account of the incident. What made it more shocking still was that Lord Meredith, the guilty party, had emerged from the encounter unscathed, while his opponent had been badly wounded—it was feared for a time, mortally wounded. This circumstance was held to cast a most discreditable light on the character of the young lord. It was no wonder that his father, in a fit of exasperation, had shipped Lord Meredith off to India to see what a prolonged sojourn in that country's torrid clime might do toward settling him.

By all accounts, he had prospered in India. Owing to the distances involved, reports of him had been necessarily few and far between, but the occasional news that had filtered into Langton Abbots had carried favorable accounts of his industry and acumen.

When his father had died unexpectedly, a few years after his migration to India, it was confidently expected that he would return home to the Abbey and settle down to a life of well-bred prosperity and ease like his ancestors before him. But Lord Meredith had confounded these expectations. Instead, he had chosen to travel farther afield—to China and Russia and even the mysterious island nation of Japan.

And now, having seen a good part of the world—and having enjoyed by all accounts more than his share of perilous adventures—Lord Meredith had decided to come home and settle at the Abbey. So Lady Laura had insisted, and Lady Laura's word was implicitly to be believed, as Catherine knew. Indeed, it seemed as if Lady Laura herself might have had a share in determining Lord Meredith's future plans. Reflecting on all she had heard of that gentleman's checkered past, Catherine thought that he and the gentle, virtuous Lady Laura made an unlikely pair, but there could be no doubt that Lady Laura was disposed to favor him. Her blushes when speaking of his intention of settling down told the story clearly enough.

"They say a reformed rake makes a good husband," Catherine told herself as she went across the common. "I hope that is true, for Laura's sake. I should hate to see her hurt."

It was completely dark by the time Catherine reached Willowdale Cottage. She was relieved to see the friendly glow of its unshuttered windows and the welcoming light thrown from the front door as her aunt came out on the porch to meet her.

"My dear, I was growing quite worried," said Aunt Rose,

the relief in her voice confirming the truth of those words. "Not but what I knew you must be perfectly all right at the Lindsays'," she added, with rather less truth. "But still I cannot think it healthy to be out in the night air. There was a prejudice against night air when I was a girl, and even now I cannot help but think there must be something in it."

"It has given me an appetite, at any rate," said Catherine, laughing as she threw off her hat and gloves. "Will you forgive me if I sit down to dinner without changing, Auntie? I'm afraid I'm a trifle late already, and you know I wouldn't offend Cook's sensibilities for the world."

"Certainly I do not mind, my dear." Aunt Rose led the way into the dining parlor, where the table was laid for two. Having seated herself at the table and seen that Catherine was seated also, she rang the bell, and the maids began bringing out the dishes. As Aunt Rose helped Catherine to roast duck, peas, and new potatoes, she inquired with interest after the inhabitants of Honeywell House.

"What had Lady Laura to say? I hope you found her and Lord and Lady Lindsay well—and her brother, too, of course. I remember your saying he had come to stay at Honeywell House recently."

"Yes," agreed Catherine, with a certain reserve. "But you know, Auntie, Sir Oswald is really only Lady Laura's half-brother. Lord Lindsay was a widower before marrying Laura's mother, and Oswald is his son by his first marriage."

She did not add that in her opinion, Sir Oswald was a blot on the Lindsay family escutcheon. He shared none of Lady Laura's sweetness and virtue. On the contrary, having found out from someone or other about Catherine's past, he had treated her ever since with a leering familiarity that was very hard to stomach. Catherine trusted that by now he had learned she was not open to his advances, but she was still glad to be spared his company whenever possible.

"Well, I hope Sir Oswald is well along with the others,"

said Aunt Rose, pursuing her former line of thought. "Is Lady Laura planning on attending the village assembly next month?"

"I don't know, for we didn't discuss it. It happens that she is giving a party of her own this next Friday. We are both invited, but I told her I would have to discuss it with you before I gave a definite acceptance."

Catherine had no real hope that Aunt Rose would refuse the invitation, for she knew her aunt's pleasure in parties of any kind. Nor was she wrong. Aunt Rose's face lit up at the magic word *party,* and she at once began to question Catherine concerning the invitation.

"Next Friday, you say? I see no reason why we may not attend, Catherine. Is it to be a large party?"

"I suspect so. The Lindsays seem incapable of doing anything on a small scale. Their 'party' will probably be more like what you or I would call a ball."

"I always loved a ball," said Aunt Rose, looking childishly pleased. "But is this not rather short notice to be giving a large party, Catherine? If it is to be on Friday, and Lady Laura is only now giving out the invitations—"

"It is rather short notice, I suppose. But I expect that is Lady Laura's doing. You know that in that household she reigns supreme. I believe there is nothing Lord and Lady Lindsay or the Honeywell House servants would not do for her if she asked. It's a wonder she isn't spoiled beyond bearing, but miraculously she is not."

"She seems a very sweet girl," agreed Aunt Rose with enthusiasm. "I must say, I was surprised when the Lindsays decided to settle in an out-of-the-way place like Langton Abbots. But I am very glad they did. Lady Laura is such a nice, well-bred, pretty-behaved girl—just the kind of girl I like to see you associating with, Catherine. You know I cannot consider the village girls really appropriate companions for you."

Catherine laughed bitterly. "I suspect most of them would consider me an inappropriate companion for them, Auntie!

Considering my scarlet past, I am lucky to be invited out at all.'' With a direct look, she added, "We need not pretend among ourselves, I hope. The plain fact is that I am damaged goods, Auntie. You know it; I know it; and so, I fear, does everybody else.''

Aunt Rose looked embarrassed but mulish, as she always did when Catherine's past was mentioned. "Everyone can know nothing of the sort, Catherine dear,'' she said, blotting her lips energetically with her napkin. "They may suspect, but they cannot know that you did anything of which you need be ashamed.''

"But I did,'' said Catherine with a twisted smile.

"Yes, but they have no proof of it,'' said Aunt Rose with energy. "And they should not assume without proof. That is the sign of a nasty mind, I always think—and that is one reason why I cannot like your being friends with the village girls. Some of them are very nice, I have no doubt, but the general tone of their minds is distressingly low.''

Catherine, remembering Mary and Isabel's conversation, was inclined to agree. To change the subject, she ventured to repeat the two girls' remarks concerning Lord Meredith. Aunt Rose was interested at once.

"And so Lord Meredith is returned to the Abbey! I am sure I am very glad to hear it. I always thought he was such a nice boy. It was a great pity that events fell out as they did for him.''

"To hear you talk, every boy you ever knew was a nice boy,'' said Catherine, smiling at her aunt. "And every girl was a nice girl. I suppose it is because people are constitutionally incapable of behaving other than nicely toward you.''

Aunt Rose flushed with pleasure at this speech but shook her head firmly. "Indeed, it is nothing of the kind. I always liked young Lord Meredith, and I always thought it most unjust that he should have been shipped off to India in that summary way. Many young men behave foolishly, after all. His papa ought to have made allowances—he was none too circumspect in his own youth, from all I have ever heard. And I suspect that if the truth about this duel business was to become known, that Radner woman would be proven to have incited the whole. I never liked her, you know. She always seemed to me a very coarse, unprincipled woman.''

"So you see Lord Meredith as an injured innocent, do you, Auntie?" said Catherine, hiding a smile. Aunt Rose saw through her pretense, however, and shook her head at her niece once more, a reluctant smile on her own lips.

"Not an innocent, no, but it is my belief that his behavior was more foolish than wicked, Catherine. And I am sure that if he did do wrong, he has atoned for it years ago. Say what you will, India cannot be a *comfortable* place, and it must be very lowering to be separated from one's home and family for so many years. I, for one, am very glad to see Lord Meredith back at the Abbey where he belongs. I hope he will be very happy there.''

Catherine concurred in this hope. Yet she could not help wondering privately if a life of travel and adventure might not be a happier one than was to be found in quiet Langton Abbots—especially for a person whose past was less than pristine.

CHAPTER III

Friday evening arrived at last, an evening much anticipated by the residents of Langton Abbots.

Catherine and her Aunt Rose were no exception. As soon as they had swallowed their dinners, they went upstairs to get ready for Lady Laura's party.

Catherine took her time bathing, then set about brushing and arranging her hair with meticulous care. She was equally meticulous when it came to arraying herself in the dress, gloves, and slippers she had chosen to wear that evening. To all appearances she was a young lady preparing for a delightful social outing, but in reality she was dreading the evening ahead: dreading it with an apprehension that was no less keen for being, by this time, tolerably familiar.

Of course there was no avoiding the ordeal that evening, as Catherine very well knew. Aunt Rose was looking forward to it eagerly, and it would not do to disappoint her. Likewise, Lady Laura was depending on her attending, and she could not disappoint her, either. Almost Catherine wished she were as immoral as Isabel and her other detractors claimed. If one were truly immoral, then one would presumably not feel guilty when one disappointed those who loved and trusted one. Catherine, surveying herself gloomily in the glass, told herself that she was doomed to suffer either guilt or its alternative, sick apprehension, all her life.

She had been to enough parties in the last nine years to have a fair idea what awaited her that evening. There was, for example, a near 100 percent certainty that she would suffer at least one direct snub from such bold antagonists as Isabel Wrexford and her mother. From antagonists less bold she would have to endure merely a series of stares, smirks, and whispers that suddenly ceased when she came into hearing distance. Even those ladies who did not snub her would in general treat her with reserve. If it had not been for Aunt Rose and Lady Laura, she would have felt friendless indeed among her own sex.

Nor could she expect better treatment from the opposite sex. It was true that gentlemen were never so deliberately hurtful as the ladies, but they could be just as cruel in an unthinking way. Either they treated her with cool and distant formality or—as in the case of Sir Oswald—they were unpleasantly familiar, behaving as though she was little more than a common harlot whom anyone might have for the asking. Sometimes the same gentleman had been known to exhibit both behaviors during the course of a single dance, depending on when his female relatives happened to be looking his way. It was this phenomenon that had decided Catherine against accepting invitations to dance on all but the rarest occasions.

So what she had to look forward to tonight was an evening spent wholly sitting on the sidelines, being treated to a series of snubs and slights and an occasional condescending kindness. Lady Laura would be kind to her, of course; that went without saying. Unfortunately, Lady Laura would probably be too busy dancing to spend much time with her friend. And if matters between Lady Laura and Lord Meredith were as Catherine suspected, then she would in all likelihood spend most of the evening with him to the exclusion of all others.

The best Catherine could hope for was to spend the evening chatting with her aunt, or with the vicar of the local church. Mr. Poole was an earnest and unattractive man in his forties who had taken over the living of Langton Abbots a little more than a year ago. Since then, he had shown a tendency to distinguish Catherine in small ways, sitting with her at parties, involving her in conversation, and coming to call on her and her aunt from time to time.

Of course it was impossible that he should pursue such a policy of open friendship with Catherine without being warned by some third party about Catherine's past. Catherine was certain that he *had* been warned about it, for the very good reason that he himself had mentioned the circumstance. At the same time, however, he had assured her that he would not let it weigh in his treatment of her.

"There is no sin so great that it cannot be forgiven a penitent heart, Catherine," he had told her, with the pompous air that was typical of all his speeches. "Remember that, and be sure that you have one friend at least who warmly applauds you in your daily struggle to 'go and sin no more.'"

Catherine had made a polite response, but inwardly she had been irritated by Mr. Poole's speech. Even if one was truly a magdalen—and Catherine supposed her two weeks in London might qualify her as a magdalen in Mr. Poole's eyes—it was not pleasant to be reminded of the fact in such a condescending way. In fact, it was downright irksome.

The truth, as Catherine owned to herself, was that her heart was not penitent at all. She spoke aloud as she surveyed her reflection in the glass.

"If I were truly penitent, I would not mind Mr. Poole preaching at me. I would not mind being snubbed by Isabel Wrexford and Lady Mabberly. I would welcome every slight and insult as the punishment I deserved for my sins. But I don't welcome it. I resent it."

CATHERINE'S WISH   43

Catherine spoke slowly, with an air of self-discovery. Again she surveyed her reflection in the glass. "Of course I am sorry, insofar as my behavior has hurt Aunt Rose. But for myself, I don't think I'm sorry at all. I did what I did at the time because I could think of no other way to escape an intolerable situation. And in fact I did escape it, although not exactly in the way I planned. If I were in the same situation again, I'd probably do the same thing, even knowing how it would all turn out.

"And not just because it got me rid of Miss Saddler and Aunt Violet." In Catherine's mind rose a memory of bustling city streets noisy with traffic and the cries of street vendors; of public houses, theaters, and assembly rooms shabby by day but full of light and color and gaiety by night; and of the pleasure she had once known in being young and free and part of that gaiety.

"There's a whole world out there that I never knew existed—a world that I never would have known existed if I hadn't run away with Angelo," she told herself. "The experience may have stripped away some of my romantic illusions, but I don't know that that's altogether such a bad thing. Sometimes, when I hear Laura and the other girls talk, it frightens me to hear how naive they are. I don't think it's any favor to girls to bring them up in such ignorance of the world. They must find out about it sometime, and when they do, they're bound to get a dreadful disappointment."

Once more Catherine thought of Lord Meredith, and of Lady Laura's betraying expression when she spoke of that gentleman. She hoped with all her heart that her friend would never experience the pain of discovering she had bestowed her heart on an unworthy object.

"For myself, I will never have to endure that pain again," she told herself. "Those two weeks with Angelo taught me more than twenty terms at Miss Saddler's would have done. I wouldn't give up what I learned in London for anything, even though I did pay a high price for it. And after all, it could have been much worse. My life may have its disadvantages now, but it's a thousand times better than it was before. Yes, it's better than it was before.''

The words brought a certain comfort to Catherine. She looked again at her reflection in the glass. What she saw was a slim girl, standing slightly over the medium height, with glossy chestnut hair drawn smoothly back into a knot at the nape of her neck. The girl's face was pale and heart-shaped; her eyes a curiously light golden-brown; and her mouth small and rather secretive.

Catherine smiled wryly at this last feature. It was no wonder if she was secretive, given the perils that self-expression must hold for a girl in her position. But apart from her mouth, she had no fault to find with her appearance. Certainly her dress was above reproach. Catherine looked with approval at her white silk dress with its deep V-neck and short shell-shaped sleeves. The skirt was plain, its single flounce surmounted by a row of delicate white-on-white embroidery whose subtlety did not detract from the elegance of the dress's lines. She might be one step away from an outcast, but she could still afford to dress as well or better than any other woman in the village.

Over the last nine years, it had become a credo with her to always appear in public serene and impeccably well-dressed. By holding her head high and going quietly about her business, she had managed to silence at least some of her critics. And if this was insufficient to silence such vocal critics as Isabel Wrexford and her mother, at least it might show them that their criticism was not going to stop her from living a full and tolerably happy life. Pinning a determined smile on her lips, Catherine turned from the glass, picked up her evening cloak and fan, and went downstairs to where her aunt was waiting.

Although it was little more than a mile across the common to Honeywell House, Aunt Rose could not think it proper to walk on such a formal occasion. Accordingly, the carriage had been called for, and with much pomp and decorum the

Willowdale Cottage ladies were driven the somewhat longer distance around the common and deposited on the doorstep of Honeywell House.

They were received with delight by Lady Laura, who came hurrying over to them as soon as they entered the saloon. She embraced Catherine, smiled warmly upon Aunt Rose, and found them comfortable seats near the improvised dance floor. "I am so glad you are here," she told Catherine in a low voice. "You will think it very foolish of me, but I was half afraid you might cry off at the last minute. Now call me a goose if you will. I know you told me you would come, and I ought not to have doubted your word."

Catherine, remembering the unwilling spirit with which she had come to the party that evening, was hard put not to blush at these words. To cover her confusion, she smiled and said, "I can hardly suppose you would miss me even if I had cried off, Laura. Such a crowd as you have this evening! I am sure everyone in the village must be here."

As Catherine spoke, however, it struck her that at least one village resident was not at Honeywell House that evening. Of course she had no idea what Lord Meredith looked like nowadays, but it seemed reasonable to suppose he would bear at least some resemblance to his youthful self. And in any case, there was no gentleman in the saloon who was not already known to her as a longtime inhabitant of Langton Abbots.

Lady Laura seemed to be thinking of the same thing, for her mouth drooped slightly. When she spoke again, her voice betrayed a note of hurt in spite of its determinedly cheerful tone.

"Lord Meredith is not here yet," she told Catherine. "I shall have to scold him well when he comes. He promised to be here in time to dance the first dance with me, and it is nearly time for the dancing to start now."

"Then be sure Lord Meredith will arrive very soon," said Catherine in a heartening voice. Her eyes flickered to the door as she spoke, and she smiled. "And if I mistake not, this is he now. He knows how to make an entrance, doesn't he?"

Lady Laura, too, looked toward the door. A vivid smile lit her face. "It *is* Lord Meredith! You will excuse me, won't you, Catherine? I must go and make him welcome, for you know he is our guest of honor this evening."

"Of course you must," agreed Catherine, smiling. She watched with indulgent amusement as Lady Laura hurried over to greet the man who had just walked into the saloon.

He was a tall gentleman with a lean, broad-shouldered physique nicely accentuated by his austere black and white evening clothes. His hair was dark, as was his complexion—the latter, no doubt, a result of his stay in the Indian sun. Yet this sunbrowned appearance did nothing to impair his natural good looks. Neither did his clean-shaven appearance, which was startlingly at variance with the masculine fashion for sidewhiskers and military-style mustaches. Altogether, he made a striking figure, standing there looking about the room with a faint smile on his handsome face.

His appearance caused a ripple of excitement to go around the saloon. People turned to look at him, first in puzzlement, then in dawning recognition. To all appearances Lord Meredith was oblivious to the sensation he was causing, but Catherine suspected he was aware of it and relishing it, too. There was a sardonic light in his eyes as he stood looking around at his fellow guests. Then his eyes lit on Lady Laura, and his expression softened suddenly to one of tenderness. He came forward to take her hands, murmuring something to her that made her laugh and change color.

"Then that's that," Catherine told herself. "He obviously does care for her." She was relieved for her friend's sake, yet there remained with her a vague sense of discontent as she watched Lord Meredith lead Lady Laura out for the first dance. Her feeling of discontent was heightened a moment later when Mr. Poole came over to speak to her, a smile lighting his homely countenance.

"Ah, Catherine! It is good to see you and your aunt here this evening, my dear. A delightful gathering, is it not?"

"Most delightful," agreed Catherine shortly.

The shortness of her answer did not prevent Mr. Poole from continuing the conversation. "You look very handsome this evening," he informed Catherine with heavy-handed gallantry. "It is a pleasant thing to see all our local beauties in full flower. I have already told Lady Lindsay that she is to be congratulated for the notion of bringing you together this evening."

"But I thought you did not approve of dancing, Mr. Poole?" said Catherine. She asked the question innocently enough, although she knew already what the answer would be. Mr. Poole had definite opinions on most subjects and no hesitation whatever about airing those opinions to anyone who would listen.

Surely enough, Mr. Poole at once embarked on a lengthy speech explaining why, although disapproving of dancing in principle, he could reconcile it with his conscience to occasionally attend a private dance in other people's homes. Catherine scarcely heard him. She was still watching Lady Laura and Lord Meredith going through the figures of a quadrille on the dance floor.

When the quadrille was over they came off the floor with the other couples. Catherine continued to watch them, finding them a good deal more interesting than Mr. Poole's homily. Lady Laura looked flushed with exertion and radiant with happiness. She was talking with Lord Meredith, smiling up at him as she spoke. Lord Meredith appeared to be listening with attention, his expression indulgently amused. But Catherine thought that once again, there was a tender emotion in his eyes as he looked down at her friend.

She had just made up her mind that he was more than half smitten with Lady Laura, and she wholly smitten with him, when he suddenly looked up. His eyes met Catherine's, and in that moment she experienced a shock such as she had never felt before.

It was not exactly a shock of recognition. Catherine had
recognized Lord Meredith earlier, when he first came into the
room, but she had experienced no shock then. This was recognition of a different sort. Catherine could not explain it; she could
only feel it, and the feeling left her weak and oddly breathless.
She sat there, gazing fixedly into Lord Meredith's eyes, until
recalled by a voice at her elbow.

"You are not attending, Catherine. Is something the matter?"

Mr. Poole's voice, sounding annoyed, came to Catherine
vaguely through the turmoil of her senses. "Nothing," she
said, wrenching her eyes away from Lord Meredith. Yet she
could not resist the urge to look back again the next moment.
Once more Lord Meredith's eyes met hers, and it was immediately borne in upon Catherine that he had suffered a shock,
too. He was staring at her as though he had seen a ghost.

Lady Laura had also noticed him staring. She turned to look
curiously in the same direction. Seeing that he was looking at
Catherine, she smiled and said something. He answered shortly,
his eyes never leaving Catherine's face. Lady Laura nodded, and
the two began to make their way across the room in Catherine's
direction.

Catherine found she was trembling. She was annoyed at
herself and rather alarmed, too. There had been moments in
the past nine years that had demanded a great deal of her, but
never had her self-possession abandoned her so utterly as it
had at the present moment. Making a heroic effort, she rose to
her feet. Mr. Poole said something, the tone of his voice expressing surprise, but his words were like so much buzzing in Catherine's ears. Her eyes were fixed on Lady Laura and Lord
Meredith, who had just joined her where she stood.

"Catherine, I must introduce to you our guest of honor,"
cried Lady Laura gaily, as soon as she was within earshot. "Of
course, you are already old acquaintances, but he does not
know that. He only knows you are a very pretty girl, and so I

thought I would give myself the pleasure of re-introducing you, so he might have the pleasure of admiring you at first hand. Catherine, this is Lord Meredith; Lord Meredith, this is my friend Miss Summerfield, whom you must remember from your boyhood days in the village.''

It never occurred to Catherine that this was a very arch and uncharacteristic speech for Lady Laura. Neither did it occur to her that the smile accompanying her friend's speech was a trifle forced. She was looking once more into Lord Meredith's eyes, and as she looked she experienced once again the jarring sense of shock and recognition that had shaken her a moment before. With it came a different kind of recognition. ''Jonathan,'' she said, the name coming to her suddenly from some disused quarter of her memory.

''Catherine,'' he returned, with a look of bemusement. ''Little Catherine Summerfield, by all that's wonderful! I never would have guessed it. It must be ten years since I've seen you—no, more than that. And so you are still living in Langton Abbots? I hadn't heard—''

He broke off suddenly, as though a recollection had just occurred to him. Catherine, watching his face, could guess what that recollection must be. But he recovered himself almost immediately and went on, a new awareness in his eyes but his voice and manner exactly as they had been before.

''And you are still living with your aunts at Willowdale Cottage? I always had the greatest admiration for Willowdale Cottage, you must know. It seemed to my youthful fancy quite an ideal residence—a regular fairy-tale dwelling, if you will.''

''Yes, I still live at Willowdale Cottage,'' said Catherine. ''But it is only Aunt Rose and I who live there now. My Aunt Violet is now living with some cousins of ours in Plymouth.'' She was pleased that her voice sounded calm and steady in spite of the turmoil of her mind. Every time she looked into Lord Meredith's dark eyes, she felt again that unsettling sense of shock and recognition. *"Jonathan,"* whispered her mind. *"Jonathan."*

"Ah, that must make a change for you," he said, smiling. "Although we were never formally introduced, I had some slight acquaintance with your Aunt Violet, Catherine. There was an affair of some purloined apples once, I believe—and another occasion involving a dispute over a damaged window."

There was a hint of mischief in his smile that suggested he was not entirely blameless in this dispute. Catherine found herself smiling back at him. "I daresay you got the worst of it, knowing my Aunt Violet," she said.

"Indeed I did. Had your other aunt not interceded for me, my plight would have been desperate indeed." He looked with a smile to where Aunt Rose sat, looking prim and ladylike in her best lavender silk. "Will you not introduce us, Catherine? I should like the opportunity to thank my savior in person."

Catherine obligingly introduced him to her aunt and then to Mr. Poole, who was still looking affronted over Catherine's earlier inattention. Mr. Poole brushed the introduction aside, however, and flashed an ingratiating smile at Jonathan. "Lord Meredith and I are already acquainted, Catherine," he said. "You must know that he holds the living of St. Etheldreda's. Seeing that he is my patron, of course I made a point of calling on him as soon as I heard he was in the neighborhood."

Aunt Rose, however, was delighted to make the acquaintance of her former protégé. She smilingly disclaimed any thanks for her good deed of years ago and told him how pleased she was to see him back in Langton Abbots.

"No happier than I am to be here, ma'am," he returned with a smile. "It is delightful renewing my acquaintance with my old friends and neighbors." Turning again to Catherine, he added with some diffidence, "I should welcome a chance to further renew my acquaintance with you, Catherine. Will you do me the honor of dancing this next dance with me?"

Catherine was caught off guard by this request. It was evident that the others were caught off guard by it, too. Aunt Rose, to be sure, was smiling approvingly, but Lady Laura was looking surprised and Mr. Poole downright disapproving. Catherine was hardly aware of their expressions, however. It was Jonathan's expression that held her, and there was something in those steady dark eyes that moved her to an unaccustomed madness. "Certainly I will," she said. Taking his proffered arm, she accompanied him onto the dance floor.

CHAPTER IV

As they began to move to the lilting strains of a country dance, Catherine looked up into Jonathan's face.

He returned her look steadily. His expression was not quite a smile, but not entirely solemn, either. A hint of laughter seemed to lurk in his dark eyes. Once more Catherine thought how different he was from the other gentlemen of her acquaintance. His lean, tanned, clean-shaven face bore no resemblance to their pale, heavy, whiskered countenances. And though his formal black and white evening clothes were quite in keeping with the fashionable mode, his height and breadth of shoulder—not to mention his self-confident carriage—served to set him yet further apart in an assembly that did not lack for distinguished guests of either sex.

For the first few minutes of the dance, neither he nor Catherine spoke. Catherine, for her part, was content merely to look at him. He seemed content to look back at her, but at last he cleared his throat and spoke.

"Allow me to compliment you on your appearance, Catherine," he said. "You were only a schoolgirl when I saw you last, and still wearing short skirts with your hair down your back. It's a shock to find you now grown into a woman, but a pleasant shock, let me hasten to add. Indeed, you're the first Englishwoman I've seen who has managed to reconcile fashion with something resembling a natural feminine appearance.''

"You do me too much honor, my lord," said Catherine gravely. Jonathan contemplated her a moment, then grinned suddenly, his teeth very white in his sun-browned face.

"I'm sorry; that wasn't a very gallant speech, was it? On my honor, Catherine, I did mean it as a compliment. You look altogether ravishing." He looked in a considering way at her white silk ball dress. "I like that style of dress. Perhaps it's only that I've been out of England too long, but I can't get used to some of the fashions I see on ladies nowadays. The hats, especially, were a shock to me. It wasn't the thing for ladies to wear jockey caps or gentlemen's beavers on their heads when I left! Call me old-fashioned, but I like to see the distinction between the sexes preserved, at least to some extent."

" 'O tempora! O mores!' " quoted Catherine, in a gently mocking voice. He laughed again and shook his head ruefully.

"Yes, it is rather humorous, isn't it? If my father was alive to hear me bewailing the manners of the present day, he would be quick to point out the irony of it all. However, that is nothing to the point. We were discussing ladies' fashions, I believe, with the rider that you, of all the ladies present, look the way a lady ought to look—in my humble opinion, at least."

Catherine was deeply gratified by this speech, although loyalty to Lady Laura obliged her to demur. "I think you are too summary in your judgment, my lord," she said. "Whatever you may think of the current fashions, you cannot deny that Lady Laura looks very lovely tonight." She nodded toward Lady Laura, who was sitting the dance out in company with George and Isabel Wrexford.

Jonathan followed her eyes and smiled. "Yes, Laura does look lovely, but she looks lovely in spite of her dress, not because of it," he explained. "And only look at that young lady there with her! I never saw such an excrescence in my life as that costume she's wearing." He looked with distaste at Isabel's much-flounced dress of orange and *eau-de-Nil* moire taffeta.

Again Catherine was gratified, not least because there was a wicked pleasure in hearing her most persistent critic maligned. She knew such an emotion to be ignoble, however, and conscientiously sought to banish it from her mind. "I suppose our modern modes and manners must appear strange to you, who have been so long away from England," she said. "What kind of fashions do the ladies in India wear?"

"Ah, that depends a good deal on the lady. Those who are living in the English settlements tend to copy English fashions—except, of course, for those who are very advanced, who prefer to copy Parisian ones. When you get among the native women, however, it's a different story. They wear what's called the saree—the traditional dress of women in India. A very pretty dress it is, too. I can't describe it very well—it's sort of a wraparound affair made out of bright-colored silk—but I brought several back with me as souvenirs, along with some brasses and the usual kind of rubbish all Englishmen feel obliged to cart home from India. You'll have to drop by the Abbey some day and have a look at it all—you and your aunt."

Catherine politely expressed her thanks for this invitation, though she could not help thinking that the chances of her and Aunt Rose dropping by the Abbey any time soon were very small. "Indeed, India sounds a fascinating place," she said. "I have often wished I could visit it. I wish you would tell me more about it, my lord, and about the other places you have visited, too. Is it true you visited China and Japan?"

"I have," Jonathan assured her, and smiled at her envious expression. "I visited them right enough, but I assure you the experience was more educational than enjoyable. Indeed, I was lucky to get out of Japan with my skin intact. But there, you don't really wish to hear about that, do you? I have often observed that there is nothing so tiresome as a person who has just returned from abroad and insists on telling everyone about his experiences."

Catherine assured him with sincerity that she would like very much to hear about his foreign experiences. "I have always wanted to travel," she added, with a barely repressed sigh. "Did you truly almost lose your life in Japan? I wish you would tell me all about it."

Jonathan needed no further encouragement but at once launched into a lively description of his foreign adventures. Catherine listened with interest, putting in a question now and then and laughing when he described some particularly humorous episode. There seemed to have been a great many such episodes in the course of his travels. As Catherine looked up at his lean dark face, alight with laughter as he described a meeting with the emperor of China, she found herself divided between equal parts of envy and admiration.

The dance drew to an end just as Jonathan finished his anecdote about the Chinese emperor. "This is too bad," he said, looking down at Catherine with contrition. "Why did you encourage me to go boring on and on like that? I didn't mean to do all the talking."

"I didn't mind," Catherine assured him. "Truly, my lord, I enjoyed it."

"Yes, but I was wanting to talk about you, Catherine. And instead, I barely let you get a word in edgewise. And now our dance is over, and the opportunity is lost to me forever. Well, there's nothing for it but for you to dance this next dance with me, too, so you may get your own back. I promise not to say one word about China, Japan, or India, but rather let you do all the talking this time around. It's only right you should have equal time, after the way I've been monopolizing the conversation."

Catherine hesitated. To dance two dances in a row with him would, she knew, make her appear very particular to such critics as Mrs. Wrexford and Lady Mabberly. But there was nothing innately improper about dancing two dances in a row with a gentleman. Certainly her inclinations were all in favor of doing so on this occasion. She could not remember ever enjoying a dance more.

"Very well, my lord. I will be happy to dance with you again," she assented with a smile.

He returned her smile but shook his head at the words "my lord." "I wish you would call me Jonathan, as you did before," he said. "We are old acquaintances, after all. Indeed, you must have noticed the brazen way I have been calling you Catherine all evening. If you do not wish to snub me, you must reciprocate by calling me by my Christian name."

"Very well, Jonathan," agreed Catherine. The orchestra had already struck up a quadrille. As they took their place on the floor with the other couples, he smiled at her again.

"We were fortunate to get a quadrille this time, weren't we? Country dances tend to defy any serious attempt at conversation. But we have now this interval more or less to ourselves, and I expect you to use it by telling me all about yourself, Catherine. What have you been doing in the years since I left Langton Abbots?"

"Nothing so interesting as you, I'm afraid," said Catherine guardedly. "For the most part, I have merely been living quietly at Willowdale Cottage with my aunt. The opportunities for foreign travel and adventure have been denied me, I am sorry to say."

He smiled and shook his head. "Perhaps you have been unable to indulge in foreign travel, but still you must have had adventures," he said. "Why, even in Langton Abbots there are opportunities for excitement and scandal—"

His voice broke off suddenly, and he gave Catherine a quick, apologetic look. She was more certain than ever that he must have heard the story of her elopement. The knowledge made her color slightly, but she was able to keep her voice even as she responded to his speech.

"Yes, I have had one adventure," she said. "But I have no doubt someone has already told you about that, Jonathan."

His color, too, had risen, but his eyes continued to meet hers candidly. "Yes, I have heard something about it," he said. "However, I would rather hear the story from you, Catherine, if you are minded to talk about it. If it's a painful subject, of course, we shall pretend I didn't mention it and talk of something else. But if you've got to the stage where you can laugh about it, then I would like very much to hear how your adventure came about."

Catherine was silent a moment, considering. "I don't mind talking about it," she said at last. "But I'm not sure I can laugh about it as yet. Though it's not without its amusing aspects, to be sure," she added with a wry smile.

"Most things aren't," he returned calmly. "It's been my experience that if you only wait long enough, the tragedy goes out of nearly everything, and all that's left is the ridiculous. How long that process takes depends on the nature of the experience, of course. It took me years to accept the fact that I fought a duel, estranged myself from my family, and spent the better part of my adult life in virtual exile for the sake of a fat, foolish, middle-aged woman who didn't care two straws for me. But now that I have accepted it, I can see the funny side of the situation. I shouldn't think your little misadventure would take anywhere near so long to recover from." He smiled encouragingly at Catherine, and she could not help smiling back.

"Perhaps not," she said. "Indeed, if I had been able to talk about it to anyone, I daresay I might be recovered from it by now. But you see, I have not had that luxury, Jonathan. The few people I would have liked to discuss it with, like my aunt, didn't want to hear about it, and the others—well, I would rather die than discuss it with any of them. In any case, they rarely allude to it in my presence, preferring instead to gossip about it behind my back. I think you are the first person who's ever asked me about it openly."

Jonathan regarded her thoughtfully. "A case of fools rushing in, perhaps," he said. "You mustn't think I mean to pry, Catherine. But if you would like to talk to someone about it, as you say, I promise you that you couldn't find a safer confidant than I am. My discretion has been perfected through long years of indulging in its reverse, and you have the comfort of knowing that I can never throw your mistakes in your teeth without leaving myself open to an uncommonly fierce retaliatory attack!"

He spoke so drolly that Catherine could not help laughing. "I suppose not," she said. "Very well, Jonathan. If you truly want to hear the story of my lone youthful adventure, then I'll tell you. But I must warn you that it is by no means so dramatic as your own, not to mention a good deal more sordid."

Speaking slowly, and choosing her words with care, she began to describe to him the events that had taken place her fifteenth and sixteenth year. She described her unhappiness at home with Aunt Violet, and her even deeper unhappiness at Miss Saddler's Academy. Jonathan was wholly sympathetic toward her plight. "If that school was worse than living with your aunt, then it must have been bad indeed," he said. "I remember your Aunt Violet, Catherine. A regular old Tartar she was, with a tongue like a razor. Even my father was afraid of her."

He subsided into silence again as Catherine went on to describe her first meeting with Angelo and the gradual development of her friendship with him. As the friendship progressed to romance, she found it harder to describe, but there was no doubt that Jonathan was a most discreet and sympathetic listener. He seemed to understand exactly what had been her feelings on every occasion and how she could have been finally driven to such a drastic measure as an elopement.

"There's nothing like opposition and ultimatums to drive a person to do something desperate, is there? Particularly when one is young and half desperate to begin with. I often think my father could have managed me quite easily as a boy if he had only been clever enough to order me to do the opposite of whatever he wanted me to do in the first place. It's a method I intend to put into use with my own children, should I ever have any."

Catherine smiled wanly. "It's true, but a rather speaking commentary on human nature," she said. "I doubt I would ever have dreamt of eloping with Angelo if Miss Saddler had not forbidden me to see or even speak to him. But her making such a point of it imbued the situation with high romance. It was just like Romeo and Juliet, you know. Before twenty-four hours had gone by, I had quite convinced myself that I loved Angelo to distraction and couldn't possibly live without him. Of course, my being so miserable at the Academy probably had something to do with it, too. I think I would have leaped at any chance of escape that had been offered me."

Jonathan nodded. "So you eloped with him," he said. "I suppose the school authorities tracked you down before you had gone half a mile and dragged you back in disgrace?"

Catherine hesitated before answering this question. "No," she admitted at last. "A lot of people seem to have that idea, and I must confess I rather encourage it, for they think badly enough of me when they imagine my elopement with Angelo was unsuccessful. The truth is a good deal worse, I am afraid." She looked up at him challengingly.

He met her gaze as steadily as before, however. "In other words, they weren't able to track you down right away," he said. "I suppose The Worst had already taken place before they did succeed in finding you?"

He spoke these words in a suitable hushed and tragic tone, yet there was a suggestion of a twinkle in his eye that showed he did not view the matter as one for tragedy. Catherine, observing it, suddenly began to feel much better. She would never have supposed she could have made such an admission without blushing—and to a gentleman, too, which ought to have made it much worse. Yet not only was she not blushing, she was actually smiling as she responded in a voice as hushed as his own.

"I'm afraid so. They didn't succeed in finding us until almost two weeks had gone by. We weren't able to marry, either, for I was too young to do so without my aunts' permission. It was Angelo's idea that they would give their consent much more readily if they knew we had been living together beforehand. But as it happened, any possibility of our marrying was long gone by the time Aunt Rose and Aunt Violet caught up with us."

"Did they wrest you forcibly from Angelo's arms and drag you away kicking and screaming, like the heroine in a romance?" inquired Jonathan with sympathy.

Catherine shook her head, her lips prim but her eyes brimming with laughter. "Aunt Violet would have enjoyed doing so, I daresay," she said. "And probably she would have done so if I had shown any sign of resistance. But after living two weeks with Angelo, I was quite ready to be wrested from his arms. Instead of being a romantic hero, he turned out to be a tiresome boy who complained constantly that he couldn't find work, yet wouldn't go out looking for any, and who spent his evenings drinking away what little money we had and bemoaning the sad state of his affairs. By the time my aunts found me, I was so sick of him that I wouldn't have married him even if they had wanted me to!"

At this, Jonathan gave such a shout of laughter that several other couples on the dance floor turned to look at him curiously. Catherine laughed, too, only dimly aware of the curious looks being directed their way. As she looked into Jonathan's smiling face, she felt as if the weight of the world had suddenly slipped from her shoulders.

It was an overwhelming relief to meet someone who not only refused to see her youthful indiscretion as a tragedy, but insisted on seeing its humorous side as well. "It is funny, isn't it, Jonathan? I can see it all clearly now. How glad I am that my aunts didn't discover me during my first few days with Angelo, when I still fancied I loved him. I probably would have insisted on marrying him in that case—and it would have been no laughing matter then, I am sure! I might as well have cut my throat and been done with life then and there.''

Jonathan nodded, his eyes still bright with laughter. ''I have often thought it a mercy that we are not invariably married to our first loves,'' he said. ''I can remember being quite infatuated with the Widow Cooper when I was seventeen or thereabouts. Indeed, I was within an ace of asking her to marry me at one point. But fortunately, my sense of self-preservation kept me from going quite so far as that.''

Catherine tried to look disapproving, but her lips were unsteady. ''Yes, I remember hearing about your exploits with the Widow Cooper when I was just a girl, Jonathan,'' she said. ''It was considered scandalously precocious of you to have seduced a woman twice your age.''

Jonathan shook his head solemnly. ''The boot was quite upon the other foot, I assure you. It was she who seduced me— and almost seduced me into offering her my hand in matrimony while she was at it.''

''A case of 'The woman gave me, and I did eat,' in fact,'' suggested Catherine in a dulcet voice.

''Precisely,'' said Jonathan, refusing to be drawn. ''I always felt the Bible was uncommonly accurate in describing the relations between the sexes. Everyone knows you women are masters of intrigue, capable of leading us poor puny masculine creatures about by the nose according to your whim. Indeed, as far as I can see, your sex has it all over ours when it comes to most things. Wouldn't you agree?''

''No,'' said Catherine frankly. ''I suppose women as a whole have a certain power over men, but the power I covet is the kind you have, Jonathan. I would much prefer to go where I liked and do as I pleased and make my own way though life, even if it meant giving up the protection women are generally afforded. And above all, I would like to be able to snap my fingers in society's face without fear of reprisals, as you have done. As a woman who has flouted convention and paid a high price for it, I cannot at all agree that your sex has anything to envy in ours."

Jonathan's face had sobered at this speech. "Put that way, I suppose not," he said. "Have you paid such a high price, Catherine? I suppose you could hardly avoid paying some penalty so long as you live in such a place as Langton Abbots. But surely your plight is not so bad as all that. Obviously you are not a complete outcast, or you would not be here tonight dancing with me."

"No, I am not a complete outcast. Aunt Rose has moved heaven and earth to get everyone to re-accept me, and for the most part she has been successful. And since Lady Laura has been here, my position has been much easier. Laura has quite taken me up, you must know, and she regards it as a personal affront if anyone dares so much as look askance at me."

A smile infinitely tender touched Jonathan's lips. "That sounds like Laura," he said. "A kinder-hearted woman never drew breath, I believe." He looked across the floor to where Lady Laura was dancing with another gentleman. "She is an angel, isn't she, Catherine?"

"Yes, she is," said Catherine, and wondered why she felt so downhearted by the admission.

CHAPTER V

For the remainder of the dance, by unspoken accord, Catherine and Jonathan discussed impersonal subjects. They talked about the leasing of Honeywell House by Lady Laura's father, the renovation of the village church, and the other changes that had taken place in the neighborhood since Jonathan's departure for India.

Although not so fraught with personal interest as before, still their conversation was absorbing. Catherine was sorry when the dance ended, supposing that she must now resign herself to sitting beside Aunt Rose for the rest of the evening. But to her surprise and gratification, Jonathan seemed as reluctant to relinquish her company as she was to relinquish his.

"A reel, eh?" he said, as the orchestra swung into a lively rendition of that dance. "I have not danced a reel in years, but that shall not deter me from making the attempt. Can I persuade you to attempt it with me, Catherine? I cannot promise to lead you always right, but I'll do my best not to step on your feet."

"I don't fear it," said Catherine, smiling. "Indeed, I am sure you will acquit yourself admirably, Jonathan." Never for a moment did she consider declining his invitation. She was too happy at his desire for her company to consider the possible consequences of dancing with him three times in a row. But she was jolted into sudden remembrance by the sight of Lady Laura's mother, who came hurrying over to intercept Jonathan as he led Catherine toward the floor.

"Lord Meredith, I wonder if you would grant me the indulgence of your company for a few minutes? I want to introduce you to Admiral Vernon, who is most anxious to make your acquaintance. I'm sure Catherine won't mind forgoing your company for this one dance, will you, dear?" She gave Catherine a tight-lipped smile. "After all, you have already danced with Lord Meredith twice this evening."

"Of course I don't mind, Lady Lindsay," said Catherine quietly. It was clear to her that Lady Laura's mother resented her monopolizing Jonathan's company. Lady Lindsay had obviously already fixed on him as her future son-in-law and felt that his place was with Lady Laura rather than with her. Looking at the matter impartially, Catherine was obliged to admit that Lady Lindsay might have some grounds for resentment. She really ought not to have danced two dances with Jonathan, much less consented to dance with him a third time. But all regard for the proprieties seemed to have deserted her from the first moment his eyes met hers.

There had been an indescribable comfort in discussing her affairs with a person who neither moralized nor condemned— who was, in fact, inclined to sympathize with her actions. And as long as Jonathan was willing to grant her that comfort, it was impossible that she should willingly deprive herself of it.

Lady Lindsay gave Catherine another tight-lipped smile. "That's right, dear. I'll ask Oswald to take you back to your aunt." With one hand she beckoned her stepson toward her, while grasping Jonathan's arm firmly with her other. "Oswald, Miss Summerfield has need of your services. Would you please see she gets safely back to her aunt?"

"Certainly, ma'am," said Oswald, bowing. "Or perhaps you

would do me the honor of dancing with me, Miss Summerfield? I've been admiring you this half hour while you was footing it with Meredith here. That's a devilish pretty dress you've got on.''

Although Sir Oswald made this speech in a respectful tone, he was all the while looking Catherine's figure up and down in a manner that was frankly lascivious. Catherine felt an acid rejoinder rise to her lips but restrained herself from giving it voice. ''Thank you, Sir Oswald, but I believe I am too fatigued to dance any more at present,'' she said shortly. ''Just take me back to my aunt, if you please.''

Sir Oswald reluctantly obeyed these instructions. Even after Catherine had resumed her seat beside Aunt Rose, he lingered at her side, trying to convince her to take the floor with him. He remarked several times on the circumstance of her dancing twice with Jonathan and hinted strongly that he would feel himself ill-used if she did not grant him the same indulgence. But Catherine said flatly that she had no intention of dancing again that evening, and after a little more fruitless teasing, Sir Oswald accepted the futility of his quest and took himself off.

Catherine was relieved to be rid of him, but it was not long before she began to wonder if she would have done better to take the floor with him after all. Her two dances with Jonathan had been widely remarked, and the greater number of her acquaintances soon found an opportunity to drop by and make some comment about her taste for Lord Meredith's society.

Aunt Rose was the first to comment on it, though she, at least, avoided any tone of condemnation. ''Lord Meredith is looking very well this evening, isn't he?'' she remarked in a thoughtful voice. ''It's a pity that he should have got so brown in India, but it doesn't disfigure him so much as it would most men. I was pleased to see the two of you dancing together, Catherine. It looked as though you were having a pleasant time renewing your acquaintance.''

Catherine gave a restrained assent to both these remarks, and

Aunt Rose said nothing more, seemingly content to let the subject drop. Other people were not so forbearing, however. Lady Mabberly made a point of coming by to mention how surprised she was to see dear Catherine dancing, and with Lord Meredith, too, of all people. The unspoken implication was that two such black sheep ought not to have been allowed at the same assembly, let alone permitted to dance with each other.

After Lady Mabberly had gone, two other ladies dropped by to say that they had not realized Lord Meredith was such a particular acquaintance of Catherine's and to ask what she had been saying to him that he seemed to find so amusing. When presently they moved on, their place was taken by Mr. Poole, who ponderously re-seated himself in the vacant chair beside Catherine and proceeded to read her a lecture on what he was pleased to term her indiscretion.

"I do not say you were wrong to dance *one* dance with Lord Meredith," he told Catherine, with the avuncular air she always found so offensive. "It would have been more prudent, perhaps, to have abstained altogether, but I think most people would have seen no impropriety in your dancing one dance together. You were, I understand, formerly acquainted, and though I fear Lord Meredith's character and conduct are not all they should be, it would perhaps be overly scrupulous to refuse his invitation on those grounds alone. He is, after all, a person of some prominence in the community."

"Yes, he holds your living, does he not?" said Catherine, not without malice. "Certainly we must none of us take any chance of offending him."

Mr. Poole returned no answer to this, but went on with a slight increase in avuncularity. 'I must confess, I think Lord Meredith would have shown greater discretion had he refrained from singling you out in such a way, Catherine. Considering his own position, and the delicacy of *your* position, he ought to have known his attentions could do you nothing but harm. Even so, however, the harm would have been minimal had he limited himself to standing up with you once. I cannot censure him too strongly for having asked you a second time. And though I dislike to criticize *your* conduct in any way, Catherine, I do think your own good sense might have warned you that you were wrong in accepting his second invitation. In your position, you know, you cannot afford the slightest breath of scandal to touch your name.''

"No, indeed. It might prove to be the straw that broke the camel's back,'' agreed Catherine with a glittering smile. Irony was lost on Mr. Poole, however. He nodded, looking solemnly pleased.

"Quite right, my dear. It's a censorious world, and though the two of us know your behavior was prompted by nothing worse than thoughtlessness, I fear others may not be so understanding. It will behoove you to be twice as much on your guard after this.''

"It's very seldom that I dance at all, let alone dance twice with the same gentleman,'' said Catherine, moved to asperity by this pompous counsel. "Perhaps from now on you would rather I removed myself from the room whenever there is dancing?''

Taking this question at its face value, Mr. Poole gave it serious consideration. "No, for that would only give rise to comment. And comment, in your position, is what you must particularly strive to avoid,'' he decided at last. "Unless of course . . . I wonder. Would it answer, perhaps, if you stood up for a couple of dances with me? I do not, as you know, approve of clergymen dancing in the general way, but for your sake I should be happy to sacrifice my scruples and make the attempt.''

With great haste and some inward amusement, Catherine begged him not to sacrifice his scruples on her behalf. "I thank you for the offer, sir, but I am persuaded it would not answer. It would merely be making both of us conspicuous and do nothing to quell the gossip my behavior has already given rise to. Besides, I should be most unhappy to think I had obliged you to perform an action that was against your conscience. Such a sacrifice as that is not to be thought of. You speak of the delicacy of my position, but your position, as an arbiter of morals in the community, is scarcely less delicate than mine."

Mr. Poole acknowledged this truth with a sigh. "Indeed, you are quite right, Catherine. I should be loath to do anything that might lessen the dignity of my office in the eyes of my flock. Very well, then: we must simply hope this business tonight will be a nine days' wonder, remarked on for a time but quickly forgotten. And I have no doubt it will be. The unwavering rectitude of your conduct for the past nine years must be a strong point in your favor, and if anyone reproaches you for your misstep tonight, you need only show yourself properly penitent to be forgiven in this world as in the next. Believe me, Catherine: A penitent heart can atone for a multitude of sins."

Catherine had no wish to enter into an argument with Mr. Poole and so only answered his speech with a slight, noncommittal smile. Inwardly, however, she reflected that her own experience in such matters had been quite different. She had found that nothing was so likely to bring down a shower of abuse and criticism on one's head as a show of penitence, whereas if one carried one's head high and showed no penitence at all, people concluded that one's sins were exaggerated and allowed one to pass on one's way unmolested.

This was, in any case, the course that she had determined to pursue after an initial period of trial and error. It had stood her in pretty good stead for the past nine years, but it was a strain sometimes to have to appear unconscious of the snubs, snickers, and whispers that inevitably followed her wherever she went. Nor was it easy to keep her expression serene and confident when she was inwardly feeling the very reverse of those emotions. She had grown adept at doing so, however, and could now maintain at least an appearance of serenity even when her heart was in a state of turmoil.

The chief difficulty was that in order to be truly effective, this mask of composure could never for a moment be dropped. And this, in turn, made it impossible to allow any human being into her full confidence. So Catherine had always told herself, but she had assured herself at the same time that it was worth the sacrifice. Still, she had often missed the comfort of a confidant. And when tonight she had impulsively abandoned her usual reserve and confided something of her real feelings to Jonathan, she had found it an immeasurable relief.

It might be that she would have to pay a high price for her unreserve at some future time. Indeed, she was already paying the price tonight, in the form of barbed remarks, smiling innuendos, and condescending lectures. But it had been worth it, even if the scandal amounted to more than the nine days' wonder that Mr. Poole had predicted. Catherine was quite certain on that score, and she felt that if it was given the good vicar to see her heart, he would find it by no means so penitent as he expected.

CHAPTER VI

As soon as Catherine had gone off with Sir Oswald, Lady Lindsay had lost no time in hustling Jonathan off in the opposite direction. She was intent on putting as much distance as possible between him and what her keen maternal eye had recognized as a threat to her daughter's matrimonial hopes.

She located Admiral Vernon's upright figure among the crowd and led Jonathan to him, talking lightly all the while of how happy she was to be able to effect an introduction between them. Admiral Vernon bowed deeply on perceiving her approach. After introducing Jonathan to him, Lady Lindsay lingered to make sure they were well launched into conversation before leaving to attend to other affairs. She felt safe leaving Jonathan in Admiral Vernon's custody, for it was well known that the admiral liked nothing better than a fresh ear into which he might pour his views on the state of the modern navy. Jonathan, who was good-natured, smiled, nodded, and made sympathetic noises in response to the old man's jeremiad, but all the while his eyes kept straying across the room to where Catherine sat beside her aunt.

She looked very lovely, sitting there with her white shoulders rising out of her silken draperies and her profile silhouetted against the dark green of the saloon hangings. Her chestnut hair gleamed beneath the light of the chandelier just over her head. He admired again the sleek simplicity of her coiffure, so striking in contrast to the cropped and curled heads of the young ladies around him. Of course Laura managed to look lovely despite cropped tresses, but she would have been lovely no matter how her hair was dressed. She was the most beautiful woman he had ever seen, and he had seen a number of them in his lifetime.

Catherine, by contrast, could not be considered a true beauty when one measured her features against the Grecian ideal. Yet there was a quality about her heart-shaped face, with its tip-tilted nose, demure mouth, and heavy-lidded golden eyes, that was as attractive in its way as Laura's more conventional pink and white beauty. Perhaps it was the intelligence that flickered behind those golden eyes—the intelligence that had been so clear during the conversation he had had with her. Or perhaps it was her smile, which started as a mere quiver at the corners of her mouth and ended by illuminating her whole face.

On a subconscious level, Jonathan felt and was disturbed by the effect Catherine had had on him during their two dances together. He tried conscientiously to dismiss her from his mind, however, and to fix his thoughts on what the admiral was saying. Although he had not yet formally proposed to Lady Laura, he was intending to do so very soon, and he felt it disloyal to be entertaining such particular thoughts of one woman when he was so near to being engaged to another. Laura was a paragon, of course: far too good for him, but then nobody could be good enough for such an angel. If the earl would only give his consent—and Lady Lindsay seemed to think it quite certain that he would, in time—then he meant to win her for his wife.

By dint of reflecting on his future bride's many perfections, Jonathan had worked himself back into a state of devoted fervor by the time he finally got free of the admiral's Ancient

Marinerlike hold. He immediately set off in search of Lady Laura. He found her just walking off the dance floor with Ben Winslow, a young gentleman who was slightly known to him from years past. Jonathan exchanged greetings with Ben, then turned to Laura with a smile. "I hope you are not engaged for the next set," he said. "I should like very much to dance with you once more, if I may. I realize I'm rather late putting forward my request, but you see, Admiral Vernon was holding me captive, and I only just got free a minute ago."

"Long-winded old bagpipe, isn't he?" said Ben with ready sympathy. "Got me cornered once at the beginning of a party and I couldn't get free of him until nearly suppertime, 'pon my word."

Lady Laura shook her head and gave Jonathan her sweet smile. "Poor old Admiral Vernon," she said. "He's a great pet of mine, but I cannot deny that he likes to talk. I am very sorry that he should have held you against your will, my lord. I would like to dance this next set with you, but it happens that I am already engaged to dance it with Tommy Mabberly. However, it may be that I can put Tommy off until the set after that. I was going to ask him if we might sit the dance out anyway, for I am feeling rather fatigued after this last dance. Reels are so exhausting."

"I'd as soon sit with you than dance with you anyway," returned Jonathan promptly. "Let us talk to Tommy and see if it can be arranged."

Tommy willingly agreed to the proposed substitution, and Jonathan led Lady Laura to a pair of empty seats in the far corner of the room. "Can I get you something to eat or drink?" he asked.

"In a minute, perhaps. For now, I would rather sit and talk." Lady Laura turned to smile at him. "Tell me, are you enjoying the party, my lord? I was just thinking how queer it must be for you here tonight, to be a stranger and yet not a stranger among these people. Most of them you haven't seen in years."

"Yes, and there are a number I haven't seen at all," agreed

Jonathan, looking around the room. "Even some of the familiar faces in the crowd don't look as I remember." His eyes were on Catherine again as he spoke. Lady Laura followed his gaze, then gave him a quick, speculative look.

"Are you speaking of Catherine Summerfield? I suppose she must have changed a great deal since you last saw her. She would have been only a girl when you went away to India."

Jonathan nodded. "Yes, she has changed a great deal since then. I wouldn't have known her to look at her."

Lady Laura nodded also, a troubled expression on her lovely face. "I would have liked to have known her before. I must confess that she greatly intrigues me, Jonathan. I have done my best to befriend her—indeed, I think we may be called friends, although I am not sure I will ever quite understand her. She seems such a strong, resolute person. It doesn't seem possible that she could ever have—but there, I ought not to speak of it." Lady Laura caught herself quickly, with a look of self-reproach. "All that took place years ago, and it has always seemed to me very unfair that she should be penalized for something that happened when she was little more than a girl. I know her position must often be very difficult, though she never makes any complaint about it. Indeed, I pity her from the bottom of my heart."

"Of course you do," said Jonathan, smiling at her. "You are an angel, and so it's natural you should pity all of us troubled mortals. You would not be yourself if you did not." He felt at that moment a deep tenderness toward Lady Laura, but mingled with his tenderness was a certain amusement. It was inevitable that a girl like Lady Laura should pity a girl in Catherine's position, but pity was not the emotion that sprang to his own mind when he thought of Catherine. Admiration, yes, and sympathy for a person who had a rocky row in life to hoe, but there was nothing pitiable about the calm, self-assured woman who had looked him in the eye and confessed frankly to having refused to marry the paramour with whom she had fallen out of love.

Lady Laura had gone on speaking in her gentle voice. "I'm afraid you exaggerate my virtues, my lord, but I do try to be a good friend to Catherine as far as I am able. I was so pleased that you should ask her to dance with you." Rather diffidently, she added, "You would not realize it, having been away from Langton Abbots so long, but it is very seldom that she dances at all. And it was so good to see her smiling for once, and laughing, too, as though she was really enjoying herself. I'm not sure if I ever saw her laugh before, and I have known her for nearly six months now."

This speech made Jonathan feel a little uncomfortable. There was nothing even faintly reproachful in Lady Laura's voice or manner, yet he was conscious of a sensation of guilt. "Yes, we were discussing old times and old friends," he said, in a would-be light tone.

He meant the words partly as reassurance to Lady Laura and partly as dismissal of the subject of Catherine, but even as he spoke he found his eyes turning again in Catherine's direction. The vicar was once more seated in the chair beside her and was saying something with a grave and consequential air. Catherine was listening with apparent interest, a faint smile on her lips. Jonathan wondered what they were talking about. There was certainly a smile on Catherine's face, albeit a somewhat ironic smile. Was it possible she was really amused by something that pompous windbag of a cleric was saying to her?

Here Jonathan caught himself with a feeling of astonishment. It was ridiculous that he should be feeling something very like jealousy for the vicar when he was sitting with the most beautiful woman in the room—the woman who was soon to be, if all went according to plan, his affianced bride. Determinedly averting his eyes from Catherine and the vicar, he looked over at Lady Laura and found she was surveying him quizzically once more.

"Of course you and Catherine would have a great deal to discuss, after so many years apart," she said. "Growing up in the same neighborhood, you must have had many friends and experiences in common. I must say, however, that I had not realized you yourselves were such good friends. Catherine gave me to understand your acquaintance was rather slight.''

Jonathan was very glad that Lady Lindsay came gliding over to them just then, sparing him from making any answer. She addressed her daughter with an indulgent smile. "How is this, my love? You beg me for weeks on end to give a dancing party, and then when I do give one I find you sitting down instead of dancing!" To Jonathan, she added, "Your conversation must be more than ordinarily fascinating, my lord, if it can keep my daughter away from the dance floor. What are you discussing?''

Jonathan opened his mouth, but Lady Laura spoke before him. "We were discussing Catherine, Mama,'' she said.

Lady Lindsay's smile faded slightly. When she spoke again, however, her voice was as lightly amused as before. "Ah, yes, poor Catherine. She is doomed to be the subject of discussion all her life, I fear.'' With an expression at odds with her sympathetic tone, she looked to where Catherine sat beside the vicar. "But after all, she is not so very much to be pitied. She appears to have found a congenial companion in Mr. Poole. And of course she had the privilege of dancing twice with you earlier, my lord.'' Lady Lindsay directed a long, level look at Jonathan. "You must take care, my lord, or you will turn the poor creature's head. A girl in her position is so—well, let us say, so peculiarly vulnerable to masculine attention.''

"I doubt her head would be turned as easily as you think, ma'am,'' returned Jonathan. "I would not have supposed any young lady could consider a couple of dances as being of much importance. Or any older lady, either, for that matter.'' He was angered by the innuendo in Lady Lindsay's words but wise enough to see that showing his anger would do more harm than good. To defend Catherine warmly would only deepen Lady Lindsay's suspicions and perhaps cause distress to Lady Laura. On the whole, it seemed best to treat the matter lightly, though he could not resist adding that last barb about older ladies.

Lady Lindsay clearly did not relish it, but to quarrel publicly was as little to her taste as his. She merely smiled and shook her head.

"Indeed, my lord, I think you underestimate your own consequence in the neighborhood. But I do not mean to pull caps with you over Miss Summerfield. She seems a very pretty, well-mannered young lady, and I know nothing to her discredit apart from that one unfortunate incident. Laura will not hear me abuse her, at any rate."

"No, I won't, Mama," said Lady Laura stoutly. Lady Lindsay smiled and shook her head once more.

"You might not think it to look at her, my lord, but my daughter possesses a remarkably obstinate nature. She *will* choose her own friends, in defiance of anything I can say. I cannot feel Miss Summerfield is altogether a fitting companion for her, but it is of course commendable of her to take an interest in a young lady less fortunately circumstanced than herself. And so I say nothing, except that I hope Miss Summerfield shows herself properly grateful for the favor shown her. There, I have done lecturing, my dears. I will leave the two of you again to your conversation while I confer with Cook about supper."

After Lady Lindsay had gone, a brief silence ensued. Lady Laura kept shooting little sideways glances at Jonathan. She appeared several times on the verge of speaking, but each time her courage seemed to fail her. Jonathan suspected she had been embarrassed by her mother's officious remarks and felt she should apologize for them, without quite knowing how to go about it. He, for his part, was wondering what he could say to resume the conversation without making further reference to the by-now controversial subject of Catherine. He finally hit on the idea of asking Lady Laura if she was now ready for something to eat or drink.

Lady Laura seized on this idea gratefully. "Yes, I wish you

would bring me something, my lord. Some punch and a few sandwiches, if you will, and perhaps a little cake.''

Promising to fulfill this commission, Jonathan left Lady Laura and went to the parlor next door, where refreshments were being served. He was filling a plate with sandwiches and lobster patties when Sir Oswald strolled into the room.

"Good evening, Oswald," said Jonathan, glancing at him briefly and then returning to his task. As always when he contemplated Sir Oswald's unprepossessing countenance with its sallow complexion and bushy black side-whiskers, he wondered how such a man could bear kinship with Lady Laura. Even if the relationship was only that of half brother and half sister, still one would have expected there to be some family resemblance. But Sir Oswald appeared to resemble none of the Lindsays, all of whom were notably fair and well-favored. Jonathan remembered hearing somewhere or other that Lord Lindsay's first wife had been of foreign birth. That might explain Sir Oswald's appearance, but it did not explain or excuse his manners, which managed to combine a polished style with an extremely coarse substance. Jonathan was no prude, but still he had been shocked on more than one occasion by the matters which Sir Oswald had seen fit to introduce for discussion.

His greeting on this occasion was entirely characteristic. "Hallo, Meredith," he said. "Don't tell me you're getting those sandwiches for the Summerfield girl? I noticed the two of you dancing earlier—and so, let me tell you, did everyone else in the room. I was green with envy, upon my word.''

"No, I am not waiting on Miss Summerfield," said Jonathan repressively. "I am getting something for your sister, as it happens.''

Sir Oswald raised his eyebrows. "Spreading your favors pretty thin, aren't you, old fellow? Don't go scowling at me, now. I've no objection to your having two strings to your bow, even if one of them's my sister.''

"What the hell do you mean by that?" demanded Jonathan, with considerable hostility.

"Just what you think," returned Sir Oswald equably. "Tell me, were you able to make any headway with the Summerfield? I've never had any luck in that quarter myself, but her dancing twice with you looked pretty particular. I envy you, my boy—upon my word, I envy you."

Jonathan drew himself up to his full height and stared at Sir Oswald in a manner that would have given that gentleman pause had he been better acquainted with him. "Miss Summerfield is an old acquaintance of mine—nothing more and nothing less. I would thank you to remember that, and to refrain from making remarks which, let me tell you, I find offensive in the extreme."

Sir Oswald smiled in an incredulous manner. "So she's an old acquaintance, is she? And I suppose that by dancing twice with her, you was merely hoping to improve your acquaintance? Doing it a little too brown, old fellow. It's common knowledge that Miss Summerfield is a—how shall I put it—a very *obliging* young lady."

Jonathan's response to this was to drop his plate of sandwiches and seize Sir Oswald by the neckcloth. Sir Oswald choked and goggled at him, too surprised to try to free himself. "I have told you once and I'll tell you again that Miss Summerfield is an old acquaintance of mine," said Jonathan through his teeth. "I consider her a most estimable lady, and if you insist on insulting her within my hearing, I'll have no choice but to call you to account for it. Do you understand?"

Sir Oswald nodded and plucked beseechingly at the hands around his throat. When Jonathan released him, he drew away, smoothing his neckcloth and eyeing him with a mixture of resentment and amusement. "I say, there's no need to half choke the life out of me, old fellow," he complained. "I won't say any more about Miss Summerfield if you don't like it, but I promise you, I am only repeating what seems to be the common opinion of her." He looked curiously at Jonathan. "You say you are an old acquaintance of hers. Tell me, then: Is there any truth in the story they tell about her?''

"What story?" said Jonathan, although he knew pretty well what story Sir Oswald must be referring to.

"Why, the story that she ran off with an Italian dancing master years ago. Tommy Mabberly told me about it when I first came to this neighborhood, and I wondered if it was true.''

"How should I know?" countered Jonathan, trusting this evasion might not be counted a lie. "I've been out of England these last ten years. But based on my knowledge of Miss Summerfield's character, I should think it most unlikely.''

Sir Oswald nodded thoughtfully. "Aye, I've wondered about that myself. The story's given pretty general credence hereabouts, but for myself I've never seen anything to support it. In fact, from my own experience I'd say that Miss Summerfield's as straitlaced as they come. I tried to steal a kiss from her once—just a kiss, upon my honor—and she almost took my head off. That don't seem much like a lady who'd elope with a dancing master, does it?''

"Indeed," said Jonathan, eyeing him with distaste. Sir Oswald did not notice his expression, however, but only nodded thoughtfully once more.

"Upon my word, I wouldn't wonder if the entire story wasn't made up out of whole cloth," he confided to Jonathan. "Work of the old tabbies, no doubt. Or possibly the young ones. Women are spiteful creatures, no doubt about it. I've often observed there's nothing they like better than to tear apart the reputation of a girl who's young and pretty. And Miss Summerfield's a devilish pretty girl—only a bit standoffish, don't you know. I hope you won't be offended if I say *that*.''

"Not at all," said Jonathan, with pretended affability. "Indeed, I would not suppose she could be otherwise, considering the liberties that you and the other gentlemen in the community apparently feel free to take with her.''

"Well, *I* won't take any more," said Sir Oswald handsomely. "I've nothing against Miss Summerfield, and my sister's devil-

ish fond of her.'' He grinned at Jonathan. ''Just as well you're
not trying to give her a slip on the shoulder! You could hardly
hope to succeed with her *and* Laura, seeing as they're bosom-
bows. They'd probably tell each other everything and upset the
whole applecart. Then wouldn't the fat be in the fire! You'd
find yourself at *point non plus* before you knew it and be
obliged to run off to India again!'' Laughing heartily at his
joke, Sir Oswald strolled out of the room, leaving Jonathan
with an increased contempt for his character and an increased
sympathy for what Catherine had been enduring for the past
nine years.

CHAPTER VII

In the days following Lady Laura's party, Catherine found herself a prey to ennui and sadness.

There was no reason for such feelings. Catherine told herself over and over again how fortunate she was. "More fortunate now than at any time in the past twelve years," she assured herself firmly. "I ought to be very grateful for all I have."

It did seem as though she had a great deal to be thankful for. She had a comfortable home, purged of the abrasive presence of Aunt Violet. She had, if not full social acceptance, at least a measure of social tolerance. And she had Lady Laura, a friend whose loyalty and devotion anyone might envy. What more could she want? Catherine did not know. She knew only that since that night at Honeywell House, the life that had formerly satisfied her had suddenly lost all its zest.

"And there's no reason for it," she told herself irritably. "If one party can unsettle me like this, then I'll simply have to stop attending parties." She could not believe that a simple dancing party could have had such an effect on her. What had happened that evening, after all? Nothing that did not happen at every village party, apart from her two dances with Jonathan. And Catherine absolutely refused to consider that two dances with Jonathan could have had such a profound effect on her. For was he not as good as engaged to Lady Laura? Everybody said so; it was only yesterday that one of her aunt's servants had alluded to his frequent calls at Honeywell House, saying, "That'll be a match, I shouldn't wonder."

Jonathan had, of course, paid her, Catherine, a few compliments during the course of the evening. But he had spoken of Lady Laura as an angel. And being called an angel must trump every other compliment that a gentleman might pay a lady, in Catherine's reckoning at least.

"Besides, I'm not foolish enough to suppose Jonathan meant anything particular by his compliments. He was only being kind. Indeed, he was very kind to me that evening." Catherine remembered how attentively he had listened to the story of her adventures and how sympathetic had been his response. She felt embarrassed now to recall how frankly she had spoken to him. "He certainly won't be tempted to call *me* an angel!" she reflected with wry humor. "My, but I was indiscreet that night. I wonder what came over me?" Catherine could not imagine, but she resolved not to let such a lapse happen again. Not that there was any danger of it. Jonathan was so fully involved with Lady Laura that he would have had no time to listen to further confidences, even had she cared to make them.

Such was Catherine's assumption, at any rate. In fact she had no definite information on the subject, for she and Lady Laura had seen little of each other for the past few weeks. This was not Lady Laura's fault. She had been as assiduous in her attentions toward Catherine as ever, but for some reason Catherine had felt reluctant to see and speak to her friend. Perhaps it was merely her low-spirited condition that made her eschew Lady Laura's society, or perhaps it was a disinclination to see Sir Oswald again. But she had a much better excuse for refusing to go abroad in the village. Another woman had been assaulted in the neighborhood of Langton Abbots, and this time the assault had taken place much closer to home.

"Actually in the village, my dear, or at least on the outskirts of it. It was that Barrett woman who lives in that little shack not far from the highway." Aunt Rose, who had been retailing this story to Catherine, lowered her voice as she added, "Of course I don't listen to ill-natured gossip, but there seems to be no doubt that she was accustomed to entertaining men in her home. But of course, that does not make it any less shocking that she should be assaulted in such a way. Poor creature, I hear she is injured quite seriously. I must ask Dr. Edwards if there is anything we can do or send to make her more comfortable."

"Shall I call upon Mary Edwards?" asked Catherine. "She generally knows her father's business as well as he does himself."

"No, my dear, I would rather you sent a note. It may be foolish, but I would prefer you did not go abroad until they catch the man who is committing these crimes."

Since Catherine had no inclination to go abroad at present, she quietly acquiesced in her aunt's desires. But when Midsummer's Eve rolled around and she received a note from Lady Laura begging her to dine at Honeywell House that evening, she could not bring herself to disappoint her.

Aunt Rose agreed she ought to go, but insisted that Catherine take the carriage rather than walk. Catherine agreed to this condition and set out for Honeywell House that evening, to all appearances quite soignée in a dress of Pomona green crepe, but in a most perturbed and apprehensive state of mind.

To her relief, the party was a small one and did not include Sir Oswald. Neither did it include Jonathan, rather to Catherine's surprise and possibly even to her disappointment, though she did not allow herself to consider such a thing. "It's just we girls tonight," Lady Laura explained gaily, as she ushered Catherine into the house. "Mama and Papa and Oswald are dining over at Mabberly Manor. But we're going to have dinner on the terrace—a sort of al fresco affair, if you will. I've invited Mary Edwards, Jeanie Bailey, Hermione Woodward, and the Percy girls. Oh, and Isabel Wrexford." Lady Laura lowered her voice. "I know you and Isabel do not get on, but I've put her as far from you at the table as possible, and I trust I may be able to make her behave herself. I hope that will be satisfactory, Catherine?"

"Perfectly satisfactory," said Catherine. Isabel might not be a favorite with her, but she had often attended gatherings where she was present and felt she could probably endure to do so again on this occasion. "Your party sounds a delightful notion, Laura. Whatever gave you the idea?"

"It just seemed the proper sort of thing to do for Midsummer's Eve. And the weather's been so sunny and warm today. It seemed such a shame to dine in a stuffy dining room when it's so lovely out-of-doors."

It *was* lovely out-of-doors, as Catherine admitted to herself. The terrace where Lady Laura proposed to hold her picnic party was a broad, balustraded stone structure that looked out over the gardens of Honeywell House. Lady Laura had hung colored lanterns in the orange trees that lined the terrace and cut flowers with a reckless hand to fill the great stone urns that ornamented its railing. The table itself was a round one just large enough to accommodate a party of eight. More flowers bloomed in a low epergne that adorned its center, and candles in glass chimneys stood ready to be lighted atop its snowy damask surface. The air was almost tropical in its mildness, carrying a faint tang of the sea, which lay only a dozen or so miles away, just beyond the green hills that fringed the northern horizon.

The company gathered around the table were almost as picturesque as the setting. Girls in silk and muslin dresses of pink, yellow, blue, and lilac laughed and chattered and turned to greet Catherine and Lady Laura as they came out on the terrace.

"Here are Catherine and Laura," cried Mary Edwards, greeting them with a glad cry. "Now we are complete. Laura, the view from your terrace is just too lovely for words. We have all been admiring it just as hard as we can.''

"Thank you," said Lady Laura, smiling. "But you know it is really not my view or my terrace, Mary. I'm sure I wish it was, but the owner of Honeywell House was only interested in leasing to Papa, not in selling.''

Jeanie Bailey, a small dark girl with a pert manner, nodded comprehendingly. "That would be Lord Westland," she said. "He's a most fearfully eccentric old gentleman—quite cracked, they say. I don't doubt it a bit, for you know all the Westlands have a reputation for being odd.''

"That they do," agreed Hermione Woodward, a vivacious redhead. "Why, every one knows Lord Westland is rich enough to buy an abbey. Why then does he live like a hermit up in Scotland and lease his home to somebody else? Not but what I'm glad he did lease his house to your papa, Laura. Indeed, I'm sure I wish he would sell it to him, so you might stay down here permanently.''

There was a murmur of agreement from the other girls. "I fancy Laura does mean to stay here, Hermione, one way or another," said Mary archly. "It may not be at Honeywell House, but there are other desirable houses in the neighborhood, you know. The Abbey, for instance, is reckoned a very fine and lordly residence.''

She smiled mischievously at Lady Laura, who blushed. "But Lord Meredith lives at the Abbey, does he not?" asked Charlotte Percy, a rather simple, literal-minded young lady. "And the property is entailed, I'm sure, like most noblemen's properties. I don't see how Lady Laura could ever buy it from him.''

Loud laughter greeted this speech, and Charlotte's sister Anne advised her not to be a goose. "Mary does not mean that Lady Laura should buy the property from Lord Meredith, Charlotte, but rather that she might marry him and so acquire the property that way.''

"I see," said Charlotte, opening her eyes very wide. "Do you mean to marry him then, Lady Laura?''

This artless question caused the girls to fall into a second fit of laughter. Anne Percy began to upbraid her sister in a furious whisper, but Lady Laura only laughed and shook her head. "No, don't scold her, Anne. It's a perfectly legitimate question, but I'm afraid I cannot answer it, Charlotte. You see, Lord Meredith has not yet asked me to marry him."

"Aye, but he means to, though," put in Mary Edwards shrewdly. "Don't say he hasn't hinted at it?"

Lady Laura smiled and looked down at her hands in her lap. "He *did* mention he was coming by tonight to talk to Papa about some very particular business," she said. "But I daresay it was only something to do with farming or livestock."

"Nonsense," declared Hermione. "You know it is not any such dull matter as that which brings Lord Meredith here tonight, Laura, or you would not be blushing like a peony. Of course he means to propose to you. And I must say, I think you're the luckiest girl in the world to have attached him. He's such a handsome creature, and so romantic-looking."

Both Catherine and Isabel Wrexford had been silent during most of this exchange. Now Isabel spoke up, her voice deceptively smooth. "Of course Lord Meredith is very handsome and romantic-looking, but he is a little too much of a flirt for my taste. I myself would look askance at marrying a man who had danced twice with another lady at my own party."

There were gasps and shocked giggles at this speech. One or two of the girls looked quickly at Catherine, then away again. Catherine felt her cheeks burning, but Lady Laura came to her rescue. "I am sure you are quite entitled to your opinion, Isabel, but for my part I confess to feeling differently," she said. "No matter how much I might care for a gentleman, I would not be unreasonable enough to expect him to live in my pocket all the time." Having made this statement, she then put an effective end to the discussion by ringing the bell beside her plate and ordering that dinner be served immediately.

The dinner was a very good one, beginning with sorrel soup and sole filet; progressing through leg of lamb and boned chicken with accompaniments of small salad, apricot fritters, and buttered French beans; and followed by a second course consisting of roast duckling à la mode and a terrine of hare with ham and pork. Its finish was a lavish dessert course of tarts, pastries, creams, and custards.

Conversation during the meal was general and desultory, as the girls devoted themselves to enjoying the banquet laid before them. But when the servants had been dismissed, and the girls sat talking lazily in the twilight nibbling on pastries and sweet biscuits, the conversation turned once more to the subject of Honeywell House and its eccentric owner.

"This really is an idyllic spot," said Lady Laura, looking dreamily out at the shadowy garden. "I don't wonder Lord Westland refuses to sell, though I can't help wishing he would."

Mary Edwards shook her head with decision. "It's not likely that he will, I'm afraid. You must know that the Westland family has owned Honeywell House forever, Laura. Even back in the Middle Ages, when people used to make pilgrimages to the well, they were living here, though not in this house, of course."

"Yes, I know about the old house," said Lady Laura. "I've seen the ruins over beyond the gardens. And I've seen the well, too, though I didn't know people used to make pilgrimages there."

"Yes," said Mary, with animation. "It wasn't so important a spot as Canterbury or Glastonbury, but our local well had quite a reputation. Why, even nowadays the girls like to wash their faces there before sunrise on Midsummer Day, in hopes they may see their future. Of course it's their future husbands that most of them really want to know about!"

"Indeed?" said Lady Laura, looking surprised. "But Midsummer Day is tomorrow, Mary. And I have heard nothing of such a custom."

"That's because it's mostly the lower classes who practice it," said Isabel with a sniff. "*I* have never washed my face in the well on Midsummer morning!"

"I have," said Jeanie Bailey cheerfully. "At least half-a-dozen times. And I know lots of other girls who've done it, too."

"Well, I have heard nothing about it," repeated Lady Laura. She sounded slightly miffed as she added, "I cannot think why no one has ever mentioned the custom to me."

"Perhaps because your future is already settled," said Hermione with a sly smile. "It's common knowledge who *your* future husband will be!"

Catherine feared this statement would lead into another discussion of Lord Meredith. and from there to another catty remark from Isabel about Catherine's two dances with him. It was obvious Lady Laura feared the same thing, for she made haste to return the conversation to the subject of the well. "Even if that was true, I would not let it deter me from making a trial of the well's powers! Does it really show one the future? You say you have tried it, Jeanie. Did it work?"

Jeanie laughed and shrugged her shoulders. "No, although I have heard stories of girls who saw all sorts of wonderful visions after washing their faces in the well. But if I am to be strictly honest, I must say that all I have ever seen in the well— and all anyone I personally know has ever seen—is water!"

She laughed again as she spoke, and everyone else laughed, too. Lady Laura joined in the laughter, but her expression was wistful. "Still, it sounds a charming custom," she said. "I tell you what, girls: I wouldn't mind getting up early tomorrow morning and trying it myself. Who'll try it with me? Catherine, will you?"

She gave Catherine a beseeching smile. Catherine was caught off guard by this request. As she was hesitating what to say, Isabel broke in with a dry laugh. "Of all of us, I am sure it is Miss Summerfield who has most cause to be concerned about the future," she said significantly. "She would no doubt be very relieved to learn there was a husband for her in it."

There were gasps and one or two giggles at this speech. Lady Laura turned upon Isabel with a look of indignation.

"Isabel, how can you? I am sure we would all like to know if there are husbands in our futures, Catherine no more than the rest of us."

"Yes, Laura dear, but you know some of us have a better chance of *getting* a husband than others. That is all I meant, and I don't think I need say any more than that. A word to the wise is sufficient, as the saying goes."

She looked pointedly at Catherine. Catherine looked back at her levelly. "Perhaps so, Miss Wrexford," she said. "But in this case, your words are quite beside the point. I have no intention of going to the well tomorrow morning."

Lady Laura looked as though she was about to protest this speech, but her reply was cut short by the entrance of the butler onto the terrace. "Excuse me, my lady, but you have a caller." he told Lady Laura. "It's Mr. Poole, the vicar. He says his business is urgent, and since Lord and Lady Lindsay and Sir Oswald have gone out for the evening, I thought you might like to see him instead. I took the liberty of putting him in the small parlor, pending your instructions."

"Yes, you did quite right," said Lady Laura with a nod. "Urgent business, you say? I cannot imagine what business Mr. Poole can have that is as urgent as all that. But I'll go to him right away."

Before she could push back her chair from the table, however, the terrace door swung open and Mr. Poole himself appeared with his hat in hand and a brazen smile on his face. "I hope you'll forgive the intrusion, my lady, but I needed to see you most urgently," he said, addressing Lady Laura.

The butler looked outraged at such presumption, but Lady Laura waved him away. "Certainly, Mr. Poole," she said, smiling at the vicar. "What can I do for you?"

"Why, it's only this, my lady. Tomorrow, as you may know, is Midsummer Day." Mr. Poole paused impressively.

"Yes, we were just speaking of it," said Lady Laura, looking puzzled. "What has that to do with your business?"

"A great deal, ma'am. Being a stranger to the area, you may

not be acquainted with certain superstitious customs pertaining to this property. There is a well, I understand, standing somewhere on the grounds, which is and has been for many years a center of pagan worship."

Lady Laura stared at him. "Pagan worship?" she said. "I don't understand. The girls were just telling me about the well—about how it is the custom in the neighborhood to wash one's face in its waters before sunrise on Midsummer Day in order to get a glimpse of one's future. But I had heard nothing of any pagan worship."

Mr. Poole drew himself up. "My lady, what else is divination and fortune-telling but pagan worship? You do not suppose it is God who speaks through such means?"

The effect of his words fell lamentably short of what was intended. Jeanie Bailey giggled, and even Lady Laura smiled. "No, I don't suppose anything of the kind, Mr. Poole," she said. "If anything, I had supposed trying to learn one's future from the well was merely a harmless amusement."

"Harmless! Harmless! I would not call it harmless, my lady. There is no saying what harm may not come through such a ritual. And that is why I have called on you tonight. It is my hope that you will heed my warnings and take measures to see that the well is secured tomorrow from all such unwholesome dabbling in the supernatural."

There was a long pause. Lady Laura appeared to be considering the vicar's words. "I don't see it," she said at last. "You will forgive me, Mr. Poole, but it still seems to me there is no harm in the local custom. I should consider it unwarrantable interference to 'secure the well,' as you propose, from anyone seeking to reach it."

Mr. Poole looked grave. "My lady, I must beg you to reconsider," he said. "You cannot have reflected on the consequences of your actions."

"Excuse me, Mr. Poole, but I believe I have," said Lady Laura with just the slightest ring of steel in her voice. "I have made my decision and must ask that you accept it as a final one. May I offer you a cup of tea?''

Mr. Poole accepted the tea but still seemed inclined to argue the subject. ''These pagan survivals are pernicious things,'' he said, morosely stirring sugar into his cup. ''In my former parish, I led a crusade to banish the maypole that the local farming folk were accustomed to erecting each year on the first of May. I also strove to eliminate certain rites and rituals connected with the celebration of All Hallow's Eve. But it is difficult, very difficult indeed, to battle such ingrained customs. Especially when the upper classes do not support my efforts.'' He looked reproachfully at Lady Laura. ''If you would only join with me in speaking against this business at the well tomorrow, we might succeed in putting an end to it.''

It was obvious that Lady Laura was annoyed by the vicar's persistence. The steel in her voice was more perceptible than ever when she spoke again. ''I have already told you what is my opinion on this subject, Mr. Poole. If you will forgive me for saying so, it all seems to me a tempest in a teapot. Not only do I see no harm in testing the well's powers, I intend to try them for myself tomorrow morning. You see now how futile is your errand.''

''You cannot be serious!'' Mr. Poole regarded her with consternation. ''My dear Lady Laura, if *you* show support for this abominable custom, then who will not follow your lead? I suppose all these young ladies will not hesitate to do so?''

He glanced around the group on the terrace. In doing so, he noticed for the first time Catherine, sitting silent in her place beside Lady Laura. ''Why, it's Catherine! Catherine, surely *you* do not mean to participate in this ritual? Say that I may count on your support, at least, even if I can depend on no one else's?''

Catherine was unhappy at being singled out for questioning in this way. She would not have answered him if left to herself, but Isabel answered for her. ''No, Catherine has already declined to accompany the rest of us to the well tomorrow,'' she said with a malicious look at Catherine. "I am sure her scruples are very understandable."

"But we hope she may change her mind," put in Lady Laura with great haste. "Do come along with us tomorrow, Catherine. I am sure there can be no harm in it, whatever Mr. Poole may say."

Catherine felt she had never before been in such an uncomfortable position. Lady Laura was looking at her; Mr. Poole was looking at her; all the girls were looking at her with curiosity or—in the case of Isabel—malicious amusement. "I have already said I did not mean to go to the well tomorrow," she said in a constrained voice. "Forgive me, Laura, but I think I must hold to that decision."

Lady Laura looked disappointed, but Mr. Poole was jubilant. "Ah, I knew I might depend on *your* support, Catherine," he said warmly.

If he had said no more than this, Catherine might have forgiven him. As it was, however, he went on in a voice that, though low, was perfectly audible to the others. "Indeed, you show commendable discretion in absenting yourself from this business. What might be allowable in an earl's daughter would be fatal to a girl in your position. You understand me, I hope?"

He paused and looked at Catherine. Catherine was by now beyond making any polite, conventional reply. "I understand only that there has been altogether too much talk already about such a trivial matter," she said coldly. Rising to her feet, she turned to Lady Laura. "I beg you will excuse me, Laura. It has been a delightful evening, but my aunt will be expecting me home."

Lady Laura opened her mouth as though to protest, then seemed to think better of it. "Of course," she assented quietly. Rising to her feet, she took Catherine's hand in hers. "I am so glad you could come, Catherine," she said, looking earnestly into the latter's eyes. "And if you should change your mind about accompanying me to the well tomorrow morning, do let me know. I should be only too happy to have your company."

Before Catherine could answer, Isabel spoke up swiftly. "You mustn't try to overcome Miss Summerfield's scruples concerning the well, Laura. The other girls and I will be glad to bear you company tomorrow morning. Won't we, girls?" The other girls made assenting murmurs. "Of course it's not something I would care to do in the usual way," went on Isabel, with a condescending smile. "But for your sake, Laura, I will be glad to lend my countenance to the affair."

What Lady Laura's reply was to this, Catherine did not hear. She had already slipped from the terrace and started toward the stables in quest of her aunt's carriage. She was determined to lose no time putting as much distance as possible between her and the others.

CHAPTER VIII

Although Catherine could not know it, that evening at Lady Laura's marked a turning point in her life.

It certainly represented the pinnacle of public mortification. Isabel's sly jabs; Mr. Poole's tactless allusions; even Lady Laura's partisanship—none would have fallen to her lot had she been an ordinary girl with an ordinary past behind her. And it seemed to Catherine now that she could bear no more of it. When, upon reaching home, Aunt Rose inquired whether she had had a pleasant time at Lady Laura's, it was all she could do not to burst into tears.

"It was well enough, I suppose," she managed to say, with assumed indifference. She then hurried upstairs to her room, flung herself across her bed, and prepared to indulge in a paroxysm of weeping.

No tears came, however. What came instead was a series of memories beginning with her term at Miss Saddler's Academy and ending with the evening just past. For the most part they were bleak memories, interspersed with numerous small humili-

ations, indignities, and insults. Of really happy memories there
were few; of untroubled hours even fewer.

"And it's not going to improve," Catherine told herself with
despair. "Aunt Rose has done a great deal, but she can never
wholly erase the past. People will always remember that I was
the girl who ran off with an Italian dancing master. If they
haven't forgotten in nine years, they never will."

In an effort to ease her misery, she reminded herself once
again that she was better off now than she had been nine years
ago. But the thought brought no comfort. It no longer seemed
enough that life should be calm, quiet, and not too painful. She
wanted something more.

"But what?" Catherine asked herself. "Surely I am not
envious of Laura and the other girls?" Exploring her feelings,
however, she found she *was* envious, not of them so much as
of their confidence in the future. One and all, they seemed
certain that love, romance, and happiness lay ahead of them.
She, Catherine, had sacrificed such certainty: sacrificed it as
Eve had sacrificed her life of innocent contentment in order to
gain a perilous knowledge.

Knowledge was a useful thing, of course. Catherine told
herself that she did not really desire to renounce her own
knowledge in order to resume her former naïveté. What she
did desire was assurance that in making the choices she had
made, she had not destroyed all hopes of happiness. "In fact,
I want a glimpse into the future," she told herself with wry
amusement. "It's enough to make me wish I believed in the
well and its powers. All I would have to do then is go and
wash my face there tomorrow with the other girls!"

No sooner had the thought crossed Catherine's mind than
she was seized by a desire to do just that. Of course it was
ridiculous. No well, however venerable, could give one knowledge of the future. Yet there *had* been curious stories in the
past of those who had seen visions in the well at Honeywell
House. An elderly maidservant of her aunts', long since
deceased, had always sworn she had seen her own future there.

"I think, myself, 'tis a matter of wishing, not of washing," she had told Catherine. "There's many that come to the well, but not many as really wishes to know their future with their whole heart—and so the well shows them nothing, or only a glimpse of what's to come. Me, though, I was sixteen and alone in the world, with never a soul to care for me and no prospects of getting on. It seemed to me that if I didn't see something ahead that'd give me comfort, I might as well die and be done with it. So I just wished with all my heart as I washed my face that morning—and I *saw*, miss. I saw my whole future just as plain as I see you now."

Catherine, at thirteen, had not been much impressed by this story. But Catherine at twenty-five now found herself wondering. The old woman had seemed very sure—and there was no doubt that she had predicted several events, including her own death, with uncanny accuracy. "I don't really believe in it," Catherine told herself. "But there's no harm in trying, I suppose." The worst that could happen, to her way of thinking, was that the well would provide a glimpse into her future and show that future to be exactly like her past. But that was highly unlikely. Much more likely, it would show her only her own freshly washed face, just as it had done for Jeanie Bailey.

Catherine felt she could live with that outcome. It was the possibilities of the excursion, not its probable results, that chiefly interested her. And there was also a certain naughty satisfaction in knowing that she was flying in the face of Mr. Poole's advice. It might be childish, but after the patronizing way he had spoken to her, Catherine would have been tempted to spurn any counsel he had given her, no matter how wise.

The only difficulties that she could see were the ways and means of the expedition. To accompany Lady Laura and the other girls to the well was out of the question. It was not that Lady Laura would mind her doing so; Catherine felt sure that on the contrary, Lady Laura would welcome her with open arms. But unfortunately, Lady Laura would not be going alone to the well. The same girls who had attended her party last night would be accompanying her there, and those girls included Isabel Wrexford.

Catherine disliked to admit that someone as contemptible as Isabel could have the power to hurt her. But the truth was that she *had* been hurt by the other girl's barbs. She shrank from seeing Isabel again—shrank from seeing any of the other girls, in fact.

"I would much rather go to the well alone," Catherine told herself. Yet on reflection, she could hardly see how such a thing could be managed. There would be other girls going to the well on Midsummer morning besides Lady Laura's group— servant girls and farmers' daughters and the like. The hour before sunrise would probably see a steady stream of female visitors to the well.

"Well, then, I'll simply have to go earlier," said Catherine aloud. "The custom merely says that one must wash one's face in the well before sunrise on Midsummer Day. If that is so, any time after midnight would do—and it's nearly midnight now."

No sooner had Catherine spoken these words than she was struck by an idea both frightening and fascinating. "I couldn't!" she exclaimed. Then she instantly contradicted herself. "Yes, I could, though. I'm wide awake and not undressed yet. Going now would be much more sensible than waiting and going in the morning. After all, it's just as dark then as now. I don't see why it should be more dangerous to go at midnight than at four or five o'clock in the morning."

Springing to her feet, Catherine began to strip off her green crepe dinner dress. She replaced it with a white muslin round dress that she had worn for a few seasons. "It's short enough to walk in, and I won't mind if it gets torn by branches and brambles," she reasoned. "I'll wear my old dark wool cloak over it. That will cover me decently if I should meet someone, but it's not at all likely that I will, at this hour." Operating on this comfortable assumption, Catherine did not bother to bind up her hair, which she had already loosened for the night, but merely pulled the hood of her cloak over her head and stepped softly out of her room.

The whole house was dark and silent. There was no sound or light from beneath her aunt's door opposite. Catherine was glad she need not bother to make any explanation for her nocturnal journey. "Aunt Rose would only worry, and really there's nothing to worry about," she rationalized comfortably. "I'll just go to the well, wash my face, and come straight back. It won't take an hour if I hurry."

Catherine tiptoed past her aunt's door, then hurried down the stairs and through the kitchens. There were several lanterns hanging near the scullery door. She took one of them, lighting it from the candle she had brought downstairs with her. She then extinguished the candle, and having slid the shade over the lantern so that only a faint glow was emitted, she unlatched the door and stepped outside.

A little shiver went through her as the night air struck her. It was not a shiver of cold. The air was as warm now as it had been earlier on Lady Laura's terrace, but the wind had picked up slightly, and it came to Catherine's nostrils charged with a racy perfume that might have been distilled from the night itself. "Silly," Catherine told herself. "It's just Auntie's roses, together with the smell of the hay that the men have been cutting." Still, she breathed deeply of the perfumed air as she went down the garden walk and let herself out through the gate opening onto the common.

At first Catherine walked in a leisurely manner, enjoying the warm, scented air and the novelty of being abroad when most other people were home in their beds. It was not until she reached the great oak that marked the halfway point between Willowdale Cottage and Honeywell House that she began to feel the first stirrings of uneasiness.

The oak was a great old tree, reputed to have stood since before the Conquest. It would have taken several fully grown men with arms outstretched to encircle its mighty girth "Someone might be standing behind it—several someones, in fact—

and I would never know they were there," Catherine thought idly as she walked past the great tree. And then—out of the corner of her eye—she thought she saw a movement.

Catherine stopped dead, looking at the tree very hard. She even ventured to slide back the shade on her lantern an inch or two and shine it upon the tree's trunk. There was nothing to be seen apart from a moth or two that came fluttering up, attracted to the light. "There's nothing there," Catherine told herself. But might there not be, even though she could see nothing now? The tree was such a large one that it would be easy for someone to stand concealed behind its bulk.

Catherine supposed she ought to walk over and make sure that no one was there. That would be the sensible thing to do. Yet sensible or not, she was completely unable to do it. She found herself remembering, all at once and with uncomfortable clarity, the two women who had been assaulted. That had been only a few miles from here, and their assailant was still at large. Suddenly, Aunt Rose's qualms about being abroad after dark seemed no longer foolish and overprotective. but rather the height of common sense.

"But I'm halfway there now," said Catherine aloud. "It would be silly to come this far, only to go tamely back home." Once more she began to walk along the path. Her feet moved rather quicker than before, however, and she cast frequent uneasy looks over her shoulder at the dark bulk of the oak. It was a relief when finally it had passed out of sight.

Yet now that her uneasiness had been awakened, she found her way crowded with terrors. She sped past the thatched huts in the spinney as though they had been the residences of assassins rather than honest workmen. The Abbey woods within their iron palisade seemed full of lurking menace, while the quarry was a black and bottomless pit as threatening as Erebus itself. Catherine was in an advanced state of nerves when she finally reached the little grove where the well stood. She stood for several minutes, reconnoitering. A little way off she could see the crumbling walls of the old Honeywell House looming dimly above the trees. At that moment, the moon burst suddenly through the clouds overhead, bathing the whole wood in a silvery light and making it appear for a moment as though the ruined house were magically whole and sound once more. Catherine drew in her breath. Then she stepped resolutely toward the little pavilion that stood just ahead of her.

The well itself was merely a waist-high circle of carved stonework, set within a larger circle of paving stones. It might once have possessed a roof or shelter of its own, but if so, such shelter had vanished centuries ago. The pavilion that enclosed it nowadays dated from the era of the new Honeywell House. It was constructed of the same indigenous gray slate, supported on slender columns with acanthus capitals.

In the moonlight, the little pavilion on its slender columns possessed an unearthly beauty. Catherine could not help admiring it, but in this instance her admiration was secondary to a feeling of relief and gratitude. The moon's glow made the grove almost as bright as day and enabled her to see that she was quite alone. Heaving a sigh of relief, she passed quickly between the pavilion's columns and made her way up to the well.

Once there, she placed her lantern on the floor and opened its shade. Light sprang forth, illuminating the uneven stone flooring around the well and the curious carvings on its curb. A few dilapidated chairs and settees stood in a corner, showing the pavilion was occasionally used as a summerhouse. Catherine was intent on the well itself, however. She went a step nearer, until she was actually standing at the curb, looking down into the still water that lay a few feet below her.

Her own face was reflected back to her as clearly as in a mirror. She remained looking at it for a moment or two, then cautiously reached out one hand to touch the water. With the touch of her hand, her image shivered and fractured into wavering fragments. A further touch made it dissolve entirely, as though it had been a looking glass that had shattered. Catherine withdrew her hand, and watched with fascination as the waters stilled, the ripples on its surface growing gradually less and less until her face looked back at her once more from the well's depths.

The water had been cool to the touch, but not so cold as she feared. "I suppose if I'm going to do this, I had better do it now," said Catherine aloud. "It must be midnight and then some."

The sound of her own voice was startlingly loud in the stone pavilion. She glanced uneasily around, then bent over the water once more. Now that the moment for action had come, she felt curiously reluctant to act. She remained standing as she was, looking down at her reflection. Her reflection looked back at her, a brown-haired, pale-faced girl with a question in her eyes. The question was a simple one: Did she or did she not really wish to know the future? Catherine thought of the evening she had just spent at Lady Laura's, and a long procession of similar evenings over the past nine years.

"I do want to know," she told her reflection. "I *must* know. Please show me the future—and please, oh, please, let it be a happy one." Shutting her eyes, she bent low over the well and splashed a little water on her face.

Though not cold, the water seemed to tingle on her skin. Catherine shivered and opened her eyes. There were still eddies dancing on the water's surface, but as she watched they stilled and subsided. Presently the water lay smooth and mirrorlike once more, reflecting her own face. Catherine stood for a considerable time, looking intently into the water. But she saw nothing apart from her own reflection. As a looking glass, the well seemed to function admirably, but as a predictor of the future it was a complete and utter failure.

So Catherine had just decided when suddenly, without warning, another face appeared in the water beside her own.

CHAPTER IX

"You misbegotten brute," said Jonathan through his teeth. Hauling on the reins with all his strength, he succeeded in bringing his plunging horse to a standstill. Reaching out to stroke its sweat-drenched flanks, Jonathan addressed it with exasperation. "Must you shy at every shadow? You nearly succeeded in unseating me that time, old fellow. And I've had enough irritation this evening without breaking my collarbone into the bargain."

The horse nickered softly and ducked his head, as though expressing contrition for his actions. Jonathan smiled and stroked him again. "No, never mind apologizing. Just get me home, there's a good fellow, and I won't ask you to make any more midnight trips through the woods. I can see they don't agree with you."

Encouraged by the tone of his voice, and spurred by the pressure of his heels, the horse began to move forward once more. Jonathan, the crisis over, settled back in the saddle and began to reflect once more on the events of the evening just past.

It had been an eventful evening, coming on top of a long and fatiguing day. For the past week he had been in London, conferring with his man of business over several matters pertaining to his estate. He had left London two days ago, expecting to reach Devonshire yesterday evening, but various small mishaps had delayed him so that he had arrived at the Abbey almost twenty-four hours later than he had anticipated. There had barely been time to wash, change, and ride furiously to Honeywell House in order to keep his appointment with Lady Laura's father.

And though he had arrived in time for that appointment, still all had not gone as he had planned. The earl had received him graciously, but at the same time he had made it clear that Jonathan was not the suitor he would have preferred for Lady Laura.

"You know she is my only daughter," he had told Jonathan. "I would not be doing my duty by her if I was to allow her to enter into marriage without assuring myself that she had a reasonable prospect of happiness. And if you will forgive me for speaking plainly, Meredith, your background and character do not tend to reassure me on that score."

What had followed had been some very plain speaking indeed. Adjectives like *profligate, dissolute,* and *debauched* had been flung about freely. When Jonathan had protested that his past misbehavior had been concomitant with his bachelor state and that he meant to turn over a new leaf with marriage, the earl had received his protestations with open skepticism and had shown how deeply he doubted Jonathan's ability to change what he clearly considered an essential part of his character.

"But it's not," Jonathan told himself with indignation. "I do mean to change. Up till now, the only one to be hurt by my behavior was myself. But it will be different when I marry. I hope I would never serve any woman as my father served my mother."

As a child, he had become early aware that his father was

not a good or faithful husband. His philanderings with other women had been notorious in the neighborhood. The late Lady Meredith, a quiet, gentle-mannered woman, had never reproached her husband for his actions, but as Jonathan grew older he could see how deeply they had grieved her. This had tended to make him a fierce partisan on her behalf, and a fierce critic of his father's behavior. And when his mother had died unexpectedly at the premature age of thirty-eight, he had blamed his father, if not for actually hastening her end, at least for rendering the last years of her life acutely miserable.

Since then, of course, he himself had had a number of more or less serious affairs with women. But those affairs had been in a different category from his father's, according to Jonathan's way of thinking. He had not been married at the time, and it was an accepted thing that young men should sow their wild oats before marriage.

Now that he was thirty, however, it was time for him to think of settling down. In Jonathan's mind, settling down was synonymous with marriage. He had given much thought to the matter and had resolved that his marriage should be very different from his mother and father's. He would find a woman of beauty, breeding, and character, a woman whom he could sincerely love and respect. He would marry her and remain faithful to her for the duration of their married lives. They would live at the Abbey, raise children, devote themselves to improving their property, and otherwise comport themselves in a sober and irreproachable manner until God should see fit to call them to their ancestors.

Jonathan, in envisioning this plan, could see no flaw with it, unless it might be the difficulty of finding a woman whom he could sincerely love and respect. But even this had not proven to be any difficulty. For upon returning to England after his travels abroad, almost the first people he had encountered had been Lord and Lady Lindsay and their daughter Lady Laura. And in Lady Laura, he had immediately recognized the woman he had been looking for.

"And whatever her father may say, I do care for her," Jonathan told himself defiantly. "I do—I do—most assuredly I do. I love Laura and respect her most truly, just as I told Lord Lindsay."

He repeated these last words aloud, as though to emphasize the strength of his feelings. Yet in the back of his mind, he could not help feeling he was being almost suspiciously insistent about his love and respect for Lady Laura. It was as though he was trying to convince himself of something he suspected was not true. Jonathan tried hard to deny that this could be the case, assuring himself over and over that he did love and respect Lady Laura very truly, but all the while he was conscious that there was something in the back of his mind that had given him sudden reservations on the subject. And that something had to do with Catherine.

Ever since he had met Catherine at Lady Laura's party a few weeks ago, he had been unable to get her out of his mind. It was not for want of trying. He had reminded himself over and over that he loved Lady Laura and intended to marry her, but somehow Catherine would not be denied. From the moment she had first looked into his eyes, he had felt something he could never recall feeling before in connection with anyone else.

It was not mere physical desire. That had been a common enough phenomenon in his life, and he trusted that by now he would have recognized its symptoms. Nor was it anything so simple of definition as love. He knew that he loved Lady Laura—loved her for her goodness and sweetness, and because she was so clearly superior to other women. What he felt for Catherine was entirely different. Looking into her eyes, he had felt as though he had discovered something—something that was at once strange and strangely familiar. It had shaken him at the time, and it shook him now to recall it. And the more he tried not to recall it, the more it obtruded on his thoughts.

Still, though he could not avoid thoughts of Catherine, he had been successful thus far in avoiding her physical presence.

Every time the idea of seeing her occurred to him—and it *had* occurred to him, many times since the night of Lady Laura's party—he had scotched it sharply. No good could come from meeting her again, and especially not when he was on the verge of becoming engaged to Lady Laura. Yet he thought of her nonetheless. He was thinking of her now as he rode through the woods toward home when suddenly he perceived a light shining between the trees. It seemed to be coming from that part of the woods that he vaguely recalled as containing the ruins of the old Honeywell House.

"Hi, what's that?" said Jonathan, reining in his horse. "Poachers?" This explanation did not seem to him likely. Few poachers would be reckless enough to stray so near Honeywell House, let alone advertise their presence with lights. Besides, this was a fixed light, not a moving one. It seemed to beckon Jonathan forward, twinkling at him provocatively through the darkness. "I'd better go see," he said aloud. Dismounting from his horse, he tied the reins to a nearby sapling, then began to advance cautiously on foot.

The woods were unfamiliar in darkness, so that it was not until he was within sight of the well pavilion that he realized where he was. The realization both puzzled and intrigued him. He continued forward, until he stood at the pavilion's entrance. From here he could see the source of the light, an unshaded lantern that beamed forth near the base of the well. Its light illuminated the pavilion and revealed its sole occupant, a young woman who seemed to be gazing into the well with curious intentness.

Jonathan advanced quietly to the woman's side. She did not stir or turn around. Indeed, she seemed oblivious to his presence, though his progress across the stone floor was far from silent. She only went on staring into the well as though contemplating something of great and absorbing interest. Jonathan leaned forward, too, curious to see what was engaging her attention.

The woman let out a gasp. Her hand flew to her breast, and she stood swaying on her feet, gazing down at the water with wide, frightened eyes. Her face was clearly reflected in the water. Jonathan, looking down at it, was stunned to recognize her as the subject of his thoughts only a moment before. "Catherine?" he said in disbelief.

His voice seemed to break the spell. Catherine spun around quickly. "Jonathan!" she said. She stared at him a moment, then sank down suddenly on the well curbing. Her breath was coming fast, and Jonathan was not certain but that she might be about to faint. He sprang forward to assist her.

"I'm sorry," he said. "I didn't mean to startle you."

Catherine allowed him to take her arm and draw her away from the well. He observed that she was trembling. "I'm sorry," he said again. "Indeed, Catherine, I had no idea I would frighten you like this. If I had, I would have been more cautious in my approach."

He spoke with real penitence. Catherine nodded. After a moment, she addressed him in a faint voice. "What are you doing here, my lord?" she asked.

"I was riding through the woods and saw your light. I couldn't imagine who could be here at this hour, so I came to investigate."

"I see," said Catherine.

Jonathan looked at her curiously. "What are *you* doing here? I saw you looking into the well just now. You didn't throw a penny in the water for luck, did you, and then decide you'd rather change it for a ha'penny?"

He smiled as he spoke, and after a moment Catherine smiled, too. "No," she said. "Does one throw money in the water for luck? I never heard of such a custom."

"It's often done with wishing wells, I believe. Though not so much in this part of the world. Indeed, now I think of it, I never heard of anyone throwing money in our local well, though I believe the girls still like to wash their faces here on Midsummer Day in hopes of seeing their futures. Oh!" Enlightenment dawned suddenly upon Jonathan. "That's it, isn't it? You were trying to 'witch' the well!'' He looked down at Catherine with dancing eyes.

Catherine did not answer but merely turned her face away. Jonathan studied her a moment. When he spoke again, his face and voice were more gentle than they had been before.

''I suppose my interrupting when I did prevented you from seeing your future,'' he said. ''That's another thing I owe you an apology for, Catherine. I seem to have made a muck of things all around.''

''It's nothing,'' said Catherine, her face still averted. ''I didn't expect to see anything in the well anyway, Jonathan. Indeed, I was foolish to even try it.''

''I don't know about that. I can understand how the prospect of seeing one's future would be hard to resist. But—forgive me for asking—isn't it more usual to try the charm just before sunrise?''

''Yes, it is more usual,'' said Catherine. ''But there were reasons why I did not care to go in the morning. And so I thought I would come now and see if the charm might still be effective.''

She continued to keep her face averted. Jonathan looked down at her thoughtfully. ''I see,'' he said.

The words were innocuous enough, but their effect on Catherine was startling. She whirled about to face him, her eyes flashing fire. ''You see, do you? Just what do you see?''

''Why, nothing in particular,'' said Jonathan, taken aback. ''It's only that—well, witching the well is rather a romantic notion, Catherine. And somehow I had not taken you for a romantic.''

''Why not?'' demanded Catherine.

Jonathan found this question as difficult to answer as her first one. ''I don't know,'' he said helplessly. ''Really, I know very little about you, Catherine. Only what I knew before—and what you told me at Lady Laura's party the other night.''

Catherine went on looking at him. Jonathan's voice stumbled slightly as he sought to explain himself. ''God knows I didn't mean anything amiss by what I said. If you tell me you are a romantic, then of course I must believe you. But after we talked together the other night, I thought—"

He stopped. "What did you think?" asked Catherine.

Jonathan took a deep breath. "I thought that you were like me," he said.

The words seemed to hang in the air between them. Jonathan looked at Catherine with apprehension. She looked back at him silently. "I thought you were like me," he repeated. "Didn't you feel it, Catherine? Or is it my imagination?"

Catherine did not answer. Jonathan went on, his voice low and strained. "I haven't been able to get it out of my mind, Catherine. I never felt anything like it before. Seeing you— and talking to you—"

"Yes?" said Catherine, as he stopped again. Unconsciously she had come a step nearer as she spoke.

Jonathan started to speak again, then stopped with a helpless gesture. "I don't know," he said. "I don't know what it was. I only know I keep thinking about you, Catherine. And when I saw you here tonight, it seemed like the answer to a prayer."

Catherine came another step nearer. "Did it?" she asked. Her eyes were steady, but a light seemed to flicker in their depths. Jonathan, looking into those eyes, was seized by a kind of madness. He reached out, caught Catherine in his arms, and pressed his lips to hers.

She returned his kiss willingly, even eagerly. Her hands came up to encircle his back and shoulders, while her lips parted beneath the pressure of his, allowing him to explore her mouth with impunity. Jonathan felt as though he were drowning— drowning in a sea of warmth and sweetness and intolerable, aching desire. "Catherine," he whispered, crushing her against him.

She made a small, acquiescent noise. Jonathan kissed her again, devouring her mouth hungrily. He had no sense that he was doing anything wrong. Indeed, he had no sense at all outside his own actions. All his thoughts were centered on his desire for Catherine. He wanted her with every fiber of his being, and with a ferocity that blinded him to every lesser consideration.

Catherine, for her part, was simply dazed by all that was happening. From the moment Jonathan had first kissed her, all her powers of resistance seemed to have been swept away. The feel of his mouth on hers was exquisitely pleasurable, so pleasurable that she felt she would die if he stopped. Yet as he continued to kiss her, it began to seem as much like agony as pleasure. Catherine found herself longing desperately for more—and when his hands slipped beneath her cloak, to caress her body and mold it yet tighter against his own, she let out a trembling sigh that was both relief and surrender.

But soon it was clear that this, too, was insufficient. Dimly at first, and then with increasing clarity, Catherine became aware of an aching within her. It was a real physical ache, a kind of yearning hunger that Jonathan's kisses and caresses only seemed to whet. She wanted not merely to see and kiss and touch him, but to be one with him. And in a dazzling flash of revelation, Catherine realized exactly what it was she wanted.

"Jonathan," she said, raising her face to his. "Oh, Jonathan!"

"Catherine," he whispered, showering kisses on her throat. Catherine shut her eyes. She could feel his hands busy at the ties that secured her cloak about her neck. By way of reciprocation she began to tug at his coat and waistcoat. Jonathan helped her remove them, then returned his attention to her cloak. A moment later she felt it slip to the ground, and then suddenly she, too, was on the ground, with Jonathan on top of her and the warm urgency of his body pressed against her own.

"Yes," said Catherine, and shut her eyes once more. She could feel Jonathan's lips on her face and neck, and his hands working purposefully at the corsage of her dress. Their touch made her tremble, partly with apprehension, partly with desire. She ran her own hands over his body, rejoicing in the broad shoulders and lean hips, warm and solid with a hard muscularity that seemed peculiarly masculine. Then she felt the shock of cool air on her skin as the neckline of her dress gave way— and then a second, even greater shock as Jonathan's mouth touched her breast.

A cry escaped Catherine. She turned her head hard to the side, breathing quickly as his lips danced across her skin with a tantalizing gentleness. "Beautiful," he whispered, "beautiful, beautiful." The words were like a litany, accompanied by a series of delicate, deliberate kisses that drove Catherine nearly wild. Her back arched of its own volition and arched again as by slow, tantalizing degrees, he drew her nipple into his mouth. What followed then was both pleasure and agony on a grand scale. Catherine found herself making little whimpering noises and running her hands up and down his back with frustrated urgency.

"Jonathan," she said in a choked voice. "Oh, Jonathan!" The words were an unmistakable plea. Still, it seemed at first as though her plea had gone unheard. Jonathan continued to kiss her breast, but presently she felt his body shift slightly, and a faint chill settled on her legs as the skirt of her dress was slowly drawn up around her waist. Catherine caught her breath, shut her eyes more tightly than ever, and braced herself for what was to come.

What came, however, was not quite what she had expected. Jonathan continued to kiss her breast, while his hands explored the area he had just bared. Gently he caressed Catherine's hips and thighs, as though teasing her by avoiding that area that most burned for his touch. When at last he did touch it, a shudder went through Catherine. She had never wanted anything so much as she wanted that touch. His hands settled down to stroke and caress her, while his mouth teased and tantalized her breast, and the combined effect was devastating. Catherine grasped his shoulders and gave herself up to pleasure. Wave after wave of it broke over her, growing greater with each kiss, each caress, each passing moment. Before long, she became aware that these waves were tending toward some definite destination. There was a pressure building within her, a sense of something imminent in the offing. In a wavering voice, she spoke Jonathan's name aloud.

His reaction was immediate, as though her voice had been some sort of signal. The pressure of his hands and mouth was withdrawn, and she felt him shift his weight atop her. Opening her eyes, Catherine found Jonathan's face was only inches away from hers. He was looking down at her, his eyes dark and unblinking. Catherine, gazing into their depths, was shaken by a sense of enormity. She felt in that moment as though she was seeing her own thoughts and feelings and desires mirrored in the eyes that were looking so steadily into her own.

"Jonathan," she whispered. He went on looking at her, and she knew with sudden certainty what he was waiting for. With one hand, she drew his face down to hers. His mouth instantly closed over hers with possessive passion, and while he kissed her she ran her other hand down, over his chest, to close at last over the tangible expression of his desire for her.

At her touch, he drew in his breath sharply. His eyes were still open, still fixed on hers, and Catherine felt another thrill at that strange, unspoken communication. He kissed her again, and as he kissed her he began to unbutton the buttons that secured his breeches. An instant later she felt his hands busy once more between her legs—and then she felt something that was not his hands, pressing against her flesh.

Catherine made a little noise in the back of her throat. Jonathan's lips were still on hers, his eyes still looking into her own, as he thrust himself against her. She felt herself yielding, felt him entering, and then he was inside her. Catherine cried out, partly with shock and partly with a pleasure so intense that it could be expressed in no other way. Filled by Jonathan's flesh, kissed by Jonathan's mouth, looking into Jonathan's eyes, she felt overwhelmed and yet triumphant: conquered and conqueror all in one.

And she knew, intuitively, that Jonathan felt the same. He drew a long, shuddering breath as he looked down at her. She wrapped her arms around him tightly, and he whispered her name as he withdrew himself from her, then thrust again. Her hips rose to meet his, an action quite involuntary on Catherine's part. Her body seemed literally possessed by his, and she could only surrender herself to the pleasure of the moment.

Over and over he drove himself into her. Gradually his thrusts resolved into a steady rhythm, and the generalized pleasure Catherine was feeling began to separate itself into distinct waves of pleasure such as she had felt earlier. As before, they seemed bearing her toward some definite destination. She had no strength to resist them, even had she wanted to. Catherine did not want to, but at the same time she did not know exactly what she did want. All she was certain of was that Jonathan must on no account stop, and this she found herself saying aloud, over and over. "Jonathan—don't stop. Please don't stop."

"I won't, Catherine—I won't," he whispered. "Never—never—never." With each repetition of the word, he drove himself home, and then suddenly Catherine found herself borne upward on a wave of pleasure more powerful and intense than any that had come before. The sensation left her gasping, and then, just as suddenly, the ground seemed to fall beneath her and she was falling into an abyss of pure, voluptuous pleasure such as she had never known or dreamed could exist. She clung to Jonathan, calling his name and dimly aware that he was looking down at her, his eyes dark and ablaze with a frenzied exultation. Then suddenly his eyes widened, and his body was shaken by a series of convulsive shudders. "Catherine—oh, Catherine—Catherine," he whispered, and Catherine, looking up at him, knew exactly what he was feeling and why. She tightened her arms around him, and he collapsed atop her, burying his face in her hair.

For a considerable time, they lay together without moving or speaking. Catherine, clasping him in her arms and staring up at the roof of the pavilion, felt a satisfaction so deep and poignant that tears sprang to her eyes. She did not attempt to check them, but let them trickle silently down her face as she continued to hold Jonathan in her arms.

At last he stirred and spoke. "Catherine," he said. "My God, Catherine!"

"Jonathan," she said, stroking his head with her hand. He turned his face to look at her.

"My God, Catherine," he said again. "That was—exquisite."

"Yes," she agreed, still stroking his hair. He looked deep into her eyes, then smiled and bent to kiss her.

"You sound dreadfully cool about it, Catherine! And yet I know you felt what I did. I know it, I tell you." Serious now, he looked again into Catherine's eyes. "Catherine, you don't mean to say you didn't, do you?"

"No," said Catherine. As she spoke, another tear rolled down her cheeks. Jonathan saw it, smiled, and bent to kiss it away.

"Come, that's more like it! Tears I can understand, for I feel rather as if I'd like to cry myself. Catherine, I never felt anything like that before—never, never."

"Neither have I," said Catherine simply. Putting her arms about him once more, she drew his head to her bosom.

He lay there willingly enough, but shifted his face so he might go on looking into her eyes. "Truly, Catherine? I am glad I could give you pleasure. I believe watching your pleasure was more gratifying than feeling my own." He embraced her fiercely. "I can't believe it really happened, Catherine. I can't believe I am lying here, holding you in my arms after just having made love to you!"

"It is rather unbelievable," agreed Catherine. Jonathan made an exasperated noise in his throat.

"Catherine, I could shake you! You give me the most exquisitely pleasurable experience of my life—one that you admit was pleasurable for you, too—and yet you can lie there talking as calmly as though we had done nothing more exciting than take a stroll through your aunt's garden!"

Catherine turned her face away. "Don't you think it's better that I should?" she asked.

"No, I don't think it's better! I want to talk to you, damn it. I want to discuss what just happened between us and what we're going to do about it."

"Do about it?" said Catherine, turning back to face him. "What *can* we do about it, Jonathan? Surely you have not forgotten about"—she paused, then went on resolutely—"about Lady Laura?"

He *had* forgotten about Lady Laura. She saw it in his face, and in the look of horror that suddenly sprang up in his eyes. Catherine was sorry for him, yet she could not prevent herself from feeling a fierce rush of triumph. Whatever thoughts or feelings might have inspired him to make love to her, they could have had no connection with Lady Laura.

When he spoke, his voice was shaken. "My God!" he said. "Catherine, I forgot. How could I forget about Lady Laura?"

"I forgot, too," said Catherine. "It wasn't until afterwards that I remembered."

She sat up as she spoke, gently but firmly displacing Jonathan's head from her breast. He immediately rolled off her and sat up, too, his expression distraught.

"But this is terrible, Catherine! You must know that Laura and I are engaged, or as good as engaged. Good God! It was only tonight that I asked her father for permission to marry her."

He and Catherine looked at each other. Catherine was the first to look away. Deliberately she stood up and began to straighten her rumpled dress and hair. "Yes, it is terrible," she agreed. "But you know I am to blame as much as you, Jonathan. Laura is my best friend, and I should have refrained from—from encouraging you on her account."

Jonathan gave her a look of reproach. "Encouraging me! You know it was not like that." He began to pace back and forth in front of the well. "What are we to do? What *can* we do?"

Catherine threw him a brief glance, then looked away again. "Nothing," she said. "There's nothing we can do, Jonathan. We must simply pretend that this did not happen."

"But I can't pretend this didn't happen!" Jonathan paused in his pacing to throw her another look of reproach. "Catherine, I tell you I felt something just now—something I've never felt before. I—Catherine, I think I *love* you. It must be that I love you. Nothing else explains it."

"But you love Lady Laura, too," said Catherine. "Don't you?"

There was a moment's silence. "Yes," said Jonathan unhappily. "Yes, I suppose I do. But it's not the same, Catherine." He looked into her eyes. "It's not the same at all."

She returned his look unflinchingly. "Even if that is true, Jonathan, I don't think it matters," she said. "You love Laura, and she has a prior claim on your feelings. Therefore we must simply forget that this happened."

"Can you forget?" said Jonathan aggressively.

Catherine was silent a moment, then spoke with difficulty. "I will try to," she said.

"Don't," said Jonathan violently. He came to her, laying his hands on her shoulders and forcing her to face him. "Don't," he said again. "Don't try to forget, Catherine. I can't bear it if you do. To have only just found each other—and now to be faced with the prospect of parting—it doesn't bear thinking of. There must be a better solution, if only we set ourselves to find it."

Catherine only shook her head. "I don't think so, Jonathan." Turning away again, she bent to pick up her cloak that was lying on the ground.

"You're not leaving?" said Jonathan in dismay as she threw the cloak across her shoulders.

"I must," she said. "I must be getting home. My aunt does not know I came out tonight. I would rather she did not know."

"Of course," said Jonathan. "But you must let me see you

home, Catherine. To see you get home safely—it's the least I can do.''

Catherine slanted him a look. "It's kind of you, but I'm afraid that would not be a good idea, Jonathan," she said. "If we were to be seen together . . .'' She said nothing more, but Jonathan saw the force of her argument. He groaned, running his hand through his hair.

"God, what a situation! Well, if I must let you go, I must, Catherine. But I'll come and call on you tomorrow, so we can discuss this business more fully.''

Catherine merely shook her head. "There's nothing to discuss," she said.

"Yes, there is!" said Jonathan. Taking a quick step toward her, he gathered her into his arms. Catherine made no move to resist him. Neither did she resist when he lowered his lips to hers and kissed her. A little shiver ran through her, and her body relaxed in his arms. But as soon as he was done, she drew herself gently away from him.

"Good-bye, Jonathan. I must go now.'' Pulling the hood of her cloak over her head and picking up her lantern, she turned and walked out of the pavilion.

CHAPTER X

Catherine made her way quickly through the woods, hardly aware of the rocks, brush, and brambles that put themselves in her way. When she reached the path across the common, she paused to drop the shade over her lantern. The moon had retreated once more behind a veil of clouds, but its radiance was sufficient to light her way along that better-marked thoroughfare. Catherine's feet followed its twists and turns automatically. Her thoughts were far away, though not so very far as regards distance. They were, in fact, back in the pavilion where she had left Jonathan.

The thought of Jonathan made Catherine tingle from head to foot. "Jonathan," she said, speaking his name softly aloud. "Jonathan! What have I done?" The thought of what she had done was so unreal, and at the same time so vivid to her, that it made her shiver.

Her thoughts were so taken up with this subject that she did not even think to be nervous as she crossed the common. She passed the Great Oak all unheeding, and spared no glance to shifting shadows and small rustles in the underbrush. Thus it was all the more shocking to her when, as she approached Willowdale Cottage, a man's figure suddenly stepped out of the shrubbery.

Catherine let out a stifled scream and took a step backwards. The man turned to look at her but made no move to approach her. He merely stood quietly in the path where he had first emerged from the shrubbery. Catherine took courage from his immobility. The thought of her lantern, too, was a reassurance, and she slid up the shade, shining it full in the man's face. He blinked in the sudden flood of light, and she saw with relief that it was merely Ned Horne.

Ned was a fixture in the village of Langton Abbots. The son of a local farmer, he was in appearance a grown man both tall and bulky of physique. His intellect, however, was still that of a child. "A touch wanting" was the villagers' consensus, and they treated Ned with a mixture of affection and contempt whenever he came shambling through Langton Abbots, his tattered coat flapping in the breeze and a vacant smile on his good-humored face. He returned their affection cheerfully and never seemed to sense the contempt that lay beneath it. Catherine had often pitied him, though it struck her as almost presumptuous to pity someone so perfectly content with his lot in life. Ned, in his childlike innocence, was much happier than most of those who held him in contempt.

As soon as Catherine recognized Ned, all trace of fear left her. He might be mentally wanting, but even his worst critics had never accused him of being dangerous. Indeed, he was generally acknowledged to be a kindhearted and gentle creature who would grieve over a dead insect or even a crushed flower with childlike abandon. So she addressed him now with a smile and relief in her voice. "Ned, I didn't recognize you for a moment. You gave me quite a turn."

At the sound of her voice, Ned came a step nearer, still blinking against the light. "It's you, is it, Miss Catherine?" he said. "I didn't know 'twas you."

"Yes, it's me," said Catherine. Ned continued to stand there, regarding her owlishly.

"You're abroad very late, Miss Catherine," he said. "The church clock struck two just a bit ago."

His voice was accusing. Catherine was taken aback by his accusation, and rather alarmed by it, too. She realized suddenly that she had been guilty of an indiscretion. If only she had turned and fled as soon as she saw Ned, he would never have known who she was. Now he did know, and if he was to go around telling people that he had seen her abroad at two o'clock in the morning, there was no telling what mischief he might not do.

"Yes. it is very late," she said. forcing another smile. "My aunt would be very worried if she learned I was out so late. You won't tell, will you, Ned?"

"Oh, no, I won't tell anybody," Ned assured her. "But you shouldn't be out so late, Miss Catherine. It isn't safe, and that's a fact."

"Not safe?" said Catherine sharply. "What do you mean? Why isn't it safe, Ned?"

A momentary glint showed in Ned's mild blue eyes. The next moment the glint had vanished, however, and he shook his head with dull disapproval. "It's not safe, that's all. A lady like you shouldn't be abroad alone o' nights. You might get hurt, like t'other ones."

His voice was matter-of-fact, almost tranquil. He might have been discussing the weather, or the latest village cricket match. Catherine looked at him closely. "What other ones?" she asked. "What do you mean, Ned?"

Again that disquieting glint showed briefly in Ned's eye. "The other ones," he repeated. "The ones as wasn't ladies. Still, you oughtn't to be abroad alone at night, Miss Catherine. It might be you next time."

Catherine stared at him. He smiled at her childishly, lifting an imaginary hat upon his head. "You needn't fear I'll say aught about meeting you this night, Miss Catherine. Good evening to you, and mind you don't forget what I've been saying."

"I won't forget," said Catherine faintly. She watched as Ned shambled off across the common.

As soon as he had vanished from sight, she continued toward Willowdale Cottage. But her steps were quicker than before, and her thoughts were running on a different subject now than her meeting with Jonathan.

What had Ned meant by his words? Obviously he was referring to the women who had been attacked earlier—the barmaid and the woman who, to use her aunt's words, had "entertained men in her home." Those attacks had been much discussed in Langton Abbots, and it was not surprising that even simple Ned Horne should have heard of them by now. But was it possible Ned had some more specific knowledge than that gained by gossip? There had been almost a knowing look in his eye when he had told Catherine that it wasn't safe for ladies to be out alone at night. The memory of it gave Catherine a disagreeable feeling.

Of course, Ned was wanting mentally, and he could not be held wholly responsible for his voice and manner. But he had certainly looked very sly and knowing when he had spoken of "the ones as wasn't ladies." And as Catherine reflected on the subject, it struck her suddenly that she had been so busy trying to defend her own reasons for being abroad at two A.M. that it had never occurred to her to question Ned about his. Was it possible that he had some connection with the attacks on the other women? Was it possible that he might not be so harmless as he had always seemed?

Catherine shivered. "It may be that I had a narrow escape tonight," she told herself. "I wonder if I ought to tell anyone about what Ned said, and about his being out tonight? But that would mean that I would have to admit I was out, too—and that would be very awkward, to say the least. I had better hold my tongue, I suppose. But still, it's very worrisome. If only there was some way I could mention it to someone in authority without incriminating myself.''

There being no apparent way to do this, Catherine resolved to dismiss the incident from mind. But that was easier said than done. The indefinite threat of Ned's words stayed with her, causing her to start nervously at every rustling leaf and waving branch. By the time she finally reached the scullery door of Willowdale Cottage, she was thoroughly rattled. With trembling fingers she extinguished her lantern and hung it with the others inside the door. She then made her way upstairs, walking as silently as she could in an effort to avoid waking anyone. Her efforts were successful. The house continued dark and silent as she slipped into her room, rapidly changed into a nightdress, and dropped down on her bed.

Sleep, however, was impossible. Catherine lay trembling, reliving the past few hours in each smallest detail. Was it possible it had only been a few hours since she had gone to the well? Her clock assured her that it was, yet in that short space of time her life had changed forever.

"Jonathan," whispered Catherine aloud. Now that she was safe at home, the incident of Ned had begun to recede in her mind. It had been only a brief, albeit disturbing moment in the evening's events, overshadowed by the enormity of what had gone before.

"Jonathan," whispered Catherine again. With her eyes closed, she could feel again his lips, his hands, as they explored her body. The mere memory was enough to make her ache for him all over again. "Oh, God," she whispered, covering her face with shaking hands. It was torture to want anything as much as she wanted him at that moment—a sweet, maddening torture that had not the slightest hope of ever ceasing. How could it cease? Catherine groaned and rolled over onto her side, hugging her knees against her chest like a child seeking comfort.

"What a fool I am," she whispered desolately.

Looking at the matter impartially, she could not deny that she had been several species of fool. It had been foolish to go to the well in the first place and more foolish still to betray her presence with a light, so that Jonathan was drawn to investigate. But neither of these things could compare with the crowning foolishness that had led her to give herself to a man who was already as good as engaged to her own best friend.

Still, Catherine very much feared that even this had not been her worst foolishness. For instead of regretting the incident properly and resolving to live it down with tears and penitence, she found herself longing to see him again—longing to look at him and talk to him and yes, make love to him once more. Catherine marveled at her shamelessness. "Perhaps Mrs. Wrexford and Lady Mabberly were right about me after all," she told herself. "Perhaps I really am an unprincipled hussy." But even this thought did not fill her with shame. The only regret she felt, the only vestige of penitence she could summon up for making love with Jonathan, was when she reflected on how she had betrayed Lady Laura.

It had been an appalling betrayal. And the fact that she had betrayed Lady Laura unwittingly rather than deliberately did not make it better, but on the contrary worse. How could she have so far forgotten Lady Laura and the claims of friendship Lady Laura had upon her as to commit such an act? How could she ever look Lady Laura in the face again, knowing that she had enjoyed intimate relations with the man Lady Laura loved?

"Oh, God," whispered Catherine, tossing restlessly on her pillow. "I didn't mean to. I didn't mean to." Yet when she thought back over the evening's events, it was clear to her that she *had* meant to. Ever since seeing Jonathan at Lady Laura's party, she had felt a strong attraction for him. He had confessed to feeling the same attraction for her, and though she could not be sure he was telling the truth, his distress and self-reproach afterwards had seemed genuine. She could not believe him the sort of man who would purposely seduce one woman while formally seeking the hand of another.

"He didn't," she told herself. "He did it because he couldn't help himself, any more than I could." And in spite of her misery and guilt, Catherine felt a surge of exultation at the memory of the mutual need and desire that had led them to make love that evening.

But it could never happen again. Catherine had realized as much almost the minute the deed was done, and it had taken Jonathan only a little longer to realize the same thing. He was Lady Laura's future husband in the eyes of the community and—what was more important—in the eyes of Lady Laura herself. She would be devastated were she to learn of what had happened that evening. "She must never suspect," Catherine resolved. "I must never betray any hint of it, as long as I live." She felt her heart sink at the prospect of such long-term concealment, but there was no help for it. She consoled herself with the thought that it might be worse.

"I see her only a few times a week, and seldom more than an hour or two at a time. Jonathan, on the other hand, will have to see her every day of his life." It struck her with a pang, however, that Jonathan might not find his task so difficult as she would find hers. Once he was married to Lady Laura, he might dismiss his interlude with Catherine along with the other indiscretions of his bachelor days and devote himself to the woman he loved. For he did love Lady Laura. He had admitted as much to Catherine that evening, and though he had also confessed a kind of love for Catherine herself, by his own admission it was "not the same."

"Of course it's not the same," Catherine told herself bitterly. "How could it be?" Her bitterness was not directed toward Jonathan, or even toward herself: It was directed toward the unkind fate that had shown her a bliss she had never thought attainable on earth, only to snatch it out of her grasp almost as soon as she had enjoyed it.

"But at least I did enjoy it," she reminded herself. "I have the memory of it, if nothing else. No one can ever take that away from me." And she felt once again a fierce surge of exultation at the remembrance of what she and Jonathan had shared.

In this manner, feeling by degrees exultant, guilt-stricken, and bitter, Catherine was gradually able to bring her experiences that evening into a kind of perspective. And once this had been done, it was a simple matter to decide the policy she must follow in regard to Jonathan from now on.

"I must not see him any more than I can help. And I must take particular care never to be alone with him again. But there, I doubt that situation will ever repeat itself. He was even more upset than I was by what happened, so likely he will do all he can to avoid me in the future. Of course he did speak of calling on me so we might discuss the situation." Catherine doubtfully considered this statement, then dismissed it with a sigh. "But by now he must see that discussion is of no use. The only thing to be done is to avoid each other. If he does try to call on me, I must refuse to see him, that's all."

Having reached this conclusion, Catherine tried to compose herself to sleep. But she continued to toss and turn for a long time, reliving those moments at the well pavilion with a mixture of guilt, misery, and exultation. It was daybreak before she slept. She woke briefly when the maid came in to open the curtains and deposit the washing water, then fell asleep again, to be wakened by her aunt's apologetic voice.

"Catherine, dear, I'm sorry to wake you. You must have been very tired to have slept so late. But it's ten o'clock, you see—and you have a caller."

"A caller?" repeated Catherine. It took her sleep-fogged brain a moment to absorb this information. Once it had, however, she sat up quickly, her eyes dark with alarm. "What caller? Who has called?"

"Why, it is Lord Meredith, dear. You look surprised—and I must say that I was surprised to see him here, too, and at such an early hour. Of course we do receive callers this early sometimes, only usually it is close friends, or a neighbor asking for a receipt, or something of that sort—"

Catherine heard nothing of the last part of this speech. At

the words *Lord Meredith,* her heart had seemed to stop, then resume its beating at an accelerated pace.

Jonathan here at the Cottage! Catherine felt dazed by the idea. He had spoken of calling, to be sure, but she had never supposed he would, and certainly not so soon after the event.

"I can't see him," she told herself. "I must not see him. It's better I should stick to the resolution I made last night and avoid him entirely." Yet in spite of her resolutions the night before, the thought of seeing and talking to Jonathan again was a seductive one. So seductive was it that she could hardly force herself to make the reply she knew she must make.

"It is very kind of Lord Meredith to call, but I cannot see him, Auntie. Please give him my regrets and—and tell him I am indisposed."

Catherine forced this reply between dry lips and sank back on her pillow. To deny herself to Jonathan had taken every ounce of strength and self-restraint she possessed. She glanced at her aunt, fearing that she might protest her words. At that moment she felt so weak and spiritless that even gentle Aunt Rose might have overruled her with ease. And there was a part of Catherine that desperately wanted to be overruled. But apparently her appearance bore out her claim of indisposition. Aunt Rose took one look at her and was instantly all concern.

"Of course! I can see you are not feeling well. I'll tell Lord Meredith you cannot see him. Do forgive me for waking you, Catherine. You so seldom sleep late, I should have known something was amiss when you did not come downstairs for breakfast."

Catherine said nothing, but only smiled wanly. Aunt Rose smoothed her pillow, kissed her brow, and advised her not to stir out of bed until she was feeling better. She then hurried away to give Catherine's message to Jonathan. Catherine, listening to the tap-tap of her aunt's slippers dying away, felt as though she had done something at once very brave and very foolish.

* * *

Jonathan received her message with outward calm but inward dismay. Having expressed concern for Catherine's indisposition and made Aunt Rose promise to notify him if it proved serious, he left Willowdale Cottage with the bewildered sense that he had just run up against a brick wall.

Of course Catherine's illness might be a real one. Many people felt exposure to night air was unhealthy, and there could be no doubt she had been thoroughly exposed to it the previous night. When Jonathan recalled exactly how exposed she had been, he found himself in the curious position of being at once aroused and appalled.

And he was even more appalled when it occurred to him that he might be directly rather than indirectly responsible for Catherine's indisposition. It was easy to disassociate the act of making love from that of simple procreation, but in actual fact one frequently led to the other. By making love to Catherine, he might well have made her pregnant.

When this possibility first occurred to Jonathan, he felt a little dizzy. His dizziness subsided when he recalled that it was rather soon for Catherine to be experiencing symptoms of pregnancy, but he was so utterly inexperienced on the subject of children and childbearing that he could not totally dismiss the possibility from mind. It was a shocking idea, but after his first shock was past, he was surprised to find how philosophically he accepted it. Indeed, there was a part of his mind that almost welcomed the idea of a pregnant Catherine. Such a development would be painful for everyone concerned, but it would also mean that his duties in the case would be clear. They had seemed anything but clear since taking leave of Catherine at the well the night before.

There was no denying that he had got himself into a fix. How exactly it had happened, Jonathan could not imagine. He only knew that he had been driven to make love to Catherine by some force as impossible to resist as it was to explain. And even now, when he had realized how wrong he had been to give way to such feelings and how dreadfully they had complicated his affairs, he suspected that if the possibility was offered to him to make love to Catherine again, he could not refuse it. The mere thought of her set him aflame with desire—a desire that was more than merely physical. He wanted her; he needed her; yes, and he loved her, too. He had told her so the night before, and since then he had come to realize just how true it was. Yet at the same time he also loved Lady Laura, and therein lay the crux of his problems.

It would have been bad enough if he had merely fallen out of love with one woman while falling in love with the other. Such things did happen, and when they happened in the early stages of courtship there was no blame to be attached to either party. But matters between him and Lady Laura had already gone so far that he could not draw back now without looking a cad. Besides, he was not wholly certain he wanted to draw back. For weeks he had been happily planning a future with Lady Laura as his wife—a future in which he would settle down to a life of rectitude and good works. It pained him to think of giving up those plans. It would be like giving up part of himself—almost, one might say, his better self. He would have to renounce the part of him that longed for stability and security and a life as different as possible from his father's.

"I can't give her up," said Jonathan aloud. "I am pledged to Laura, and I mean to marry her." Yet when he thought of giving up Catherine, the idea was equally painful. Perhaps it was even more painful. What he had experienced with Catherine went beyond any mere physical union. It had been a transcendent experience, in which he and she had been one in the truest and most literal sense. In all his many dealings with women, he had never felt anything like it. It had been an experience such as the poets had described in their highest flights of verse—verses that he had always secretly supposed to be much exaggerated. But he knew the truth of the matter now. And knowing it, it was inconceivable that he should deliberately turn his back upon it. He longed to see Catherine again—not necessarily to make love to her, though he longed to do that, too. But it would have been enough just to look at her, to talk with her, to gaze into her pale golden-brown eyes and see again his own soul reflected back.

Jonathan groaned aloud. "I can't give her up," he said. "I can't. Oh, God, what am I to do?"

He had hoped that by calling on Catherine that morning, he would be able to clarify his feelings. Having once decided what he felt, he might then be able to divine what duty was really asking of him in regard to both her and Laura. But Catherine had refused to see him. Perhaps she was truly ill, but the more Jonathan thought about it, the more certain he became that she had simply refused to see him. She had told him last night that his duty was to Lady Laura. This was her way of emphasizing that duty. And Jonathan was not altogether certain but that she was right.

"Perhaps I ought to call on Laura," he told himself. He felt an indefinable shrinking from the idea, but when he thought about it, he realized that was only natural. It was, after all, less than twelve hours since he had been lying in Catherine's arms. Yet it had also been barely twelve hours since he had asked Lady Laura's father for her hand. Lady Laura would probably be expecting him to call today. He ought to call, and perhaps by calling on her, he would find that all his worrying had been needless. Lord Lindsay had plainly shown his disapproval of Jonathan's courtship of his daughter. If Lady Laura were minded to take her opinions from her father, then she might well have abandoned all idea of marrying Jonathan and would tell him so with her customary directness and honesty. He would then be free of any further obligation in that direction. And though Jonathan was not entirely sure he wanted to be free of Lady Laura, he had to admit that such an outcome would greatly simplify his plight. Remounting his horse, he set off at once for Honeywell House.

CHAPTER XI

Jonathan found Lady Laura at luncheon with a party of young ladies.

The footman who admitted him to Honeywell House did not think to inform him of this circumstance, so that Jonathan walked in upon the party unprepared. He stopped short with an exclamation of dismay.

Upon his entrance, half-a-dozen inquisitive feminine faces turned to look at him. Lady Laura's face, however, promptly lit up with a glowing smile.

"Lord Meredith!" she exclaimed, rising to her feet. "You must sit down with us, my lord, and have a glass of wine and something to eat. Haywood, give Lord Meredith a glass of wine," she instructed the butler. "And see that another place is laid for him."

Jonathan tried to protest, saying he had not meant to intrude on their party. Lady Laura advanced on him smilingly, however, took him by the arm, led him to the vacant chair beside Hermione Woodward, and made him perforce to seat himself. "No, no, you shall not escape us so easily, my lord!'' she told him. "We are glad to have your company, aren't we, girls?''

The girls one and all murmured their assent, except for Isabel Wrexford. That young lady merely eyed him with an air of knowing contempt. "You are early to call upon dear Laura today, my lord,'' she said.

"And so are you, Miss Wrexford,'' he returned. "I had not expected to find a party here at this hour.''

Lady Laura laughed. "Oh, my lord, that was easy to see when you came in! You looked quite horrified.'' She smiled at him warmly. "But I am persuaded none of us was so thin-skinned as to take it personally.''

Jonathan managed to smile back at her, but it was a feeble smile. To encounter Laura alone after what had transpired between him and Catherine would have been awkward enough. To have half-a-dozen interested witnesses to the encounter increased the awkwardness a hundredfold. Lady Laura seemed to sense his constraint, for she went on easily, not waiting for him to reply.

"I daresay you wonder what kind of a party you have walked in upon, my lord. The fact is that we have been celebrating Midsummer's Day in the traditional Langton Abbots fashion. You must know the girls told me yesterday of the custom of washing one's face at the well on Midsummer morning. So we decided to go there in a party early this morning to wash our faces—and now we have returned to enjoy a biscuit and a glass of wine and compare our visions.''

Still Jonathan said nothing. He thought of Catherine as he had seen her the previous night at the well, and the thought sent a tingle down his spine. He shifted in his seat, throwing an uncomfortable look at Lady Laura. She caught him looking and smiled again, her blue eyes warm with trustful affection. Jonathan felt miserable. He had had no chance to talk to her privately as yet, but it was plain from her looks and words that she had no intention of discouraging his suit, whatever her father's attitude might be. Obviously there would be no simple solution to his problems. If he wanted to end his relationship with Lady Laura, then he would have to be the one to end it. He would have to look into her lovely, smiling, trustful face and tell her that he no longer cared for her and wished to marry her.

And that was impossible. Yet it was equally impossible that he should forget about Catherine and go blithely ahead with his courtship of Lady Laura. Jonathan sat morosely, twisting the stem of his wineglass between his fingers, until he was startled by a remark from Isabel.

"Laura, you have not asked Lord Meredith why *he* was at the well this morning." Looking directly at Jonathan, she added, "But there, perhaps he merely went to wash his face on Midsummer morning like the rest of us."

"I? Good lord, no." Jonathan stared at Isabel. "What makes you think I was at the well this morning?"

"Well, you were, were you not?" said Isabel, giving him stare for stare. "Or are you denying it, my lord?"

Jonathan did not know whether to deny it or not. Fortunately, before he was forced to commit himself, Lady Laura intervened. "Now Isabel, we don't know that Lord Meredith was at the well this morning," she said. She flashed Jonathan an apologetic smile. "All we know is that we found your riding crop at the well pavilion, my lord—or a riding crop very much like yours."

Jonathan did not reply. In his mind's eyes, he was seeing himself the night before, dismounting from his horse to go investigate the light he had seen in the well pavilion. His riding crop had been in his hand then, but he remembered now that he had dropped it soon after entering the pavilion because he had had to go to Catherine's aid when she had been startled by his sudden appearance. And considering all that had happened after that, it was perhaps not surprising that it had never occurred to him to pick it up again.

Looking up, he found that all the young ladies were regarding him with lively interest. Try as he might, he could not keep himself from flushing. "Perhaps I did leave my crop at the

Pavilion," he said. "But it cannot have been this morning that I left it. I slept rather late this morning and did not leave the house till nearly ten."

Lady Laura opened her mouth to speak, but Isabel spoke first. "But you must have left it this morning, my lord," she said, her voice more deceptively sweet than ever. "For you had it with you yesterday evening. I saw you when you were out riding, around about nine o'clock it was. I daresay you did not see me, for I was in the lane close against the hedgerow, but I saw you very clearly. You were riding toward Honeywell House, and I noticed very particularly that you had your crop with you then."

Jonathan, looking into Isabel's malicious pale blue eyes, felt an overwhelming urge to wring her neck. But he merely smiled back at her coolly. "Did I? If you say so, then I must believe you, Miss Wrexford. But in that case, I cannot think how my crop came to be at the pavilion. Perhaps it is not my crop after all. I had not noticed it was missing.

"I am sure that it is yours, my lord. It has your coat-of-arms upon it. Wait just a moment, and I'll get it."

As she spoke, Isabel pushed back her chair from the table. Before she could rise to her feet, however, Lady Laura spoke with unwonted sharpness. "Never mind the crop now, Isabel. I will show it to Lord Meredith later, and if it is his, he can take it with him. It is ridiculous to make such a piece of work about such a petty thing. May I give you some dessert?"

Isabel accepted both dessert and Lady Laura's rebuke with sullen meekness, and for a while talk at the table dwindled into silence. Jonathan paid it little heed. He was alternately cursing his own carelessness at leaving his crop at the well the night before and rejoicing that it had not been something even more incriminating. It was not until some minutes later that a few words broke in upon his thoughts. "The third such attack in weeks! I cannot understand why they have had no luck in finding the man responsible."

Jonathan looked up. The girl who had spoken these words,

Jeanie Bailey, caught his eye and turned to address him with appeal in her voice. "Cannot something be done to stop these attacks, my lord? It is getting quite ridiculous. Why, my mama will hardly let me stir out of the house nowadays without one of the servants in attendance."

"Has another woman been attacked, then?" asked Jonathan. Jeanie nodded, and Mary Edwards, the doctor's daughter, spoke up in her turn.

"Yes, it happened just last night. It was one of old Mrs. Percy's maidservants. Apparently the girl had sneaked out of the house to meet her sweetheart, down by Old Church Road."

Jonathan nodded. Old Church Road, so named because of the ancient chapel it had once led to, was well known in Langton Abbots as a local lovers' lane. "Yes, I know the place," he said. "A very secluded spot."

"Yes, and I must say, it was foolish of her to go out alone when she knew this creature was still at large," said Mary, with a shake of her head.

Jonathan thought of Catherine, going alone to and from the well the previous night. The thought that something similar might have happened to her made him feel physically ill. "Was the woman badly injured?" he asked faintly.

"No, oddly enough, she was not. Apparently she was standing there, waiting for her sweetheart, when this man grabbed her from behind. But he had hardly done so when her sweetheart arrived and began calling for her. And her attacker was apparently so much startled that he let her go and ran away."

"She was lucky," said Hermione emphatically.

"Very lucky," echoed Jeanie.

"Much luckier than she deserved," said Isabel with a disagreeable laugh. "She sounds as unprincipled a creature as the others who were attacked. No nice girl would steal out of the house in the middle of the night to meet a man. If I were Mrs. Percy, I would give her her notice at once."

Some of the girls protested this speech, others agreed with it, and a short argument ensued. It was Lady Laura who put an end to it. "At any rate, we may now hope that the man who has perpetrated these dreadful acts will soon be caught," she said. "Was the girl or her sweetheart able to give any kind of description of him, Mary?"

Mary shook her head regretfully. "No, the girl did not see him at all, for he attacked her from behind, as I said before. Her sweetheart did catch a glimpse of him as he was running away, but it was very dark, and apparently the man was wearing some kind of mask or hood over his head."

The girls all shivered at this, and Anne Percy said that she, for one, was never going to set foot outdoors alone again until the man was apprehended. "Really, I can't think why he hasn't been apprehended already," she said. "It's hard to believe any stranger could stay in the area for weeks and weeks and not be noticed."

"Unless it is not a stranger," said Hermione with a shudder. "It might be anybody, really. That is what makes it so frightening."

"But it must be a stranger," countered Anne. "Nothing of this sort has ever happened in the neighborhood before. It must be someone newly arrived to the area—some tramp, perhaps."

The other girls all murmured agreement—all except Isabel, who turned to look at Jonathan. "Why, you are newly arrived in the area, are you not, my lord?" she asked. "And as I recall, the first of these attacks took place not long after you arrived."

She spoke innocently enough, but the implications of her speech were clear. A sudden hush fell over the table. Hermione Woodward drew her chair suddenly away from Jonathan's in an involuntary movement. Several of the other girls eyed him with a mixture of curiosity and fearful speculation.

Jonathan felt cold anger rising in him. He had always thought Isabel Wrexford a disagreeable girl, but now he perceived she was a public menace. "That is so, Miss Wrexford," he said in a measured voice. "But surely you do not suspect me of being responsible for these attacks?"

Isabel opened her eyes wide. "Oh, no, my lord! It only

seemed to me an odd coincidence that they did not start until you returned to the neighborhood. And you were actually abroad last night when the latest one took place, were you not?''

There were many things Jonathan longed to say in reply to this speech. Most of them were not fit for the ears of ladies, however, and before he could think of one that was, Lady Laura had risen from her seat. Her face was aflame with righteous indignation.

''Isabel, that is a monstrous accusation!'' she said. ''I am sure none of us believe Lord Meredith had anything to do with these dreadful attacks.'' Her voice trembled with emotion as she went on, her eyes resting on each of the girls in turn. ''If any of you believes otherwise, then I beg you will say so now. I do not care to associate with anyone who could imagine so unjust and iniquitous a thing.''

No one said anything, and after a minute Lady Laura sat down again and began to eat her dessert as though nothing had happened. The other girls followed her example, but conversation at the table was scanty after this incident, and it was clear the mood of the party had been spoiled. As soon as dessert had been eaten, first one girl and then another excused herself on the plea that she must return home.

Isabel was one of the last to leave. ''Thank you so much for inviting me, Laura,'' she said, bestowing a stiff hug and frigid kiss on Lady Laura. ''A most delightful party. We must organize a similar outing next year, by all means.''

''Certainly,'' said Lady Laura, but her voice was cold, and she did not return Isabel's kiss.

As soon as all the young ladies were gone, Lady Laura turned to Jonathan. ''Shall we go to the drawing room, my lord?'' she asked.

Jonathan nodded. He felt unhappily certain that the coming interview would be a painful one, but there seemed no way to avoid it. Together he and Lady Laura went to the drawing room. As soon as the drawing room door was closed behind them, Lady Laura drew a deep breath. "I shall never invite Isabel Wrexford to this house again," she said. "Never!"

"You certainly need not do so on my account," said Jonathan, trying to speak lightly. "What a poisonous-tongued harpy! If she were a man, I would have had to call her out for some of the things she said today."

"I know. I know." Lady Laura went over to the fireplace and began to rearrange the ornaments on the chimneypiece in an abstracted manner. After a moment, however, she stopped and turned again to Jonathan with an apologetic smile. "You must forgive me, my lord. The things she said about you quite upset me, yet it is absurd that I should have taken them so to heart. Of course no one could believe you were responsible for attacking those unfortunate women."

"I certainly hope not," replied Jonathan. "But I must confess that Miss Wrexford's remarks caused me a certain unease. I hadn't realized it before, but it does look as though a very pretty circumstantial case might be built up against me."

"Don't!" said Lady Laura. "Don't even think such a thing, my lord." She came closer, laying her hand on Jonathan's arm. "My lord, no one who knew you could suppose you guilty of anything wrong," she said, looking up at him warmly. "You, who are so good, so noble—no, you need not shake your head, my lord. Other people might not recognize it, but I, at least, can see the natural nobility of your character."

Jonathan felt a little nauseated. He took a step backward, trying to laugh. "My dear Lady Laura, I appreciate your desire to defend me," he said. "But you know you mustn't go to the opposite extreme and try to canonize me. I assure you that I am very far from being good and noble."

Although he had begun his speech lightly, there was real feeling in his voice as he spoke these last words. Lady Laura merely shook her head, however, and regarded him with a confident smile.

"But you are, my lord. I know you, you see, as others do not. As Papa does not, for instance." Something like a frown passed over Lady Laura's face. "You must know that Papa told me what had passed between you last night. I was quite angry with him when he told me about it. Of course he meant it for the best, but he simply does not understand you as I do."

The look of love and trust in her eyes was too much for Jonathan. He turned abruptly away. "My dear, I think he understands me better than you do," he said with his face averted. "I am not half good enough for you."

"You are, my lord! Indeed you are." Lady Laura came forward once more, again laying her hand on his arm. "You must not despair because of the things Papa said last night. I am sure he will come around in time to the idea of our marrying." She looked shyly up at Jonathan. "Perhaps it is forward of me to mention it, my lord, when you have not yet made me a formal proposal. But Papa told me that you had offered for me, and I wanted there to be no misunderstanding between us. Of course I would prefer to marry with Papa's consent, but if necessary I will marry without it. Mama, at least, likes you and approves of you, and there is no reason why we may not consider ourselves engaged, even if the engagement must remain a secret for the time being."

Jonathan could only nod in reply. Each word Lady Laura spoke made him feel worse. By setting aside her father's objections and accepting his suit as an accomplished fact, she had just effectively elevated him to the position of her fiancé. And much as he had coveted that position in the past, he felt it was impossible that he should occupy it now.

"Laura, I am greatly honored—but truly, I think your father's qualms are justified," he said haltingly. "It would be wrong for you to tie yourself to me in any way while he disapproves of a marriage between us."

Lady Laura gave him a look that was half amused and half hurt. "My lord, I am already tied to you," she said. "If you do not know my feelings for you, then you must be a less perceptive man than I have always taken you for. And I shall consider myself engaged to you even if you yourself choose to repudiate that engagement in the face of Papa's disapproval.''

After this, there really was nothing more to say. Jonathan could think of nothing, at any rate. He took leave of Lady Laura and left Honeywell House in a sorely exercised state of mind.

CHAPTER XII

In the week that followed her encounter at the well with Jonathan, Catherine lived as a virtual hermit. She kept close to Willowdale Cottage, never straying farther than the shrubbery and retreating inside the house if she saw anyone approaching. She refused all invitations to parties and other entertainments, and kept to her room when visitors came to call.

Of course the visitor she dreaded most was Jonathan. Sending him away the first time had been hard enough, and Catherine was afraid she might not have the necessary strength of will to do it a second time. But as the days slipped past without his coming, she began to relax. It appeared he had taken her advice and rededicated himself to Lady Laura. Of course it hurt a little to think she could have been so easily set aside; in point of fact, it hurt more than a little. It was a thought so supremely painful that Catherine sometimes wondered how she could endure it. Whatever Jonathan might be capable of, she knew she could never forget what they had shared that night at the well. But it was right that he should forget if he could, and

Catherine was resolved to bear her pain stoically and not feel hurt by his neglect. The neglect that really hurt her, much more than Jonathan's, was Lady Laura's.

In her first access of shame and guilt, she had felt as though she could never look Lady Laura in the face again. But that feeling had passed, and by the time a week had gone by she was feeling a positive longing to see her friend again. No doubt this was partly caused by the loneliness of her self-imposed exile, and it was possible that morbid curiosity had something to do with it, too. But whatever the motivation, her desires were doomed to be thwarted. Not a word came to her from Honeywell House—not a note, or an invitation, or a friendly visit.

Catherine was at first surprised by this silence and then, as time went on, increasingly resentful. It was true that Lady Laura had reason to eschew her friendship, if she only knew it, but Catherine was sure she did not know it. It was inconceivable that Jonathan should have told her what had passed between them. So why then did Lady Laura not come? By now Jonathan would have formally proposed to her, and she would be his acknowledged fiancée, with all the happiness that position entailed. It seemed to Catherine that in her happiness, Lady Laura might have spared a crumb of comfort for her less fortunate friend.

Catherine was reflecting morbidly on these things as she went across the common on a warm July day, a little more than a week after her and Jonathan's meeting at the well. It was the first time she had strayed from the grounds of Willowdale Cottage in all that time. Although she still wished to avoid Jonathan, he had shown no inclination to approach her since the morning after their encounter, and she had decided she no longer needed to keep so close to home. Besides, her state of exile was grating on her. She felt lonely and restless and hoped a long walk might do something to relieve her malaise.

Her feet, from long habit, carried her instinctively along the path to Honeywell House. When Catherine realized this, she stopped for a moment, then continued along the path with sudden resolution.

Of course she would not actually go to Honeywell House. She was too proud to call on Lady Laura when Lady Laura had shown no desire for her company. Besides, it was only too likely that if she did go to Honeywell House, she would find Jonathan there, rejoicing in his role as Lady Laura's successful suitor. Catherine shuddered at the thought of meeting him in such circumstances. No, she would not go to Honeywell House, but there was nothing to keep her from going to the well if she liked. In the week and a half that had passed since her last visit there, Catherine had conceived a great desire to see the well again. She had relived the events that had taken place there so many times that they were beginning to seem slightly unreal in her mind. By seeing the place where her encounter with Jonathan had taken place, she hoped to revive her memories of that night, memories that she never wished to forget despite the pain that was their invariable accompaniment.

There was nobody at the well pavilion. Catherine made sure of this fact before approaching it. She entered the pavilion cautiously and stood looking around her. The little building looked very different in daylight, disappointingly innocuous and ordinary. There was the place she had set her lantern, just beside the well curb. There was the place where she had stood to wash her face and where she had seen Jonathan's face appear beside her own in the water. And there, a little way apart, was the place where she and Jonathan had made love, and where he had afterwards stood and said he loved her.

Catherine traced all these places with her eye as she stood in the entrance to the pavilion. She could remember well enough the way the events of that night had unfolded, but there was nothing to show that they had unfolded here as opposed to any other place. It was very disappointing. She had not really supposed the flagstones would bear the mark of her and Jonathan's lovemaking, but she had expected to see or experience something more than she was seeing or experiencing. Catherine turned away with a feeling of disillusionment, and found herself face-to-face with Jonathan.

"You!" she exclaimed, taking a step backwards.

He did not answer but only stood looking at her. The sight of him struck Catherine like a physical blow. She gazed back at him, overcome by the coincidence of meeting him in such a manner. He was looking as handsome as ever, his dark hair swept back from his brow, and his lean, broad-shouldered physique encased in a well-tailored blue topcoat and biscuit-colored pantaloons. Yet it struck Catherine that his face was a trifle worn and haggard-looking. Before she had considered the consequences, she spoke again, impulsively. "Jonathan, are you unwell?" she asked.

"How should I be well?" he asked, and his voice was harsh. His next words, however, were spoken in a gentler tone. "Thank God you're here, Catherine. I've been wanting to talk to you in the worst way."

"Have you?" said Catherine.

He flashed her a look of reproach. "You must know that I have. I came to call at your aunt's cottage the very morning after we—after the evening we met here. She said you were unwell, but I was afraid it was only an excuse not to see me. It was, wasn't it?"

"Perhaps," said Catherine, turning away. "But I thought it better that we should not see each other again after what had happened. You know I told you so at the time, Jonathan. And if I had known I would find you here today, I would not have come."

"But you did come," said Jonathan. "And you see I came, too. Don't you think that's something more than a coincidence, Catherine?"

"I don't know what you mean," said Catherine. Jonathan went on looking at her steadily.

"What I mean is that you came back here—back where it happened. And so did I. And I think we did it for the same reason."

Catherine said nothing. She stood still a moment, and then, summoning all her strength of will, she turned and walked out of the pavilion.

Before she had gone three steps, Jonathan was beside her. "Catherine, I must talk to you," he said.

"You had much better not," said Catherine, averting her face. "There is really nothing to say, Jonathan. I told you so before."

"Do you really believe that?" Jonathan studied her profile as they went along the path. "It cannot be that you didn't feel what I felt the other night. And yet almost I am tempted to believe you care nothing for me. You seem so cold, so detached. But you aren't. I *know* you aren't, Catherine. I know it."

Catherine whirled around to face him. "Jonathan, I cannot talk about this," she said. "And I don't see the point in doing so. What happened between us was certainly unfortunate, but—"

Here Jonathan interrupted her, his voice indignant. "Unfortunate! How can you say so? Now I am sure you cannot have felt what I did. If you had, you could never regret it."

"I do regret it," said Catherine softly. "For your sake, and for Lady Laura's."

"But for your sake, Catherine?" Jonathan's eyes held her own. "Do you regret it for your sake?"

Catherine stared at him a moment, then wrenched her eyes away and began to walk along the path once more. Jonathan followed after her. After she had gone a few paces she whirled to address him again.

"You have no right to ask me such questions!" she said. "No right at all! Go back to Lady Laura and let me be."

"I can't," said Jonathan, and there was misery in his voice. "I can't, Catherine. If you only knew! This last week and a half has been hell for me."

"It doesn't matter," said Catherine in an uncompromising voice. "You are engaged to Laura, are you not?"

Jonathan shrugged his shoulders despairingly. "It seems so," he said.

"It *seems* so?" There was scorn in Catherine's voice.

Jonathan colored defensively. "It's not so bad as it sounds, Catherine," he said. "After what happened between you and me the other night, I thought that—that it might be better to break matters off with Laura. I hadn't even proposed to her yet, and God knows her father wasn't happy at the idea of having me as his son-in-law. But somehow—I don't know how it happened, but somehow Laura took my proposal for granted." With a groan of misery, Jonathan ran his fingers through his hair. "She considers us engaged, Catherine! She told me she cared for me, and—and that she wouldn't change her mind even if I did. Do you see what a position that puts me in?"

Catherine was silent a moment, then nodded. "Yes," she said. "Yes, I see, Jonathan."

Once more she began to walk along the path. Once more Jonathan followed after her. "I hope you do see, Catherine." he said. "That's why I wanted to talk to you. I wanted to see you and make you understand. There are a million things I've wanted to say to you. I feel as though you must hate and despise me."

"I don't hate you," said Catherine unsteadily. Jonathan gave her a wry smile.

"But you do despise me," he said. Catherine was silent. "I don't blame you for it, Catherine," he said. "I despise myself, you see." Running his fingers through his hair again, he added, "It seems there ought to be some way out of this situation. But for the life of me, I can't see what it is."

Catherine spoke with difficulty. "Of course there is a way out, Jonathan," she said. "You know it as well as I do."

Jonathan shook his head. "Not that way, Catherine," he said. "I can't give you up, and that's flat."

He spoke the words very quietly. Catherine did not reply. For a time they went along the path in silence. At last Jonathan drew a deep breath. "Catherine, I—" he began, then stopped.

Ahead of them, just around a curve in the path, the sound of voices could be heard approaching.

Catherine heard it, too. "I mustn't be seen with you, Jonathan," she said sharply. "You must go back the way you came—back to Honeywell House."

"It's too late for that," said Jonathan. Looking around quickly, he spied a dense thicket of laurels not far from the path. A moment later both he and Catherine were behind the thicket, while a party of village women walked past them on the path, chatting and laughing and quite unconscious of the two who were hidden only a few feet away.

As soon as they had passed out of sight, Jonathan drew a deep breath. "That was a near thing," he said.

"A very near thing," agreed Catherine. She rose to her feet. "You must see that we cannot risk being seen together again, Jonathan. I haven't much reputation left, but what I do have those women would simply love an excuse to tear to shreds."

"Harpies," said Jonathan angrily.

Catherine laughed unsteadily. "It would hardly be unjustified, Jonathan. You must admit that, at least!" She looked at him, smiling. He looked back at her a moment, then leaned forward and kissed her. Gentle though it was, the touch of his lips was like a match to tinder. It seemed to set every fiber of Catherine's body instantly aflame.

It was a full minute before she could speak again. "Why did you do that?" she asked.

"You know why, Catherine," he said, and repeated once more his previous statement. "We need to talk."

"Not here," said Catherine. She had just sense enough to stipulate that. Further protest was beyond her. She felt light-headed, and there was a stifled sensation in her chest, as though she was unable to draw her breath properly.

Jonathan gave her a long look, then reached out and took her by the hand. Catherine accompanied him without a murmur. Instead of following the path back to Willowdale Cottage, however, he took a turning that Catherine recognized as leading toward the Abbey and his own home woods. At the paling that bounded the woods, he paused to unlock the little footgate that led onto the heath. Catherine hung back, regarding him with a troubled mien.

"We are going to the Abbey?" she asked. "I cannot. It would look very peculiar, you know. And your servants would be sure to talk."

"Yes, I know," said Jonathan. "We're not going to the Abbey. There's a gamekeeper's cottage a little farther along here that hasn't been used in a year or two. I thought we might talk there. It ought to be tolerably private, if not very luxurious."

He threw Catherine a fleeting glance. She did not reply, but the breathless sensation in her chest intensified as she accompanied Jonathan into the woods. They had not gone far before they encountered the gamekeeper's cottage, a small low-eaved house surrounded by a fenced yard containing a couple of sheds and outbuildings. Here, too, there was a gate, and Jonathan glanced around carefully before unlocking it and leading Catherine through. The cottage itself was unlocked. Jonathan pushed open the door, and glanced apologetically at Catherine. "I'm afraid it's rather musty," he said. "As I said before, it hasn't been used in a year or two."

"I don't mind," said Catherine. A glance showed her that the cottage's interior consisted of a single room, sparsely furnished with a spindle bedstead, a pair of cupboards, and a deal chair and table. Catherine seated herself in the chair, and after a little hesitation Jonathan seated himself on the bedstead, which was bare of linens but still covered by a dubious-looking feather bolster. For a moment they sat, looking at each other in silence.

It was Catherine who broke the silence. "You said we needed to talk," she reminded him.

"Yes, we do," agreed Jonathan at once. Nevertheless, it was several minutes before he cleared his throat and spoke again. "Before I say anything else, I must thank you for agreeing to hear me today, Catherine. It's more than I expected or deserved, after the way I behaved to you the other night."

Here he stopped in amazement, for Catherine was laughing. She laughed and laughed, tears streaming down her face as she sought to regain her composure. "Oh, Jonathan!" she said. "You speak as though you injured me, rather than—rather than—"

She was unable to go on, but it was enough. A reluctant smile creased Jonathan's face. "Rather than making love to you?" he said. "I am glad you see it in that light, Catherine. But there are different kinds of injury, you know. And I am afraid that by behaving so thoughtlessly—so selfishly—I have injured you nonetheless."

Catherine spoke firmly. "It is not I you have injured, but Lady Laura," she said. "You need not think of me at all in this, Jonathan."

"That's impossible," said Jonathan, looking at her directly. "It is you I think of most of all." He hurried on before Catherine could reply. "Ever since that first night at the party, I haven't been able to get you out of my mind. I think about you all the time, and—and dream about you at night. I do, Catherine. And when we made love the other night, I felt as though all my dreams had come true."

He waited, but Catherine did not speak. "I know it's wrong to be telling you this, Catherine, given the circumstances," he said. "But it seemed even more wrong not to tell you how I felt. I love you, Catherine." Rising from the bed, he came over to where she sat. "If only I were free—"

"But you are not free," said Catherine, rising also. "I understand, Jonathan. It's unfortunate, but there it is."

"Unfortunate!" said Jonathan explosively. "I would say rather that it is damnable." He caught Catherine by the shoulders. "I *love* you, Catherine. I would rather have you than anything else on earth. Even more than my honor." Lowering his lips to hers, he kissed her, a fierce and possessive kiss that had in it an element of despair.

Catherine returned the kiss with a passion equal to his own." "Oh, Jonathan," she whispered. She began to pull at his clothes, and he complied willingly, casting aside his own garments and tearing at her own, wrenching aside hooks and buttons with a reckless disregard. Having reduced both her and himself to nudity in short order, he then swept Catherine up in his arms and carried her to the bed.

Catherine, looking up at him, was struck by how unreal it all seemed. Here she was, lying shamelessly nude atop a sagging bolster in a gamekeeper's cottage in broad daylight. And here was Jonathan, as nude as herself, looking down at her. Yet it seemed the most natural thing in the world—the most natural, and at the same time, the most wonderful. The sunlight filtering through the shuttered windows brought out the olive glow in Jonathan's skin as he leaned forward to kiss her. It illumined tiny golden flecks in his dark eyes as he looked down at her. "Beautiful," he whispered, and kissed her again.

The touch of his lips was tantalizing; the feel of his skin against hers exquisite. Catherine shut her eyes, then opened them again, unwilling to miss any part of what he was doing to her. He bent to kiss her breast, and she ran her hand through his hair, exulting in its dark silken splendor. She admired the solid breadth of his shoulders, and the lean muscularity of his body as he straightened again to kiss her lips. "Beautiful," he whispered again. "God, you're beautiful, Catherine."

"You're beautiful, too," said Catherine, and meant it. Twining her arms around his neck, she drew his lips down to hers. He kissed her again, his eyes gazing into hers as his mouth melded with her own. Catherine shivered with excitement. She could feel that he was aroused, sense the hard pressure of his sex between her legs, and the sensation excited her even more. She ran her hands along his back, and lifted her hips in an encouraging manner. Jonathan needed no further encouragement. With a stifled moan, he thrust himself into her. "Oh, God, Catherine," he gasped.

Catherine, staring into his dilated eyes, felt as though she was experiencing his pleasure as well as her own. The experience was overwhelming. Shuddering, she shut her eyes, then opened them again. "Jonathan," she said. "Oh, Jonathan!"

He, too, shuddered and whispered her name as he thrust once more. Soon his thrusts became a rhythmn, and Catherine began to feel the same sense of uncontrollable excitement building within her. But the pleasure of watching Jonathan's pleasure was so much more immediate than her own that she was scarcely disappointed when he suddenly cried out and collapsed weakly atop her. "Jonathan," she whispered, running her hands through his hair. "Jonathan."

"Catherine," he said, burying his face in her hair. "I wanted you so much. I wanted you so much I couldn't help it." He turned his head to look at her. "Will you forgive me, Catherine?"

"Of course," said Catherine. She had no very clear idea what he was asking her to forgive, although she understood vaguely that it had to do with the strange and overpowering rush of pleasure she had felt before. But that had seemed so far above and beyond any reasonable expectation that she had hardly expected to feel it again.

"It's all right," she said, and kissed him.

Jonathan kissed her back, his mouth lingering on hers in a more leisurely manner than it had previously. "It's not all right," he said. "I want to give you pleasure, not merely take it for myself."

"But you did give me pleasure," said Catherine, slightly surprised. He merely smiled, however, and kissed her again, slowly and lingeringly. Presently his lips strayed from her own to kiss her hair, her throat, her ear. Catherine, lying relaxed on the bolster, shut her eyes and sighed. The kisses continued, light as a butterfly's touch, moving lower now, until his mouth closed over her breast. Catherine caught her breath at this and arched her back in voluptuous pleasure. His mouth continued on her breast for some time, teasing and insistent. Catherine turned her head from side to side, breathing hard and feeling tormented in her longing for release—a release she was sure could not come.

When his mouth moved from her breast she was both relieved and disappointed. When it moved lower, however, she was frankly incredulous. She raised herself on her elbows, staring at Jonathan with wide eyes. He pressed a trail of kisses along her hips and stomach that seemed to burn like fire in Catherine's dazed senses. "Jonathan!" she said urgently.

He raised his head to look at her. For a long moment his eyes held hers; then deliberately, he lowered his head to kiss her again. This time, however, his lips moved lower, past hips and stomach, moving with inexorable delicacy toward that part of her that most longed for his attention. At the touch of his mouth on her inner thigh, Catherine sank back trembling on the bolster. She shut her eyes, felt him caressing her most private areas with incredible delicacy; felt the insistent warmth and wetness of his mouth surrounding and enveloping her, and it was too much. She cried out, then cried out again as a wave of intolerable pleasure bore her up to dizzy heights, then deposited her trembling and gasping back on earth, never to be quite the same again.

"Oh, God!" said Catherine, and raised herself on her elbows once more. "Oh, God, Jonathan! What did you do to me?"

At the sound of her voice, Jonathan ceased kissing her. He, too, raised himself on his elbows, regarding her with dark-eyed intensity. "Gave you pleasure, I hope," he said.

"Oh, yes," said Catherine. She began to laugh weakly. "You did that, Jonathan—yes, indeed!"

Jonathan rose and moved forward in the bed until his body lay over hers once more. Catherine put her arms around him and embraced him fiercely. "Jonathan," she whispered.

"Catherine," he said. Catherine looked into his eyes and felt again a swelling sense of euphoria. "Nothing—nothing could exceed this moment," she told herself. "This is the pinnacle of my existence." Then she felt him entering her again; saw his eyes darken and kindle as her body yielded to him; felt him tremble as he took full possession of her; and promptly forgot all else in the sheer intensity of the experience. As she looked into his eyes, the pleasure she was experiencing and the pleasure she was giving suddenly became one, as though her mind and Jonathan's were as intermingled as their bodies. And the result was magic. She lost all sense of her own body, except as a vehicle for her pleasure and his. Her hands and hips and mouth moved of their own accord. She knew what he was thinking, what he was feeling, and exactly what to do to heighten her pleasure and his.

It was a pleasure that seemed to go on forever. Catherine wanted it to go on forever. Yet all the while it was changing imperceptibly, becoming a pleasure less leisured and deliberate and more urgent and frenzied. At last there came a moment when Jonathan began to call her name over and over, his voice rising with each repetition. Catherine looked into his eyes, saw what was happening, and suddenly felt her own body contract around him as she was lifted on a wave of pleasure. Once again the world spun around her. When it settled, she found Jonathan lying limply in her arms, both their bodies moist with exertion and a moisture in her eyes that was not exertion at all.

She could not speak, but only held him tightly, listening to his labored breathing and feeling the pounding of his heart against her own. For a long time they lay thus. Catherine would have been happy to lie with him in her arms forever, but finally Jonathan stirred, sighed, and lifted his head. "Catherine?" he said.

Catherine regarded him silently. He looked back at her a moment, then sighed again. "It's no use," he said. "There aren't any words, Catherine. Only—I love you. Never forget it, whatever happens."

"I won't," said Catherine, and clasped him tighter. He went on looking at her, his eyes dark and solemn.

"You do love me, too, don't you, Catherine?" he said. "I wasn't just imagining that you felt what I felt?"

He spoke the words humbly, almost timidly. Catherine, looking into his eyes, saw there a vulnerability that caught at her heart. She drew his face down to hers and kissed him. "No, Jonathan," she said. "You were not imagining." He returned her kiss lingeringly, and a shiver went through her.

"Catherine, my love, my love," he responded, looking solemnly into her eyes. "What are we to do?"

CHAPTER XIII

In the conversation that followed, Catherine maintained that there was no difficulty at all in determining what she and Jonathan ought to do. "You know this cannot happen again, Jonathan," she said, rising from the bed and beginning to resume her scattered clothing. "Or rather, it must not happen again. If Laura considers that you are engaged to her, then you *are* engaged to her. You have admitted yourself that you love her, and not so very long ago you desired such an engagement as much as she did."

Jonathan winced. "What a blackguard you make me sound," he said. "I wish I could make you understand how I feel, Catherine."

Catherine turned to look at him. "I think I do understand," she said. "Of course you could not help loving Laura. She is so good and beautiful."

"Yes, she is. But you know you are beautiful, too, Catherine."

"But not good," said Catherine. She looked at Jonathan, half-smiling, but with a sadness in her eyes. "You can hardly claim that I am good, Jonathan. Not after what has just happened!''

Jonathan started to speak, then stopped. "That's not true, Catherine," he said.

"It *is* true," insisted Catherine. "Even if I had not—" She stopped, then went on resolutely. "Even if I had refused to let you make love to me, Jonathan, I still would not be like Laura. She is, I believe, naturally good and virtuous and kindhearted. And I am none of those things."

"Well, neither am I," said Jonathan.

They looked at each other for a moment. Presently Jonathan went on, in a different kind of voice. "That's it, I suppose. Of course I don't mean to insult you by saying that we are two of a kind, Catherine. There can be no doubt that my behavior, both now and in the past, has been much worse than yours. But I do think we—well—*feel* alike." He went on, groping for words. "When I am with you, it's as though all pretenses are stripped away. And it's so intoxicating. Not just making love to you, though goodness knows that is intoxicating, too. It's like falling downhill—easy to start and impossible to stop."

Catherine gave a shaky laugh. *"Facilis descensus Averni,"* she suggested. "The descent to hell is generally held to be an easy one."

Jonathan did not smile. "Making love to you isn't hell, it's heaven," he said. "Though I will admit it has put me in a hellish dilemma."

Catherine, who had sat down to put on her shoes and stockings, glanced up at him. "There is no dilemma, Jonathan. What we did may have felt like heaven, but it was wrong nevertheless. Your duty is clear if you will only follow it."

Jonathan regarded her incredulously as she finished tying her garters and began to put on her shoes. "How can you be so matter-of-fact about it?" he said. "To calmly counsel me to do my duty, when you know it would mean I would never see you again—or at least never see you again like this. I can't bear it."

Catherine said nothing, but only went on putting on her shoes. When she was finished, she looked up again. "But what is the alternative?" she asked. "You say you love Laura, and that she loves you, too. Not only that, but the whole village, including Laura herself, look upon the two of you as engaged. What place does that leave for me?"

Jonathan stared at her. "Good God," he said, and his voice was shaken. "Catherine, what have I done?" For several minutes he sat in silence, and his misery was so obvious that in the end Catherine could not bear it. She came over to him, seating herself on the bed and putting her arms around him.

Jonathan embraced her fiercely in return, burying his face in her hair. "Catherine, I can't bear it," he whispered. "I didn't mean for it to happen like this."

"I know it," said Catherine. He was still a moment, then went on, his face still buried in her hair.

"It's so damnably ironic. You know I've been an idle, dissolute sort of fellow all my life, Catherine. I never made any pretense of being anything else. But when I came home, I meant—I honestly meant—to turn over a new leaf."

"I know it," said Catherine, stroking his hair. "I know you did, Jonathan."

He turned to look at her. "And now to have this happen! It'd be funny if it weren't so painful. I used to be so critical of my father for keeping mistresses during his marriage to my mother. And now I find I'm doing practically the same thing—perhaps even a worse thing. And I don't know how to set it right." His arms tightened around Catherine. "I don't know how to set it right. No matter what I do, someone will end up being hurt. Either you or Laura—and I can't bear for it to be you, Catherine."

"But you couldn't bear to hurt Laura, either," said Catherine. "I know I could not." Gently she disengaged herself from his arms and stood up. "I know I am right, Jonathan," she said. "We must not meet again like this. It is right that you should be with Laura, not me."

"Perhaps so. But it doesn't feel right," said Jonathan. He looked up at Catherine with burning eyes. "Nothing has ever felt more right than being with you. Afterwards I feel guilty enough, but at the time it doesn't seem possible that there can be anything wrong about it."

Catherine turned away. In a tremulous voice, she said, "I have the idea that other people have said much the same thing, Jonathan—and that they have used the same argument to justify some rather dubious dealings. The fact is that one's feelings are not always a true guide. Feelings can so easily lead one astray. I believe in this case you and I would be better guided by duty." Picking up her hat and gloves, she added, "I must be going home. My aunt will be wondering what has become of me."

Before she could reach the door, however, Jonathan rose quickly to his feet. "Wait, Catherine! You're not going yet? There are things I must tell you—things I forgot to mention before."

Catherine turned back reluctantly, yet with a faint unsteadiness about her lips. "Are there indeed? I cannot think how they can have come to slip your mind."

Her eyes just glanced over Jonathan's unclad form. He looked down at himself, smiled self-consciously, and turned away to draw on his discarded underlinen. "I can't either! But it really is essential that I talk to you, Catherine. I have done something rather indiscreet that may possibly affect you, though I certainly hope not."

"What is it?" said Catherine, looking at him searchingly.

"The other night when we were at the well, I very foolishly went off and left my riding crop behind. And it was found by Laura and some other girls when they went to wash their faces the next morning."

Catherine was still a moment, considering this information. "I see," she said. "I suppose that *was* a trifle indiscreet. But I cannot see that it is so very important, Jonathan. Even if they were able to recognize the crop as yours—"

"They were," said Jonathan grimly. "And what is worse, that insufferable Wrexford girl was able to pinpoint the time I lost it as being sometime after nine o'clock the previous evening. She asked a lot of very uncomfortable questions about what I was doing at the well pavilion that night. I did my best to put her off, but I know she is convinced she has stumbled on a secret of some sort, as indeed she has. Of course, I don't suppose it would ever occur to her to connect my presence at the pavilion with you. But I thought it as well you should be on your guard. No one knows you went there that night except me, do they?"

"No, no one. Oh!" Catherine's eyes suddenly widened. "Yes, one person *does* know, Jonathan. And I think you should know about it, for really the circumstances were rather odd."

Rapidly she described her meeting with Ned Horne on the way back from the well and the suspicion that had occurred to her that he might be responsible for the recent string of attacks on local women. "Really, his manner was very strange, Jonathan. His warning me like that, and the way he looked at me—it made me quite uncomfortable."

"Ned Horne?" said Jonathan, looking surprised. "It never would have occurred to me to connect him with these attacks. Why, he has lived around here since I was a boy. And I always supposed he was quite harmless, poor fellow."

"Yes, so did I. But he *was* out on Midsummer's Eve, Jonathan. And you know another woman was attacked that night, not so very far from where I met him. It might be as well to make a few inquiries about whether he was out the nights the other attacks occurred."

"Yes, of course," said Jonathan with a nod. "That can be done easily enough. I'll drop a word in Sir Thomas Mabberly's ear and see that the proper inquiries are put in motion. No, better yet, I'll see to it myself." He glanced at Catherine. "I've a personal interest now in putting a stop to these attacks. You didn't know, did you, that I am under suspicion of having perpetrated them myself?"

"You?" said Catherine, wide-eyed. "But that's ridiculous, Jonathan! Who would suspect you of doing such a thing?"

"Miss Wrexford again. She hinted—oh, so delicately!—that it was peculiar how the attacks began about the same time I returned to the neighborhood."

"That's nothing," scoffed Catherine. "She was just being spiteful, as usual."

"Yes, she most certainly was. But the experience was rather uncomfortable all the same. When she pointed out what an amazing coincidence it was that one of the attacks actually took place on a night I was known to be abroad—well, I could feel everyone eyeing me askance. I tell you, it was very uncomfortable. I wouldn't be surprised if the constable doesn't come to call on me one of these days."

"I heard about Mrs. Percy's maidservant being attacked Midsummer's Eve," said Catherine slowly. "But you couldn't have done that, Jonathan."

"No, I was otherwise occupied that night," said Jonathan, looking into her eyes. "Unfortunately, only you know that, Catherine. And I can hardly produce you as a witness to my whereabouts."

"No," agreed Catherine. "But really I cannot believe it will come to that, Jonathan. No one could seriously believe you could have committed such crimes. And unless it can be proved you were abroad the nights of the other attacks, there could be no real case against you."

"That's true," said Jonathan. "I daresay I could produce an alibi for those other nights if need be. Well, that is a reassuring thought, but still I would rather Miss Wrexford had held her tongue. My behavior of late is not something I care to have subjected to public scrutiny!"

"Nor mine," said Catherine. Rather bitterly, she added, "But you know everything one does in Langton Abbots is subject to public scrutiny, Jonathan. That's another reason why we must not meet like this again."

"I suppose not," said Jonathan. He had finished dressing

by now, and he stood looking down at Catherine. "I suppose not," he said again. "I see the point of what you're saying, Catherine. But it's so hard to let you go. If only I could believe it would all work out for the best—"

"It will," said Catherine quickly. "I am sure it will, Jonathan." She held out her hand, and he took it silently. "Good-bye, Jonathan," she said.

Jonathan did not speak, but only pressed her hand. Catherine looked at him a moment, then turned away, conscious of tears starting in her eyes. "Good-bye, Jonathan," she said, and left the cottage without waiting for a reply.

When she reached home she found that her aunt, predictably, had been alarmed at her long absence.

"My dear, I was quite worried about you! I do wish you would not walk out alone. I simply cannot think it at all proper—and until they catch the man who has been attacking those unfortunate women, I cannot think it at all safe, either."

"I daresay they will catch him soon," said Catherine, turning away under pretense of removing her hat. After all that had taken place between her and Jonathan that afternoon, she had little interest in this well-worn theme of her aunt's. But her aunt's next words brought her sharply to attention.

"—only a rumor, of course, but still there's no smoke without fire, as I often say. And it's a fact that none of these attacks took place until he returned home. But still, I can hardly believe it of him. Such a handsome young man—and with such charming manners, too. It simply doesn't seem possible that he could—oh, it doesn't bear thinking about."

"What doesn't bear thinking about?" said Catherine sharply. Her aunt looked at her in surprise.

"Why, what I was just telling you, my dear. About the rumor that Lord Meredith is responsible for these attacks. I do not like to believe it of him, but it does seem as though the coincidence is too much to dismiss. And there's no denying he was very wild in his youth. That business with the Cooper woman, you know, was really scandalous.''

''Yes, but hardly in the same class as these attacks,'' said Catherine in a hard voice. ''From all I ever heard, it was the Widow Cooper who was the aggressor in that affair, and not Lord Meredith.''

This plain speaking sent Aunt Rose into a flutter. ''Catherine! Really, you ought not to speak of such things. Though there's no denying that the Cooper woman was a bold creature, quite capable of tying her garter in public.''

This speech momentarily distracted Catherine, causing her thoughts to hearken back to her interview with Jonathan that afternoon and certain dealings involving the tying and untying of her own garters. But she sternly resisted this beguiling train of thought and returned her mind to the subject at hand. ''I don't believe for a minute that Lord Meredith had anything to do with these attacks,'' she said forcefully. ''It's a ridiculous idea. And I am surprised at you for giving it a minute's credence, Auntie. Why, I thought you liked Lord Meredith!''

''I do like him, my dear. That's why I was so disturbed when I heard this rumor. I would hate to believe him responsible for anything so vicious as these crimes, but I was calling on Mrs. Percy this afternoon, and she told me that Mrs. Wrexford had told her in confidence that Lord Meredith had been proved to be abroad late that same night her maidservant was attacked. You must admit it looks rather suspicious, my dear.''

''I will admit nothing of the kind! I expect there were dozens of people abroad that night if we only knew it.'' Catherine bit back the urge to say ''*I was myself,*'' and went on with increasing wrath. ''Yet no one suspects those other people of being guilty, only Lord Meredith. And why? Because years ago, he conducted himself in a manner that the people hereabouts are pleased to call immoral. And so they assume he is guilty of these other crimes as well!''

Aunt Rose blinked at her vehemence. ''I am sure I would

like to believe Lord Meredith is not guilty, my dear," she said. "Only the evidence seemed rather suggestive, that is all."

"What evidence? The evidence that Lord Meredith was abroad that night? I can't believe Mrs. Wrexford would base such an outrageous accusation on such a slender foundation. Yes, I can, though. God knows I've had to put up with enough insinuations from her these last nine years, and from her daughter, too. They both delight to put the worst possible construction on anything one might say or do."

"Don't tell me they have dared make accusations against your character, Catherine!" said Aunt Rose, looking indignant. "If that is so, I shall certainly have to have a word with Mrs. Wrexford."

This speech made Catherine sigh and smile at the same time. "Don't bother, Auntie. Neither Mrs. Wrexford nor her daughter make accusations, only insinuations—and you know insinuations are quite impossible to counter. That's what makes it so infamous that they should have made Lord Meredith the target of their insinuations in this instance. I daresay the poor man will be plagued with suspicion all his life, unless they find out who is really committing these crimes."

"You seem quite convinced of his innocence," said Aunt Rose, eyeing her with curiosity.

"I am convinced," said Catherine.

She said nothing more after this, and Aunt Rose said nothing more, either. But later that evening, when they were eating their dinner, she surprised Catherine by saying, "I have been thinking over what you said about Lord Meredith, Catherine, and I believe you are perfectly right. He was always such a nice boy. I know it's said that people change over time, but I don't believe that's really true, and I certainly haven't found it true in my experience. Lord Meredith may have committed a few indiscretions in his lifetime, but I don't believe he has suddenly become a violent and vicious criminal. And if anyone dares hint such a thing in my presence, I intend to give them a piece of my mind. Gossip is such an iniquitous thing. In general, you know, I do try not to listen to it, and I am quite ashamed that I gave it any credence in this instance. I am sure such a gentleman as Lord Meredith could never have committed such heinous acts.''

This speech was some balm to Catherine's feelings, but she continued to fulminate silently on the accusations against Jonathan for the rest of the evening and into the night.

"Auntie is right. Gossip *is* an iniquitous thing,'' she told herself, as she tossed alone and restless in her bed that night. "No one knows that better than I do. But somehow I mind it more on Jonathan's account than on my own. To imagine he could have committed such sickening acts! It's laughable.'' She thought of how gently Jonathan had touched her that afternoon, and of how she had responded to his touch. The thought made her writhe in a curious mixture of shame and remembered pleasure.

"I can't think how I can have behaved so shamelessly. I truly meant not to see him again, and certainly I had no intention of making love to him again. Yet somehow it ended up happening just the same. I suppose in my heart I really wanted it to happen—oh, yes, of course I did. Otherwise I would never have consented even to talk with him privately, let alone accompany him to that gamekeeper's cottage. It's a lamentable fact, but I haven't any moral strength at all where he is concerned. Just seeing him makes me forget all my resolutions about keeping my distance. And whenever he touches me, I'm like wax in his hands.''

The thought of Jonathan's hands made Catherine shiver and shut her eyes in pleasurable remembrance. Yet mingled with the pleasure was an ache of loss. Never again would she experience the bliss she had felt that afternoon. Never again would she know Jonathan as other than the husband of her best friend. By giving into temptation that afternoon and on the night of Midsummer's Eve, both she and Jonathan had taken a risk that might even yet result in disaster. To take such a risk a third time would be pure madness.

Based upon this rationale, Catherine could only conclude that she was mad. How else to explain the urgent longing to see him again that had beset her as soon as she had parted from him? And she very much feared that no amount of risk was sufficient to deter her if a suitable opportunity presented itself.

"But it isn't my risk alone," she reminded herself. "If it were, it would be one thing. But Jonathan has even more to lose than I do in this situation. Indeed, I'm not sure he understands exactly how much he does stand to lose."

Catherine, for her part, felt she did understand. It was not that Jonathan had said much concerning his relationship with Lady Laura, for overall he had been quite reticent on the subject. But the same mysterious bond that allowed her to understand his thoughts and feelings without words made her quick to grasp what qualities had drawn him to pursue Lady Laura. And she divined what it would mean to him to relinquish that pursuit. It would be relinquishing not only Lady Laura herself, but the dreams and ideals he had cherished when he had first determined on marrying her.

"He would hate me for it," Catherine told herself. "Not right away, perhaps, but sooner or later he would come to despise me. And I would despise myself. The decision we have made is the only possible one we could have made under the circumstances."

Catherine was quite sure of this, though she could not force herself to feel happy at the idea of being separated from Jonathan. There was some comfort to be gained by reflecting that he had not appeared any happier than she at the prospect. "It's very wrong, I know, when he is to marry Laura," she told herself. "But still I can't help being glad." And having reached this conclusion, she managed at last to fall asleep.

CHAPTER XIV

The weeks that followed were nothing if not educational for Catherine. She learned that it was possible to feel both miserable and exultant at the same time and in very nearly the same degree. She learned how easy it was to make good resolutions and how desperately difficult to keep them. And she learned that physical and emotional desire, once well and truly awakened, are very unwilling to subside once more into a state of quiescent slumber.

She thought of Jonathan every hour of every day, and almost every hour of the night. She imagined him going about his daily activities: paying calls, inspecting his tenants' properties, meeting with his bailiff. And in the evening, she imagined him calling at Honeywell House, where he would doubtless be received by Lady Laura with all the affectionate ceremony proper to their betrothed state.

Such imaginings were very painful to Catherine. Yet painful as they were, she could not help indulging in them. She also could not help wondering now and then if Jonathan was thinking of her. As time went on, it began to seem more and more a presumptuous idea. Why should he think of her, when he was with Lady Laura? "Because he loves me," she told herself fiercely. Yet in some ways, that seemed the most presumptuous idea of all.

She herself had urged him to be loyal to Lady Laura and think of her no more. But now that he seemed to have taken her advice, Catherine found there was a part of her that frankly rebelled at his doing so. She was seized by wild longings to write to him or call on him: to purposely put herself in his way and see what happened. She managed to repress these longings as they arose, but it was always a struggle. And just at present, there was nothing to distract her from the struggle. She could not walk or drive abroad without a chance of meeting Jonathan. She hardly dared visit even the local lending library in order to exchange her books. In desperation, she flung herself into housecleaning, taking on every dirty, strenuous job that the cottage afforded.

Aunt Rose protested against this zeal, saying there was no need for it. "The house had a thorough cleaning just before Easter, as it always does. And if it needed cleaning again, then we keep maids enough to do it. I certainly should not expect *you* to undertake it, my dear!"

"I don't mind," said Catherine. "Indeed, I want to do it."

Aunt Rose shook her head at this curious taste, but made no further demur to her niece's labors. The house was turned out, sorted through, and thoroughly cleaned from attic to cellar. Catherine then began to cast her eye on the garden as her next project, much to the displeasure of her aunt's gardener. She was conferring with him one day about a proposed alteration to some flower beds when she became aware she was being watched. Turning, she saw Lady Laura regarding her gravely from the other side of the garden gate.

"Laura!" she exclaimed, her eyes widening in surprise.

Lady Laura continued to regard her gravely. "May I come in?" she asked. "Or would it be better if I called another time, Catherine? You look as though you are busy."

"No, not at all. Do come in, Laura." Stripping off her garden gloves, Catherine opened the gate for Lady Laura to pass through. Lady Laura was exquisitely clad in a white gauze dress with trimmings of pale blue ribbons, and a bonnet of tulle and lace crowned her blond head. Catherine felt rather embarrassed about her own, more serviceable clothing. She pulled off her earth-stained apron and did her best to smooth her hair and dress as she ushered Lady Laura into the house.

In the parlor they found Aunt Rose, who rose to greet Lady Laura with an exclamation of pleasure. After the usual civilities had been exchanged, she began to question Lady Laura about her recent doings and those of her family. Catherine was glad to be spared the duty of making conversation. In her first surprise and pleasure at seeing her friend, she had forgotten the more awkward aspects of their meeting, but now they had returned to her in full force. She was glad to be spared a tête-à-tête with Lady Laura.

"I hope you and your family are well, Lady Laura? It has been quite a time since I've seen you. Indeed, I had rather feared you might be ill, you have been so seldom at the Cottage these last few weeks."

"I am quite well," said Lady Laura. Catherine fancied she looked a little conscious as she spoke these words. "It *has* been some time since I've called, but you see I have been very much occupied. I hope you will forgive me, Catherine," she went on, turning to Catherine. "I am afraid I have been neglecting you."

Catherine was made uncomfortable by Lady Laura's searching gaze. "I quite understand, Laura," she said. "Of course you have other things to occupy you just now." Steeling herself to her task, she went on resolutely. "I hope you will accept my best wishes—you and Lord Meredith. I am not mistaken in believing you are engaged, am I?"

Lady Laura regarded her with a gaze more searching than ever. "No," she said. "But we have not made the engagement public as yet. How did you know we were engaged, Catherine? I have told no one about it as yet.''

Catherine felt her face go hot. For a panic-stricken moment she was sure she had betrayed herself. Then she recalled the conversation at the Midsummer's Eve party, and her confidence returned. ''Oh, but surely—you know you spoke of Lord Meredith coming to call on your father that evening we were all together,'' she said. ''At your Midsummer's Eve party, it was. And naturally I assumed he was coming to ask for your hand.''

''Yes, of course. I remember now,'' said Lady Laura. She hesitated a moment, then went on with an air of constraint. ''The fact is that my father has offered certain objections to my marrying Lord Meredith. But Mama and I are confident we can talk him over eventually. And in the meantime, Lord Meredith and I have agreed to consider ourselves privately betrothed.''

Catherine nodded. Lady Laura continued to study her face. ''I have not seen you since that night, Catherine. Have you been well? You look very pale, and I think you are a little thinner, too.''

Catherine opened her mouth to answer, but Aunt Rose spoke out first. ''Yes, I've been saying the same thing. She has been working too hard, I think. She insisted on having a complete turnout of the house, even though it was just cleaned at Easter. And now that that is done, she speaks of overhauling the garden. I am sure I should be completely knocked up if I were to work half as hard as Catherine has these past few weeks. Of course she is very strong, but still I cannot think it healthy for her.''

''Yes, Catherine is very strong,'' said Lady Laura. Her eyes dwelt on Catherine with an almost brooding expression. ''I wish I were as strong as she is.''

''I'm not strong at all,'' said Catherine. The words burst out of her, and she looked at Lady Laura, half afraid of the meaning the other girl might read into them. But Lady Laura went on speaking as though she had not heard Catherine's outburst.

''I could tell the moment I met you how strong you were—

not just in body, but in mind. In fact, I think it was that which drew me to you. I am such a weak creature myself. I can't help admiring those who are stronger than I am.''

''I'm not strong at all,'' said Catherine again, almost desperately. ''It's you who are strong, Laura. I have always admired your strength of character.''

Lady Laura looked at her, half-smiling but with a wistful expression in her eyes. ''I have no strength of character at all. I used to think I did, but lately it has been borne in upon me just how weak I really am.'' As though feeling she had become unduly personal, she hurried on in an abrupt change of subject. ''But there, I am forgetting the purpose of my call. I came here today, not only to apologize for neglecting you these past few weeks, Catherine, but to invite you and your aunt to a party Mama and I are getting up. I hope—that is, *we* hope—that it may be possible to announce my engagement to Lord Meredith that evening.''

Catherine looked down at the engraved card that Lady Laura had just pressed in her hand. ''It's very good of you, Laura,'' she said slowly. ''But—''

''Don't say 'but'!'' said Lady Laura quickly. ''I want you to come, Catherine. You *must* come. I would rather not hold the party at all if you are not to be there.''

Both Catherine and Aunt Rose stared at her. Lady Laura forced a laugh, but her eyes were direct and urgent as she addressed Catherine. ''You understand me, Catherine? You must come, even if it's only for an hour or two. Do please say you will.''

''Yes, of course I will, since you desire it, Laura,'' said Catherine. She tried to infuse a little cheerfulness into her voice, but in truth she felt anything but cheerful. The idea of attending Jonathan and Lady Laura's betrothal party was deeply distasteful to her. And her distaste was compounded by the suspicion that Lady Laura might have an ulterior motive in inviting her there. She had looked and behaved so strangely during the interview that Catherine was forced to the unavoidable conclusion that she must suspect something of the relationship that existed between her and Jonathan. Yet in that case, why would Lady Laura be so urgent about inviting her to her party? Merely to show Catherine that Jonathan belonged to her? It was the kind of thing Isabel Wrexford might do, but somehow it did not seem like Lady Laura.

On the other hand, Lady Laura did not seem much like Lady Laura today. Certainly she did not seem like the Lady Laura Catherine had used to know. She expressed pleasure at Catherine's acquiescence, but her voice and manner were very stiff, and when presently she rose to take her leave she merely bowed to Catherine without smiling or extending her hand. Catherine returned the salute with a heavy heart. But the next moment Lady Laura had thrown her arms around her and kissed her with all her old fervor. "Catherine, I didn't mean it," she whispered. "Do forgive me."

"Of course I will," said Catherine warmly. And such was her relief that it never occurred to her until afterwards to wonder what Lady Laura was asking her to forgive.

Afterwards, of course, she did wonder. Try as she might, she could think of nothing for which Lady Laura ought to beg her forgiveness. Indeed, as Catherine reflected unhappily, the boot was quite upon the other leg. But Lady Laura could not know that, or she would not have made such a point of inviting her erstwhile friend to her betrothal party.

"I wish I need not go. Indeed, I ought *not* to go," Catherine told herself over and over again during the days that followed. To attend any party where Jonathan would be present must be an unwise act at best. On the present occasion, it would be nothing short of madness. She could gain nothing from the spectacle of him dancing attendance on Lady Laura—nothing but a heartache. Yet Catherine did not feel she could refuse Lady Laura's invitation on that account. Indeed, she felt she deserved all the heartache she could get as penance for the feelings she had harbored and still harbored for her friend's fiancé.

This was Catherine's rationale for attending the engagement party, in spite of her past and present feelings for Jonathan. But she knew well enough that such a rationale was mere whitewashing. The plain fact was that she longed to see him again, even if it was unwise, and even if it cost her a heartache. So for better or worse (and feeling pretty certain that it must be for worse), she made her preparations for the party, looking forward to it with a mixture of dread and anticipation.

Aunt Rose, too, had chosen to attend the party that evening at Honeywell House. Catherine was glad of her aunt's support as they entered the house and gave their names to the footman. She caught a glimpse of herself in a mirror as the footman led them toward the saloon, and she reflected grimly that on this occasion, at least, Lady Laura could not accuse her of being pale. Her cheeks were flushed, and her eyes feverishly bright. As the footman flung open the door of the saloon and announced, "Miss Payne. Miss Summerville," she took a deep breath and stepped forward across the threshold.

The saloon looked almost exactly as it had on the evening of Lady Laura's last party. Looking around it gave Catherine a curious sense of déjà vu. It was on that evening that she had encountered Jonathan for the first time after his years of absence. They had exchanged a few words and danced two dances together, and the meeting had forever changed her life. Even if she never exchanged another word with him, she could never be the same girl she had been that night: restless, discontented, and filled with indefinable longings.

Her longings were clearly defined now, as Catherine reflected wryly to herself. She was longing to see Jonathan, and yet fearing to see him, too. Again she glanced around the room, her body tense with expectation. There were plenty of people in the saloon, and a goodly number of them gentlemen, but though Catherine looked closely at each blue- or black-coated figure, she could not discern Jonathan among their number.

"Perhaps he decided against coming when he found out I was to be here," she told herself. "That would disappoint Laura, of course, seeing that this was to be her betrothal party. But even so, it's better that he and I should not meet. Yes, assuredly it is better." Yet she could not really make herself believe it. Unconsciously, she had been building upon the prospect of at least seeing him that evening, and to be balked of that prospect left her feeling bitterly disappointed.

As she and Aunt Rose waited for their turn to greet their hostess, she roused herself to take one final look around the room. Once again, she failed to see Jonathan, but she inadvertently caught the eye of Mr. Poole, the vicar, who had just entered the room. His face at once brightened. He came hurrying over to Catherine and her aunt with a broad smile on his face.

"Catherine! It is delightful to see you again, my dear. And you, too, of course, Miss Payne." Having exchanged greetings with Aunt Rose, he turned back to Catherine. "Upon my word, Catherine, it really is delightful to see you again," he repeated in a lower voice. "I have seen so little of you these last few weeks that I had begun to fear for your health. You have been well?"

"Well enough," said Catherine evasively.

"I am glad to hear it," said Mr. Poole. "Very glad to hear it indeed." He smiled again, but his voice sharpened slightly as he added, "Still, I must say that I take it amiss that you should have been absent from divine service so often these past few weeks, if you had not ill-health to excuse you."

He paused, but Catherine said nothing. After a minute he went on, lowering his voice still further. "I must say I have been disappointed, Catherine. I have taken great interest in your spiritual growth and development. Not merely a pastoral interest, you understand, but a personal one. It seemed to me you were making a most encouraging progress. And I cannot help but think regular attendance at divine services would assist you in progressing even further."

Catherine merely nodded and turned away, under pretext of

fastening a loose button on her glove. She wished desperately that Mr. Poole would go away. His heavy rhetoric and unwanted advice were maddening at all times, but in her present state of misery they were as irritating as a buzzing fly. Like a fly, however, no mere passive measures on the part of his victim were sufficient to discourage Mr. Poole. He continued to address Catherine in a confidential voice.

"Indeed, Catherine, you cannot know how grieved I have been to find you missing from my flock these last few Sundays. It was bad enough when I fancied your absence due to illness, but now that I find out otherwise, I am puzzled as well as grieved. May I ask what occasioned you to absent yourself from my services?"

Catherine felt a wicked urge to say that she had taken to attending services at the Methodist chapel instead. Mr. Poole had a fanatical dislike of all dissenters, and the presence of a small but thriving Methodist congregation in Langton Abbots was a source of much vexation to him. But she had an innate respect for Mr. Poole's office, even if not for the man himself, and so she forced herself to answer him politely. "I would rather not discuss the matter, if you please, Mr. Poole. Rest assured that I have good and sufficient reasons for absenting myself from church."

Mr. Poole looked grave. "I have no doubt you believe your reasons to be good and sufficient, Catherine," he said. "But it is easy to be led astray by one's own desires and doubts in these matters. If you could bring yourself to confide in me, I think it might be as well." Clearing his throat, he went on pompously. "I am your spiritual adviser, you know—at least, so I have liked to fancy myself. And I would take it as a great compliment if you would tell me all your little cares and concerns and let me try to assist you." He paused, looking at Catherine expectantly.

Catherine regarded him for a long moment. She did not know it, but there was a half-smile on her lips and a light of amusement in her eyes. The idea of confiding her "little cares and con-

cerns'' to Mr. Poole was a horrifying one, but an entertaining
one as well. She wondered what his reaction would be. Would
he merely draw back in shock and disgust, or would he go so
far as to denounce her publicly before everyone as a scarlet
woman? "I ought to have worn a red gown instead of this blue
and green one, so as to better fit the role," thought Catherine
with inward merriment. Then all at once she stiffened. She had
just become aware, in the mysterious way one does become
aware, that someone was looking at her. And even before she
turned her head, she felt an inward certainty whom she would
see.

It was Jonathan. Clad in his black evening clothes, with his
dark hair sleeked back in formal style, he had just entered the
saloon from the adjoining refreshment parlor. He stood looking
at Catherine, and the expression in his eyes made her catch her
breath. It was anger—fierce, furious, blazing anger, such as
she had never seen in any man's eyes before. For a moment
he stood regarding Catherine with the same smouldering gaze,
then came toward her. "Catherine," he said.

His voice rang out above the buzz of conversation in the
saloon. A number of people turned to look at him. One of those
people was Lady Lindsay. She glanced at him, then at Catherine,
and then, moving quickly, stepped out of the receiving line to
grasp him by the arm. "Lord Meredith," she said in a high,
clear voice. "There you are, my lord. Laura was just looking
for you."

Catherine watched as Lady Lindsay led him over to where
Lady Laura, in a frothy gown of sky-blue gauze, was talking
with several of her friends. She received him joyfully, addressing him with some remark that caused him to smile slightly
in spite of his obvious perturbation. Even as he answered her,
however, his eyes turned again toward Catherine. And once
again Catherine caught a glimpse of anger blazing in their
depths.

Catherine felt shaken. She could not imagine what she had
done to deserve such reproach. For surely it had been reproach

she had read in Jonathan's eyes? Catherine thought it was, and immediately her mind jumped to the conclusion that he must resent her presence at his and Lady Laura's betrothal party.

In the stress of the moment, she had forgotten all about Mr. Poole. But she remembered him again when he addressed her in a voice sharp with disapprobation. "Upon my word! Lord Meredith makes pretty free with your name, does he not, Catherine? I wonder at his effrontery."

Shaken or not, Catherine could not let this remark go uncontested. "You make free with my name, too," she reminded Mr. Poole. "And I have known Lord Meredith much longer than I have known you." *And much more intimately,* she could not help adding to herself.

"Yes, but the circumstances are different. I am your vicar— your spiritual adviser, as I said before—and I stand almost in the role of a father to you. It is fitting I should address you by your Christian name. But what is Lord Meredith?"

The question was rhetorical, but Catherine answered promptly. "A very old friend and neighbor," she said.

Mr. Poole looked annoyed. "Yes, I daresay. But I tell you plainly, Catherine, that you would do better to eschew his acquaintance just the same. Of course I do not mean to criticize Lord Meredith—who is, after all, my employer. But I am only voicing public opinion when I say that he is not a gentleman I would advise any young lady acquaintance of mine to encourage. Particularly not a young lady in your position. It is as I told you before: the delicacy of your position obliges you to avoid even the shadow of impropriety."

"Yes, you have certainly told me that before," said Catherine with an edge to her voice.

Mr. Poole went on without heeding the interruption. "And that is why I dislike to see you on terms of even common civility with Lord Meredith. Let me speak frankly, Catherine. Given the worldly position he occupies, he cannot be expected to respect your own. I would not put it past him to make"— Mr. Poole sank his voice to a whisper—*"improper advances."*

Catherine looked at him. Mr. Poole looked back at her solemnly. "Forgive me for speaking of such things, Catherine," he said, squeezing her hand. "But I would protect you from any and all such pitfalls."

"Do you seriously imagine Lord Meredith would make improper advances to me, when he is engaged to Lady Laura?" returned Catherine in a silky voice. "It would seem to me a most unwise proceeding, not to say any worse of it."

"True . . . true. Yet men of his stamp are not beyond such moral equivocation. And it is possible Lord Meredith is even more unprincipled than we suspect. I have recently heard a most disturbing rumor—"

Catherine stiffened, but at that moment the couple ahead of her moved forward in the receiving line. This meant that she and Aunt Rose were also obliged to move forward to make their greetings to their hostess. Lady Lindsay received them both politely, but the smile she bestowed on Catherine did not quite reach her eyes.

"Ah, Catherine!" she said. "I am so glad to see you, my dear. How lovely you look tonight." Her eyes jealously appraised Catherine's gown of peacock blue and green brocade, lingering on the spray of peacock feathers that ornamented her chestnut hair. "Such a striking costume and really most original. But I should be afraid to wear it myself. Green and blue together are so trying to one's complexion—and I had always heard peacock feathers were bad luck."

Catherine thought Lady Lindsay sounded as though she rather wished than feared this was the case. But she returned a conventional thanks to Lady Lindsay's compliment, and Mr. Poole, who had overheard the whole exchange, spoke up eagerly.

"Oh, be sure there is nothing amiss about peacock feathers, my lady. I am pleased to see Catherine ignore that foolish superstition. You know superstitions in any form are anathema to me. I am very proud of her for showing her indifference to them." With an avuncular smile, he patted Catherine's arm.

Catherine, annoyed, drew her arm away sharply and moved

on down the receiving line. Here she found herself face-to-face with Lady Laura. She had steeled herself for that meeting, but it happened that Jonathan still stood beside Lady Laura, so that she was forced to face both of them at once. It was a moment inexpressibly painful for Catherine. The moment was rendered even more painful by the look on Jonathan's face. He was staring down at her with the same smouldering expression with which he had regarded her earlier. Even as Catherine smiled and greeted Lady Laura she could feel his eyes burning down at her. The consciousness oppressed her, and her voice shook as she tried to answer Lady Laura's friendly inquiries.

"Yes, I am well—quite well, thank you. It was so kind of you to invite me, Laura. Your party looks to be a great success. I hope—I hope it will be."

"Thank you, I hope so, too," returned Lady Laura gravely. "You are acquainted with Lord Meredith, of course." She turned to Jonathan. "My lord, here is Catherine. Does she not look lovely tonight?"

Jonathan did not immediately answer this question. He went on looking down at Catherine as he had done before. Catherine looked back at him, being quite helpless to do otherwise. It was a moment electric in its intensity. When Jonathan finally spoke, his words were a ridiculous anticlimax. "Yes, certainly," he said. "She looks charmingly this evening. It is a pleasure to see you again, Catherine."

Catherine murmured something in reply, not knowing what she said. Rather doubtfully she held out her hand to him. She half expected he would ignore or reject it, but his own hand instantly closed over it. The touch of his hand sent a thrill through Catherine. She shut her eyes briefly, then opened them again with a weak attempt at a smile. "Good evening to you, my lord," she said. Reluctantly he released her hand, and she moved away, feeling as limp as if her knees had suddenly turned to water.

Aunt Rose had encountered old Mrs. Percy, a friend of hers, with whom she was exchanging animated conversation. Catherine stood passively by, smiling politely but not really listening to what was being said. Her thoughts were on other matters. She jumped slightly to hear a voice in her ear. "Miss Summerfield! I was hoping you might be here this evening. And now I find all my hopes gratified."

Catherine turned reluctantly. She had recognized the voice as belonging to Sir Oswald, Lady Laura's half brother. A glance confirmed this recognition. Sir Oswald was handsomely dressed in a black evening coat with pearl-white breeches and waistcoat, but though his appearance did credit to the name of Lindsay, Catherine still shrank from him. She disliked the boldness with which he looked her up and down, and the intimacy of his manner as he took her hand and bowed over it.

"Allow me to congratulate you upon your appearance," he said. "You look lovely tonight—lovely as a picture. Would it be too much to hope you might do me the honor of standing up with me for the first set?"

"Thank you, Sir Oswald, but I do not intend to dance this evening," said Catherine, drawing her hand away. She felt a pang in her heart as she made this statement. Unacknowledged to herself, she had been cherishing a hope that Jonathan might ask her to dance as he had done at Lady Laura's last party. But all such hopes had been put to flight by Jonathan's unfriendly reception. Even if that had not been the case, she had no wish to dance with Sir Oswald.

Sir Oswald looked displeased by her refusal, according her merely a curt bow in reply before stalking off. Catherine cared nothing for his displeasure. But she felt low in spirits nevertheless as she turned back to her aunt and Mrs. Percy. She wondered how on earth she was to endure the evening that lay ahead of her. She had just cut herself off from any possibility of dancing; Jonathan appeared to be angry with her; and though Lady Laura did not appear angry, still there was something so strange and untoward in her manner that Catherine shrank from approaching her. Or perhaps it was merely her own guilty conscience that made her shrink from approaching her friend. Catherine was just wondering again dismally how she was to pass the two or three hours that remained before she could decently go home when the question was answered for her by Mr. Poole's coming up to her and taking her by the arm with an air of calm presumption.

"There you are, Catherine," he said. "Shall we find a couple of empty seats? I am most anxious to continue our conversation."

CHAPTER XV

Under the circumstances, Catherine could think of nothing better to do than accept Mr. Poole's invitation.

She had no wish to talk further with him, of course. But the evening must be got through somehow, and if she could only divert him from the subject of her own spiritual progress (or lack thereof), she trusted she might pass an hour or so in a harmless and not completely disagreeable manner. Mr. Poole was a well-educated man who could talk fluently on many subjects of greater or lesser interest. Perhaps more importantly, he was absolutely above reproach. No one would criticize her for sitting with the vicar.

So Catherine reasoned, and this reasoning was a strong incentive to accept the vicar's invitation. She felt she could not afford criticism concerning her conduct that evening. Already she had caught one or two people looking at her queerly, and the numbers of whispers and murmurs such as usually accompanied her public appearances had seemed even greater than usual. Perhaps the guests had taken their cue from Lady Lindsay, whose hostility toward her had been only thinly disguised. Or perhaps it had been Jonathan's calling out her name in that conspicuous way. Catherine did not know, but she sensed a quality in the atmosphere that made her uneasy. She hoped it might be assuaged by behaving with the utmost decorum during the remainder of the evening.

But behaving with decorum did not mean encouraging Mr. Poole to probe her thoughts and feelings. When he made an attempt to take up the subject of her non-church attendance a second time, she distracted him with an adroit question on the subject of superstitions. "I remember when I was here with the other girls on Midsummer's Eve, you spoke of certain customs that you had succeeded in banishing from your former parish. Something about a maypole, was it not?"

This was a very successful strategy. Mr. Poole expanded under her interest, pouring out a lengthy account of the battles over various superstitious observances that he had instigated in his former parish. "It is very difficult, dealing with such deep-rooted superstition. Why, those ignorant people were actually convinced that the success of their harvest depended on their dressing up and dancing around a maypole on the first of every May!"

He sounded so incredulous that Catherine could not help smiling. "I suppose such superstitions are common in rural communities," she said.

"Yes, but that makes them none the less pernicious," returned Mr. Poole warmly. "And even those who ought to have known better were wont to encourage the villagers in their superstition. I had quite a struggle with the squire of the place— a most ignorant and prejudiced old man. He insisted that the villagers had a right to dance around the maypole if they chose, but fortunately there were several other educated and influential persons in the community who felt as I did. And in the end we succeeded in getting the maypole moved off the village green." He broke off speaking to smile at Catherine. "It is good of you to indulge me in the recounting of my trials and tribulations, Catherine. You are a most indulgent and sympathetic listener.''

This was true in a sense, for Catherine had been sympathizing most heartily with the villagers bereft of their traditional maypole. She merely smiled in a noncommittal fashion, however, and said, ''Do tell me more, Mr. Poole. Did you not say something also about the villagers having had some kind of festival at All Hallows' Eve?''

Mr. Poole willingly launched forth on this fresh subject. Catherine listened with only half an ear, for she was busy looking around the room for Jonathan. The idea that he was angry with her had disturbed her so deeply that at first she had been unable even to consider it rationally. She felt more rational now, but still the idea of Jonathan's anger was very disturbing. ''It is unjust that he should be angry at me for coming tonight,'' she told herself. ''After all, I am only here at Lady Laura's invitation.''

But Catherine's own inherent honesty refused to let this pass. ''No, I'm not here only because of Laura,'' she owned to herself. ''He knows I am not, and that, no doubt, is why he is angry with me. I'm afraid he is justified in being angry, too. It was weak of me to give in to temptation this way, but I have been so miserable these last few weeks! And now I will be even more miserable, knowing I have ruined what good opinion I had left in his eyes. For I *did* ruin it—I know I did. It's obvious from the way he was looking at me earlier that he hates and despises me now.''

Yet in spite of her conviction on this point, Catherine still could not keep her eyes from searching for Jonathan. She looked long and hard about the room, but neither he nor Lady Laura were visible among the crowd. This seemed at first odd, but then Catherine realized it was not odd at all. He and Lady Laura were an engaged couple—engaged privately, if not yet publicly. And there was nothing surprising about an engaged couple seeking out a place of privacy to indulge in a little light lovemaking, such as was appropriate to their engaged status.

The thought of Jonathan making love to Lady Laura was like a knife in Catherine's heart. She flinched under the pain of it, and Mr. Poole noticed her flinch. "Why, Catherine, are you cold?" he said, breaking off his discourse to regard her with concern. "I saw you shiver just now. There *is* a fearful draft in here. I noticed it when we first sat down, but I am afraid I paid it no heed. I ought to have been more careful of you."

"It's nothing," said Catherine, drawing her shawl around her shoulders. "I am not cold, Mr. Poole."

"But I fear that you are, my dear. And not surprising, either. It is a most unseasonably cool night for August, and this saloon is certainly very drafty. Suitable for those who dance, perhaps, but not for those who merely sit and talk." Mr. Poole flashed Catherine an arch smile. "And of course we two are not among the dancing contingent. Perhaps we had better seek out some other place for our talk. Should you mind removing to the conservatory? I see the Lindsays have opened it for the party, and it should be warm enough in there."

"I don't care," said Catherine dully. She truly felt as though she cared for nothing at that moment. Since Jonathan had forsaken her, all the world appeared in her eyes like dust and ashes. Besides, there was nothing improper about going to the conservatory with Mr. Poole. It opened off the parlor that adjoined the saloon, and all evening people had been wandering in and out as they waited for the dancing to begin.

Mr. Poole seemed in no wise offended by Catherine's unenthusiastic assent. "Your trust does me great honor, my dear," he told Catherine. "Let me just inform your aunt of our intentions, and then we may go."

Aunt Rose was duly informed and raised no objection to the proposed expedition. Catherine rose to her feet and accompanied Mr. Poole out of the saloon, through the parlor, and from there into the warm, moist, flower-scented air of the conservatory.

Once there, she was more interested in looking for Jonathan

than admiring the impressive display of flowers and foliage inside the conservatory. But neither he nor Lady Laura seemed to be about, a fact that allowed Catherine to relax even if it did not precisely cheer her. "You are a lover of flowers?" asked Mr. Poole, as Catherine idly fingered the leaves of a fuchsia.

"Yes, certainly. Who is not?" said Catherine. She spoke absently, her thoughts still busy with the same ever-present subject. In the distance, she could hear the musicians tuning their instruments in the saloon. That meant the dancing would soon begin, with Jonathan and Lady Laura no doubt leading off. Catherine was just as glad to be spared that sight. She could not help envisioning it, however, even in spite of Mr. Poole's best efforts to entertain her with remarks about flowers taken from various classical authors.

"—the orchid, of course, was well-known to the ancients. Pliny the Elder described and named it—though not, perhaps, very decorously! However, we need not concern ourselves with that. I must confess that I have never cared much for orchids myself." He paused to examine a display of orchids, their grotesque flower forms towering over the low-growing plants. "They are parasites, I believe. I will confess they are not without attractions, but for my part, I much prefer a wholesome English rose." He pointed to a handsome display of hothouse roses nearby.

"Yes, very lovely," said Catherine.

Reverened Poole broke off a small white rose and offered it to Catherine with a whimsical smile. " 'Sweets to the sweet!' You know I think of you as being like one of these roses, Catherine. Lovely and spiritual, and yet with a pleasing air of humility withal."

Catherine regarded him and the proffered flower incredulously without making any move to take it from his hand. "I don't think I'm any of those things, Mr. Poole," she said. "Indeed, I am a great deal more like those orchids you did not admire!"

"You must allow me to know you better than you know yourself," said Mr. Poole firmly. Again he offered the flower to Catherine. But she took a step backwards, putting her hands behind her back.

Mr. Poole did not seem displeased by her reluctance. "Ah, you are as modest as you are lovely, Catherine," he said with a smiling shake of his head. "But you need not fear there is any impropriety in accepting this flower from my hand. I offer it in a spirit of respect and esteem, not mere flirtation. Take the rose, Catherine—aye, take it, as you have already taken my heart."

Catherine looked at Mr. Poole in amazement. She felt sure he must be joking. But the look on his face convinced her that he was not. There was a smile on his lips, but it was a magnanimous smile such as a man might wear who had just conferred a most generous and unlooked-for favor.

As though guessing her thoughts, his smile broadened. "No, Catherine, you are not mistaken," he said. "Ever since making your acquaintance, I have cherished feelings of the sincerest admiration and respect for you. And as I have come to know you better, those feelings have ripened into love. Yes, love, Catherine! I love you and wish to make you my wife. Take now this rose, and make me the happiest of men."

He sought again to put the rose in Catherine's hand, but instead of taking it Catherine took another step backwards. The rose fell onto the floor, and several of its petals were dislodged. "You must be joking," she said flatly.

With an expression of annoyance, Mr. Poole stooped to pick up the rose. "No, certainly not," he said. "It would be most improper to joke upon such a subject." Recovering himself, he gave Catherine an indulgent smile. "But of course, it is only that I have taken you by surprise. I daresay you did not look for such an offer, Catherine—indeed, how could you? But now you have heard me, you must see the advantages such a marriage would hold for you."

Catherine was revolted by his self-satisfied manner. Even

more revolting was the idea of Mr. Poole as a husband. She, much more than most young women, knew what the conjugal duties of marriage entailed. She did not bother to hide her revulsion as she said, "Thank you, but I beg you will say no more on this subject, Mr. Poole. Your offer, though kindly meant, is not one I should ever be able to accept."

If Mr. Poole's expression had been satisfied before, it was staggered now. He regarded Catherine with astonishment and more than a hint of indignation. "Do you mean to say," he demanded in an incredulous voice, "do you mean to say you are *refusing* me?"

"Yes," said Catherine concisely.

Mr. Poole regarded her silently for some minutes longer. "I must say I am surprised," he said at last. "May I ask what prompts you to refuse my offer, Catherine? I had thought it must be acceptable to you, else I would not have made it."

Catherine chose to answer his question with one of her own. "Why did you think your offer must be acceptable?" she said. "Surely there must be an element of uncertainty in any proposal of marriage, or it would not be necessary to make one."

Mr. Poole accorded this statement an incredulous smile. "Come, come! We are not children, Catherine. I daresay there is uncertainty in some cases, but in this instance I thought there could be no doubt."

"Why not?" said Catherine.

Mr. Poole seemed surprised but not discomposed by her question. "Why, because of the peculiarities of your situation. Catherine. I don't mean to disparage you in any way, but we both know that situated as you are, you can hardly expect to pick and choose among bridegrooms. I thought you must be glad to have as husband an honorable, disinterested man who was willing to overlook the irregularities of your past."

"Your honor and disinterestedness do you great credit," said Catherine dryly. "But you see, I don't love you, Mr. Poole."

To her astonishment, Mr. Poole received this statement with

equanimity. "No, I daresay not. It is quite to your credit that you should not, for until now I have given no indication of my feelings. Now that you know them, however, it will be quite proper for you to return them."

Catherine could only look at him in amazement. "But I just said I don't love you, Mr. Poole!" she said. "There is no question of my returning your feelings. Indeed, I am quite incapable of returning them."

This statement earned her another indulgent smile from Mr. Poole. "Ah, Catherine, you have fallen into a common error," he said. "There is, alas, a mistaken notion abroad that men and women are alike in their feelings. Nothing could be further from the case. A man may love without encouragement and even without hope, but no gently bred woman knows or can know the nature of true love before she is married. It is quite proper that she should feel some degree of attachment for the man she marries, of course. I do not dispute it, though I think there are cases when even this attachment may be dispensed with. But it is for her husband to awaken those strong and enduring feelings of love that are woman's sublimest glory."

Catherine looked at him for a long moment. "If you will pardon me for saying so, that is arrant nonsense, Mr. Poole," she said.

"And I say it is not," he returned, looking ruffled. "You have not the experience I have in such matters, Catherine. I assure you that if you were to do me the honor of marrying me, you would learn to love me in time."

Catherine was torn between laughter and anger at his conceit. "And I assure you that you are wrong, Mr. Poole," she retorted. "It is quite impossible that I should ever love you."

"You seem very certain," said Mr. Poole, looking at her narrowly. "But you can hardly be certain on such a subject, unless—unless it be that your feelings are already engaged elsewhere? But surely that is not the case, Catherine. I would be very sorry to think you capable of such a thing."

"Think whatever you like," said Catherine shortly. "Only
believe me sincere when I say I will not marry you, Mr. Poole."

"But I cannot believe you sincere, Catherine. How can I?
You are, admittedly, a young woman of good family and considerable personal charms, but you are also encumbered with a
past that must make any honorable and decent-thinking man
hesitate to offer for you. You really cannot hope to receive a
more advantageous offer than the one I have just made you.
And if you are imprudent enough to cherish a prior attachment,
then let me say that is all the more reason you ought to accept
my offer. In your situation, such an attachment can only lead
to the most dangerous consequences."

Catherine was struck by this speech, which seemed to show
an almost eerie prescience. More striking still was what happened next. Without warning, the branches of a nearby orange
tree were thrust aside, and Jonathan stepped out from behind
it. He stood there, looking from Catherine to Mr. Poole with
a forbidding expression on his face.

CHAPTER XVI

It had been a long evening for Jonathan.

He had endured many such evenings in recent days. In fact, each day of the past few weeks had seemed to hold a full lifetime of pain and perplexity. At times he felt as though he was caught in the meshes of a trap. The more he struggled, the more entangled he found himself, until at last he ceased to struggle and gave himself up to despair.

The very nature of the trap made escaping from it all the more impossible. The bonds that held him were of the lightest and most ephemeral kind, but for that very reason they bound him all the more tightly.

If Lady Laura's behavior had been in any way wrong or unreasonable, he would have had no compunction in breaking with her. But he had to admit there was nothing wrong or unreasonable about anything she had said or done during the past few weeks. She assumed that he wished to marry her, and such an assumption was quite understandable in light of his conversation with her father. Likewise, there was nothing wrong or unreasonable in the unfailingly modest, tender, and affectionate manner she showed toward him on all occasions. It made him deeply ashamed of himself. If he could not quite bring himself to wish he returned her feelings, he could at least wish they might have been bestowed on some worthier object than he had proven to be.

Unfortunately for both of them, Lady Laura's feelings for him showed no signs of diminishing. She had given her heart into his keeping with perfect faith and trust, and now Jonathan was faced with a choice between either betraying that trust or betraying his own heart. It was a dilemma that turned him sick. If it had been only his own happiness that was at stake, he hoped and believed he would have made a willing sacrifice of it so as not to cause Lady Laura pain. But there was Catherine's happiness to be thought of, too. And as Jonathan reflected on that subject in all its complexity, it seemed to him that what hung in the balance was a deeper thing than mere happiness. After what had passed between Catherine and himself, first at the well and then later at the gamekeeper's cottage, he felt he belonged to Catherine—belonged to her in some deep and intrinsic way that had nothing to do with mere legal or religious ceremony. To deny the reality of that union would be like denying his own soul.

But he could hardly explain all this to Lady Laura. In fact, during the past few weeks he had found it difficult to talk to her at all, so ashamed and unhappy was he. He thought she had noticed his mood, but if she had, she had abstained from remarking on it. Her manner toward him was exactly what it had been all along: warmly admiring of all he did or said, and warmly indignant toward anyone who dared criticize him. This latter quality was an especial trial to Jonathan. He felt how little he deserved such a defender, but unfortunately this, too, was a matter he could hardly explain to Lady Laura. So he drifted through the days, tacitly accepting his engagement while yet chafing under its bonds.

The party that evening had been neither his nor Lady Laura's idea, but rather Lady Lindsay's. She, even more than her daughter, seemed anxious to see their engagement publicly announced. "Of course Lord Lindsay will come around in time," she assured Jonathan every time they met. But as yet the earl had shown no signs of "coming around," and Jonathan suspected that evening's party was a way of forcing his hand.

It was not an idea to make him happy, but neither did it greatly increase his unhappiness. The public announcement of his engagement could not make him feel one bit more entangled than he already was. Lady Laura believed they were engaged, and her opinion was all that mattered—hers and Catherine's. And both women, in their way, had made their opinions clear in the matter.

That being the case, Jonathan felt he was obliged to go along with Lady Lindsay's plans and appear at the party that evening as Lady Laura's escort. But he was certainly not enthusiastic about the prospect. Indeed, so far from enthusiastic was he that he entertained thoughts several times of throwing over the whole thing, closing up his house, and going back to India without a word to anyone.

But of course such a proceeding was out of the question. He had courted and won Lady Laura's love, and now he owed her a duty—a duty that consisted in this instance of attending her party this evening. And he thought he owed a duty toward Catherine, too, though in what that duty consisted he was not nearly so clear. What was clear, however, was that he must meet her that evening. Lady Laura had told him that she would be present, making such a point of it that Jonathan had been rendered uneasy.

He wondered if she could have somehow got wind of his relationship with Catherine, As far as he knew, there was nothing to link Catherine and him together except for the riding crop he had foolishly left behind at the well pavilion. That ought not to have incriminated Catherine in any way even if it incriminated him, but it was nonetheless possible that Lady Laura might have put two and two together and come up with the correct sum. There were times when her beautiful blue eyes seemed to see a good deal more clearly than he would have liked, even in spite of her determined blindness regarding his character.

Keeping this in mind, Jonathan resolved that he would be very discreet that evening. He would pay Catherine exactly that amount of attention that was consonant with their public relationship, and no more. He had gone to Honeywell House firm in this resolve, but his resolve had begun to crumble the moment he entered the saloon. He could so vividly remember the last occasion he had been there. All the events of that night came back to him: how he had come to Honeywell House with a cheerful, untroubled heart, meaning to woo Lady Laura, and then had looked across the room and seen Catherine.

The remembrance of that moment sent a jolt through him, exactly as it had done on that evening so many weeks ago. And with it came a remembrance of Catherine's physical presence so strong that Jonathan became momentarily blind to everything around him. With an effort he wrenched himself back to his present surroundings. But the experience left him in an absurdly nervous state, jumping every time he was addressed and watching with anxious gaze the doors of the ballroom. His heart leaped up every time a woman entered and sank when he saw it was not Catherine. After a while, he fancied his preoccupation had become apparent to Lady Laura, and this unnerved him still further. Muttering an excuse about getting something to drink, he fled to the refreshment parlor.

A glass of punch somewhat restored his equanimity, but he was still in a highly nervous state. Within a matter of minutes he would be seeing Catherine again. The thought ran through his mind like a refrain, making it impossible to think of anything else. Afraid he might betray himself in this mood, he remained in the refreshment parlor for a considerable time, drinking punch and nervously pacing the floor, until he was fairly certain Catherine must have arrived, along with most of the other guests. It was a "now or never" sort of moment when Jonathan finally pushed open the door and reentered the saloon.

And he saw, not twenty paces from him, Catherine talking to Mr. Poole.

Not merely talking to him, but smiling at him. And not a mere polite smile, but one of genuine amusement that lifted the corners of her mouth and lighted her golden eyes. It struck Jonathan that he had never seen her looking more lovely. Her dress of peacock blue and green brocade set off the pale perfection of her skin and the tawny splendor of her glossy chestnut hair. When she turned her head, he saw the whimsical headdress fashioned from the tips of peacock plumes that was set just above the chignon at the back of her head.

It was altogether an exotic and provocative toilette, and once again, Jonathan thought he had never seen her looking more lovely. Then he revised that opinion, remembering her as she had lain in his arms that afternoon at the gamekeeper's cottage. The remembrance sent a surge of what felt like liquid fire pulsing through his veins. She had been his that afternoon in every way that mattered. And now here she was, being monopolized by an officious clergyman. What was yet more unpardonable, it appeared that she was actually enjoying the experience. There could be no doubt that Mr. Poole was enjoying it. He might be a clergyman, but there was a distinctly unclerical gleam in his eyes as he regarded Catherine. Without conscious thought, Jonathan took a step forward. "Catherine!" he said in an imperative voice.

Even before he called her name, she had turned to look at him. For a moment she stood regarding him, the smile dying from her lips and her eyes growing wider and wider. Jonathan felt at that moment a whole catalog of emotions: love, desire, hurt, jealousy, and an elemental and possessive passion. He wanted nothing so much as to sweep Catherine up in his arms, carry her off to some place of privacy, and make love to her in such a manner that she would forget all about presumptuous clerics. He took another step toward her, but long before he had reached her side, fate, in the form of Lady Lindsay, intervened.

"Lord Meredith! There you are, my lord. Laura was just looking for you."

The sound of her voice restored Jonathan to sanity. Of course he could not carry Catherine off over his shoulder like a primitive man—not without causing an open scandal. He stood quietly as Lady Lindsay upbraided him for his long absence from the saloon with a severity that was only half joking. Likewise, he made no objection when she led him over to her daughter, saying she knew he must be eager to return to his dearest Laura. But the fire was still coursing through his veins, and even as he tried to smile and chat with Lady Laura, he could not keep his eyes from straying to Catherine.

It was only a minute or two later that she came forward with her aunt to greet Lady Lindsay. Mr. Poole, behind them, was drawn into conversation with an elderly gentleman, and Jonathan heaved an inward sigh of relief. It appeared as though he had become upset over nothing, and he chided himself for jumping to conclusions. But the respite proved only temporary. A few minutes later, Mr. Poole excused himself to the elderly gentleman and went over to where Catherine stood with her aunt. A brief conversation ensued, and then, to Jonathan's incredulity, he saw Catherine accompany Mr. Poole to an unoccupied sofa, where they both sat down and became engaged almost immediately in earnest conversation.

Soon after this, Lady Laura suggested they take a turn through the conservatory before the dancing started. "It's becoming dreadfully crowded in here, though of course I ought not to complain. I am glad so many of our friends and neighbors were able to attend. But if you do not mind, I would like to get away from the noise and press of people for a few minutes."

Jonathan accepted the suggestion with alacrity. He, too, welcomed a chance to get away from the saloon. It was not the press of people, however, but rather the actions of one particular person that were causing him discomfort. In the conservatory, he accompanied Lady Laura up and down the rows of plants and flowers, obediently admiring everything she pointed out to him but brooding inwardly on Catherine's behavior.

It was not that her behavior had been wrong in any way. He had to admit that it was quite in order for a young lady to chat with a clergyman in full view of a roomful of people. But with a lover's quick perception, he had divined that Mr. Poole, too, was in love with her, and it was this thought that made him see red. He felt Catherine must be aware of the clergyman's feelings. Yet instead of discouraging him, she seemed bent on encouraging his attentions by every means possible.

What could she mean by it? Jonathan could think of several things she might mean by it, and they were none of them comfortable things. He recalled the last conversation they had had together, in which she had urged him to do his duty and marry Lady Laura. Was it possible that Catherine, too, considered she had a duty of that sort? Might she have considered her situation in the light of St. Paul's famous advice, and decided that marriage with Mr. Poole would provide an outlet for feelings that were unacceptable when applied to himself?

"She can't," Jonathan told himself fiercely. "She can't marry him, that's all."

The mere thought of Mr. Poole daring to look to Catherine as a wife made him so angry that it would have been a relief to knock the improvident cleric down, or at least to expel him from his post as vicar of St. Etheldreda's. But when he considered the matter, he realized he could not risk the gossip that either of these measures would provoke. He had already been indiscreet that evening, addressing Catherine in a manner that was hardly suitable to a mere acquaintance. If anyone had noticed, it might have had truly unfortunate consequences. He consoled himself with the thought that Lady Laura seemed not to have noticed, and as his fiancée she would have a right to resent it if anyone did. The thought made him glance sideways at Lady Laura. She was walking along, looking gravely up at his face.

"There you are, my lord," she said. "I am glad to see you

with me again. You must know that though your body has been walking along with me in the most dutiful fashion, your mind has been somewhere else entirely.''

This was so true that Jonathan could not think of anything to say to it. Lady Laura went on, seeming not to notice his confusion. ''I think it is nearly time for the dancing to begin,'' she told Jonathan. ''Do you care to take part? I can find another partner if you do not.''

Her voice was in no way reproachful, but it made Jonathan feel guilty all the same. He recognized that he had been behaving abominably to Lady Laura, in spite of all his resolutions to do otherwise. ''Yes, of course I wish to dance,'' he said. ''You are an angel to bear with me and my moods, Laura. Let us go back to the saloon at once.''

Yet even as he turned to go back to the saloon, his thoughts were diverted once more from the subject of Lady Laura. There were only a few people in the conservatory now, for most of the guests had returned to the saloon to take part in the dancing. But as he and Lady Laura moved toward the door, he heard voices in the next aisle over—a man's voice and a woman's. The woman's voice was pitched very low, but low though it was, there was something familiar about it that resonated in Jonathan's ears. He turned his head sharply to look. A series of hanging baskets obscured the view, but he thought he could distinguish a flash of peacock blue and green amid the foliage and flowers.

So far as he knew, there was only one young woman wearing peacock blue and green that evening. And that woman was Catherine.

As soon he was back in the saloon, he set about verifying his suspicions. Surely enough, neither Catherine nor Mr. Poole were anywhere to be seen in the saloon. If Jonathan had suffered agonies of jealousy before at the mere sight of Catherine smiling at the clergyman, this discovery intensified those feelings a hundredfold. His one desire was to go back to the conservatory, locate Catherine and Mr. Poole, and demand of the latter exactly what the hell he thought he was doing.

Yet it was impossible to gratify this desire. Jonathan recognized it, even in the midst of his emotional turmoil. The orchestra was playing, couples were taking their places on the floor, and Lady Laura was smiling and holding out her hand to him. Slowly Jonathan took it and led her out onto the floor.

Having made a sacrifice of his desires, he tried to make it a complete sacrifice by devoting his full attention to Lady Laura. In this he was not completely successful, for he could not help keeping an eye on the door to see if Catherine and Mr. Poole might presently reenter the saloon. But this did not absorb his whole attention by any means. He was able to devote the greater part of the dance to doing his duty by Lady Laura. He asked her questions and listened carefully to her answers, and when the dance ended he flattered himself that he had been uncommonly successful in his pretense. He smiled at her as they walked off the floor together.

"Well, you cannot accuse my mind of wandering free of my body on this occasion, at least," he told her. "Both have been here with you all the time."

"Yes, but not your heart, my lord," she said.

She said it so quietly that at first Jonathan was not sure he had heard her aright. He stared at her, and she smiled faintly. "Never mind, my lord. I do not mean to reproach you. Indeed, I think I speak truth when I say none of us truly has our heart in this party tonight. I, for one, will be very glad when it is over." In a lighter voice, she added, "But in the meantime, I must do my duty by my guests. Here is Tommy Mabberly, come to collect me for the next dance. You may be excused, my lord. Go and see if you can recover that lost heart of yours."

Jonathan was too glad to be free to ponder what she might mean by these last words. Pausing only to mutter a brief greeting to Tommy Mabberly, he made his way to the conservatory.

There were still quite a few people in the conservatory, as Jonathan discovered. Peering amid the trees and potted plants,

he surprised Jeanie Bailey in the act of being kissed by Ben
Winslow. He also interrupted a couple of young gentlemen
who were breathlessly watching a spider ascending a thread of
silk, upon which a handsome wager was apparently riding. He
had almost come to the conclusion that Catherine and Mr. Poole
were not in the conservatory at all when, pushing aside some
obtrusive tree branches, he found himself face to face with
them. Catherine was looking very pale, while Mr. Poole was
very red and holding a rather battered white rose in his hand.

To Jonathan, the sight of that rose was like the proverbial
red flag to a bull. He spoke the first words that came into his
head. "What's going on here?"

The question was addressed to Mr. Poole, but it was Catherine
who answered it. "We are exploring the conservatory, my
lord," she said, looking steadily at Jonathan. "I hope you have
no objection?"

Jonathan, of course, had any number of objections. But Catherine's manner of speaking reminded him once more of the
need for discretion. He damped down his temper, therefore,
and sought to answer Catherine's question in a more neutral
tone of voice. "No, of course not. I merely wondered where
you had got to, Catherine. You must know I was wanting to
ask you to dance with me."

Catherine opened her mouth. but Mr. Poole spoke first.
"Catherine is not dancing this evening, my lord," he said, in
a smug voice that made Jonathan long to hit him. "And as I
do not care to dance either, we decided to improve our time
by coming here to admire the beauties of nature."

Jonathan made no response to this, but turned to address
Catherine directly. "Is this true?" he asked. "You are not
dancing at all tonight?"

"No, I am not," said Catherine. She looked as though she
would have liked to say more, but in the end she only reiterated
the words. "I am not dancing tonight."

"So you see, my lord, your errand is fruitless," chimed in

Mr. Poole. "You had best return to the saloon. I am sure there are many ladies there who will be glad to stand up with you."

The statement was clearly intended as a dismissal, but Jonathan was not about to let himself be dismissed. The white rose and various other evidences made him suspect he had interrupted a romantic interlude of some sort. Come what may, he was grimly determined that it should not be resumed.

So he smiled with false affability and said, "If Catherine will not stand up with me, then I don't care to dance, either. I might as well stay here and admire the beauties of nature with you."

It was evident that this speech did not please Mr. Poole. "I am sure Catherine and I would be honored by your company, my lord, but I fear you would find merely looking at flowers and plants very dull work," he told Jonathan. "You had much better go back to the saloon."

"If you think looking at flowers and plants is as dull work as all that, then perhaps *you* had better go back to the saloon," retorted Jonathan. "I would be glad to stay here with Catherine."

Mr. Poole looked vexed. "I did not say I found looking at flowers and plants dull, my lord. I only said I thought *you* would find it so. I did not know you had a liking for such things."

"I expect there are many things you do not know about me, Mr. Poole," said Jonathan, now with real sharpness in his voice. "It so happens that there is nothing I would like more at the present moment than to explore this conservatory."

Mr. Poole was silent for a moment, then spoke with an air of reluctance. "You force me to speak plainly, my lord. In any other situation I hope I should welcome your company, seeing that you stand as my patron and employer. But it happens that Catherine and I were having a very particular conversation when you appeared—a conversation in which it would be awkward to have a third. You understand me, I hope."

At this juncture, Catherine spoke up unexpectedly. "On the

contrary, Mr. Poole,'' she said. ''The conversation you refer to was already finished long before Lord Meredith appeared. There is no reason why he may not remain in the conservatory if he wishes.'' With a glance at both men, she added, ''For my part, however, I think I had better return to the saloon.''

Mr. Poole looked annoyed but made an effort to recover his authority. ''Of course, if you think it better, Catherine. I shall be glad to take you back to the saloon.''

''You need not trouble yourself in the matter, Mr. Poole,'' said Jonathan. *''I'll* take her back.''

Mr. Poole looked at him narrowly. ''I thought you wished to remain in the conservatory, my lord,'' he said.

Jonathan said nothing, but took Catherine's arm. Mr. Poole looked at them both, and it was easy to trace the progression of his thoughts in his expression. First bewilderment, then suspicion, and finally shocked comprehension succeeded one another across his face. Turning to Catherine, he addressed her as though Jonathan was not there. ''Catherine! Remember of what we were speaking. Remember that I offer you an honorable position, in which you may work out your salvation with fear and trembling. Stand firm in it, and reject the temptations of the Evil One!'' And having made it clear with a glare to whom this last statement referred, he turned and walked out of the conservatory.

CHAPTER XVII

After Mr. Poole had gone out, Jonathan looked at Catherine. "That's a new experience," he said. "I've been called a great many things in my life, but that's the first time anyone's ever referred to me as the Evil One!"

Catherine could not help smiling, but her eyes were worried. "Jonathan, what shall we do? I am sure Mr. Poole guessed the truth—or at least part of the truth. Why did you come after me?"

"Because I could not help it," said Jonathan. The words burst from him, and he went on speaking rapidly, his voice strained and pitched only a little lower than before. "I tell you I could not help it, Catherine. I knew I ought not to follow you here, but when I saw that fellow making sheep's eyes at you— well, it was more than I could take. You don't care for him, do you, Catherine?"

Once more Catherine smiled, even in spite of her worries. "You know I do not. There is only one man I care for, God help me."

Jonathan grasped her hand. "Don't speak like that, Catherine! I don't want you to love anyone else. I couldn't endure it if you did.''

"If I did love anyone else, it certainly wouldn't be Mr. Poole,'' said Catherine.

She meant it as a joke, but Jonathan was past joking. With an oath, he gathered her into his arms. "I won't let you love anyone else," he whispered. "I won't!'' Lowering his lips to hers, he kissed her, a hard, possessive kiss that seemed intent as much on subduing as seducing. The net effect on Catherine was much the same. By the time he was done, her breath was coming raggedly, and it was all she could do to utter the most feeble of protests.

"Jonathan, we can't,'' she said. "Not now—not here.''

He caught at the ambiguity of the words. "Where, then? You must meet me, Catherine. Meet me at the keeper's cottage tonight—later, after the party.'' Again he kissed her, and that kiss stilled the last protest in Catherine's throat. She swallowed and nodded.

"Yes, I will meet you, Jonathan,'' she said. "Tonight, at the keeper's cottage.''

They parted soon after, Catherine insisting that she must return to the saloon alone rather than risk being seen in his company. As she left the conservatory, she glanced nervously to the left and right to see if there was anyone about who might have observed her and Jonathan's embrace. But to her relief, the conservatory appeared quite empty. They had been reckless— astoundingly, insanely reckless. And not only had she engaged freely in the recklessness, she had pledged herself for further recklessness that very night. The thought tightened her stomach with mingled fear and anticipation.

Afterwards, Catherine retained only the vaguest memories of the rest of the evening. She sat beside Aunt Rose with downcast eyes, speaking only when someone addressed a direct question to her. It seemed to her that unless carefully guarded, her eyes and voice might betray what she was feeling. But what was she feeling? She tried to sort out her emotions, but they were a hopeless jumble—part fear, part shame, part excitement, and part shameless exultation. "I am betraying Lady Laura," she told herself. The thought gave her pain, yet never did she seriously consider not keeping her rendezvous with Jonathan. Shame might be her portion afterwards, but at the moment shame was a mere abstract concept that could not compare with the burning reality of her love and desire for him.

Even so, she made no effort to hurry the evening on. She was content to let events take their course, secure in the knowledge that Jonathan was waiting for her at the end of it. When Aunt Rose finally decided that they should take their departure, she acquiesced quietly, putting her shawl over her shoulders with careful precision and gathering up her fan and reticule. She could not, of course, escape saying farewell to Lady Laura, and in some strange way she did not even want to. It seemed all a part of the evening's events, a necessary ordeal through which she must pass.

She followed Aunt Rose docilely up to where Lady Laura stood near the saloon door. She observed with detached surprise that her friend seemed to be engaged in some sort of family conference. Both Lord and Lady Lindsay were there, and so was Sir Oswald, though that gentleman seemed to be taking no part in the conversation. He was standing a little apart from the others with a cynical and rather bored smile on his face. His expression changed when he saw Catherine, however. He turned to her with an eagerness that made her involuntarily draw back a step. "Miss Summerfield!" he said. "There you are. I wondered what had become of you."

Though the remark was a conventional one, Sir Oswald's voice was charged with meaning. Catherine looked at him quickly. It struck her that he was eyeing her with even more than his usual lascivious interest, but she merely bowed quietly and expressed her pleasure in the evening's party. "But you're not going already?'' said Sir Oswald. ''I must forbid you to go, Miss Summerfield. We have hardly talked at all, and I was greatly looking forward to improving my acquaintance with you.''

Again his voice was charged with meaning. Catherine misliked both it and his words and wondered uneasily if something lay behind them. But she reminded herself that Sir Oswald's manner was never other than offensive; this, no doubt, was merely another manifestation of its offensiveness. So she bade him good night with cool reserve and turned her attention to the other Lindsays, to whom Aunt Rose was already tendering their farewells.

It was immediately obvious to her that their manners were not as usual, either. All three of them seemed tense and tight-lipped, as though they had been in the midst of an argument. Lady Lindsay's farewell to Catherine was brief to the point of curtness, and though Lady Laura's was more affectionate, she, too, seemed distracted by some inner concern. Of the three, the Earl gave the best imitation of his normal manner. He wished Catherine and Aunt Rose a genial good night and urged them to return soon to Honeywell House. These sentiments were clearly not mirrored by his wife, however, who listened to the earl's polite effusions with a face that would have curdled milk.

As Catherine left Honeywell House with her aunt, she pondered what these things could mean. She could not guess the subject of the Lindsays' discussion, but she doubted that it had anything to do with her. Both the Earl and Lady Laura had seemed a trifle distant, but without personal animosity in their manner toward her. And though Lady Lindsay obviously disliked and distrusted her, she had been exhibiting dislike and distrust toward Catherine for some weeks now. Catherine wondered if Lady Laura's mother suspected something of the true state of affairs between her and Jonathan, or if she merely thought her an unfit companion for her daughter.

''If she does think so, she is perfectly right,'' Catherine

acknowledged to herself. "I am no fit companion for Lady Laura. I must break with her entirely after tonight, come what may. This is the last time I shall ever visit Honeywell House."

She found peace in this decision, although it was a rather melancholy peace. But even such a peace as that was lost to her when she recalled the meeting that still lay ahead of her that night. She tingled from head to foot when she reflected that in a very short time she must traverse the common to the gamekeeper's cottage, where Jonathan would be awaiting her. The thought of him made her ache with simultaneous love and misery.

"I must see him," she told herself with despair. "I cannot bear to give him up. I would rather be a Judas to my best friend than stay away from him tonight."

It was certainly a fair night for a midnight rendezvous. The moon was full, with not a vestige of cloud in the sky to obscure its silvery light. The air was cool for August, with a chill in it that presaged the coming autumn. It made Catherine shiver and thrill at the same time as she sat gazing out the carriage window at the moonlit landscape.

As soon as she reached home, she excused herself to her aunt, went upstairs to her room, and shut the door. She did not bother to undress, but merely sat down in a chair and waited.

The clock by her bedside ticked away the minutes as the household slowly settled down for the night. She heard Aunt Rose speaking to the cook-maid downstairs about some detail of the breakfast menu and admonishing one of the other servants about a duty that had been neglected. Later she heard her aunt's footsteps coming up the stairs, followed soon after by the heavier tread of the servants. Now she could hear her aunt moving about in the room across the hall, making her preparations for bed. Little by little those sounds died away, and all was quiet in her room. The whole house was silent, with only an occasional creak of aging timbers or the rustle of a mouse behind the wainscoting.

Catherine rose. The shawl that she had worn to Lady Laura's

was still draped around her shoulders, but she removed it and instead took from her wardrobe the dark cloak she had worn to the well on Midsummer's Eve. Wrapping it around her, she left her room, went silently down the stairs, and out the scullery door.

She did not bother to take a lantern with her as she had on the last occasion she had walked abroad at night. The bright moonlight made it unnecessary, for one thing, and for another Catherine wished to avoid drawing attention to her presence. But she found a third reason as her feet went quickly and silently along the path over the common. Without a lantern, she seemed more a part of the night, a part of its mysterious noises and stirrings and as anonymous as any of the small creatures she heard rustling in the darkness as she passed.

She reached the entrance to the Abbey woods without difficulty. The footgate was already open, swinging gently on its hinges, showing that Jonathan had been there before her. Catherine looked about carefully and even ventured to call his name softly, but there was no answer. She supposed he must be waiting for her at the cottage. A shiver of excitement shook her as she passed through the gate, pulling it carefully closed behind her. A short walk brought her to the enclosure around the keeper's cottage, and here, too, she found the gate unlocked. Looking closely, she was able to make out a light burning dimly within the cottage.

Catherine hesitated a moment, then pushed open the gate. On the threshold of the cottage she hesitated once more. She did not know whether she ought to knock, or simply go in. As she was hesitating, the door opened by itself. Jonathan's arms came out to embrace her, and Jonathan's voice sounded in her ear, a voice fierce with triumph but strained with emotion. "Catherine," he said, "Catherine!"

"Jonathan," said Catherine. She was dimly aware of being pulled into the cottage and the door kicked shut behind her. Jonathan's mouth was on hers, devouring her with a passion that was almost painful in its urgency. His hands fumbled with the fasteners of her dress. Catherine found herself responding to his kisses with a similar urgency, a similar passion. Under the heat of that passion her clothes simply melted away, slipping from her body piece by piece until she was naked. She did not realize that he was naked, too, until he swept her up in his arms and carried her once more to the spindle-legged bed. As he laid her down upon it, she was vaguely aware that it was softer and more comfortable than the last time she had lain there. But that detail scarcely impressed itself on Catherine's mind. She was looking at Jonathan, not at the bed; looking into the dark eyes burning into hers as he gazed down at her.

"I *know* you love me," he said. "I know you love me, Catherine. You wouldn't say it before, but I know you do. Say it—say it now."

"I love you, Jonathan," said Catherine in a soft voice.

She saw the fire leap up in his eyes, but he continued to look down at her with that same steady gaze. "And I love you, too, Catherine," he said. "So much that I would sooner be damned than let you go to anyone else. Because you are *mine,* Catherine—my own, my only love."

"Yes," said Catherine. It was such a simple, self-evident fact that she could not deny it.

At her assent, Jonathan's eyes seemed to blaze even hotter. "Then say it, Catherine," he said. "Say you are mine, and that you love me."

"I am yours—and I love you. Oh, Jonathan," she gasped. He had entered her as she spoke, and it was as though their love were suddenly a concrete thing, not merely a spiritual one but a driving force that abetted and intensified the urgency of their need for each other. And it was too much to be borne. Catherine felt it—felt the piercing sweetness of it in an uprising of pleasure so great that it was almost pain. She called out his name, and he called hers, and a moment later they were lying in each other's arms, stunned at what they had just experienced.

"My God, Catherine!" said Jonathan at last.

"My God, Jonathan!" returned Catherine. She began to laugh weakly. He raised himself to look into her eyes.

"Why are you laughing?"

"Because it is either that or cry." Catherine tightened her arms around him. "I do love you, Jonathan—God help me."

Jonathan was silent for a moment. "That is the second time you have said that, Catherine. But you know God is commonly held to help those who help themselves. Have you ever considered that might hold true in this situation, too?"

"What do you mean?" said Catherine.

Jonathan was silent a moment. "I mean that we love each other," he said. "That much is obvious. And we were meant to be together; that is obvious, too. And there is nothing real keeping us apart, only loyalty to an idea—an idea that I now believe was a mistaken one from the beginning."

"Not to an idea," said Catherine. "Lady Laura is not an idea, Jonathan."

He made a gesture of impatience. "I know it! I know she is not. I have been very wrong in my behavior toward her— very wrong and very contemptible. But two wrongs don't make a right, Catherine."

"What do you mean?" said Catherine again.

Again Jonathan made a gesture of impatience. "I mean I can never be the man Laura thinks me. To imagine I could come here and settle down and become a pattern card of propriety—it was a foolish notion from the beginning."

Catherine studied him carefully. "I don't think it was such a foolish notion, Jonathan," she said. "I think it was a very noble and commendable one."

Jonathan turned his face away. "Be that as it may, it was obviously an unrealistic one. And so—and so I have been thinking, Catherine." He turned back to face her. "It seems to me that since I have made such a mess of the situation, it would be better to simply throw the whole business over and go away."

There was a moment's silence as Catherine considered this

statement. "Go away?" she repeated. "Where would you go, Jonathan? To China or India?"

"To China or India or anywhere! Anywhere but here. And Catherine—Catherine, I want you to come away with me."

Catherine said nothing. Jonathan went on, his eyes kindling. "Only think of it! We would be together—together always, wherever we went. I would marry you, of course, once we were out of England. Then we might see the world at our leisure. We could travel to the Continent and Asia, see things other people only dream of. Indeed, it would be like a dream come true to me, Catherine. There is nothing I would rather do."

"It seems to me that not so very long ago your dream was to settle down in Langton Abbots and live the life of a respectable citizen and landowner," said Catherine, looking into his eyes.

Jonathan's eyes wavered under her gaze. "Yes, I daresay it was," he said. He was silent a moment, and Catherine was silent, too. After a moment he went on, his voice almost pettish. "But that dream was an unrealistic one, Catherine. I know it now. And so I think it better that I should cut my losses—leave here, and make a life for myself—for us—somewhere else."

He paused, looking at Catherine. Still she said nothing. "Don't you agree, Catherine?" he said. "Don't you think it would be better to be content with what I *can* do, rather than attempt what I have already proven I cannot? Think of it! We might be together when we pleased, and love each other without intrigue, or deception, or guilt."

Catherine sighed. "Do you really think it would be without guilt, Jonathan?" she said.

"Why not?" said Jonathan sharply. "I do intend to marry you, Catherine. I said that before, if you remember."

"Yes, I remember. But what I mean is, do you really think you could simply abandon Lady Laura and everything else you have here and be happy with me? I don't think you could, Jonathan."

"Yes, I could!" he said passionately. "I would give anything to be with you, Catherine! Anything at all." In a lower voice, he said, "I know I said before that you were mine, Catherine— that you belonged to me. But it's really the other way around. It is I who belong to you, and there will never be anyone else who cares for me as you do. Because you *understand* me, Catherine. There can't be any true love without understanding. I know that now, and I only wish to God I had found it out sooner."

He buried his face against her shoulder. Catherine tightened her arms around him. After a moment she began to speak in a quiet, measured tone.

"It's no use, Jonathan," she said. "I can see it, even if you do not."

He said nothing. Catherine gently stroked his hair. "But I think you do see. You could never be really happy, knowing you had run away and abandoned the duties that belong to you here. We spoke of this before, you know, the last time we were here. And you agreed with me then that you must forget about me, and devote yourself to doing your duty by Lady Laura. What has changed since that day?"

Jonathan raised his head to regard her with blazing eyes. "What has changed is that I know now I cannot forget you. Seeing you tonight—you cannot know what it was like! It was torture to try to dance and make small talk and pretend you were nothing to me but the merest acquaintance."

Catherine's lips trembled. "Yes, I do know. It was torture for me, too. And that is why I think it best that I should leave Langton Abbots, Jonathan."

He regarded her speechlessly for a moment. At last he spoke, in a voice in which anger and reproach strove for supremacy. "You say that! You, who have just been telling me *I* must stay and do my duty?"

"Yes, because you have a real duty here, Jonathan. Our situations are entirely different. It is right that you should stay, for you have your responsibilities as a landlord to keep you here, as well as your engagement to Lady Laura. But there is no reason why I may not go if I choose—''

"And you do choose?" demanded Jonathan angrily. "You choose to run away and leave me, just like that?"

Catherine shut her eyes. "You must see how it is. There is simply no other way, Jonathan. If I was to stay, we could not help ourselves from meeting like this again. You know we could not, Jonathan."

A tear escaped the corner of her eye. There was silence for a moment, and then Jonathan sighed and wiped it away with his hand. "Yes, I know," he said. "But there must be some other way, Catherine. I can't bear to see you go away. And to have you go away on my account makes it worse still."

"Ah, but that is the easy part," said Catherine. She gave him a tremulous smile. "Don't overestimate my sacrifice, Jonathan. I feel I am doing you good, you see, and as long as I feel that, I can do anything." With a self-mocking twist of her lips, she added, "The feeling is not original, of course. I believe there have been numberless poems and songs and books written to vaunt the beauty and nobility of self-immolating love. There is nothing your truly heroic lover likes better than a sacrifice; didn't you know?"

"I only know that I cannot bear it," said Jonathan in a low voice. He rose from the bed as he spoke and stood looking morosely at the floor. After a minute, however, he sat down heavily on the side of the bed again and buried his face in his hands. "I cannot bear it," he said again. "I feel that it is all my fault."

"Not *all* your fault, Jonathan," said Catherine, trying to smile. "I had a share in it, too, I think." She rose and seated herself beside him on the edge of the bed. In doing so, the bed itself caught her attention. She looked down at it curiously, and Jonathan, catching her look, smiled wanly.

"A featherbed," he said. "And sheets, and pillows. I wanted it to be fit for you, Catherine." In an access of fresh emotion, he added, "I wish it was different. I wish *I* could have been different. There is nothing I would not do for you."

"I know it," said Catherine, stroking his shoulder. "I know it." Her face was thoughtful, however, and after a moment, she went on in a hesitant voice. "The servants must have thought it odd, your bringing these things here."

Jonathan shook his head. "They don't know anything about it. I took them from one of the guest bedchambers. I'll see they're put back before they're missed." He looked down at Catherine. "You know I have more care for you and your reputation than that, my love. Though I admit I wasn't terribly discreet at the party tonight!"

"No, you were not," agreed Catherine. "But then I wasn't, either. And that's another reason I must go. We are getting more and more reckless. It's as if we want to be found out."

Jonathan was quiet for a moment. "Perhaps we do," he said. "At least, *I* do. I admit it, Catherine. There's a part of me that would be delighted to be obliged to marry you."

Catherine nodded. "Yes, I know," she said. "I think I do understand you, Jonathan. And I understand also how fatal it would be if we were forced to marry under those circumstances."

Jonathan did not dispute the matter. Instead, he leaned down and kissed her. Catherine returned the kiss, and by common accord they began to make love again—silently, but with a mutual desperation that communicated itself in every action. When they were done, Catherine rose and began to resume her scattered garments.

Jonathan did likewise. As they were preparing to leave, however, he caught her by the shoulder. "You're sure, Catherine?" he said. "You're sure we ought not to take—the other way?"

Catherine understood what he was speaking of. She smiled sadly. "Quite sure," she said.

"Then at least kiss me good-bye," he urged. "You must do at least that much."

Catherine laughed and sighed at the same time. "You know that if I kiss you, I shall never get around to saying good-bye."

A reluctant smile lit Jonathan's face. "I suppose not," he said. "How well you do understand me, Catherine."

"Well enough," said Catherine. With a significant look, she pointed to an object that was lying on the floor. "You are forgetting your riding crop again, Jonathan." And with this remark, she turned and hurried from the cottage.

CHAPTER XVIII

Catherine insisted on returning to Willowdale Cottage alone and on foot, despite Jonathan's pleas to accompany her. "I cannot feel right about letting you go alone. We still have a lunatic at large, you know, whose favorite pastimes seem to be torture and rapine. At least let me follow you home, Catherine, if you will not allow me to accompany you. I'll be very discreet and follow at a distance. And perhaps when you reach home, you can put a candle in your bedchamber window, so I will know beyond doubt that you are safe and sound."

Although Catherine argued that these measures were unnecessary, it soon became clear that Jonathan intended to follow her home whether she gave him permission or not. She assented grudgingly to his plan, therefore, and resigned herself to the inevitable escort. But as she made her way back through the shadowy woods and across the moonlit common, she was not really sorry to know she had a private guard following behind her. Jonathan was as discreet as he had promised, following behind her at a distance and moving so quietly that oftentimes she was not certain he was really there. But every time she had made up her mind that he had turned back, she would catch sight of him, a figure on horseback silently rounding a curve in the path or silhouetted briefly against the sky as he crested a hill.

She reached home without meeting anyone and quickly made her way up to her bedchamber. Once there, she lighted a candle, placed it in the window, and peered out through the casement. She thought she could make out Jonathan's figure standing beneath some trees at the end of the lane, and a moment later she was sure of it, as he raised a hand in salute—a hand that bore aloft a gold-topped riding crop. Then he wheeled his horse and set off back across the common. Catherine remained at the window, listening, until the last sound of hoofbeats died away.

A glance at her bedside clock showed her that it was almost morning. She supposed she might still garner a few hours' sleep if she made haste, but it hardly seemed worth the effort. She was certain she could not sleep anyway. So she merely changed her evening dress for a morning one, washed her face, brushed her hair, and was ready to go downstairs as soon as she heard a stirring in the kitchen quarters.

When her aunt came downstairs an hour or so later, she remarked with surprise on Catherine's early rising. "I had not expected to see you for at least another hour yet, my dear. Indeed, we kept such late hours last night that you would have been quite justified in keeping to your bed till noon."

Catherine thought to herself what a mercy it was that her aunt could not know just how late were the hours she had kept the previous night or what had motivated her to keep them. Then she became aware that Aunt Rose was still speaking, her voice betraying an air of concern.

"Is it possible you are falling ill, Catherine? You look very pale and tired this morning. Instead of having breakfast, I believe you had better go back to bed, and let me send you up a tray later."

"I am quite well, Auntie," said Catherine. "I don't feel like going back to bed." She did not feel like having breakfast

downstairs, either, but reckoned that at least it would be more
of a distraction from her private thoughts than lying alone in
bed would be. As it happened, however, breakfast proved to
be even more of a distraction than she had bargained for. She
and Aunt Rose had hardly taken their seats at the table when
Agnes, the Cottage's senior maidservant, came rushing into the
parlor in a state of great excitement.

"Oh, ma'am! Oh, miss! Dr. Edwards's maid was just here
to borrow a cup of arrowroot, and she told us the most shocking
news. Oh, I never thought there could be such doings in Langton
Abbots, never!"

"Not another of those dreadful attacks!" said Aunt Rose.
turning pale. "Oh, Agnes, say it isn't so?"

"Nay, 'tis something a deal worse, ma'am. There's been
murder done!"

Agnes pronounced these last words with relish. Aunt Rose
uttered a squeak, and even Catherine could not stifle a gasp.
"Murder!" she said. "Agnes, are you sure?"

"Certain sure, miss. It was Dr. Edwards's Nancy who told
us. She said the doctor was called out early this morning by a
farmer over Wybolt way, who'd got up early to cut his oats
and found a woman's body lying in the ditch."

"How early?" said Catherine, at the same time that Aunt
Rose asked, "What woman, Agnes? Was it someone we
know?"

Agnes elected to answer Aunt Rose's question rather than
Catherine's. "I wouldn't think so, ma'am. I didn't hardly know
her myself, to talk to. But I'd heard tell of her, all right, and
so had most folks hereabouts." Agnes lowered her voice to a
discreet murmur. "She was old Dunham's daughter over at
Dunham Farm. Always very free with the men, she was, and
never minding she came of a respectable family. She'd go off
with anyone as would buy her a new dress or bonnet. There
were plenty to predict she'd come to a bad end, but I'm sure
we none of us wished such a fate upon her, poor soul."

"When was she found?" said Catherine again. "When do they think the—the attack took place?"

Agnes threw her a curious look. "I'm sure I couldn't say, miss. All Nancy said was that the doctor had to go out very early this morning, before it was properly light. But as for when she was murdered—nay, that I couldn't say, miss."

Catherine asked no more questions. But her mind was working busily as Agnes went on to give her and Aunt Rose such other details of the crime as the intrepid Nancy had reported.

It gave Catherine an eerie feeling to reflect that she might well have been abroad last night at the same time as the woman's murderer. But she reminded herself that this was only surmise. The woman could have been killed days or even weeks before her body was discovered. Catherine hoped it might be so. She also hoped the murder would turn out to be unrelated to the attacks that had already occurred—a private quarrel, perhaps, between the murdered woman and some discarded lover. For if it developed that this crime had been committed the previous night by the same unknown assailant who had attacked the other women, then Jonathan would inevitably find himself under suspicion once more. He had been abroad the night before, as his servants would no doubt know, and they would know likewise that he had not returned home until nearly dawn. And the only person who could prove that his time had not been spent murdering old Dunham's daughter was herself.

"But I'm probably worrying needlessly," Catherine told herself. "It may be that whoever committed this crime will be quickly located, and Jonathan's name will be cleared without any assistance from me. Besides, I'm not sure I *could* clear his name, even if I was to come forward. He was already at the cottage when I arrived, so I cannot say for certain when he got there. And I can't prove he went straight home afterwards, either."

For a moment a horrible suspicion hovered at the periphery of Catherine's mind. Perhaps Jonathan had *not* gone straight home afterwards, as she supposed. Perhaps he had not gone home Midsummer's Eve after meeting her at the well, either. Perhaps—

But Catherine pushed the thought from her mind with resolution. "I *know* him," she reminded herself. "I know him, and I know he could never do such dreadful things." She was ashamed of having harbored such a suspicion, even for a moment. But it proved how infectious fear and suspicion could be if even she, who knew him best, could imagine he might be guilty. How much more convinced must be those who did not know him and had relied on hearsay as evidence of his character!

It made Catherine shudder to imagine it. "Let us hope some evidence will soon turn up that will absolve him of all these crimes," she told herself. "I have no doubt it will—not a doubt in the world."

She kept her ears open for the rest of the day, hoping to hear some news that would confirm this hopeful view. There was certainly no shortage of news on the subject. All the residents of Langton Abbots were buzzing about the murder that had taken place in their midst. The servants came in almost hourly to report some detail that had just been discovered, and several neighbors called to discuss the subject with Aunt Rose and shudder over the danger they now imagined to be lurking everywhere.

Catherine learned that the murder was thought to have taken place the previous night, some time not long after midnight. This, of course, was hardly the news she had been hoping for. She heard also several people speak of Jonathan in guarded tones, though no one went so far as to openly accuse him of the crimes. But Catherine could not take much comfort from this circumstance. If such kind and charitable souls as Mrs. Percy and Miss Berryton could bring themselves to whisper of Jonathan's guilt, then such unkind and uncharitable critics as the Wrexfords would no doubt be shouting their suspicions from the rooftops.

All this was very bad. But as Catherine sat listening to Mrs.

Percy and Miss Berryton talk, it occurred to her that there might be another reason for their reticence. Several times when Jonathan's name was mentioned, she had looked up to find their eyes resting on her with a curious and speculative gaze. And once Miss Berryton had started to say something about him, then broken off with an embarrassed look in her direction.

Catherine had no difficulty interpreting these looks. It was clear that the relationship between her and Jonathan was now suspected and talked about by the Langton Abbotsites. Even if the talk was not yet fully accredited, it would continue to grow and flourish as long as both she and Jonathan lived in the same neighborhood. Catherine, who had been debating since that morning whether she might not owe it to him to stay in Langton Abbots until he was cleared of suspicion, now found her mind suddenly made up for her. If matters had gone so far that her name was being linked publicly with his, then the best thing she could do for him was to leave the neighborhood as quickly as possible. That would eliminate at least one source of gossip, and she trusted the other would soon die out of its own accord, once the true assailant of the unfortunate women had been identified. So she waited until Mrs. Percy and Miss Berryton had finally taken themselves off, then addressed her aunt with a confidence she did not feel.

"Auntie, I have made up my mind to leave Langton Abbots."

Aunt Rose, who had been placidly drinking tea, choked and put her cup down hastily. "Leave Langton Abbots?" she exclaimed. "My dear, you don't mean it!"

"Yes, I do. I have been considering the idea for some time now, and it seems to me it would be best."

Having made this statement, Catherine waited in trepidation. She was sure Aunt Rose would demand to know why she wanted to leave Langton Abbots. Such an inquiry would be very awkward, for Catherine had no reason to give her. To tell her the truth was out of the question, and she could not bring herself to lie. But the matter was made unexpectedly easy for her by her aunt's attributing to her a motive she had never even thought of. "Because of this business last night," said Aunt Rose, nodding vigorously. "Yes, yes, I see your point, Catherine. Much as I dislike the thought of leaving Langton Abbots, I must confess that I, too, could hardly be comfortable staying here as long as the chance of such a thing happening again remains. Better we should leave for a few weeks or months and return when they have succeeded in capturing the madman who is responsible for these crimes. But where would we go?"

Catherine, who had been prepared for long hours of argument, was stunned to find her decision embraced so quickly. "I don't know," she was forced to confess. "I hadn't got as far as considering that."

"There's always London," said Aunt Rose dubiously. "Grillon's hotel—I have stayed there twice before, and I know it for a very genteel, respectable place. I think I could bring myself to stay there for a month or two if it was necessary. But London is such a big place, and I have always heard there is a great deal of crime there. It might be a case of jumping out of the frying pan and into the fire. Perhaps it would be better to go to a smaller city—a watering place, perhaps, or a seaside resort. Indeed, a spot of sea bathing might do you good, Catherine. You have been looking rather peaked lately."

"Whatever you think best, Auntie," said Catherine, only too relieved to resign the matter into her aunt's hands. "Anywhere at all will suit me splendidly, so long as it isn't here."

Aunt Rose reached out to pat Catherine on the shoulder. "You poor dear! I had not realized you were fretting so about these crimes. If I had, I would have suggested we leave sooner. But we won't lose any time about leaving now we've made up our minds." She rose briskly to her feet. "I'll set the maids to packing, and I'll write to my friend Lucilla Harvey. You know she has a house in Bath, and she has always spoken of the Bath waters as being very healthful. Perhaps she may know of a suitable lodging we could obtain there on short notice."

Miss Harvey was duly written, and a reply was received back by the very next post, informing Aunt Rose and Catherine that they might occupy her own house if they liked. "It seems she is leaving to visit her nephew and his wife in York, so that the house will actually be standing empty for the next six weeks. I call that quite providential!"

"Quite," said Catherine, without enthusiasm. A borrowed house in Bath was hardly the solution she had had in mind when she had envisioned leaving Langton Abbots. But it was a goodly distance from Devonshire, which was the most important thing, and it would be a stepping-stone from which she might later move into more permanent lodgings. Indeed, it was not the details of the move so much as its effect on Aunt Rose that chiefly troubled Catherine. It did not seem fair to ask her to leave her beloved cottage in Langton Abbots, yet Catherine knew her well enough to be sure she would consider it her duty to accompany Catherine if Catherine insisted on living elsewhere.

"But there's no point in borrowing trouble," she told herself: "By the time such a question arises, a solution may have already presented itself. It's enough that we're leaving Langton Abbots as soon as we may. It can't be soon enough for me."

Yet now that the die had been cast, she found herself not so much glad as sorry to be leaving Langton Abbots. In spite of all she had endured there—Aunt Violet's tyranny, the pinpricks and jabs of gossip, and the more recent sufferings that had been the natural accompaniment to her love for Jonathan—she found that the village was very dear to her nonetheless. She looked at Willowdale Cottage and thought there never had been such a delightful or desirable dwelling place. The village with its rows of whitewashed houses, neat garden plots, and gabled shop fronts now struck her afresh with its haphazard charm, and the surrounding countryside with its wooded valleys and fertile pastures was so lovely that it made her heart ache when she looked upon it. When she reflected she would probably never see it again, it seemed almost more than she could bear.

But difficult as it was to take leave of these familiar places, the leaving of familiar persons was a hundred times more difficult. Of course it was Jonathan she was sorriest to leave behind. She had already made up her mind to leave him, however, and the thought that she was doing it for his own good did something toward easing her misery. But there was no such ease to be gained in the dozens of other leave-takings that fell to her part during the next few days. Although neither she nor Aunt Rose had made much publicity of their leaving, news of it had nevertheless filtered out in the inevitable way news always did in Langton Abbots, and they were besieged by callers.

Some of those callers were friendly and well-intentioned, desiring merely to wish Catherine and Aunt Rose farewell and press upon them some parting gift. Others came quite shamelessly to pry. There were several who even dared hint that Catherine and Aunt Rose's precipitate departure might be motivated by something besides the recent string of crimes. The fact that this was indeed the case in no way mitigated the offensiveness of such hints in Catherine's eyes.

Aunt Rose, of course, always refuted these suggestions with an air of gentle, ladylike amusement that was very effective in quelling her would-be inquisitors. Catherine found it entertaining to see Langton Abbots' chief gossips thus confounded, but at the same time she could not help feeling guilty. Aunt Rose really believed that both she and Catherine would soon be returning to Willowdale Cottage. How would she react when she found her niece would not be returning with her? At best, it would put her in an awkward position with her neighbors; at worst, it might keep her from returning to Langton Abbots at all. All Catherine could do was hope, as before, that some solution might present itself before the time for such painful revelation came to pass.

In the meantime, she endured the calls of her friends and neighbors with as much composure as she could muster. There was one caller who tried her composure more than the others, however. That caller was Mr. Poole. He came on a day when her aunt was out of the house, and the maidservant who admitted him was so awed by his grave, clerical demeanor that she instantly ushered him into the parlor, giving Catherine no chance to deny herself. "Here's the vicar, miss," she announced, then precipitately withdrew.

It was the first time Catherine had seen Mr. Poole since the night he had proposed to her in the conservatory. She felt all the strain of meeting him again after such an interview, but greeted him pleasantly, offered him a chair, and told him that her aunt was out. "Perhaps you had better call back a little later, Mr. Poole. I know she would be happy to see you."

Mr. Poole bowed gravely "Of course I would be delighted to speak to Miss Payne. But it happens the chief of my business is with you, Catherine." He looked at her searchingly. "It is true that you are leaving Langton Abbots?"

"Yes, quite true," acknowledged Catherine.

Again Mr. Poole bowed. "I am sorry to hear it. I hope, however, that your absence will not be a long one?" Again he fixed her with a piercing gaze. "I spoke to Mrs. Percy, and she seemed to think your plans were rather indefinite."

"So they are," said Catherine briefly. Mr. Poole continued to regard her with an intent gaze.

"But you do intend to return to Langton Abbots eventually, Catherine? I hope you do not mind my asking such a personal question. But you see, your answer is important to me."

Catherine did mind Mr. Poole's asking such a question, and the temptation was great to give him a sharp set-down. But when she thought about it, it seemed to her that her best course would be to answer him honestly. Once he knew she was really leaving, he would probably waste very little more time on her, and she was eager to bring the present interview to a close. Moreover, she suspected him of being the main source of the rumors about her and Jonathan in the village. If he could be convinced that she really intended to leave Langton Abbots, then he would probably cease to spread any more such rumors, and they would eventually die off if there was no new scandal to fuel them. So she said quietly, "My plans are not yet fixed,

Mr. Poole. But as things now stand, I doubt very much that I shall be returning to Langton Abbots.''

Mr. Poole looked graver than ever. "I am sorry to hear it, Catherine. Perhaps your motives are better than I give you credit for, but in this case I fear you have not chosen the better part.''

"Indeed?" said Catherine, regarding him with amazement. "And what would you consider the better part, Mr. Poole?''

"Marriage with me, of course,'' was his astounding answer. "When I took leave of you last time, I told you to consider well before you rejected my offer absolutely. It appears you have not taken my advice. But I felt it my duty to call on you one last time and try to make you see reason.''

Catherine's brows drew together. "Then it will be my duty to tell you once more that I cannot possibly accept your offer, Mr. Poole,'' she said. "I hoped I had made that clear during our last conversation.''

Her words brought a flash of anger to Mr. Poole's eyes. When he spoke again, however, his voice was as calmly assured as ever. "You said something of the sort, but you will forgive me if I failed to take you seriously. The reasons you adduced for refusing me were, in my opinion, wholly inadequate.''

Catherine could only stare at him. "I told you I did not and never could love you!" she said. "That seemed to me a perfectly adequate reason for refusing you.''

"If it was your real reason," said Mr. Poole significantly. "Come, come, Catherine. I am sufficiently a man of the world to understand the situation as it stands. It is plain to see that you have an attachment to my employer, Lord Meredith. I do not wish to rebuke you, but you must know how impossible it is that such an attachment could ever bring anything but shame and sorrow to you and those connected with you. I, on the other hand, offer you an honorable place as my wife, with all the perquisites attached to that situation. There seems to me no question as to which alternative is the better one.''

Catherine drew a deep breath. "Yes, that might be true, were

I obliged to choose between marrying you and certain shame and dishonor. But there is nothing that says I cannot reject both the alternatives you name.''

It was obvious that Mr. Poole had never considered this idea. For a moment he looked flabbergasted; then his face cleared, and he shook his head with a pitying smile. "Catherine, Catherine! I understand you, I think. But you know that in your situation you cannot hope to attract a more eligible suitor than I am."

"I don't expect—" began Catherine indignantly, but Mr. Poole cut her off. He went on speaking, his face still reflecting the same air of indulgent pity.

"You do not seem to realize how fortunate you are in having attached such a man as myself, Catherine. Nor have you realized how unlikely it is that you should be so fortunate again. Let us be frank. Sincere as my attachment is, I must admit that I have felt certain qualms at the idea of taking a young woman to wife who has demonstrated such a—well, let us be charitable and call it *unsteadiness* of character. Were I not so sincerely attached, I must have relinquished my suit in disgust long ago."

"Well, then, we must hope your qualms will recompense you for the pain of relinquishing your suit," said Catherine, rising to her feet. "There's no point in discussing this any further, Mr. Poole. There is nothing you could say or do that would induce me to marry you."

Mr. Poole also rose to his feet, looking at her incredulously. "I believe you are serious," he exclaimed. "You really mean to refuse me?"

"Yes, I do. Now let us say good-bye and part on good terms if we may, Mr. Poole. I don't suppose we shall meet again."

Instead of taking the hand she offered him, Mr. Poole stood regarding her with fixed attention. "You really mean to refuse me," he repeated incredulously. In a voice of gathering wrath, he added, "It is as I supposed before. Your infatuation for Lord Meredith has overridden all your principles. Well! I think I see the matter clearly now. This talk of going away is merely a blind, of course. We may expect next to hear of you established somewhere in the keeping of your paramour!''

"I don't—" began Catherine again, but again Mr. Poole cut her off. He spoke vehemently, almost spitting out the words in his wrath.

"I had not supposed you so lost to decency, Catherine. And I am sorry—sorry beyond words that it should be so. No doubt you imagine, like many another, that you can avert the fate that awaits you. But I would bid you to be careful, Catherine. You must have observed, this last month or two, what becomes of women of light character."

The protest Catherine had been about to make died on her lips. She stared at Mr. Poole. "What do you mean?"

"I mean that the Lord strikes down those who choose the way of the transgressor." A fanatical light gleamed in Mr. Poole's eye, and his voice became both soft and sibilant. "One after another He has struck them down—the scarlet women in our midst. Oh, yes, His ways are strange, and His instruments not those we ourselves might choose, but I have seen His hand clearly in all that has passed." Looking at Catherine, he added matter-of-factly, "And now His hand is poised to strike you down, too, Catherine."

Catherine did not speak. She continued to stare at Mr. Poole with a growing sense of horror.

Her brain told her that what she suspected was impossible. It could not be that Mr. Poole had had anything to do with the attacks that had taken place around Langton Abbots in the last few months. As vicar of the parish church, he, if anyone, ought to be immune from suspicion. Yet when she considered it, there was a dreadful kind of logic in the idea. Mr. Poole had spoken as though the unknown assailant were an instrument of God, and that assailant's acts in accordance with God's will. It was an insane idea, of course, but after hearing Mr. Poole talk, it had become clear to Catherine that if not actually insane, he was at least verging on insanity where this one subject was concerned. He could not else have spoken approvingly of acts that must fill any normal person with horror and disgust.

And there was his conceit, too—the same conceit that had made him so certain Catherine must marry him and so outraged when he found she would not. She had heard that madmen were often conceited. Suppose he fancied it was his role to punish those women in his parish who flouted the Seventh Commandment? It seemed a monstrous notion, yet there had surely been something strange and meaning in the way Mr. Poole had warned her that God's hand was poised to strike her down. Remembering the fanatical gleam in his eye, Catherine felt there were depths in his character that might conceal any number of horrors.

Once more she looked at him, seeking for some proof that might either confirm or banish her suspicions from her mind. Mr. Poole, having made his threats, seemed to have recovered his composure. He stood regarding her now with a gentle, almost pitying smile on his face. It was a smile that showed clearly that he considered her fate to be already sealed, and in a way it was more horrible than when he had threatened her openly. Catherine began to back away from him. "Good day, Mr. Poole," she managed to say, then turned and ran from the room.

CHAPTER XIX

It took Catherine a considerable time to recover from her interview with Mr. Poole. Even after her first shock and horror had passed, she had still to settle the thorny question of what she ought to do next.

Someone in authority clearly needed to know all that Mr. Poole had said and implied. But who would that someone be? Jonathan's name sprang immediately to Catherine's mind, but she put the notion away from her regretfully. Of course her motive for seeing him in this instance would be impersonal, but she knew well enough that she could never be completely impersonal where Jonathan was concerned. She still loved him and longed to see him in spite of her resolutions, and she simply did not dare to meet him again as long as she cherished such feelings.

So if Jonathan was eliminated as a possibility, who else remained? Sir Thomas Mabberly? He was the local magistrate and therefore the most obvious person to consult in such a case. But a visit to Mabberly Manor would necessarily bring her into contact with Lady Mabberly, one of her fiercest critics and detractors. Catherine shrank from such a contact. She might, she supposed, talk to the local constable or to Dr. Edwards. Either of them would probably be a suitable person to whom she might confide her suspicions. But Catherine feared that neither man would have the necessary power to act against a person like Mr. Poole, who himself occupied a position of considerable power in the village.

After much thought, she determined to seek her aunt's opinion in the matter. Aunt Rose might appear at first glance a sweet, slightly dithery old lady, but she possessed an underlying shrewdness and common sense that Catherine had come to respect over the last twelve years. So Catherine gathered her courage together, and as soon as she could find a moment alone with her aunt, she described to her all that had passed between her and Mr. Poole that afternoon.

Aunt Rose was astounded. "He said that!" she exclaimed. "He dared to bracket you with those—those other women, Catherine?"

"Yes, he did. But it wasn't that which concerned me so much, Auntie. It was the way he spoke, as though these attacks were—well—divinely ordained. It was disgusting and rather frightening, too. And I could not help wondering whether he might not have some personal role in all that has happened."

Aunt Rose, however, was more preoccupied with the insult that had been dealt her niece's character than with any discussion of Mr. Poole's role in the recent string of crimes. "I shall certainly write the bishop and tell him what has passed," she said indignantly. "To think that Mr. Poole would dare imply such a thing! Up till now I have always thought him a very good, orthodox clergyman—though, to be sure, I have not always agreed with him on certain points of doctrine. But if he could insult you in such a manner, Catherine, then the matter must be dealt with immediately. I am not quite without connections, though I do live very retired, and Mr. Poole must learn he cannot insult a Payne, or a Summerfield, either, without paying the consequences. I shall insist upon a full apology."

"I don't care about an apology, Auntie! All I care about is seeing that Mr. Poole is stopped, if it is indeed he who has committed these dreadful crimes."

Aunt Rose looked shocked. "You cannot really believe he has committed these crimes! I think you must be mistaken there, Catherine. To imagine that Mr. Poole could—no, it's quite impossible. Besides," she added, in a thoughtful voice, "I don't think he *could* have perpetrated them, Catherine, dear. You know he boards with Mrs. Stanley, and she is the most inquisitive creature alive. I doubt he could stir a step out of the house without her knowing it, let alone run about the countryside at night committing murders and such. And I think, too, that he was actually in London visiting his sister when the first of these crimes took place, so he cannot possibly be responsible."

Catherine was shaken by her aunt's words but not convinced. She remembered the fanatical gleam in Mr. Poole's eyes when he had spoken of divine retribution. It seemed to her that he might have committed the crimes even despite the handicap of an inquisitive landlady. And though his being in London during the time of the first attack seemed to clear him of suspicion, Catherine felt the matter deserved further investigation. It would, after all, be easy enough to claim he was in London when he was actually somewhere much nearer at hand.

But if Aunt Rose had not convinced Catherine of Mr. Poole's innocence, she had at least convinced her that it would be futile to confide her suspicions to anyone else. If Aunt Rose did not believe her, there seemed no chance that anyone else would. Catherine reached this conclusion reluctantly, after much private agonizing. She disliked leaving Mr. Poole free to attack and perhaps kill some other woman, but as things now stood she felt she had no alternative. Finally, feeling she must do something, she wrote all her suspicions in a letter, to be delivered to Jonathan once she was safely away from Langton Abbots. He had as big a stake in the matter as anybody, she reasoned, and with all the facts in his possession, he could make a full investigation of the affair and determine if Mr. Poole was indeed the guilty party.

She wrote this letter on the afternoon of the day preceding her and Aunt Rose's departure. Nearly everything else regarding their departure was already done. Their trunks were packed; the furniture was swathed in holland covers; and a post chaise and four had been ordered for ten o'clock the following morning. Catherine, as she wrote, was conscious of a lump in her throat. It was difficult to write to Jonathan—difficult to write what was virtually a final farewell to him and yet keep her letter strictly impersonal. It was also, she found, difficult to convey the full menace of Mr. Poole's words by a simple recital of them. Between these two difficulties, Catherine bogged down over and over again. She would start one letter, grow dissatisfied, tear it up and begin anew, only to repeat the whole process over again. She was still wrestling with the task when the maidservant Agnes tapped on the door of her bedchamber.

"Begging your pardon, miss," she said. "You've a note here from Lady Laura. It was brought round by her woman just a few minutes ago."

Catherine sat looking at the little three-cornered note a considerable time before she opened it. It gave her a strange feeling to contemplate Lady Laura's note, not least because she had been in the act of writing to Jonathan when it arrived. Even though her letter to him had been a determinedly businesslike communication such as Lady Laura or anyone might have read, still it gave her a sense of guilt. At last, gathering her courage, she broke the seal, unfolded the note, and read the following:

Dear Catherine,

I have just learned that you are leaving Langton Abbots. Will you do me the honor of waiting on me

*before you go? There is something I particularly wished
to discuss with you. I am,*

> *Yours affectionately,*
> *Laura Lindsay*

*P.S. Do please come, Catherine. I will send the carriage
to you at eight o'clock unless I hear from you otherwise.
Please, please, do come!*

> *Yours, etc.*
> *L.L.*

Catherine read this note through several times with growing
unease. It was a strange epistle, she thought, beginning formally
but ending in what was almost a plea. The more Catherine
thought about it, the uneasier she became. What could Lady
Laura want of her? Was it only that she wished to say farewell
to Catherine, or did the business she "particularly wished to
discuss" have something to do with Jonathan?

"It doesn't matter," Catherine told herself. "I will not see
her. Even if she has heard some rumor about Jonathan and me,
her mind will soon be set at rest. Within a few months, at most,
she will learn I am not coming back to Langton Abbots. There
is no need to harrow up both our feelings with a painful scene."

Yet as soon as Catherine had convinced herself that she
might legitimately refuse to see Lady Laura she began to swing
around to the other viewpoint. Lady Laura had written her a
kind and affectionate note, begging her to come and wait on
her before she left Langton Abbots. It was a request that was
quite justified by the friendship that had existed between them
in the past. And even if they were now more rivals than friends,
it still seemed to Catherine that she had a duty to call on Lady
Laura one last time. She had injured her friend dreadfully, as
she well knew, and she felt her conscience would bother her
less if she acceded in this final request.

Even if Lady Laura wished only to reproach her, Catherine
still felt she ought to call. In fact, she was not sure but that

she would prefer Lady Laura to greet her with reproaches rather than kindness. At the very least, it would be one less thing to feel guilty about. So Catherine argued with herself, first inclining one way, then the other, for the rest of the day. Right up until eight o'clock she was not sure if she meant to go or not. But in the end, duty and a sense of morbid curiosity won out. When the maid informed her that the Earl's carriage was at the door, Catherine put on her hat and shawl, informed her aunt that she was going to say good-bye to Lady Laura, and left the cottage with a fast-beating heart.

All the way to Honeywell House, she sat staring out the carriage window. The setting sun illuminated the landscape, highlighting the lush growth of summer foliage that was yet untouched by the approach of autumn. It was a beauty that ought to have wrung Catherine's heart, considering how much she loved it and how she never expected to see it again. But she was so gnawed by anxiety that she was incapable of appreciating beauty or anything else. All she could think about was the coming interview. It was one thing to know she deserved rebuke, quite another to put herself purposely in the way of receiving it, as Catherine told herself. But there was no rebuke in Lady Laura's manner when she received Catherine, in the handsome drawing room where she and Catherine had spent so many hours together.

"Catherine, I knew you must come," she said. Approaching to where Catherine stood, she looked at her for a moment, then enfolded her in her arms. "You did not mean to leave without saying good-bye to me?" she whispered.

Catherine was overcome by a deep sense of shame. She could not speak, but only returned Lady Laura's embrace in wordless misery. "Catherine, I only heard today that you were leaving," Lady Laura went on, her voice choked with tears. "I could not believe it when I heard it. Why, why did you not let me know? I know I have neglected you shamefully these last few weeks. But—"

"You haven't neglected me," interrupted Catherine. Her

own voice was choked with tears as she went on eagerly, "It's not your fault, Laura. I thought it best to go away as quietly as possible. Of course you were busy with—with other matters. With your engagement," she added bravely.

A strange look passed over Lady Laura's face. "My engagement," she repeated. "Yes, I suppose that has occupied me a good deal of late."

"That would naturally be the case," said Catherine. She tried to make her voice light, even teasing. But Lady Laura shook her head.

"It isn't so simple as that, Catherine." She looked at Catherine soberly. "Perhaps you are not aware that the engagement has still not been publicly announced?"

Catherine was surprised. "Has it not?" she said. "I had thought you and your parents intended to announce it, at the— at the party you gave the other night." She could not restrain a flush, as she recalled the other things that had taken place that night. But Lady Laura did not seem to notice.

"No, we did not announce it then. Mama wanted to, but Papa was still opposed to the idea, and as for me, I simply could not make up my mind. We had a tremendous argument about it." Lady Laura smiled ruefully. "You probably noticed us talking together as you were leaving. It was all rather embarrassing, and I do not wonder that Lord Meredith took leave of the party soon afterwards."

Catherine found herself flushing deeper than ever. "I see," she said in some confusion. "So your father convinced you to wait?"

"Yes. Only I don't know that it was really he who convinced me. If I had wanted to, I am sure I could have carried my point even against Papa's objections. But the fact is that I did not want to, Catherine. I was almost glad of an excuse not to announce the engagement. And yet I do still want to marry Lord Meredith." Lady Laura's eyes were very clear and blue as she looked at Catherine. "The truth is that I am a coward, Catherine. You may laugh if you like, but it's true. I have neither the courage of my convictions, nor the strength to abandon them.''

Catherine did not laugh. ''You're not a coward, Laura,'' she said.

Lady Laura smiled faintly. ''It's very good of you to say so,'' she said. ''But I don't think you really understand what I am like, Catherine—any more, perhaps, than I really understand you.''

The silence that followed this speech might have been embarrassing, had it not been cut short in an unexpected fashion. The doors to the drawing room swung open, and Sir Oswald sauntered in, a genial smile on his face. Lady Laura turned to him, frowning. ''What is it, Oswald?'' she asked.

Sir Oswald smiled more genially than ever. ''I thought I heard voices,'' he explained. ''And so I thought I'd pop in and see what was doing. Well, well, Miss Summerfield, as I live and breathe!'' He surveyed Catherine with bold-eyed admiration. ''This is a surprise—a most delightful and unlooked-for surprise, upon my word. Laura, why did you not let me know sooner that Miss Summerfield was here? I call it very selfish of you to try and keep her to yourself.''

Lady Laura did not return his smile. ''I am having a private interview with Miss Summerfield, Oswald,'' she said. ''That is why I did not notify you that she was here. If you would please excuse us?''

''Certainly, certainly. Glad to oblige.'' Still smiling genially, Sir Oswald turned and sauntered back out of the drawing room.

As soon as the door had closed behind him, Lady Laura looked at Catherine. ''You must forgive the interruption, Catherine. Oswald means well, I am sure, but he is sometimes rather—intrusive.'' Not waiting for Catherine to respond, she went on in a serious voice. ''About this trip of yours, Catherine. I had heard you were going to Bath?''

Catherine nodded. ''That is true. At least—'' She stopped, then went on in a self-conscious voice. ''I—that is, my aunt and I—may possibly extend the trip to include other towns as well. Our plans are rather indefinite.''

Lady Laura nodded thoughtfully. ''And it is true you are leaving tomorrow?'' she asked.

''Quite true,'' said Catherine. She was finding it harder and harder to meet Lady Laura's eyes.

''And will you be returning soon? You know Papa only holds a year's lease on Honeywell House. I had thought he intended to renew it at the end of the year, but lately he has been talking as though he may not. So you see, Catherine, if you do not return here within a few months' time, I may be gone myself.''

Embarrassed or not, Catherine could not control herself at this. ''But Laura!'' she exclaimed. ''Even if your family leaves Honeywell House, surely you will remain here? If you are to marry Lord Meredith—''

''Yes, yes, of course,'' said Lady Laura, almost impatiently. ''But let us leave Lord Meredith out of the question for the moment. Will you or will you not be returning soon to Langton Abbots?'' Lady Laura looked at her steadily. ''Is this to be a final farewell?''

''Yes, Laura. I think it will be,'' said Catherine softly.

Lady Laura looked at her for a moment, then leaned forward and kissed her on the cheek. ''Then you must write me,'' she said. ''Promise me that you will write, Catherine. Write me as soon as you get to Bath. I must know how you are and what you are doing, or I cannot be happy myself.''

This request filled Catherine with dismay. She foresaw all manner of unhappy complications arising from a correspondence with Lady Laura, not least of which would be the unhappiness of receiving bulletins of Lady Laura's married life with Jonathan. Since their friendship was doomed to be severed, it seemed to her better that it should be severed completely. But when she tried to protest against Lady Laura's demands, she found Lady Laura unexpectedly firm.

''I must insist, Catherine. It is essential that you write to me." As though sensing Catherine's thoughts, she added, "If you prefer, I will not write to you in return. But I *must* insist that you write to me. So many things can happen in life, Catherine—so many sad and unexpected things. I would not want to lose touch with you entirely."

She looked so wistful that Catherine found herself relenting. Indeed, Lady Laura had so successfully countered her arguments that she could think of no reason for not relenting. It appeared that Lady Laura would not insist on flaunting her own happiness in Catherine's face, and she reasoned that no harm could come of writing her an occasional letter. Of course she would rather not have written if she could have avoided it. She knew her own weakness if Lady Laura did not, and if Lady Laura meant to marry Jonathan, it still seemed to her better that she have no contact with either of them. But writing to Lady Laura alone was at least relatively harmless, and since she seemed to desire it so much, Catherine felt she could not refuse her request.

"Yes, I will write to you, Laura," she said.

Lady Laura kissed her again and told her how grateful she was. "You don't know what it means to me, Catherine," she said, looking at Catherine earnestly. This was so literally true that Catherine could think of no reply. Once again she was conscious of a gulf separating her from Lady Laura, a gulf not merely of rank and position, but of essential personality. She was sure that had she stood in Lady Laura's place, she would have wanted nothing more to do with herself.

But just as it was natural in Lady Laura to command, it was natural in Catherine to follow her friend's commands. So she assented docilely to all Lady Laura's directives about writing her long and frequent letters. She also made no demur when, at the last minute, Lady Laura insisted on giving her a token to remember her by. "I want you to have this, Catherine," said Lady Laura, as she unfastened the little gold cross on a chain that she habitually wore around her neck.

Catherine was very close to tears by this time, and she could only nod, blinking, as Lady Laura fastened the chain around her neck. They were standing by the carriage by this time. As Catherine turned to step inside, she was arrested by a familiar voice. "Going home already, Miss Summerfield? I'll give you a lift. I was just headed that way myself, and there's no sense in taking two carriages."

Catherine stopped short in dismay. The last thing she desired at such a juncture was to share a carriage with Sir Oswald. He stood there, smiling at her in his usual lascivious fashion and offering her his arm to assist her in mounting the carriage steps. Under the circumstances, Catherine did the only thing possible.

"Thank you, but I will not put you to so much trouble, Sir Oswald," she said. "I would rather walk home."

This refusal obviously displeased Sir Oswald, but he made an effort to hide his displeasure behind an amused and indulgent manner. "Walk home! At this hour? No, indeed, Miss Summerfield! It is almost dark, and I am sure your aunt would think Laura and me most remiss if we did not do you the honor of seeing you safely home."

As Catherine was seeking for a reply to this speech, Lady Laura came to her aid unexpectedly. "The sun is just now setting, Oswald," she said. "If Catherine walks quickly, I am sure she can reach home before it grows dark. And I am sure I do not blame her for wishing to walk home. She is leaving Langton Abbots tomorrow, you know, and I daresay she would like to take a last look at all her familiar haunts before she goes."

"Yes, I would," agreed Catherine gratefully. She kissed Lady Laura one last time, bade a cold farewell to Sir Oswald, and set off across the grounds toward Willowdale Cottage.

CHAPTER XX

As Catherine threaded her way amid the formal gardens of Honeywell House, she rejoiced in her narrow escape.

It had been difficult to tell Sir Oswald to his face that she would rather walk home than share a carriage with him. Fortunately, Lady Laura seemed to have understood her dilemma. With her usual kindness and tact, she had given Catherine an excuse that would spare her Sir Oswald's unwanted escort while at the same time sparing his feelings.

"That's the kind of thing that comes naturally to Laura," Catherine reflected, as she skirted an Italian garden and plunged into the surrounding woods. "She has a kind of instinct about how best to spare people's feelings, even the feelings of someone who has injured her as I have. She *is* an angel, and there's no doubt Jonathan would be better off with her than me. That is some comfort—indeed, it's the only comfort I have. But I suppose that's better than having no comfort at all."

The thought of Jonathan with Lady Laura sobered her, as it always did. She tried to put the thought away from her and concentrate on the future but found it difficult. Tomorrow she would begin a new life, in a new place and among a new set of people, but tonight she knew a strange, nostalgic desire to dwell on the life that had been familiar to her one last time. The fancy struck her that she might do in reality what Lady Laura had suggested by way of excuse. Why should she not take a final look at the places that had been dear and familiar to her? And there was one place above all others that she desired to look at one last time. The well lay amid the trees only a few rods from her present path. Catherine's feet led her there almost without conscious volition. A few minutes later she was standing in the shelter of the pavilion. looking down into the waters of the well.

From the depths of the water, her own face looked back at her gravely. Catherine contemplated it for some minutes. There was sadness in her eyes, but also, she thought, a measure of peace.

"Because I am doing what is right," she told her reflection aloud. She drew a deep sigh and turned away, only to find herself face-to-face with Jonathan.

"Jonathan," she whispered. For a moment, surprise held her frozen. Yet her body felt anything but frozen. The blood coursed through her veins in a fiery flood that was part shock, part consternation, and part fierce, elemental desire. Becoming aware of this latter emotion, she took a quick step backwards. Her heel struck the curb of the well, throwing her off-balance. As she stood swaying, trying to recover herself, Jonathan came to her aid, just as he had done that night so many weeks ago. He caught her round the waist and half-pulled, half-lifted her away from the curb of the well. As soon as she could, Catherine drew away from him, but she found herself trembling uncontrollably. She folded her arms over her chest and turned away, fighting an urge to burst into tears.

After a moment, Jonathan spoke. "Can you ever forgive me, Catherine?" he said. "It's hard to believe I could be clumsy enough to frighten you twice in the same way."

"You didn't frighten me," said Catherine. "You only surprised me." She threw him a look over her shoulder. "What are you doing here?"

He did not answer, and after a minute Catherine threw him another look. He had moved over to the well and was standing at the curb, looking down into its waters. "What are you doing here?" said Catherine again. Once again he did not answer. He only went on looking into the water with an abstracted gaze.

"You are leaving Langton Abbots tomorrow," he said.

It was a statement, not a question. Catherine nodded. Then she realized he was not looking at her and forced herself to speak. "Yes, I am leaving tomorrow," she said.

He turned to look at her then. Catherine once more looked quickly away, but not in time to avoid seeing his face. "You are leaving tomorrow," he repeated. "And yet you came here tonight?"

Unlike his previous remark, this *was* a question. Catherine tried to answer it as best she could. "I don't know why," she said falteringly. "I suppose—I suppose I wanted to see the well one last time."

Jonathan did not answer. Instead, he drew a deep sigh and sat down heavily on the well curb. After a minute, Catherine came over to join him.

"I have been to call on Lady Laura," she said.

"Have you?" said Jonathan, rather mechanically. "That was kind of you."

"No, the kindness was all on her side. She wanted to see me before I left and say good-bye. And she gave me this." Catherine held out the cross around her neck.

Jonathan glanced at it, then at Catherine's face. He seemed about to speak, but Catherine forestalled him. "I know how you feel, Jonathan. At least, I think I do. But I am sure we are doing the right thing. Seeing Laura tonight, and talking with her, has made me more sure than ever that we have done rightly."

"I am glad you are so sure," said Jonathan. "I don't feel sure at all myself."

He turned to look at her. Catherine looked back at him for a moment, then rose to her feet. "I had better go," she said.

Jonathan also rose. "I'll see you home," he said.

"No, you will not," said Catherine firmly. "Don't be absurd, Jonathan. You know we must not be seen together. Besides, were you not on your way to visit Lady Laura?"

Jonathan let out his breath in a long sigh. "Yes," he said. "I suppose I was." He stood where he was for a moment, looking moodily down at his feet. After a minute, he raised his eyes to look at Catherine. "But she is not expecting me, Catherine. It was only that I felt restless—restless and unhappy. And I thought I ought to call on her—but I ended up here instead."

Catherine made a gesture as though to stop him. He smiled wryly and went on in a sober voice. "Never fear, I don't mean to say any more than that, Catherine. But since I find you here, I do think I ought to see you home. I don't believe you should be out alone after dark."

Catherine's thoughts flew to Mr. Poole. "I don't think I need worry about that tonight," she said. "It's Sunday, and there's Evensong tonight." Mr. Poole always held Evensong services on Sunday evenings, and Catherine was comforted by the thought. If he was busy celebrating Evensong, he could hardly be out raping and murdering women.

Jonathan looked at her curiously. "What does being a Sunday have to do with it?" he asked. "Do you know something that I don't, Catherine?"

Catherine was strongly tempted to take him into her confidence. But a glance at the deepening twilight convinced her that she had better stick with her original plan. To explain her suspicions of Mr. Poole would take time, and it was growing darker every minute. If someone was to witness them having a twilight tête-à-tête in the pavilion, it would only add fuel to the scandal that she was trying so desperately to quench.

Nor was this Catherine's only reason for wishing to get away. She was realistic enough to see that every minute she was alone with Jonathan was a test of her strength. Thus far she had passed the test, no doubt because she had been strengthened by her interview with Lady Laura. But even so, she had found it a fearful effort to keep the conversation decorous and impersonal, and she sensed Jonathan was having to make an effort, too. It seemed best not to try either of their strengths too far.

"I have an idea, yes, but it's nothing I care to discuss at present," she said, turning away. "You may as well go on to Honeywell House, Jonathan. I'm sure I shall be perfectly safe."

There was a long pause. Catherine could feel Jonathan looking at her. Once more she found herself trembling. Making an effort, she spoke aloud in a clear, strong voice. "Go, Jonathan!" she said. "Go."

Again there was a long pause. Catherine trembled more than ever, sensing that the issue was balanced on the narrowest of razor's edges. But at last, Jonathan heaved a sigh. "Very well," he said. "Good-bye, Catherine."

Catherine made no response, but stood still, waiting. She heard Jonathan's footsteps cross the stone floor of the pavilion, a horse's nicker, and then, a moment later, the sound of hoofbeats slowly fading into the distance.

Catherine turned around, feeling as weak as though she had just run a footrace. The first object that met her eyes was Jonathan's riding crop. It lay near the curb of the well, its gold trimming glinting handsomely in the last rays of the setting sun.

"Oh, Jonathan!" said Catherine. "How could you?" She found herself laughing helplessly, even as the tears rolled down her cheeks. For several minutes she could do nothing but stand there, weeping and laughing by turns, until the storm of emotion passed. Wiping away her tears, Catherine stooped to pick up the crop.

"I can't leave it lying here, that's certain," she told herself. "I'll take it home with me. Tomorrow I can have one of the servants ride over to the Abbey and give it to him along with the note I wrote about Mr. Poole. Of course that may cause more gossip, but at least I can take comfort in the fact that it will be the last gossip I can possibly cause in Langton Abbots. So long as that is the case, I daresay Jonathan and I can both stand it.''

Holding the crop at her side, so that it lay concealed among the folds of her skirt, Catherine cautiously left the pavilion. It was all but dark now, the sun having just slipped behind the horizon. The western sky was illumined only by a fading orange glow. Catherine found it difficult to negotiate the tenuous path amid the trees. But her thoughts were so absorbed with Jonathan that she hardly noticed.

"I shall never see him again," she told herself. "This is the last time—the very last time I shall ever see or speak to him.''

The knowledge was painful, a real physical pain that seemed to constrict her heart like a cruel hand. So badly did it hurt that when she tripped over a tree root and struck her shin against a stump, that pain seemed slight in comparison.

Catherine paused for a moment, rubbing the sore spot absently. Jonathan's crop had fallen from her hand when she had stumbled and now lay amid a pile of last year's leaves. As she leaned over to pick it up, her ears caught the sound of a snapping twig somewhere nearby. It was a small sound, but it startled Catherine. She turned quickly. Her eyes searched amid the trees, but the dark had gained by leaps and bounds since she had left the pavilion, and she could distinguish little.

"It's nothing," she told herself with an inward shrug. "Some animal, perhaps—or perhaps nothing at all.'' Yet even as she tried to reassure herself, he ears caught another small sound. This time it was a mere rustle, such as might have been made by the wind playing among the fallen leaves. But there was no wind. Catherine, looking around her, realized that it was an abnormally still evening. The leaves hung motionless on the trees, and the air was charged with an eerie silence. And in that silence it was easy to hear—or to imagine that she heard—the sound of stealthy footsteps drawing nearer.

Catherine's skin crawled. She told herself that the sound was only imagination. Even if it was not imagination, there was no reason to suppose it represented danger. Yet all her instincts told her otherwise. As she stood listening with straining ears, she could almost feel some invisible menace drawing closer with every stealthy and deliberate step.

When another twig snapped, sounding like a shot in the dark wood, Catherine waited to hear no more. She turned and ran for all she was worth. And her instincts were quickly vindicated, for almost immediately she heard footsteps pounding after her—footsteps that were stealthy no more, but rather swift and grimly determined.

Instinct had led Catherine to run, and instinct likewise guided her path. She ran toward the common, in the direction of home. Before she had gone far, she realized how foolish she had been. It would have been much better to have run toward Honeywell House, which lay much closer at hand and offered a certain source of refuge and assistance. The nearest dwellings in the other direction were only a few laborers' huts, and even if she was lucky enough to reach them in time, there was no certainty that their occupants would be willing to open the door to her, assuming they happened to be home in the first place.

But it was her only hope, and so Catherine ran toward the common, her heart pounding and her breath coming in shallow gasps. Behind her she heard the thud of her pursuer's footsteps. They sounded so close behind her that she did not dare to look back. Once, however, she heard a crash and a muffled oath, as though her pursuer had fallen foul of some obstacle. Catherine's heart gave a leap of hope, but even then she did not look back. She ran faster instead, praying fervently that the pursuit might be ended. But soon she heard footsteps pounding after her once more: a little farther behind her now, it was true, but as grimly purposeful as ever.

"Please let there be someone on the path," she prayed with

desperation. A servant on an errand; a farmer returning from the local tavern; even a traveling peddler would have been an inestimable boon to her. But when at last she burst out of the woods and onto the path, she saw with despair that it was quite deserted.

To her left stretched the heath, a bare and empty plain washed by the last lingering remains of twilight. To her right yawned the quarry, a black pit like an open mouth in the near darkness. It looked indescribably menacing, but beyond it lay the laborers' huts and her only hope of salvation. Catherine ran faster, but her pursuer ran faster, too, unhindered by trees and underbrush as on the narrow trail through the woods. She could hear his labored breathing growing gradually closer until she imagined she could feel his breath on the back of her neck. It was like a nightmare to Catherine—a nightmare whose most frightening quality was knowing that there could be no awakening to save her. With sudden desperation, she halted and wheeled around to face her pursuer.

It was obvious he had not expected this. He took a step or two backwards, as though confounded by his victim's show of defiance. But then he recovered himself and rushed forward, his hands outstretched toward Catherine's throat.

Catherine shrank back with an involuntary cry. She had expected, at the very least, a human attacker. But this was a monster: a black, formless, faceless thing with glittering eyes of menace. For a moment her senses swam. She raised her hands, trying to ward off this vision of evil. And then she became aware that she was still holding Jonathan's riding crop in her hand.

Without thought or hesitation, Catherine acted. Raising the crop high, she struck directly at the creature's formless head.

He drew back with a whispered epithet. The next moment he came toward her again with renewed fury, but that instant's hesitation had been sufficient to show Catherine that he was both vulnerable and human. The formless head was merely a black silk mask; the shapeless body a dark cloak. The discovery heartened her, and she struck again with all her strength. Again he swore and drew back. Catherine screamed loudly. "Help!" she cried. "Help!"

"Shut up!" he whispered harshly. "Shut up! There'll be no help for you—not after I'm done with you." A string of even worse threats followed, as he made another effort to get his hands around her throat. Catherine slashed at him with the crop and managed to strike him full in the face. As she drew back to strike him again, however, he caught hold of the loop at the crop's tip and tried to wrench it from her grasp. Instinctively Catherine hung on for dear life.

"Help!" she cried again. Pull as she might, the man was stronger than she was. She could feel both the crop and herself drawn slowly toward him. With a strength born of desperation, Catherine made a last, furious effort to pull it back. At the same time she screamed at the top of her lungs, "Help! Help!"

What happened next was confusion. Her attacker let go of the crop so suddenly that Catherine fell backwards onto the ground. There was loud cursing, a sound of running footsteps, and then a sudden, horrific scream. And as Catherine lay cowering on the ground in a state of terror and confusion, she became aware of another, most welcome sound. It was the beat of an approaching horse's hooves. She scrambled to her feet again, just as a rider swept past on the path toward the quarry.

"Help!" she screamed. "Help!"

The rider turned and came about with a suddenness that set his horse rearing. "Catherine?" he said. "My God, Catherine!"

With a sensation of indescribable relief, Catherine recognized Jonathan's voice. "Jonathan!" she cried, running toward him.

He dismounted quickly, just in time to catch her in his arms. "Catherine!" he said again. "Catherine, what's happened?"

But Catherine was unable to answer. Relief coming on top of shock and horror had been too much for her. Her legs gave way abruptly; she sank to the ground and burst into tears.

As though from a great distance, she heard Jonathan's voice, questioning her frantically. "Catherine, are you injured? Ought

I to fetch a doctor?'' He sounded so nearly hysterical that
Catherine thrust aside her own hysteria in order to calm him.
Laughing shakily, she shook her head.

"No, I am not hurt at all, Jonathan," she said. "But it's a
wonder I wasn't. Indeed, I am not at all sure why I escaped.
Did you frighten away the man who was attacking me, or did
someone else?''

She looked up at Jonathan. He was staring down at her.
"The man who was attacking you?'' he repeated. "My God,
Catherine! You don't mean to say you were being attacked?''

Catherine regarded him with surprise. "Yes, Jonathan, that
is exactly what I mean," she said. "Didn't you hear me calling
for help?''

"That, yes," said Jonathan slowly. "I was on my way to
Honeywell House when I heard someone calling for help. And
so I rode back as quickly as I could. But I never imagined—
my God, Catherine!" He stared down at her with horror. "Do
you think—could it have been the man who attacked those
other women?''

Catherine shivered. "I think it must have been," she said
in a low voice.

"Who was it?'' said Jonathan sharply. "Who was it that
tried to hurt you, Catherine?''

Catherine shook her head. "He was wearing a mask, so I
never saw his face," she whispered. "But he ran after me, and
tried to—tried to grab me around the throat." She put her
hands to her throat with a shudder of remembrance. "And from
the things he said—yes, it must have been the same man. It
was horrible.''

"My God!" said Jonathan again. He sat down abruptly
beside Catherine, looking deeply shaken. "I knew I should not
have let you go home alone. It's my fault—all my fault.''

"Indeed it is not," said Catherine strongly. "On the contrary,
I think it must have been you who saved me. The man who
was attacking me ran away just before you came up. And if it
had not been for your riding crop, I never would have had even

a chance to call for help." She began to laugh wildly. "It was a good thing you left it at the pavilion, Jonathan. I did not think so at the time, but it turned out to be quite providential!"

"My riding crop!" said Jonathan blankly. He looked down to where the crop lay on the ground beside her. "What did my crop have to do with it?"

"Everything," said Catherine, and explained how she had taken the crop with her, intending to return it to him, and how she had ended up using it to defend herself. "I hit him three or four times, but then he caught hold of it and tried to take it away from me. And he had almost succeeded when suddenly he let go and ran off. And then you rode up. I still don't understand exactly what happened or why, but I am very glad to be safe."

Jonathan was looking around him uneasily. "Not so very safe," he said. "For all we know, that fellow could still be lurking somewhere hereabouts." He rose to his feet. "I'd better get you home, Catherine. There's no time to lose. As I say, that fellow may still be lurking somewhere hereabouts, and if I can call a party of men together quickly enough, we might be able to capture him. If he was on foot, he can't have got far."

Catherine suddenly clapped a hand to her mouth. "I don't think he did get far! Jonathan, the quarry!"

Jonathan looked at her in puzzlement. "The quarry?" he repeated. "It would be a good hiding place, I'll admit. But there's only the one path to the bottom, and it would be pretty difficult to negotiate in the dark."

"Not just difficult: it would be impossible. And that awful scream! It must have been, Jonathan! It must have been."

"I did hear a scream, just as I rode up," said Jonathan slowly. "But I supposed that was you, Catherine. You said you were calling for help—"

"Yes, and I did scream, too, but not that time." Catherine shivered. "Not that time, Jonathan. I'm almost sure the man who attacked me must have fallen in the quarry."

Jonathan turned to look at the quarry. "It's possible, I suppose," he said. "He was in a hurry to get away, no doubt, and of course it is getting dark. But still I find it hard to believe he didn't see the quarry in time to avoid it."

Catherine shook her head. "He was wearing a mask, remember," she said. "And if his mask had become twisted, or if his eyes were injured . . . you know I hit him in the face, Jonathan. Not once but several times, as hard as I could."

For a moment she and Jonathan looked at each other. "We'll have to make sure," said Jonathan at last. "Or rather, *I'll* have to make sure." He frowned. "But I can't leave you here alone, Catherine. I suppose I had better take you to your aunt's before I do anything else." He extended a hand to her. "I'll take you home first, then knock up Edwards and the constable and a few others to come with me. We'll make a thorough search of the area and find out just what happened."

Catherine allowed him to raise her to her feet, but her face was grave. "I already know what happened," she said. "That awful scream! I am sure I could not be mistaken."

"Perhaps not, but we'll have to make sure," repeated Jonathan. He glanced indecisively at his saddle. "Can you ride pillion, Catherine? I don't like to ask it of you, but you know that time is of the essence in this business. Just possibly that fellow really didn't fall into the quarry, in spite of what it sounded like. And even if he did, he might not have been so badly injured that he couldn't get up and get away. We must find out as soon as possible."

Catherine merely shook her head. "I am sure he didn't get away," she said. "But I don't mind riding pillion, Jonathan. If you will help me into the saddle, I will manage very nicely."

Jonathan assisted her onto his horse's back, then swung himself into the saddle in front of her. Catherine wrapped her arms around him and laid her face against his back. He turned his head to look at her and seemed about to speak, but in the end he merely urged his horse forward in a brusque voice. The horse obediently started along the path. As they passed the quarry, they both instinctively turned their heads to look. Its open pit still yawned dark and shadowy, but the moon had risen now, and its silvery light made it possible to discern a patch of something even darker that was lying at the bottom of the quarry.

"He was all in black," whispered Catherine. "A black cloak, and a black mask."

Jonathan nodded. He put up a hand to pat one of her hands that was resting on his shoulder. "We will have to make sure, of course. But it could be. I hope it is. This has been an ugly business—a very ugly business." In a sober voice, he added, "Pray God that this will be the end of it."

"Yes," was all Catherine said. She laid her face against his back once more, and they continued along the path in silence.

CHAPTER XXI

When Catherine and Jonathan rode up to the Cottage gate, Aunt Rose came rushing out to them with a mixture of relief and anxiety evident on her face.

"There you are, my dear!" she exclaimed, as Jonathan swung Catherine down from the saddle. It was clear she was puzzled to find her niece riding pillion with Lord Meredith. But any questions she might have asked were forgotten as soon as she got a good look at Catherine.

"My dear, whatever has happened? Are you ill?"

"I am afraid she has had a bad shock," said Jonathan, as he helped Catherine onto the porch. "Nothing worse than that, I hope, but quite enough in its way." Turning to Catherine, he added, "You know I hate to leave you like this. But I think this business needs to be settled one way or another as soon as possible. You are sure you will be all right?"

"Quite sure," said Catherine with a wan smile. "Don't worry about me, Jonathan. I will be quite all right now that I am home." She shivered.

"You *are* ill!" exclaimed Aunt Rose in concern. "You must

be, if you can shiver on a sultry night like tonight. I daresay you have taken a chill. We must get you inside, and I'll have the maids draw you a nice warm bath.''

Catherine made no demur to this suggestion. But as Aunt Rose was leading her inside the cottage, she paused to address Jonathan once more. ''You'll let me know as soon as you find out something definite?''

''The minute I know, I'll come and tell you all about it,'' said Jonathan. ''That's a promise, Catherine.'' He looked long and earnestly into her face, then turned and hurried back to where his horse was tethered.

As soon as Aunt Rose had helped Catherine inside the cottage, she set about satisfying her curiosity. ''I was surprised to see you come home with Lord Meredith, Catherine,'' she remarked as she transferred her own shawl to her niece's shoulders and rang for the maid. ''How did that come about? And what did he mean when he said that you had had a shock? What kind of a shock?''

Catherine started to speak, then covered her face with her hands. ''I can hardly bear to talk about it,'' she whispered. ''It was all so dreadful.'' With sudden resolution, she uncovered her face again. ''But I think I would feel better if I did talk about it.'' She smiled a twisted smile. ''Besides, I may as well get used to it. I will likely have to tell the story over again to the constable, and to Sir Thomas Mabberly, and probably to others as well.''

''To the constable?'' repeated Aunt Rose with wide eyes. ''And to Sir Thomas? Catherine, what on earth has happened?''

''You had better sit down, Auntie, before I tell you about it. I am afraid it will come as an even worse shock to you than it did to me.''

As soon as they were seated within the parlor, Catherine told her aunt the whole story. She described her visit with Lady Laura; how she had decided to walk home from Honeywell House, and how she had encountered Jonathan at the well. She skimmed lightly over the conversation that had ensued between

Joy Reed

them, but described how Jonathan had left his crop behind, and how that same crop had come to her aid later with startling results.

Aunt Rose listened with eyes and mouth wide open, making frequent exclamations of horror and sympathy. "My dear! What a narrow escape!" she said at the end of Catherine's recital. "You ought to have some stimulant after a dreadful experience like that. Some brandy, perhaps." She rose to her feet. "I'll go ask Cook if there is any in the house."

"Never mind the brandy, Auntie," said Catherine. "I will be well enough, I think, if I have a cup of tea and that bath you were speaking of."

"Yes, of course, of course," agreed Aunt Rose. She hesitated, then went on in a hushed voice, "Catherine, this man who attacked you . . . Do you think he might have been the same one who attacked those—those *other* women?"

"I think there can be no doubt, Auntie," said Catherine. "You know it would be too much of a coincidence to have two such men on the loose in a little village like Langton Abbots. I think it was the same man, and Lord Meredith thinks so, too."

Aunt Rose nodded. "Yes, of course." She paused for a moment, then went on in an even lower voice. "Catherine, *who was he?* It sounds as though you got a fair look at him. You must have some idea."

Catherine blinked. Strangely enough, this question had not occurred to her. The man who had attacked her had seemed a monstrous entity unto himself, and she had never considered that he must have another identity. "I don't know who he was," she said slowly. "He was wearing a mask and a loose cloak. I didn't get much idea of what he really looked like."

"We can be sure it was not Lord Meredith, at any rate," said Aunt Rose in a voice of satisfaction. "Of course I knew he could not be guilty of such dreadful crimes, but still it is a satisfaction to have it proven."

Catherine smiled a little. "It is indeed," she said. "But I

would know the man who attacked me could not have been Lord Meredith, even if he had not ridden up when he did. This was a shorter man than Lord Meredith, and a smaller man, too. More like—well, more like Mr. Poole.''

Aunt Rose shook her head, however. ''I do not think it can have been Mr. Poole, either, Catherine,'' she said. ''He had Evensong services this evening, you remember.''

''Yes, I remember. But it is just possible, you know, that he asked Dr. Astley from over in Wybolt to take the service this evening, as he sometimes does. You didn't attend Evensong yourself, did you?''

''No, I didn't,'' admitted Aunt Rose. ''I worked so hard today getting ready for our journey tomorrow that I decided I would rather stay home and rest tonight. But Agnes went, I believe.'' Reaching for the bellrope, she pulled it twice. Agnes appeared in answer to the summons, and Aunt Rose addressed her with brisk authority. ''Agnes, I know you attended Evensong this evening. Did Mr. Poole officiate at the service?''

''Why, yes, he did, ma'am,'' answered Agnes, looking surprised at the question. ''Just like he always does.

''Do you know what time he finished?''

Agnes ruminated. ''As to that, I couldn't say, ma'am. I didn't look at the clock when I came in. But it wasn't so very long ago—half an hour, perhaps, before Miss Catherine came in.'' She looked at Catherine with interest.

Aunt Rose also looked at Catherine. Catherine nodded slowly. ''He *could* have managed it,'' she said. ''If he went straight to Honeywell House after the service, I think it is just possible.''

''But he didn't, miss.'' Agnes spoke up unexpectedly. ''Just as we all was leaving the church, a boy came running up to say that old Mrs. Linwood over at the Alders was in a bad way, and could he come see her? And Mr. Poole put off his cassock in a hurry and said he'd go. And I saw them drive off together myself—him and the boy.''

Catherine and Aunt Rose exchanged glances. "That does appear rather conclusive," admitted Catherine.

"Yes, it does," agreed Aunt Rose. Turning to Agnes, she said firmly, "That will do, Agnes. You may go back to the kitchen now."

Agnes went, but with visible reluctance. It was obvious that Aunt Rose's questions had aroused her curiosity. "I suppose now the servants will guess something has happened," said Aunt Rose, looking after her with a sigh. "But it can't be helped."

"No," agreed Catherine absently. "They find out everything sooner or later."

"But at least Agnes's evidence seems to vindicate Mr. Poole. I must confess I am glad. I would not like to think he committed such dreadful crimes." Her face twisted into a look of perplexity. "The only question is, if *he* did not, and Lord Meredith did not, then who did?"

"We'll find that out when they search the quarry, I expect," said Catherine with a shudder. Aunt Rose came over and put a hand on her shoulder.

"Forgive me, my dear," she said penitently. "You have been through a great deal this evening. I should not be troubling you with questions this way." Again she patted Catherine's shoulder. "Let us get you a bath, and then you should go to bed and try to get some sleep."

"A bath would be most welcome. It's silly, no doubt, but after my meeting with that—that creature, I feel actually unclean." Catherine rubbed her arms with an expression of distaste. "I wish I could wash away the whole memory of this evening. But as for getting any sleep, I don't think I can, Auntie. Indeed, I would rather not even try. You know Lord Meredith promised to return and tell me as soon as there was any news."

"Yes, but that will not likely be until morning, my dear. You know that if he and the other men must search the quarry, they will no doubt wait until daylight to do it."

Catherine had her doubts about this, but Aunt Rose spoke

with great firmness, and it was easier to give way than to argue the point. The bathtub was filled, a clean nightdress produced, and Aunt Rose herself performed the task of turning down Catherine's bed and tucking her into it. "Sleep well, my dear," she said, kissing Catherine's brow. "Do try not to think anymore about this nasty business. What happened was very unfortunate, but it is all over now."

"Yes, it is over," agreed Catherine. She lay looking reflectively up at the ceiling, then glanced at her aunt once more. "As for being unfortunate, however, I'm not sure I agree. The more I think about it, the more I feel I have been very fortunate indeed." She tried to smile, but her voice broke a little as she added, "I have taken so many things for granted for so many years. I don't think I will ever do so again. I feel like St. Paul with the scales fallen from his eyes—and even more like Lazarus! It's as though I've been given a second chance at life—a second chance that I did not deserve, or dare even hope for."

Aunt Rose looked sober. "Yes," she said. "Yes, I see what you mean." With unaccustomed emotion, she bent to kiss Catherine again. "Oh, my dear, we have both been spared a great deal," she whispered. "It quite terrifies me to think of it." As though embarrassed by this confession, she drew hastily away. "But I don't mean to keep talking on and on. Try and sleep now, Catherine. And if you need anything to settle your nerves, just ring the bell. I think there are still a few drops of laudanum in that old bottle Violet bought years ago."

Catherine promised to ring for laudanum if she needed it, but she had no anticipation of needing it. Her nerves felt not at all amiss. It was true that she was not at all sleepy, but she hardly cared for that. Her present mood was sober, thoughtful, and—more than anything else—deeply thankful. Indeed, her whole soul seemed to be singing a psalm of gratitude and thanksgiving.

"I am very fortunate," she told herself over and over. "No

matter what happens after this, I can endure it. It is a great thing just to be alive after such an escape.''

Hour after hour she lay there, thinking over all that had happened that evening. She was aware of the passage of time, as the clock struck off the hours one by one, but not in any conscious way. Once she thought she heard voices in the distance, and the barking of dogs. She sat up in bed and looked toward the window. Some lights were moving in the distance along the path that led to the quarry. Some time after that she heard several horsemen ride past on the high street at a furious pace, followed soon after by a carriage moving at an equally rapid rate of speed.

Again Catherine sat up in bed and watched until the taillight of the carriage had disappeared into the night. She suspected that all these things had some connection with what had happened to her that evening. For a moment she found herself wishing she was out there, too, in the thick of the action and excitement; then she recalled how narrowly she had survived her last brush with action and excitement and decided with a shudder that she was glad to be where she was. Once more she lay down in bed. Before long, she had fallen again into a reflective trance.

It lasted until about three o'clock in the morning, when she was startled by a soft rattle from somewhere close at hand. Catherine sat up in bed, looking about her. Again the rattle sounded, and this time she realized it came from the window. She got up and went to the window. A third rattle came as she was standing there, and she saw it was caused by someone below who was tossing handfuls of gravel at the glass. It was too dark to see the someone very clearly, but his height and breadth of shoulder struck Catherine as very familiar.

Opening the pane, Catherine thrust her head out the window. ''Jonathan?'' she called.

''Yes, it's I,'' Jonathan's voice came softly in reply. ''May I come inside, Catherine? I have some news for you—news of a very particular sort. And I don't like to shout it from here.''

"Just a moment, and I'll come down and let you in," said Catherine.

Turning away from the window, she caught up her bedside candle. Lighting it hastily from the tinderbox, she set it on her dressing table. She tied her dressing gown over her nightdress, ran a comb through her hair, then took up the candle again and went softly downstairs. When she unlocked the front door, she found Jonathan waiting just outside. "Come into the parlor," she whispered, as she beckoned him inside. "We can talk there without waking my aunt."

Jonathan followed her into the parlor and stood watching as she lit the candles one by one from her own candle and hastily pulled the holland covers off a couple of chairs. She then seated herself in one chair, and Jonathan sat down in the other. "What is your news?" she asked. Looking closer at his face, she was frightened by what she saw there. "Jonathan, what is it? What has happened?"

He shook his head slowly. "I hardly know how to begin. What a night this has been! I feel as though I'd aged about twenty years in the last six hours."

"What has happened?" asked Catherine again. "Did you make a search of the quarry?"

"Yes, I did—or rather, we did. I rounded up a party of men from the village with torches and lanterns and dogs, and we all went down into the quarry. And we found the man who had attacked you down at the bottom, right enough, just as you had predicted."

"Dead?" said Catherine. The word was a mere whisper.

"Yes, dead," said Jonathan. He paused, looking searchingly at Catherine. "Catherine, do you know? Have you already guessed who he was?"

Catherine shook her head. "I had thought it was Mr. Poole at one time," she said. "But since then I have come to believe I was mistaken."

"It wasn't Mr. Poole," said Jonathan. He paused again, then spoke with sudden resolution. "Catherine, it was Oswald."

"Oswald?" said Catherine incredulously. "*Oswald?*"

She stared at Jonathan. He nodded, his face grim. "Yes, I could hardly believe it myself. In fact I didn't believe it when we first found him. I thought there must be some mistake—that somehow there had been two men, and the one who assaulted you had got away. But I don't think there can be any doubt, Catherine. He was wearing a mask and a dark cloak, just as you described him. And there were marks on his face—marks such as might have been made by a riding crop."

Catherine shuddered. "Oswald!" she said again. A moment later she exclaimed, "Poor Laura! Does she know? Has anyone told her?"

"No," said Jonathan, "no." He looked down at his feet for a moment, then raised his eyes to Catherine's face. "She will have to be told, of course. But the earl thought it better not to disturb her with the news until morning."

Catherine nodded. "Yes," she said. "This will come as a dreadful shock to her." She sat for a moment, thinking deeply. "But of course it must be a dreadful shock to all the Lindsays. Lord Lindsay must feel it most of all. Oswald was his heir, and his only son."

Jonathan's face hardened. "As to that, I wouldn't be too sure," he said. "I don't think Lord Lindsay was as shocked as he might have been."

"What do you mean?" asked Catherine, looking at him in surprise.

Jonathan shook his head, his face grimmer than ever. "As soon as I found out it was Oswald in the quarry, I knew Lord Lindsay would have to be told. I rode over to break the news to him while the other men were taking up the—the body. He was very distressed, of course, as one might expect." Jonathan paused, his eyes darkly shadowed, as though seeing the scene again in his mind's eye. "But when I explained, as delicately as I could, that it appeared his son had been responsible for the attacks that had taken place around Langton Abbots, he took my breath away by saying he had known it all along."

"Jonathan, you don't mean it!" gasped Catherine. "He knew Oswald was responsible for hurting those poor women—and actually killing one of them? And yet he did nothing about it?"

Jonathan's lip curled. "According to his way of thinking, he had already done everything necessary! He explained to me that it was about a year ago that he first became aware of his son's predilection for forcing himself on women against their will. Apparently there was some trouble about it while they were all living in London—trouble that the earl managed to have hushed up only with great difficulty. So he put Oswald in a private sanitarium for a few months while he looked about for a house in the country where he might bring him. Of course he could not take him to his *own* country house!" Jonathan's voice dripped sarcasm. "That would never have done, for it might have damaged his reputation in his home county."

Catherine shook her head wonderingly. "So that is why the Lindsays came to Langton Abbots. We all wondered about it at the time, but I am sure none of us guessed the real reason. I cannot believe Lord Lindsay could have connived in such a way!"

"You do not know the half of it," said Jonathan grimly. "When I expressed the same sentiment, he explained to me quite seriously that he chose Langton Abbots because it seemed likely to offer the fewest temptations to his son. He said—"

Jonathan broke off suddenly with a self-conscious look.

"He said what?" asked Catherine. "I don't see why Langton Abbots should offer less temptation than any other village."

She paused, looking at Jonathan inquiringly. After a moment he went on, but his voice was hesitant, and he had trouble meeting Catherine's eye.

"It seems that Oswald prefers to attack women of—well, women of a certain reputation," he said. "That is Lord Lindsay's story, at any rate, though I don't suppose there's any truth in it."

Catherine nodded slowly. "I see," she said. "And so Lord

Lindsay thought this neighborhood sufficiently free of that particular kind of woman to risk bringing his son here.''

Jonathan eyed her uneasily. ''Yes, that was his reasoning.
But it was faulty reasoning, as I pointed out to him. In the last
few months Oswald has attacked at least four women, one of
them fatally.''

''Five women,'' said Catherine. ''You are forgetting me,
Jonathan.''

Jonathan hesitated, then nodded. ''Yes, that is true. But I
thought it best not to mention you when I was discussing the
matter with Lord Lindsay, Catherine. At least, I did mention
you in a general way, but not by name.''

''That was considerate of you,'' said Catherine. It was impossible to tell from her voice if she was speaking ironically or
not. Once again Jonathan looked at her uneasily, but before he
could respond, she took up the conversation again. ''How did
you account for Oswald falling into the quarry, if you did not
mention me?''

''I merely told Lord Lindsay that I had heard calls for help
while I was on my way to Honeywell House,'' said Jonathan.
''When I rode over to investigate, I came upon a young woman
who was fighting off the attack of a masked man. The man ran
off as soon as I came up, and in his hurry to escape he must
have lost his way and run over the edge of the quarry. And I
said that while I was investigating who he was and what had
become of him, the woman apparently slipped away, thinking
it better not to be publicly involved in the matter.''

''A good story,'' said Catherine, nodding her head in a
judicial manner. ''A good story, Jonathan—and very nearly
true, too.''

''It *is* true, in every respect that matters,'' said Jonathan,
meeting her eyes gravely. ''You know I could not allow your
name to be bruited about, Catherine. Not in a matter like this.''

''But obviously it already is bruited about,'' pointed out
Catherine. ''Otherwise Oswald would not have selected me as
his victim.''

Jonathan did not immediately reply. Catherine looked at him searchingly. "You do see that, don't you, Jonathan?" she said. "My being singled out for such an attack is like a public indictment of my character."

Again Jonathan hesitated before replying. "I think you are taking this too personally, Catherine," he said. "Oswald probably took opportunity as much into account as the character of his victims. Besides, you cannot consider that he was a balanced or rational judge of character. At the very least he must have possessed some mental instability, and it may have been more serious than that. Lord Lindsay told me in confidence that there was madness in his first wife's family. Apparently her father ended life in an asylum, and she herself was subject to fits of melancholy and hysteria. She actually made away with herself in the midst of one of her melancholic fits when Oswald was just a boy."

Catherine merely shook her head. Jonathan eyed her with concern. Before either of them could speak again, however, an interruption occurred. The parlor door flew open, and there stood Aunt Rose, a stiff and militant little figure armed with a candle in one hand and a watchman's rattle in the other.

"Auntie!" exclaimed Catherine.

"Catherine!" exclaimed Aunt Rose. She looked relieved, but also greatly embarrassed. Her embarrassment grew even greater when she noticed Jonathan. "I heard voices downstairs and thought it was burglars," she explained. "And so I came to investigate."

"That was very plucky of you, Auntie, but also a little risky, wasn't it?" said Catherine, regarding her with a smile. "After all, if we had really been burglars, we might have attacked you."

Aunt Rose nodded vigorously. "Yes, that is why I brought the rattle. Even if I was attacked, I could hardly have helped making some noise as long as I was holding it. And it is so dreadfully loud that it could not help rousing the whole household." She set the rattle carefully on the parlor table, then turned to Jonathan. "I am surprised to find you here, my lord."

There was curiosity in her voice, and also a certain reserve. "Lord Meredith has brought us some news, Auntie," said Catherine, interpreting the reserve correctly. "Of course it is an unconventional hour for calling, but he knew I would want to hear it as soon as possible."

She went on to relate to her aunt the substance of Jonathan's news. Aunt Rose was deeply shocked to hear that Oswald had been responsible for the recent attacks. And she was warmly indignant against Lord Lindsay for having conspired in his son's crimes, however passively.

"Iniquitous—positively iniquitous," she declared. There is no excuse for his not acting immediately to put his son under restraint, as soon as he suspected he was guilty. Indeed, I believe I am right in thinking he would actually be legally liable to some extent for Oswald's crimes."

She looked at Jonathan. Jonathan shook his head. "He would be if he was an ordinary man of ordinary estate," he said. "But being the Earl of Lindsay, I am afraid he will escape without censure from the law. Indeed, he has already declared his intention of having the whole business hushed up if possible."

"Hushed up?" exclaimed Catherine. "But he can't, Jonathan! As matters now stand, every woman in the neighborhood is afraid to step outside her own doorstep, let alone go for a walk or run an errand! And they will all continue to be afraid until they know for certain that the culprit has been caught. When it is a matter of such serious and numerous crimes, I think the neighborhood has a right to know the truth."

"Yes, I pointed that out to the earl. But he was singularly unsympathetic to his neighbors' feelings. I suppose one could expect nothing less, seeing that he has allowed his son to prey on them without hindrance these last few months."

" Yes, and that is bad enough," said Aunt Rose decisively. "He should not be allowed to stand in the way of justice now."

"I don't intend that he shall," said Jonathan. "In fact, I told him so when I spoke to him this evening. He was inclined to take a high hand with me, but I told him that there were several other people under suspicion for the crimes, one of whom happened to be myself. And all of us will remain under suspicion until the true facts of the case are made known to the public."

"What did he say to that?" asked Catherine.

"He hemmed and hawed a good deal, and talked about the honor of his name. I told him my name meant a good deal to me, too, and that I would prefer not to be whispered about as a possible murderer."

"And what did he say to that?" asked Catherine again.

Jonathan did not immediately answer, but Catherine could tell by his face that the earl's further remarks had not been pleasant ones. "He said, as I recall, something to the effect that since I seemed to have spent most of my life getting myself talked about for one thing or another, he could not see that a little more gossip could hurt me," said Jonathan slowly. "I am afraid that from that point on, the conversation became rather personal. He said a number of things about me and my character, and I responded with a few things about him and his. He did his best to bully me and even threatened me with an action if I made the matter public without his permission. But I wasn't having any of it. Indeed, I would have liked to tell him I'd plaster the truth on every milepost between here and London, action or no action."

"I wish you had!" said Aunt Rose, pursing her lips with a martial air. "*That* would show him."

"Yes, it would. But unfortunately, I could not take quite such an imperious line as that. I am in a rather delicate position as regards Lord Lindsay, and his concerns must be mine whether I like it or not."

Jonathan glanced at Catherine as he spoke, but it was Aunt Rose who responded. "Because you are engaged to Lady Laura," she said, nodding sagely. "Indeed, I am very sorry for her, poor girl. And for her mother, too—it must be a dreadful shock to find one's near relation is a murderer and worse. Indeed, one cannot but sympathize with the earl's wish to save his family pain, whatever one may think of his other conduct.''

''Yes, that is true,'' said Jonathan. ''And that is why I hesitate to publish the truth, even in spite of the claims of justice. Although Lady Laura and I are not formally engaged, still there has been a degree of understanding between us that must compel me to take her feelings into consideration.''

''You say you and Lady Laura are not formally engaged?'' said Aunt Rose, looking astonished. ''I am surprised to hear it, my lord. Everyone speaks of it as an established thing.''

''Yes, and Laura herself believes it is an established thing,'' said Catherine, before Jonathan could speak. ''I talked with her this evening before all the excitement took place, and in the course of the conversation, she declared she intended to accept Lord Meredith's proposal, even if her father did not like the match.'' Lifting her head, Catherine looked directly into Jonathan's eyes. ''Surely you do not mean to cry off now, Jonathan? You know Laura will need you now more than ever, once she learns about her brother.''

''I know it,'' said Jonathan, returning her gaze steadily. ''I have no intention of crying off, Catherine.''

''Of course he does not,'' said Aunt Rose indignantly. ''How can you even imply he would do such a thing, Catherine? Certainly Lord Meredith will not cry off from his engagement.''

''I am sure he will not,'' said Catherine. Again she raised her eyes to Jonathan's face. ''I must say, however, that it seems too bad to me that your connection with Lady Laura means you must suffer an unjust suspicion for the rest of your life.''

''Ah, but it shouldn't come to that. You see, after Lord Lindsay and I had wrangled for an hour or two and called each other a variety of hard names, we were able to come to a compromise.''

''What compromise is that?'' asked Aunt Rose, looking skeptical. ''Surely there can be no compromise with the truth!''

''No, but there may be in the way it is distributed. According to Lord Lindsay's wish, there will be no formal publication of Oswald's guilt, but I am permitted to make a private disclosure of the facts in order to clear anyone else who may be suspected of the crimes. And given the way gossip travels in this place, that will be as good as a formal publication.'' Jonathan threw a fleeting glance at Catherine. ''In fact, I pointed out to Lord Lindsay that there really wasn't a hope of keeping the matter quiet. A round dozen men accompanied me down into the quarry, and even if I hadn't told them that we were searching for the man suspected of committing the recent string of atrocities, they would have guessed something was amiss from the way Oswald was dressed. It shouldn't be long before every soul in Langton Abbots knows the truth, and that's all that matters to me.''

''Yes, that seems a fair compromise,'' agreed Aunt Rose. With a shake of her head, she added, ''I ought not to say so, perhaps, but it seems to me fortuitous that Sir Oswald should have met his end as he did. As long as Lord Lindsay was willing to shield him, it would have been difficult to bring him to justice any other way. Besides, this way spares his family the ordeal of a formal trial and his victims a great deal of painful publicity. It almost seems like the work of providence.''

Jonathan agreed, but in a quiet voice. He glanced at Catherine once or twice, but she said nothing and kept her eyes fixed on the toes of her bedroom slippers. After a moment or two of further musings, Aunt Rose rose to her feet.

''It was very kind of you to bring us the news, my lord,'' she said. ''I know Catherine was anxious to hear what had happened, and I will confess to having been curious myself. But it is time now we let you go. I am sure you must be longing for your bed, after the fatiguing evening you have passed.''

This was such an unmistakable dismissal that Jonathan could do nothing but take his leave. In doing so he tried hard once more to catch Catherine's eye, but she was careful to avoid it. ''Good night, Catherine,'' he said, bowing over her hand. ''I hope to see you again soon, so we may talk some more about this business.''

There was a faint question in his voice, but Catherine ignored it. ''Good night, Jonathan,'' she said. ''Thank you for taking the time to come here and tell me what happened. And if you think it would not come amiss, please convey my sympathies to Lady Laura and to Lord and Lady Lindsay when next you see them.''

''I'll do that,'' said Jonathan. He cast Catherine a last, wistful look. ''Good night, Catherine.''

''Good night,'' said Catherine, turning away. She did not turn back again until the door had closed behind him.

CHAPTER XXII

After Jonathan had gone, Catherine returned to her bedroom and tried her best to sleep.

She did manage to doze off, just as dawn was beginning to streak the eastern sky. But when Aunt Rose came downstairs to the breakfast parlor at nine o'clock, she found her niece already there, seated at the table and clad in a neat traveling pelisse and a veiled bonnet.

"Good heavens, are you down already?" exclaimed Aunt Rose. Her eyes took in the details of Catherine's costume, and her surprised look became downright incredulous. "Why, Catherine dear, you look as though you are expecting to go on a journey! I know we had planned to go to Bath today, but surely what happened last night alters things?"

Catherine made a great show of inspecting the contents of the different dishes on the table before answering her aunt's questions. "I don't see that we need change our plans, merely because of what happened last night," she said, rejecting all the dishes on the table and contenting herself with a cup of coffee. "You know we have been planning to go to Bath for almost a week."

"Yes, but that was because of those dreadful attacks," said Aunt Rose. "Now that Sir Oswald is dead—and may God have mercy on his soul—there is no need for us to leave Willowdale Cottage."

"No need, perhaps, but I should like to anyway. The arrangements have all been made, and Miss Harvey's servants are expecting us. Cannot we go anyway?"

"We could," said Aunt Rose slowly. "But I don't see why, Catherine. Why should we go away and leave our friends and home when we do not have to?"

"Of course we do not have to. But I should like to anyway." Catherine raised haunted eyes to her aunt's face. "I can't explain, Auntie. I can only say that after everything that has happened, I feel as though I simply must get away from Langton Abbots. If you do not care to go, then perhaps I could take Agnes with me and go alone. But I must get away from here, at least for a while. I *must.*"

"I see," said Aunt Rose. She was quiet a long time, looking at her niece. Then she nodded with sudden decision. "I see," she said again. "It's true you had a terrible experience last night, Catherine dear, and I expect it would do you good to get away from Langton Abbots for a while. But of course you cannot go alone. If you go, I shall go with you." Blotting her lips with her napkin, she rose from the table. "I am afraid we shall be a little later leaving than we originally planned," she said apologetically. "Supposing that our plans were changed, I did not dress for traveling this morning. And my trunk is not quite packed, either. But if you will give me a couple of hours, Catherine, I should have everything ready. I'll ring for Agnes and let her know we will be leaving Langton Abbots after all."

It was only a little more than two hours later when Catherine and Aunt Rose left Willowdale Cottage and entered the hired post chaise that had been sent around from the local posting house. Agnes, looking very important, entered the chaise after them and seated herself on the small rear-facing perch seat. The other servants were to stay behind and tend to the cottage in their absence. It gave Catherine a pang to reflect that she could not say good-bye to them as she wished without betraying the fact she did not intend to return to Langton Abbots. And she could not say openly that she did not intend to return without grieving her aunt, perhaps unnecessarily.

"No doubt she will become reconciled to the situation in time," Catherine told herself. "It will be soon enough to tell her my intentions when she begins to speak of returning home. There is no need to upset her now, at the beginning of our journey." So she had contented herself by making all the servants generous presents before she left and thanking them warmly for their services on her behalf. And as she sat staring out the post chaise window at the home that had been hers for the past twelve years, she did her best not to look as though she never expected to enter it again.

Soon enough the postilions were given the order to start. Willowdale Cottage was left behind them, and Catherine sat looking out the window, trying to reconcile herself to the prospect of the new life that lay ahead of her.

It was, in her opinion, absolutely necessary that she begin a new life. It was as necessary now as when she had first made up her mind to do it a week ago. Indeed, it might be argued that it was even more necessary now than then. There had been a moment the previous evening when she, like Aunt Rose, had believed there was no longer any need to leave Langton Abbots. When Jonathan had taken her in his arms beside the quarry, and she had realized she was saved from a terrible fate through his intervention, she had felt as though they were bound anew by a tie that could not be sundered by anything on earth.

But that had been mere self-deception. She had begun to realize it even as she and Jonathan were riding home together, and talking to him later that night had made her see the truth yet more clearly. She might feel as though she was bound to him, but he was bound in honor to Lady Laura—bound by ties that he could not break without injuring all three of them. The situation was, in fact, exactly as it had been before, with the added difference that Lady Laura had just suffered a catastrophic loss that would naturally make her turn more than ever to Jonathan for support. In the difficult days ahead she would be trusting in his love to comfort and sustain her. And Catherine understood perfectly that he could not betray that trust without doing violence both to Lady Laura and to his own conscience.

"So that's that," she told herself. The thought of life without Jonathan was a bleak one, but she reminded herself that life on any terms was better than the alternative. So recently had she escaped death and violence that even heartache and loneliness seemed desirable by contrast.

By dwelling diligently on these thoughts, she was able to keep herself in a not-too-dismal frame of mind. She responded cheerfully to her aunt's frequent questions and comments and even found a certain mild distraction in the changing landscape outside the chaise window. They reached Bath on the second day of their travels, and with the help of a passing chairman who directed them to the Royal Crescent, they and their baggage were eventually deposited in front of Miss Harvey's elegant home. No sooner was this done than Miss Harvey's butler appeared to take charge of them and it.

"This way, if you please, ma'am. This way, miss," he told them. "Your rooms are all ready for you, and Cook has dinner almost ready to set on the table."

The dinner was a good one, and as Aunt Rose helped herself to artichokes and green goose, she expressed herself pleased with her new quarters. "A very pleasant and elegant house," she told Catherine in a low voice. "And the servants all seem to know their business." She bestowed a gracious nod on the footman who had just refilled her wineglass. "I have no doubt we will be very comfortable here."

Catherine expressed the same conviction, but she still felt desolate when she reflected that there were now a hundred miles between herself and Jonathan. "Now I am gone, he will soon forget me," she told herself. "I will be nothing but a memory to him, and perhaps not even that." Then she pulled herself up with a mental rebuke. It was right that Jonathan should try to forget her, seeing that he was planning to marry another woman. Forgetfulness was both right and proper under those circumstances, and if she was half in earnest about starting life anew, she ought to be doing her best to forget him, too.

In the days that followed, she did try her best to forget the past and start a new life. She and Aunt Rose visited the Pump Room and wrote their names in the subscription books at both the Upper and Lower Rooms. They visited the lending library and the theater, and attended a concert of ancient music. Aunt Rose was at first rather dubious about appearing at any of the larger public assemblies, but being assured by Miss Harvey's butler that these were perfectly unexceptionable gatherings, she ventured to attend one and discovered there several old acquaintances whom she had not seen in years. She flitted about the rooms with a beaming face, chattering like a magpie and looking as happy as any schoolroom miss making her first appearance in society.

Catherine, too, had a pleasant time that evening, though her enjoyment was of a quieter sort than her aunt's. She had lived so long in the restricted society of Langton Abbots that she could not get over the novelty of appearing as an ordinary young lady untrammeled by a scandalous past. Whenever one of the women present swept her a curious look or one of the men an admiring one, she found herself flinching inwardly from the contemptuous whispers and stares she was sure must follow. But no contemptuous whispers or stares materialized. She did overhear one young lady describe her as "a plain, countrified creature, without a particle of style," but since this young lady's escort had just asked Catherine to dance with him, her comment was not exactly disinterested.

This gentleman, a Captain MacFarland, danced twice with Catherine and seemed much taken with her. "I've enjoyed dancing with you, Miss Summerfield," he told her at the conclu-

sion of the second dance. "You won't by any chance be
attending the ball at the Lower Rooms on Thursday, will you?"

"I do not know," said Catherine. "My aunt has not spoken
of it."

Captain MacFarland shook his head. He was a handsome
young man with merry gray eyes, a large and flourishing mus-
tache, and light brown hair with a hint of ginger in it. "But
you must, Miss Summerfield," he said. "Do try and talk your
aunt around. The party'll be as stale as flat champagne if you're
not there."

Catherine laughed. "If it is as large a party as this one, I
cannot think my presence will make or mar it to any great
extent," she said.

"Yes, it will," said Captain MacFarland in a positive voice.
"It'd be like rum punch without the lemons or soup without
salt." His face was smiling but thoughtful as he regarded Catherine. "I've danced with at least a dozen girls this evening.
They were all nice girls, mark you—and some of 'em deuced
pretty girls, too. But there's something about you that sets you
apart from the rest, Miss Summerfield. It's not just the way
you look, though that's outstanding enough (did I tell you that
you were the handsomest lady in the rooms tonight? I didn't?
How shamefully remiss of me!). And it's not the way you talk,
for you've hardly talked at all. Indeed, all I've been able to
learn, after nearly an hour of hard questioning, is that your
name is Miss Summerfield; that you like Bath pretty well; that
you have lived with your aunt in Devonshire for the last twelve
years, and that you prefer lemonade to orgeat."

Again Catherine laughed. "I do not know what more you
expect to learn during the course of two dances, Captain Mac-
Farland," she said. "That is all true information as far as it goes."

"Aye, but it doesn't go far enough," complained Captain
MacFarland. "Most young ladies'll talk your ear off once you
get 'em started. But all you do is smile and answer 'yes' and
'no' in the most provoking way. I do believe there's some

mystery about you, Miss Summerfield. You're not a princess in disguise, by any chance?"

"No," said Catherine. She smiled as she spoke, but she could not help thinking that in the midst of his teasing Captain MacFarland had come uncomfortably close to the truth. The thought was a disturbing one, and there was a certain distance in her voice as she added, "I am certainly not a princess in disguise, Captain MacFarland. And I think you had better not depend on my attending the ball at the Lower Rooms on Thursday. I doubt my aunt will care to attend two large parties in one week."

She had not supposed Captain MacFarland would notice her disquiet, but he saw through her once again with the same uncomfortable penetration. "I have offended you, haven't I, Miss Summerfield? I do beg your pardon." Dropping his voice, he added, "Of course when I suggested you might be a princess, I did not mean to suggest you bear any resemblance to our present royal princesses. Fine girls, all of 'em, but they're none of them what you could call beauties."

Catherine could not help smiling at this speech, and Captain MacFarland smiled, too. "That's better," he said. "We are friends again, I hope. And if you *should* attend the ball at the Lower Rooms, then mind you save the first two dances for me."

Catherine assented, but in a manner that was still a trifle cool and distant. She did end up attending the ball at the Lower Rooms, however, and she did have a pleasant time in a mild way. Captain MacFarland was very attentive and amusing; so were several other gentlemen; and she made the acquaintance of a young lady, the daughter of one of Aunt Rose's old friends, who professed an immediate desire for friendship. This girl, Miss Diana Harlinger, went out walking with her on the following day, while Captain MacFarland took her out driving the day after that; and before long nearly every day was devoted to outings and entertainments of some sort.

And yet, beneath all the gaiety, Catherine was conscious of

a sense of emptiness. Diana was a lively and amusing companion only a few years younger than herself, yet when Catherine listened to her innocent chatter about beaux, fashions, and Bath society, she found herself feeling eons older and wise to the point of disillusionment. Likewise, Captain MacFarland was a handsome, gallant, and (everyone assured her) extremely eligible gentleman. Yet it was impossible for Catherine to take his attentions at all seriously.

In the beginning, she had been afraid that his interest might lead him to make inquiries about her. She shrank from having him or any of her other new acquaintances learn the more lurid chapters of her past. But as time went on, she worried less and less on this score. She realized it was inevitable that someone, some day, would rake up her connection with Angelo and perhaps her connection with Jonathan as well. And once the first distaste of this notion had passed, Catherine found she did not care.

She had long chafed at the difficulties of her existence in Langton Abbots. Yet now that she was able to pass as an ordinary girl with an ordinary happy past behind her and an ordinary happy future in front of her, she found life almost unbearably insipid. Indeed, so perverse is human nature that she was sometimes tempted to tell her new friends the truth about herself, just to see their shocked reaction. If Bath society grew hostile toward her, she could always move on to somewhere else—and one place seemed very like another in Catherine's reckoning just then. She was reflecting on these thoughts with a sense of melancholy one day when she and Captain MacFarland were out driving. It did not occur to her that her thoughts might show in her face until he addressed her in a grave voice.

"Is something wrong, Miss Summerfield?"

Catherine looked up in surprise. "No, nothing," she said. Summoning a smile to her lips, she added, 'I beg your pardon, Captain MacFarland. I am afraid I was woolgathering and forgot for a moment where I was."

Captain MacFarland did not return her smile. "Where did you think you were? It seems not to have been a very hospitable place, to judge from your expression."

"I suppose I was thinking of home," said Catherine slowly. "It's a very odd thing, but I believe I am homesick.

"And why should that be an odd thing?" said Captain Mac-Farland, studying her with curiosity. "I have always heard Devonshire was very beautiful."

"It is—oh, it is." Into Catherine's mind came flooding a recollection of just how beautiful was that country, with its green wooded hills, highland pastures, and rocky seacoast. And just beyond the edges of that memory hovered another memory—a memory she fought to keep down with all her strength.

Captain MacFarland continued to study her profile. "I would give a good deal to know what you are really thinking about," he said in a conversational tone. "You wouldn't care to confide in me, by any chance? I assure you that you might depend on my discretion."

"It's nothing," said Catherine. She had to stifle a hysterical urge to laugh as she spoke. Captain MacFarland's words had reminded her of that long-ago interview with Mr. Poole, and the way he, too, had urged her to confide in him. On the whole, Catherine thought she would rather have confided in Captain MacFarland than Mr. Poole, but the habits of a lifetime disinclined her to confide in anyone. There was only one person who had ever really understood her; only one person who had ever been able to fully sympathize with her feelings and impulses. And she was cut off from him as surely as if he had ceased to exist.

She did not realize she was crying until a large tear rolled down her cheek and splashed onto the front of her dress. She blinked furiously and turned her face away, hoping Captain MacFarland had not noticed. But as she had discovered on previous occasions, Captain MacFarland had an uncomfortable habit of noticing almost everything.

"What is it?" he said, checking his horses and turning to

Catherine. "Miss Summerfield, what is it? Do please tell me
what is the matter. And don't say it's nothing," he added, as
Catherine opened her mouth to speak. "You would not be
crying if it was nothing."

Catherine gave him a watery smile. "I might," she said.
"Indeed, I am not crying about anything in particular, Captain
MacFarland. You need not concern yourself in the least."

"But I do concern myself." The captain's voice was uncus-
tomarily harsh, but it softened as he went on speaking. "I want
to help, Miss Summerfield. Tell me what is distressing you,
and what I can do to remedy the situation. I assure you, I am
game for anything between manslaughter and pitch-and-toss if
it will assist you in any way."

Catherine gave a shaky laugh. "You are very obliging, Captain MacFarland! But I don't think I will trouble you for your
assistance."

The captain's face did not relax its set look. "It's no trouble,
Miss Summerfield. You must have realized by now how I feel
about you. It would be a pleasure—no, a privilege—to assist
you in any way."

Startled, Catherine turned to look at him. He smiled ruefully.
"That's taken you off guard, hasn't it? But indeed I do care
for you, Miss Summerfield. I hadn't meant to declare myself
just yet, but since I have—well, I don't mind admitting that
I've fallen for you hard. If you could see your way clear to
returning my feelings, it would make me very happy."

He paused, looking searchingly at Catherine. There was a
look of distress on her face, and she was shaking her head
slowly. "Oh, no! I am so very sorry, Captain MacFarland.
Please believe I never meant to encourage you to declare yourself. Indeed, I never supposed your attentions were serious.
Diana told me—" She broke off with a look of embarrassment.

"Diana told you I was the horridest flirt in Bath, I suppose,"
said the Captain, smiling grimly. "And so you never supposed

I was serious? There's a facer for me! But I assure you that I *am* serious, Miss Summerfield. How can I make you believe me?"

"I do believe you," said Catherine gently. "But I'm afraid it doesn't make any difference, Captain MacFarland. I like you very well, but—"

"But you like me as a friend and not as a would-be suitor," finished Captain MacFarland with an even grimmer smile. Catherine nodded mutely. He sat in silence for several minutes, then shrugged his shoulders with a wry smile. "Well, never mind. Only—if there is anything I can do for you, Miss Summerfield, I beg you will let me know. You need not be dissuaded from asking just because you can't return my very flattering feelings," he added with a touch of self-mockery. "I may not hold the place with you I wish, but I am still perfectly willing to fulfill the offices of a friend—or better yet, a brother. What I mean is, I have a sister myself. If she was in difficulties—if some fellow had mistreated her, for instance—I'd think it my duty to at least talk to the fellow and perhaps kick him in the backside if circumstances warranted. And I'd be happy enough to fulfill the same office for you."

He looked at Catherine in a questioning way. She shook her head and tried to smile. "You are very kind, Captain MacFarland," she said. "But I think you have misunderstood the situation. No one has mistreated me, and I know of no one whose backside needs kicking!"

"Don't you?" Captain MacFarland gave her another intent look, then smiled suddenly. "There's another facer for me! What a conceited dog I am. I simply assumed that if you couldn't bestow your heart on me, it must have been because you'd already given it to some other fellow. Now call me a conceited ass, if you like! I am sure I deserve it."

Try as she might, Catherine could not refrain from coloring. She hoped against hope that Captain MacFarland would not notice, but like all such hopes, it proved to be vain. "So there is someone else!'' he exclaimed. ''Well, that makes me feel a trifle better. My conceit might recover from this blow after all. Do you and your aunt go to see the conjuror at the Bell this evening, Miss Summerfield?''

''Yes, I believe so,'' said Catherine. She was grateful to Captain MacFarland for changing the subject in such a circumspect way. They talked perseveringly of the conjuror all the way home, and the captain was twice as gay and flirtatious as usual, as though to reassure Catherine that his conceit had not been dealt a deathblow. As they parted, however, his manner grew serious once more.

''If there is ever anything I can do for you, I hope you will let me know. Perhaps you thought I was merely trifling when I said that earlier, just as you supposed I was trifling about other things. But I assure you that I am serious in this as in the other, Miss Summerfield. It would greatly assuage the pains of rejection if I might at least feel I had been useful to you.''

Catherine was touched and promised to let the captain know if he could be useful to her. This was hardly a contingency she anticipated, however.

''What can he or anyone do for me?'' she asked herself, as she went slowly into he house. ''I already have everything any reasonable human being could want or need. The fact that I want something unreasonable is my own silly fault. Captain MacFarland cannot help me get it, and neither can anyone else, any more than if I were crying for the moon.''

In this dark mood she went into the house and found her aunt poring over a newspaper in the front drawing room. She looked up with a smile as Catherine came in.

''There you are, my dear. Did you have a pleasant drive with the captain?''

''Yes, very,'' said Catherine in as cheerful a voice as she could muster. ''It was very pleasant indeed.''

''That's good.'' Aunt Rose returned to her perusal of the newspaper. ''I was just reading about Dr. Mustapha,'' she explained to Catherine. "The *Bath Journal* says he is a genuine eastern prince and possesses powers 'unparalleled in all the known world.' "

"You *are* excited about seeing this conjuror tonight, aren't you, Auntie?" said Catherine, smiling in spite of her depression. "I hope he will not disappoint you."

"Oh, be sure he will not, my dear. It says here that 'he has performed before Royalty on several occasions, to great acclaim.' And you know I have never seen a conjuror before." Aunt Rose's voice took on a reminiscent tone. "There was a conjuror performing once at a fair Violet and I attended when we were girls. I wanted to see him most dreadfully, but Violet said all conjurors were wicked humbugs and that we ought not to waste our money on encouraging them. I do hope it is not wicked to want to see Dr. Mustapha." Aunt Rose's face wrinkled into a look of concern. "But if Royalty patronizes him, I cannot see that there is anything improper about our patronizing him, too."

Catherine assured her aunt that there could be nothing improper about attending a conjuror's performance, thinking meanwhile that it was just like Aunt Violet to object to such an innocent diversion. "What time is the performance tonight?"

"The *Journal* says it begins 'at eight o'clock sharp.' I have already sent one of the footmen down to the Bell to secure our seats. But perhaps it would be as well to get there early anyway. There will likely be a great many people wanting to see Dr. Mustapha, and I would not want to risk missing any part of his performance because we were late coming in."

Catherine agreed that it would not hurt to arrive at the Bell beforetimes and consented to an early dinner so as to ensure their having plenty of time to find their seats by half past seven. Then she went to her room to change, reflecting with some amusement that her aunt seemed likely to hustle them out the door by six if her eagerness continued unabated. She herself had no great eagerness to see the great conjuror's performance, but then she had no eagerness to see anything or anyone—

except, of course, for the one person whom circumstances barred her from ever seeing again. As she dressed for the evening ahead, she found herself wishing with wry amusement that Dr. Mustapha was able to conjure away a heartache.

CHAPTER XXIII

Catherine was a little uncertain about what to wear to a conjuror's performance. Like Aunt Rose, she had never had occasion to attend one before. But supposing it must be something similar to a musicale or concert, she chose a dress of coral pink watered silk that she had worn to a concert of ancient music a few weeks before. Her only ornament, apart from her gold earrings, was the cross and chain Lady Laura had given her. This had become a kind of talisman for Catherine since leaving Langton Abbots. She wore it constantly, and its presence around her neck served both to remind her of the old life she had put behind her and the new and better one that she meant to make for herself.

In this costume she accompanied Aunt Rose to the Bell, where they were, inevitably, the first guests to appear; Aunt Rose's anxieties had led them to arrive a full hour before the performance was to begin. An obliging servant showed them into the performance room, however, and seated them with great pomp in a pair of dusty red plush chairs situated front and center from the equally dusty red plush curtain.

"These seem like good seats," Aunt Rose whispered to Catherine. "You do not mind sitting so close, do you, Catherine? I have always heard a conjuror's performance depended solely on the quickness of the hand. And so it seemed to me we had better sit where we can see his hands properly."

Catherine assured her aunt that she did not mind sitting close to the stage, and settled back in her seat to inspect the details of her somewhat shabby surroundings. Before long, other members of the audience began to arrive, providing her with something else to look at. Dr. Mustapha's audience was by no means so exclusive as that attending the assemblies at the Upper and Lower Rooms. It seemed to consist largely of shopkeepers, serving girls, and other similarly humble persons. But there were enough members of the gentility present to reassure Aunt Rose that she was doing no wrong in attending, and when the elderly Countess of Lycaster hobbled in, accompanied by her lapdog and companion, Aunt Rose's assurance was complete.

"You know Lady Lycaster would not be attending if there was anything wrong in it," she whispered to Catherine exultantly. "She is a very strict churchgoer. I have heard she takes nothing but green tea and a biscuit on Fridays and Holy days."

Catherine was not much interested in the details of the countess's penitential diet, but she nodded politely and went on looking at the audience. She observed Captain MacFarland come in with several of his brother officers and bestowed a smile and nod upon him. Diana came in a little later with her mother, and the two of them made their way with some difficulty to their seats at the front, in the row directly behind Catherine and Aunt Rose. "I've just seen the most divine man, outside in the street," Diana whispered to Catherine. "I wonder if he is going to come to the performance tonight, too? You can't miss him if he does. A regular Corsair, with dark hair and the most ravishing eyes. I only saw him once, and I'm already in love with him."

As Diana had been in and out of love with twenty different gentlemen in the last few weeks, Catherine did not pay this statement any particular heed. "Your Corsair had better hurry if he expects to find a seat," she whispered back. "I believe the performance is about to begin."

She proved to be correct in this belief. A diminutive boy, dressed in an eastern-looking costume of red and gold, appeared on the stage to announce in shrill accents that the great Dr. Mustapha was now ready to thrill and confound all comers in a performance unequalled in the history of Bath. The dusty curtains swung open, and Dr. Mustapha himself came out, to the accompaniment of scattered cheers and clapping from the audience.

The great conjuror proved to be a solemn-faced man of middle age. Even without the adjuncts of a turban, beads, and brocade Turkish trousers, he would have been a striking-looking individual, being very tall and thin to the point of emaciation. Taken all in all, he made a most satisfactory appearance, although Catherine suspected his swarthy complexion owed more to walnut stain than to royal Arabian blood. But if his ancestry was questionable, there was no disputing his powers of performance. Handkerchiefs, glasses of wine, and a live bird in a cage were made to disappear and reappear with blinding rapidity. Sixpences were drawn from the ears and mouths of astonished audience members; and eggs, flour, and sugar were recklessly compounded in a lady's bonnet, only to be subsequently turned out as a fully baked and frosted cake.

Aunt Rose sat enraptured throughout the entire performance, her eyes wide and her lips slightly parted in a beatific smile. Catherine, for her part, was as amazed as her aunt. For a while she forgot her own, all-encompassing concerns, and when Dr. Mustapha concluded the show with a bow and a modestly expressed hope that the audience had enjoyed his humble talents, her applause was as loud as anyone's.

"Catherine, that was wonderful," exclaimed Aunt Rose, clapping for all she was worth. "I never saw anything so diverting. But I simply cannot imagine how he did all those things. I was watching his hands as closely as I could all the time and yet I never saw a thing amiss. How did he get those sixpences out of people's mouths and make that cake in that woman's bonnet? Upon my soul, I am almost tempted to believe that Violet was right and there is something uncanny about conjurors.''

"Don't be silly, Auntie," said Catherine absently. She was watching Dr. Mustapha, who had descended from the stage and was making his way among the audience. His dark face was lit by a melancholy smile as he received their compliments and congratulations. Diana, who had come over to join Catherine as soon as the show was over, was also watching him. Then she gripped Catherine's arm with sudden excitement. "It's the Corsair!" she hissed. "Right there, standing near the doors. Oh, he *is* an enchanting creature! Don't you think he's handsome, Catherine?"

Catherine looked toward the doors. A gentleman was standing there—a tall, dark gentleman, who was looking directly at her with grave dark eyes.

It was Jonathan.

Catherine did not pause to think, or to respond to Diana's question. She was out of her chair and down the aisle in a twinkling, leaving Diana gaping after her. Jonathan came forward to meet her. He opened his arms as though to gather her in, and Catherine very nearly allowed him to do so. But it occurred to her, at the very last moment, that this would be an indiscreet proceeding, and so she stopped short, trembling from head to toe. "Jonathan," she said. "Jonathan!"

Although she spoke only the one word, there was a vibrant note in her voice that made a number of people turn to look curiously at them both. Jonathan came a step closer, catching her hands in his.

"Catherine." he said in a low voice. "Thank God I've found you, Catherine. It seems as though it's taken me forever to track you down."

Catherine swallowed hard. "But you should not have tracked

me down, Jonathan," she said. "We agreed—we agreed it would be best if I went away."

"Because of Lady Laura," said Jonathan, nodding. "But you see I have a message for you from Lady Laura, Catherine. She charged me to put it directly into your hands, and what could I do but obey?"

"A message?" said Catherine blankly.

Jonathan took a letter from his pocket and offered it to her. "A message," he said. "Why don't you sit down while you read it, Catherine? There are plenty of empty chairs now the performance is over."

Catherine dropped down into the nearest vacant chair. The letter consisted of several closely written sheets. Her eyes widened as she scanned the lines of Lady Laura's elegant Italian handwriting:

My dear Catherine:

 Did you forget your promise? You know you were pledged to write to me as soon as you arrived in Bath. I expect you thought I would prefer to be left to myself, after all that has happened. I cannot deny that these last few weeks have been very difficult for me. Oswald's death was a great shock, and the manner of his death an even greater one. Even now I can scarcely grasp that he was responsible for the terrible things that happened in the neighborhood. But I do not mean to dwell on that, except to say how sorry I am for all those he injured. Perhaps it is indiscreet of me, but I cannot help suspecting you were one of the injured, Catherine. Lord Meredith declares he did not recognize the woman whom Oswald was attacking just before he met his death, but I have sometimes suspected he was merely preserving a chivalrous reticence. If so, I will preserve the same reticence. Lord Meredith has assured me that he arrived in time to prevent any real or lasting injury to the woman in ques-

tion, and with the grace of God she will recover in time from the shock of the experience. I pray that she does, and that I and all my family may receive the same indulgence.

Having said that, let me return to the object of my letter. That object, put simply, is to state that I henceforth renounce any claim on Lord Meredith and consider him to be quite free to engage himself wherever he pleases.

You will wonder at my making such a statement, when only a few weeks ago I declared myself determined to marry him. He would have married me, I have no doubt, and fulfilled his duties toward me conscientiously. But of late I have begun to question whether I really want a husband on such terms. I think it was first brought home to me a few Sundays ago, when Mr. Poole preached a sermon on Abraham and Isaac. I was struck with a fancy that the story in some ways paralleled our own situation, and that my own role resembled that of God! It was a disquieting thought, Catherine. God may demand of a man the sacrifice of the thing he loves most, but I, Laura Lindsay, am not God. In demanding such a sacrifice of you and Lord Meredith, I feel now I was being both unreasonable and very selfish.

You will notice I speak quite plainly of the feeling existing between you and Lord Meredith. No good purpose can be served now by ignoring or glossing over the truth. From the first moment you two met, on the night of the party I gave to welcome him to the neighborhood, I was aware of it, though I did my best to pretend otherwise. But no one knowing either of you in the slightest degree could doubt you were strongly attracted to each other.

It was, I may say, a source of considerable chagrin to me. There have even been times when I resented you quite fiercely, Catherine, feeling you had taken Lord Meredith's love away from me. But I have come to see that such resentment was unjust to you both. In fact you took noth-

*ing from me—nothing that I had or ever could have had
from Lord Meredith, even had he married me without
knowing of your existence. And that being the case, it is
only right and proper that I should relinquish him to you.*

Trusting that you and Lord Meredith will find happiness together, I am—

> *Yours affectionately*
> *Laura Lindsay*

*P.S. In re-reading this letter, I find I have conveyed the
impression that I am renouncing Lord Meredith solely
from motives of selflessness and nobility. Nothing could
be further from the case. On the contrary, my motives
are both selfish and purely personal. Having witnessed
the degree of attachment that exists between you and
Lord Meredith, I find myself desirous of experiencing the
same species of attachment. And until I find a man in
whom I inspire such passionate and devoted love, and
who inspires in me the same emotion, I should much
prefer to remain a spinster.*

> *Yours, etc.,*
> *L.L.*

Catherine read this amazing letter through from start to finish, then looked up at Jonathan. He was looking down at her with a smile both rueful and tender. ''Jonathan, do you know what Laura has written here?'' she demanded. ''Has she already told you?''

''That she will not marry me? Yes, she has told me that. But I did not read the letter before she sealed it up, Catherine. What else did she say?''

For answer, Catherine handed him the letter. He read it through deliberately, betraying only by a slight raising of the brows that its contents were a surprise to him. ''Well!'' he said at the end. ''What an extraordinary document!''

''Extraordinarily generous and forgiving,'' said Catherine in a low voice. "You see how she has taken all the blame on herself ? And she has made it sound as though in giving you your freedom, she was merely acting out of motives of self-interest."

"Yes, I do. But she has also put her finger on several great truths." Jonathan looked into Catherine's eyes.

They had been so busy talking that they had both forgotten the presence of the other people around them. At this juncture, however, they were suddenly made aware of the circumstance by the sound of several voices speaking at once.

"There you are, Catherine!"

"Good evening, Miss Summerfield."

"Catherine, you wretch, how could you steal my Corsair! Introduce us, won't you?"

Catherine looked up to find Diana, her aunt, and Captain MacFarland all converging upon her. Diana and Aunt Rose looked merely curious, while Captain MacFarland looked suspicious as well as curious, especially when his eyes turned toward Jonathan. Jonathan gave him a surprised look in return, then looked at Catherine. She colored richly. But Aunt Rose eased the situation by recognizing Jonathan with an exclamation of pleasure. "Lord Meredith! I never expected to see you in Bath! What brings you here?"

"He has brought me a note from Lady Laura," said Catherine. As she spoke, she refolded the letter hastily, intending to put it safely away in her reticule.

Before she could do so, however, their party received an addition in the form of Dr. Mustapha. "Good evening, ladies, gentlemen," he said with a bow.

"Good evening," said Aunt Rose, turning to him with delight. "Oh, Dr. Mustapha, I must tell you how much I enjoyed your performance. I never saw anything so diverting. The way you made those sixpences appear in people's ears and mouths! It was most entertaining."

"You enjoyed that, did you?" said Dr. Mustapha, smiling. "Then perhaps you will allow me to perform the same service for you.'' In a twinkling, he had extracted a shining sixpence from Aunt Rose's ear. She gasped, put a hand to her ear, and let out a crow of laughter.

"How ridiculous! However do you do it?"

Dr. Mustapha smiled mysteriously and shook his head. "Ah, that is nothing! I have much greater powers than that." In a move that took Catherine by surprise, he reached down and plucked the letter from her hand. "Among other things, I possess the ability to read letters without even opening them," he announced in a dramatic voice. "Perhaps you would like me to divine what is in *this* letter?"

"Yes!" said Diana and Aunt Rose eagerly.

"Yes," drawled Captain MacFarland. He was still looking very hard at Jonathan.

"No!" exclaimed Catherine and Jonathan simultaneously.

Dr. Mustapha looked at them both with a light of laughter in his eyes. "You think not? Well, I have no wish to be indiscreet. But I can tell you this much. I see romance, and courtship, and a betrothal at the end of it. In fact"—In a lightning-quick gesture, he suddenly produced a small box from out of the air—"I should not be surprised if I had not the betrothal ring right here."

"How the deuce—!" exclaimed Jonathan. He made a grab for the box, but Diana was quicker. Taking the box from Dr. Mustapha, she eagerly opened it. "Oh!" she exclaimed. "What a lovely ring!"

"So it is," agreed Aunt Rose. She looked at Dr. Mustapha with perplexity. "But I don't understand. Whose ring is it?"

"It's mine," said Jonathan. Reaching forward, he removed the box from Diana's hand in a peremptory manner. "But how it came to leave my pocket and get into this fellow's hands, I do not know." He looked angrily at Dr. Mustapha.

Dr. Mustapha gave him an apologetic smile and shrug. "Forgive me, good sir. I could not resist the temptation."

"What kind of stone is it?" said Diana, addressing Jonathan eagerly. "I never saw one that color before."

"It's a sapphire," said Jonathan shortly.

"A sapphire! But I thought sapphires were blue."

"Yes, but they come in other colors, too. This kind come from Padparadscha in Ceylon. They're quite celebrated for them there," said Jonathan, even more shortly. "I was in the East a few years ago and brought several of them back with me."

"Well, it is certainly very pretty and exotic-looking. Why, it is just the color of Catherine's dress!"

Everyone looked at Catherine and her coral pink dress. Once again she found herself coloring. Captain MacFarland looked at her with comprehension in his eye. "So it is," he said. "What a remarkable coincidence!"

Catherine felt matters had gone on long enough in this manner. She rose to her feet. "We have been so busy talking that I have not yet had a chance to introduce you all to Lord Meredith," she said. As she was making Jonathan, Diana, and Captain MacFarland known to each other, Dr. Mustapha excused himself with a smile and went over to talk to Lady Lycaster and her companion. "A rum fellow," said Captain MacFarland, looking after him. "Seems to be a first-class conjuror, though."

"Yes, indeed," said Aunt Rose. She looked at Catherine and Jonathan, her brow slightly furrowed. "But I did not quite understand what Dr. Mustapha was saying about that letter you two were looking at. Was he right about what it said?"

"I hope so," said Jonathan. He looked intently at Catherine. So did Captain MacFarland and Diana and Aunt Rose. Catherine felt their eyes on her, but her own eyes were fixed steadily on Jonathan as she made her answer.

"To some extent he was right," she said. "But it remains to be seen whether he was right in all the particulars."

"Well, I suppose we shall have to wait and see," said Aunt Rose. "Would you all care to return to our house for supper?"

"I should like to, very much," said Jonathan promptly.

"So should I," said Diana with equal promptness. She was

still looking admiringly at Jonathan. But Captain MacFarland shook his head, a wry smile on his lips.

"No, Diana, I think you have another engagement," he said, and drew her aside to whisper into her ear. What he said was not audible, but Diana's response came clearly to the others.

"Oh! Do you think so? Well, I have no wish to be *de trop*." With a last, regretful look at Jonathan, she turned to Aunt Rose and excused herself gracefully from the supper invitation. "But I shall call on you tomorrow, and I shall expect to hear all about it then," she said, squeezing Catherine's arm.

Captain MacFarland took leave of them next. "Good evening, Miss Summerfield," he told Catherine, and added in a lower voice, "I begin to see which way the wind blows. But I remain steadfastly devoted to your service, even if there is nothing more I can do than save you from Diana's company tonight."

Catherine, conscious of Jonathan's eyes upon her, did not respond to this speech. She merely murmured good evening and turned away.

She and Aunt Rose returned alone in their carriage to the Royal Crescent, while Jonathan followed in his own carriage. As they drove through the narrow streets, Aunt Rose marveled at Jonathan's presence in Bath. "It was a great surprise to me to see him here, after everything that has happened. Of course he did say that he and Lady Laura were not formally engaged, but I daresay they are by this time, and poor Lady Laura is probably reluctant to let him out of her sight until such time as they can be properly married. I do not accuse her of accepting Lord Meredith for wrong motives, you understand. But under the circumstances, it would not be wonderful if she was anxious to leave Honeywell House and all that must remind her of her brother."

"But she and Lord Meredith are not engaged, Auntie," said Catherine. "I know for a fact that Lady Laura has refused him—refused him in a most final and decisive manner. There will be no marriage between them."

"Is that so!" said Aunt Rose, astonished. "I am very surprised to hear it, my dear. Do you suppose Lord Meredith is much cut up about it? He did not appear so this evening."

"No," agreed Catherine in a quiet voice. "But appearances are sometimes deceptive, Auntie. He may be more cut up than he appears. I shall not know until I have talked with him—talked with him alone, that is. Should you mind very much?"

"I suppose not," said Aunt Rose, looking puzzled. "But why should you—oh!" She broke off suddenly, her eyes widening. Catherine was pretty sure she had just caught an inkling of the truth, but she said no more about it during the drive, much to Catherine's relief. As soon as they reached home, Aunt Rose ordered a pot of tea and a tray of refreshments sent to the drawing room. "You and Lord Meredith may talk in here, my dear," she said, carefully avoiding Catherine's eye. "I'll be upstairs in my sitting room if you want me." She kissed Catherine's brow, then hurried off. A moment later there was a knock on the door, and shortly thereafter the butler appeared in the drawing room doorway with a more than usually portentous expression on his solemn face.

"Lord Meredith, to see Miss Summerfield," he announced.

CHAPTER XXIV

Catherine did not speak or move as Jonathan came into the drawing room. She remained sitting where she was on an upholstered settee by the window. He came toward her, looking rather hesitant. "Catherine?" he said.

Catherine indicated the settee beside her. He seated himself there, then looked about the room. "Your aunt is not here?" he asked.

"No," said Catherine. "I told her I wished to speak to you alone."

Jonathan looked startled at first, then smiled with relief. "That's good," he said. "I've grown so used to having to steal odd minutes with you here and there. It will seem like luxury to be able to talk without feeling someone is watching and wondering all the time what we are saying. I wish I could have managed the same trick this evening!" His smile grew rueful. "That conjuror fellow put one over on me properly. I still don't know how he managed to get that ring out of my pocket without my noticing."

"He certainly created a sensation," said Catherine. Both her voice and her face were expressionless. Jonathan surveyed her thoughtfully.

"At the time I was quite furious at him," he said. "But apart from spoiling my thunder a bit, I trust he did no harm." He paused, looking at Catherine. "I had intended to make you a proper proposal this evening, you know—to offer you my hand and heart in due form. That is why I brought the ring with me to the performance. Did you know?"

Catherine nodded slowly. "I suspected, at least."

Jonathan gave her a slightly incredulous smile. "Well you might suspect! You know how I feel about you, Catherine. And you have read Laura's letter. Did you think I would not fulfill my duty to you as soon as I was free to do so?"

"I don't want to be a duty." Catherine spoke with quiet desperation. "We have argued so much about duty these last few months. I am quite sick of the word."

A brief silence followed this statement. "Perhaps 'duty' was an unfortunate word to use," acknowledged Jonathan at last. "But you know there are duties and duties, Catherine. Some are performed only with great reluctance, while others are so delightful in prospect that one cannot be happy until they are performed. And that is how I feel about marrying you."

Catherine glanced at his earnest face, then looked away. "I wonder," she said. "Have you ever really thought what it would be like to be married to me, Jonathan?"

Jonathan's eyes glowed. "Have I not! You must know I have, Catherine. To be with you all the time, and never have to hide the way I feel about you from anyone—that's as close to heaven on earth as I could wish for."

Catherine looked at him gravely. "It would not *all* be heaven, you know," she said. "The people of Langton Abbots still gossip about my elopement with Angelo, even after all these years. They are not likely to stop just because I married you."

In an impetuous manner, Jonathan consigned all the inhabitants of Langton Abbots to a very warm place. "That's all very well," said Catherine, smiling faintly. "But I don't think you've properly considered the matter, Jonathan. Where did you envision our living after we were married?"

Again there was silence. "I don't know that I'd envisioned it at all," admitted Jonathan. "All I'd envisioned was being with you. But that is the important thing, isn't it, Catherine? As far as I can see, the rest is mere detail."

"It isn't." Catherine spoke firmly. "I know how important the Abbey is to you, Jonathan. I know when you first returned here, you dreamed of settling down to become a model landowner—"

"Yes, but that was in the beginning," said Jonathan impatiently. "I told you weeks ago that I was perfectly willing to give that dream up in order to be with you."

"I remember," said Catherine. She went on, choosing her words carefully. "At the time, you were pledged to marry Laura. You asked me to run away with you, so you might escape that obligation."

"Yes, I did," said Jonathan truculently. "I daresay I ought to be ashamed of it. But you know at the time it seemed the only solution, Catherine. And shameful as it would have been, I still would have done it in order to be with you."

"But you see now that it was not necessary, Jonathan," said Catherine. "Circumstances have changed."

"Yes, they have changed," agreed Jonathan. He was looking more and more puzzled as he regarded Catherine. "But the change is all for the better, isn't it? I fail to see the problem, Catherine. You know I would still be happy to run away with you—in fact, more than happy. To travel and see the world with you is a dream quite as appealing in its way as staying in Devon. There are lots of places in the world worth seeing, some quite as pretty as Langton Abbots. And almost all of them are more exciting!"

"Yes, no doubt," said Catherine, regarding him with a level gaze. "But Langton Abbots is your home, Jonathan. And if you were to cut yourself off from it for my sake, I know you would regret it."

Jonathan's brow creased. "That may be," he said. "But even admitting it was true, I don't see not marrying you because of it. If it comes to a choice between you and the Abbey, then my decision is already made."

"But I don't want you to choose between me and the Abbey!" said Catherine with exasperation. "That relegates me to a duty once again. And I simply refuse to be a duty to you."

"Then what do you suggest?" Jonathan's voice was deceptively mild, but his expression was frustrated as he looked down at her. "You must know how much I want to marry you, Catherine. But you seem very determined to find reasons why I should not. Is it that you do not want to marry me?"

He looked at her steadily. Catherine's eyes fell before his gaze. "I do want to marry you," she said in a low voice. "But even more, I want you to be happy."

"And you think I will not be, if I am married to you?" Jonathan's voice was full of amusement. "My dear, I have already told you I cannot be happy without you."

"But neither could you be happy abandoning your responsibilities! And if you did not abandon those responsibilities, then you would have to endure hearing people gossip and whisper about your wife as long as you remained at the Abbey. And I'm afraid that would not make you happy, either."

Jonathan looked at Catherine very hard. "I would not like it, certainly, if someone criticized you to my face," he said. "I think I would undertake to put a stop to such impertinence rather quickly! But as far as mere gossip is concerned—well, you know I have always cared very little for the opinions of other people, Catherine. If it was up to me—" He stopped.

"If it was up to you, what?" prompted Catherine.

"Why, if it was up to me, I should say we ought to do just as we please and let other people go hang," said Jonathan slowly. "But I could hardly ask that of you, Catherine. I know how difficult it has been for you, living in Langton Abbots these past nine years."

An odd smile had begun to spread over Catherine's face.

"It hasn't been easy, certainly," she said. "There was a time when I thought I would do anything to escape it. But now I have been in Bath a few weeks, I find myself almost missing all the criticism and controversy! I'm afraid the truth of the matter is that I am simply not a very conventional woman at heart—no, nor even a very respectable one. I never have been, and I know now I wouldn't want to be even if I could."

An answering smile had begun to spread across Jonathan's face. "Well, neither am I a conventional or respectable man," he said. "And that being the case, I can think of nothing more suitable than that we two should marry and live in the manner that pleases us best. We can travel when we feel like it, and when we tire of traveling, we can come back to Langton Abbots and devote ourselves to being the lord and lady of the manor and a delightful source of gossip to the Langton Abbotsites."

Catherine shut her eyes. "It sounds like a dream," she whispered. A moment later she opened her eyes, her expression troubled. "But there's one problem with your plan, Jonathan—one complication you haven't thought of."

"What complication do you mean?" asked Jonathan, in a voice of only mild exasperation. "Surely it cannot be an important one?"

Catherine made a despairing gesture. "Important enough! I am speaking of Lady Laura, Jonathan. As long as she is living at Honeywell House, we could hardly be happy living at the Abbey. She doesn't say anything about it in her letter, of course, but I know what suffering it would cost her to see us married and living there together. As generous as she has been to me, the least I can do is spare her that."

Jonathan took her hand in his. "My dear, if you are seeking to wriggle out of marrying me by means of that excuse, then you will have to seek other means," he said. "Prepare yourself for a shock. Lady Laura is no longer living at Honeywell House. The Lindsays were already making preparations to leave at the time she wrote that letter to you, and by this time I have no doubt they are long gone. You must know that public opinion against the earl has been very strong in the weeks since Oswald's death. He maintains that he gave up his lease on Honeywell House because the neighborhood has painful associations for him and his family, but I think myself the place simply became too hot for him. So he and the other Lindsays are gone from Langton Abbots—and so is your last excuse for not marrying me.''

As Jonathan spoke these words, he took the ring box from his pocket. Opening it, he took out the ring and slipped it on Catherine's finger. ''A perfect fit,'' he said triumphantly.

''Yes,'' said Catherine. Her expression was sober as she looked down at the coral-pink stone on her finger. Jonathan observed it, and his own expression became sober, too.

''You know if you don't care for the ring, Catherine, we can always get you another one. I hoped it would suit you, but that was only a hope. I certainly did not mean to presume in any way.''

Catherine looked up in surprise. ''But it does suit me, Jonathan! The ring is a beautiful one. I wouldn't think of changing it.''

''Then what is the trouble? There must be some trouble, or you would not look so sad.''

Catherine looked again at the ring on her finger. Then she reached up to touch the cross at her throat, and a sigh escaped her lips. ''It's not trouble, exactly,'' she said. ''I was only thinking about Lady Laura. Poor Laura; she has ended with nothing, and I have so much. It hardly seems fair.''

Jonathan possessed himself of her hand once more. ''Yes, but you know what you have wouldn't suit Lady Laura, Catherine,'' he said gently. ''She recognized that herself in the end.'' He touched the ring on her finger. ''Even this ring wouldn't have suited her—and how much less the bridegroom that went with it! No, things are better as they are. I am sure Laura will someday find a bridegroom who is really worthy of her, and then she will be as happy as she deserves.''

"And you will not mind that?" said Catherine, looking at him squarely.

Jonathan met her look with a confident smile. "No, why should I? I am no dog in the manger. Having already won my own heart's desire"—he squeezed her hand—"I am generous enough to wish all humanity could be equally lucky."

Catherine sighed. "That is exactly how I feel," she said. They sat together in silence a moment, just looking at each other. "It still seems like a dream," said Catherine presently. "I can hardly believe it is true that we are to be married."

"Married—yes, married." Jonathan looked startled, as though suddenly awakened to some forgotten recollection. "Lord, yes! What a fool I am. There's no time to be lost. Catherine, when will you marry me? You don't want a long engagement, I hope?"

This last question was spoken with so much anxiety that it made Catherine smile. "No, I hardly see any point in that," she said. "We are, I think, well enough acquainted to dispense with that nicety!"

"My point exactly," said Jonathan. Drawing her toward him, he began to kiss her, showering kisses on her face and neck. "Catherine, will you marry me soon?" he said, between kisses. "Tomorrow? Or even tonight if it can be arranged?"

Catherine, who had shut her eyes in the midst of these proceedings, opened them to regard him with amazement. "Are you mad?" she said. "How could we be married tomorrow, let alone tonight?"

"Nothing could be easier, so long as we have a special license. And I do have one. All I have to do is find a clergyman who will perform the ceremony, and the thing is done."

"But—" Catherine was sure there must be a host of objections to such a plan, but it was difficult to think coherently with Jonathan's lips dancing across her skin. "But—did you really come here with a special license, Jonathan? You must have been very sure I was going to say yes!"

He stopped kissing her to regard her gravely. "No, I wasn't

sure at all. But if you did say yes, I wasn't going to give you a chance to back out of it! And I was pretty sure you wouldn't want a parish wedding, Catherine. It would be awkward to ask Mr. Poole to marry us, after all that's happened.''

Catherine laughed. ''Yes, so it would,'' she said. Jonathan began to kiss her again, and she shut her eyes and sighed. ''I suppose I can hardly protest that marrying in such haste would be improper and unconventional,'' she said. ''We have already established that we are both thoroughly improper and unconventional people. The only real objection I can see to the plan is my aunt. I am sure she is not expecting me to marry you—or if she is, she has only just begun to expect it in the last hour or so. She will certainly not be prepared for a wedding on such short notice!''

''Then let us call her down and prepare her,'' said Jonathan. He bestowed a last lingering kiss on Catherine's lips. ''I want to complete this business tonight, if at all possible.''

His tone, and the wistful way he eyed Catherine, left little doubt as to just which business he was referring to. Catherine merely laughed, however, and got up to pull the bell rope. ''Please ask my aunt if she can come downstairs for a moment,'' she told the servant who answered the summons. ''Lord Meredith and I would like to talk to her.''

It was only a moment later that Aunt Rose arrived in the drawing room, agog with curiosity and anticipation. ''You wanted to talk to me, Catherine dear?'' she said, looking eagerly from her niece to Jonathan.

It was Jonathan who answered the question. ''We need your assistance, Miss Payne. Catherine and I are engaged and would like to be married as soon as possible. Do you think we might manage the business tonight, if we put our heads together?''

Aunt Rose's mouth fell open. ''Married?'' she said. *''To-night?* But—but you have only just become engaged!''

''Yes, but our attachment is a long-standing one,'' said Jonathan gravely. ''I know this comes as a surprise to you, Miss Payne, but if you think about it, you must see that there is really no reason why we should wait now we have made up our minds to marry. If I have learned nothing else these last few weeks, it is that life is too uncertain a business to dally where important matters are concerned. I would like to make sure of Catherine, now that I have her.''

''There's something in that,'' admitted Aunt Rose. She regarded her niece with a worried frown. ''But I cannot like to see Catherine married with no bride clothes or breakfast or even a proper wedding dress! It does not seem fair to her, my lord.''

''But you see, I don't care about bride clothes, or breakfasts, or wedding dresses, Auntie,'' said Catherine. ''All I really care about is my bridegroom. A shameless confession, but there it is.'' She smiled at Jonathan, who promptly signified his approval of these words by taking her hand in his and kissing it.

Aunt Rose's face softened. ''I don't think it is shameless at all,'' she said. ''In fact, I think it is very much to your credit. There are too many girls who consider their wedding and trousseau to be of the first importance, while their bridegroom is merely secondary. But—don't you think you might regret it if you wed in such haste?''

''I think I should regret it more if I did not,'' said Catherine, looking at Jonathan.

Aunt Rose also looked at Jonathan, and then at her niece once more. What she saw seemed to convince her, for all she said was, ''You always were a headstrong girl, Catherine. I expect that you know what will suit you best. Even if I thought otherwise, I don't suppose I could convince you of it! But if you and Lord Meredith mean to be married immediately, how are you to manage about the clergyman and the license?''

''Lord Meredith has promised to take care of those details, Auntie. It will be for you and me to plan the others.'' Catherine smiled at her aunt. ''It might be a little unconventional, but I had hoped you might give me away at the altar. You have been father and mother to me for almost half my life. Will you, Auntie?''

"I, give you away?" repeated Aunt Rose. An amazed and delighted look spread across her face. "My dear, I would be honored. It's unconventional, of course, but I would be honored." She sighed. "But I do wish you could have a bridesmaid or two to attend you at the altar, Catherine. Indeed, we really ought to find someone to stand up with you, for there must be witnesses if the ceremony is to be valid."

At this opportune moment, there was a knock on the door. Jonathan, Catherine, and Aunt Rose all turned around to look. "Who could it be at this hour?" wondered Catherine. Her question was answered a moment later when Diana burst into the room, followed closely by Captain MacFarland.

"I did my best to stop her, but she saw your house was still lit up and insisted that we stop and call on you," he said, addressing Catherine apologetically. "I hope we did not arrive at a bad time?" His eyes rested on Jonathan with gloomy curiosity.

The nuances of this speech were lost on Aunt Rose, who was still caught up in the excitement of planning a wedding. "On the contrary, you have both arrived at a very good time," she told Diana and the captain jubilantly. "We are going to have a wedding! Catherine and Lord Meredith are going to be married, and it may be that they will be married tonight if Lord Meredith can find a clergyman who is willing. And I was just saying that I wished Catherine could have a bridesmaid—and now here you are, Diana! And perhaps Captain MacFarland will help us, too, by acting as a witness to the ceremony?"

It was probably fortunate that Diana's cries of rapture prevented Captain MacFarland from making any immediate reply. "Catherine, are you really to be married?" she cried. "And may I really be your bridesmaid? What fun! I am so glad I wore my new primrose satin tonight. Mama said it was too elaborate for a conjuror's performance, but I had a *presentiment* that I ought to wear it. And you are to marry Lord Meredith? My dear, I had no idea you were even engaged! How dark you have kept it all. If it had been me, now, I should not have been able to keep it a secret for a minute. I would have cried it in the streets like a watchman, so everyone might hear."

"We none of us doubt it, Diana," said Captain MacFarland, smiling grimly. He turned again to Catherine. "Do you really mean to be married tonight?"

"If Lord Meredith can find a clergyman," said Catherine. She looked at Jonathan. "Do you really think you will be able to at this hour, Jonathan?"

"Yes," said Jonathan. Despite the brevity of his reply, his tone left no doubt that he meant to succeed in his quest or die trying. Captain MacFarland looked at him thoughtfully, then spoke with sudden resolution.

"It may be that I can assist you, my lord. I have a cousin who is a canon here at the Abbey. Shall I see if I can bring him to you?"

"That would be very kind of you," said Jonathan, giving him a surprised look. "Thank you very much, Captain—MacFarland, isn't it? Catherine and I are greatly indebted to you."

He extended his hand to Captain MacFarland. After an instant's hesitation, the captain took it. "Not at all," he said. "I am happy to be of help." He hesitated again, then went on in a formal voice. "Allow me to congratulate you, my lord. I have not known Miss Summerfield long, but from what I have seen of her, I should say you are a very fortunate man."

"Yes, I am," said Jonathan. He looked down at Catherine. Captain MacFarland looked, too, then turned away hastily, saying he would go and fetch his cousin. He made no definite answer when Aunt Rose pressed him once more to stay and be a witness to the ceremony. But Aunt Rose did not perceive the vagueness of his reply, being distracted by Diana, who was resolved that the wedding should be as complete as a wedding so hastily conceived and executed could possibly be.

"We can make this table the altar, with cushions here for Catherine and Lord Meredith to kneel on," she told Aunt Rose. "Have you any potted plants or flowers? It would look lovely if we arranged them in a half circle around the hearth. There now, I'll put these candlesticks on top of the table, and the prayer book in the center, and it will look perfectly elegant. If only we had some wedding favors. It seems shabby to have a wedding without wedding favors.'' She surveyed with discontent the unadorned front of Jonathan's black jacket. ''A yard or two of lace and ribbon is all it would take, and of course a needle and thread.''

Aunt Rose obligingly rang for these articles, and as soon as they arrived Diana sat down to stitch up a set of wedding favors. By the time the clergyman appeared, all the members of the wedding party were properly garnished with a rosette of ribbon and silver lace. The drawing room was festive with candles and flowers, and the cook in the kitchen was hard at work frosting a cake that had been originally intended for dinner the following day.

The clergyman was a small, middle-aged man with mild blue eyes behind gold-framed spectacles. He came into the room smiling and carrying a large, bridal-looking bouquet.

''Good evening, ladies. Good evening, sir,'' he said, bowing first to Aunt Rose, Catherine, and Diana, and then to Jonathan. ''My name is Tompkins—Randolph Tompkins. I have the honor to be a canon at the Abbey here in Bath.'' He looked around the drawing room in a shortsighted way. 'My cousin, Captain MacFarland, said you were in need of the services of a clergyman.''

''Yes, these two young people wish to be married,'' said Aunt Rose, indicating Catherine and Jonathan. ''But where is Captain MacFarland?''

''He could not return with me. Another engagement, I believe he said. He charged me to deliver his apologies and regrets, along with his best wishes to the bridal couple. Oh, yes, and he also asked me to give this to the bride-to-be.'' With a beaming smile, he held out the bouquet to Catherine.

Catherine took it, with an embarrassed glance at Jonathan. ''Thank you,'' she said. ''That was very thoughtful of Captain MacFarland.''

"Indeed it was," agreed Aunt Rose. "What a pity he could not stay to witness the ceremony!"

Jonathan looked hard at both the bouquet and his bride-to-be. All he said, however, was, "It was indeed thoughtful of Captain MacFarland. He seems a most sensible and estimable man."

Diana, for her part, was delighted with the bouquet. "It's exactly what you needed to complete your bridal toilette, Catherine," she said. "Let me just tuck a few of these roses in your hair, and then you will be ready to be married."

"But we need another witness, since Captain MacFarland cannot be here," said Aunt Rose with a worried frown. "I suppose one of the servants might stand in as a witness. Why, yes, of course, Agnes! I wonder I did not think of her before. She has been in service at the Cottage so long that I am sure she would never forgive either of us if she was not present at your wedding, Catherine. I'll ring for her right away."

Agnes was duly summoned, and as soon as she had appeared (clad in a resplendent cap, and clutching a handkerchief in preparation for all the tears she meant to shed), the ceremony began.

Under the circumstances it could not be anything but a very brief and simple ceremony. To Catherine, however, it seemed indescribably moving. The drawing room was lovely and festive in its array of candles and flowers; the little clergyman read the service in a voice unexpectedly strong and resonant; Aunt Rose gave her away with tears of mingled regret and happiness shining in her eyes; and Diana and Agnes wept steadily through the whole ceremony. At the penultimate moment, when the bridal couple were called on to repeat the vows that would make them husband and wife, Jonathan looked deep into her eyes as he pronounced the words, "I will." And something in the way he looked and spoke made Catherine's heart turn over.

Her own "I will," came out barely audible. The clergyman heard it, however, smiled, and went on to pronounce the benediction. She then found herself being kissed by Jonathan with an enthusiasm that made Aunt Rose blush and the clergyman turn discreetly away. That, at least, was something she knew very well how to cope with. She was then kissed in succession by Aunt Rose, Diana, and Agnes, the latter weeping and declaring, "I never saw such a beautiful bride as you made, Miss Catherine—no, not in all the years I've been in service. And to think of your marrying Lord Meredith and becoming his lady, all so sudden like this! Lady Meredith! I can scarcely take it in, and that's a fact."

Lady Meredith! The words rang strangely in Catherine's ears. But Jonathan only laughed and gathered her close. "Truth to tell, I'm having trouble believing it myself," he told Agnes. "But I have many years to convince myself of its veracity, please God. And I hope I never become so assured that I take it for granted."

"Very prettily spoken, my lord," said Aunt Rose warmly. "Now you must have some champagne and a slice of wedding cake. It's really sponge cake, of course, but you see Cook has put your initials on it, and I'm sure it will be delicious even if it's not quite a traditional wedding cake."

Everyone agreed that the cake was delicious despite not being traditional, and as soon as it and the champagne had been eaten and drunk, Jonathan announced his intention of taking his bride away with him. Aunt Rose's mouth fell open in sudden consternation.

"But where will you go, my lord?" she said. "I never even thought of it until now, but of course you will be wanting to take a wedding trip. And Catherine has not the proper things for a bride—and even those things she does have are not packed! I don't see how you are to manage. Perhaps you would like to stay here for a night or two, until we can get her things ready? I can easily have the maids make up one of the bedchambers."

Jonathan looked at Catherine. She looked back at him, and between them there passed an unspoken communication. Jonathan smiled.

"Thank you, Miss Payne, but I do not think we will put you to so much trouble. Nor do we need to trouble ourselves with the idea of a wedding trip just now. No doubt we will do a good bit of traveling later on, but not just at present.''

"But where do you mean to go, then?'' demanded Aunt Rose, looking mystified. Again Jonathan looked again at Catherine. Smiling, she answered the question for him.

"I think Lord Meredith and I would prefer to go home, Auntie. Wouldn't you rather return to Langton Abbots than stay in Bath?'' she asked Jonathan. He laughed and gathered her close once more.

"Yes, I would, dear wife. You have discerned the longings of my inmost heart. There is nothing I would like better than to return to the Abbey and make you acquainted with your new home.'' His eyes sparkled. "I remember, months ago, that I invited you to come and see all the souvenirs I collected in India. You chose to ignore that invitation at the time, but now you have a second chance to accept it. Shall we proceed to the Abbey with all due speed?''

"Yes,'' said Catherine simply.

Aunt Rose looked from one to the other of them in amazement. "But surely you do not mean to drive to Devonshire tonight!'' she said. "On your wedding night?''

Her voice was scandalized. Catherine and Jonathan glanced at each other, then quickly looked away again. Both of them were experiencing difficulty in keeping their faces straight.

It was Catherine who spoke first. "I don't mind traveling on my wedding night if Lord Meredith doesn't,'' she said. "I should prefer to reach Langton Abbots as soon as possible. And if we start now, we might be there as early as tomorrow afternoon.''

She glanced again at Jonathan. He nodded solemnly. "Yes, it seems the most practical plan. I'll have my groom run round to the nearest posting house and get my carriage harnessed to four fast horses, while Catherine's maid throws a few things in a bag for her. The rest of her things can be sent down later.''

Aunt Rose threw up her hands. "Oh, very well! But I tell you plainly, I have never heard of such a way of being married. The two of you seem resolved to do everything as differently as possible from the rest of the world! I simply cannot understand either one of you."

"Yes, but we understand each other," said Jonathan, smiling at Catherine. "And that is the important thing."

Aunt Rose continued to grumble and shake her head as she gave the order for Catherine's things to be packed. Diana, however, whispered, *"I* think your wedding is the most romantic thing possible, Catherine. And I would not at all mind being married the same way, if it would bring me a bridegroom as handsome as Lord Meredith!"

Before long, Jonathan's groom appeared to announce that the carriage was at the door. Mr. Tompkins had already been sent home, with a handsome tip to recompense him for the trouble of coming out at night, and so it was only Agnes and Diana and Aunt Rose who saw the newlyweds off. "Oh, dear, oh, dear! I don't know how I shall go on without you, dear," said Aunt Rose, hugging her niece as though loath to give her up. "I can't think that we are really to be parted, after all these years. The Cottage will be so lonely without you."

"We shall not be so very much parted," said Catherine, giving her a hug in return. "Lord Meredith and I will be often in Langton Abbots, Auntie."

"That's true," admitted Aunt Rose. "But just at first I shall find it very hard, I am sure." She drew a deep sigh. "I declare, I'm minded to accept Mrs. Harlinger's invitation and accompany her and Diana to Brighton this winter. It would be a way of distracting my mind, if nothing else. Besides, I've always had a great fancy to see Brighton."

Catherine laughed. "Then I should accept Diana's mother's invitation by all means. Why, Auntie, what a traveler you are getting to be! First Bath, and now Brighton. Before long you'll be visiting India and China like Lord Meredith!"

Aunt Rose started to protest this idea, then stopped. "I

might!'' she said, an awestruck smile spreading across her face. "I just might, Catherine. Now I am started, there's no saying where it will end." She hugged Catherine again and bestowed a fervent kiss upon her. "And I owe it all to you. If it had not been for you, I never would have set foot out of Langton Abbots. It just goes to show how useful it is to be jolted out of one's routine once in a while. But you will see that Esther airs all the rooms and that the apples and pears are properly laid in while you are down in Langton Abbots, will you not? I could not embark on my travels with a clear conscience if I knew things were not being attended to at Willowdale Cottage.''

Catherine promised to see that the Cottage was properly maintained in her absence, and Aunt Rose let her go with a last, tearful embrace and a last outpouring of good wishes for the future. Agnes and Diana, too, showered good wishes upon her while weeping similar quantities of tears; so that it was a wonder the street was not too flooded to get the carriage through, as Jonathan remarked. But the postilions and horses were equal to the challenge, and soon the carriage was threading its way through the narrow streets of Bath, embarked on its long journey to Devonshire.

Jonathan, inside the carriage, leaned back against the upholstered squabs and eyed his wife in a considering way. "We managed that business neatly," he said. "I find myself agreeing with Agnes, by-the-by. There never was such a lovely bride as you, Catherine, whatever the shortcomings of the ceremony itself may have been."

"And I agree with Diana that there never was such a handsome bridegroom," returned Catherine, laughing. "And I refuse to admit that there were any shortcomings to our being married this way, Jonathan. Married! I cannot believe we really are married. No matter how I try, it still seems like a dream."

Jonathan nodded. "So it does to me. So it always will, I suspect, no matter how many years we are together." He took Catherine's hand in his. "You really don't mind, I hope, that we are not to have a wedding trip immediately? I promise to make it up to you, the moment the Abbey is in a condition to leave."

"Of course I don't mind," said Catherine, squeezing his hand. "What I told my aunt is perfectly true. All I want is to be with you, Jonathan. And in a way, it seems right that we should begin our married life in Langton Abbots. That's where everything began between us, and I think we ought to establish ourselves there before doing anything else, even though it may be difficult in some ways."

"Nothing will be difficult if I have you with me," said Jonathan. He raised her hand to his lips. "Let's see. Our first order of business shall be to impress the Langton Abbotsites with our new respectability. It will be only a surface respectability, I'm afraid, but they needn't know that." He smiled into Catherine's eyes "Then we will devote ourselves to getting the Abbey into proper shape. With you to help me, that shouldn't take long. And then, once those things are done, we may indulge ourselves with a proper wedding trip. What would you like to see first?"

Catherine shook her head, smiling. "I don't know, Jonathan. I have been so few places in my life. Almost anywhere would be new and exotic."

"We might travel to the Continent, to begin with," said Jonathan thoughtfully. "I've never been there myself, you know. What with the war with France and my own misbehavior, I was kept from making a proper Grand Tour. But the war will soon be over now, they say, and there are a great many places on the Continent worth seeing. France, and Germany, and Switzerland—and Greece, of course—"

"And Italy," suggested Catherine, all unsuspecting. "Don't forget Italy, Jonathan. Rome, and Venice, and Milan—I should like to see them all."

Jonathan gave her a penetrating look. "You don't have any other reason for wishing to visit Italy, I trust?" he asked.

"No, why should I?" asked Catherine in surprise. Understanding came to her an instant later, and she laughed. "Are you thinking of Angelo? I assure you that *I* wasn't. That is definitely a closed chapter in my life.'' She smiled at him. ''Any feelings I had for Angelo were over years and years ago. And even at the height of my infatuation, they never compared with the feelings I have for you.''

Jonathan nodded, looking rather shame-faced. ''Of course. I didn't mean to throw that episode up to you, Catherine. Only— Italian men have the reputation of being rather seductive, you know. I don't know if I like the thought of putting my very lovely wife in the way of temptation.''

Again Catherine laughed. ''It wouldn't be temptation, Jonathan. I assure you that I have entirely lost my taste for Italian men. I prefer Englishmen nowadays.'' She reached up to kiss his cheek.

Jonathan immediately caught her in his arms and pulled her into his lap. ''Oh, you do, do you?'' he said. ''Well, you will have to adduce more convincing proofs than that, my lady.''

Catherine obligingly adduced such additional proofs as she could think of, whereupon Jonathan adduced a few in return, causing Catherine to express a wish that they had remained in Bath overnight after all. ''Of course I am anxious to reach Devonshire, but we might have waited one night, I suppose.'' She threw him a teasing look. ''Indeed, I was surprised that you consented to spend our wedding night traveling, Jonathan. Earlier you had seemed more interested in—well, in other things!''

''So I was. So I am,'' said Jonathan. Pulling off her hat, he began to pluck the pins from her hair one by one in a purposeful manner. ''And with your consent, I shall proceed immediately to those other things now.''

''Oh, Jonathan!'' Catherine's eyes widened with incredulity and laughter. ''Could we? In a *carriage?*''

''I think we could,'' said Jonathan gravely. And he went on to prove to Catherine that in spite of a few small obstacles and inconveniences, the thing was not only possible but eminently enjoyable.

Afterwards, Catherine reclined across the banquette with her head in Jonathan's lap. "What a beautiful night this is," she said dreamily. The window shades, which had been discreetly drawn during the earlier part of the drive, were open now, and from where she lay, she could see the star-spangled expanse of the night sky. "A beautiful night," she repeated. "Look at the stars, Jonathan! They look close enough to touch."

"I would rather look at you," he responded. "Not only are you every bit as beautiful as the stars, you really are close enough to touch." But at Catherine's urging, he consented to look out the window and so was just in time to see a tiny light streak across the sky and then vanish into nothingness.

"A shooting star," said Catherine in an awed voice. "Jonathan, did you see it?"

Jonathan nodded. "Yes, I did. Amazing, isn't it? And a lucky portent if I ever saw one."

"Do you think so?" said Catherine, shifting her gaze to him. "Are shooting stars so very lucky, then?"

"The luckiest thing there is," said Jonathan solemnly. "For a newly married couple to see a shooting star on their wedding night means they are sure to enjoy a long lifetime of wedded bliss."

Catherine regarded him with skeptical golden-brown eyes. "Are you sure you didn't just make that up, Jonathan?" she said. "I never heard of that particular story before."

"I might have made it up," allowed Jonathan with a conscious smile. "But it sounds well, doesn't it?"

"Yes, very well indeed," agreed Catherine, returning his smile. "And what is more to the point, I don't see why it shouldn't turn out to be true."

"Nor do I," said Jonathan. They were both silent a moment, looking up at the stars once more. After a minute or two, Jonathan spoke again. "Come to think of it, I *have* heard of one superstition connected with shooting stars," he said. "A real superstition, I mean—not one of my own invention."

"Yes?" said Catherine, shifting her gaze to his face again. "What superstition is that?"

"That anyone seeing a shooting star is entitled to make a wish. According to my calculations, that should mean we have a wish each, Catherine. What do you wish for?"

Catherine smiled and shook her head. "I already have all my wishes, Jonathan," she said. A moment later she spoke in a dreamy voice. "Do you remember the night you caught me at the well at Honeywell House?"

"I am not likely to forget it anytime soon," said Jonathan, speaking with dry significance.

Catherine laughed and colored. "No, of course not. But you never knew what I was really doing there that night." She sat up in order to face Jonathan squarely. Her lips were still smiling, but her eyes now held a deeper and more serious light. "I was wishing that the well would show me a glimpse of the future that night, Jonathan. And what I saw was you—and now it has come about that I am here with you as my husband and the most wonderful future imaginable ahead of me. It's enough to make me believe there must be something in the powers of the well after all."

Jonathan leaned over to kiss her. "Then call me a believer, too," he said, "for it's certain that what the well gave me is all I could ever hope or desire."

"Do you think so?" said Catherine, smiling at him.

"I know so," said Jonathan, and kissed her once again.

Look for the second installment of the Wishing Well Trilogy
EMILY'S WISH
coming in November 2000.

Desperately fending off the advances of her late employer's nephew, Miss Emily Pearce fears she may have killed the man and flees into the night. Stumbling across the grounds of Honeywell House, she looks into the old wishing well—and is stunned to see the face of a handsome gentleman reflected back. No ghostly vision, it is Honeywell House's summer tenant, celebrated author Sir Terrence O'Reilly, who catches her as she faints into his arms! Drawn to this captivating beauty and her mystery, he offers her a position as his secretary. But as their passion blossoms, so does a merry chase of wits and wild hearts. For despite the unexpected arrival of his former fiancée, Sir Terrence's only desire is to convince Emily she is the true heroine of the greatest love story of all—their own.

ABOUT THE AUTHOR

Joy Reed lives with her family in Michigan. She is currently working on the second installment of her Wishing Well trilogy. Look for *Emily's Wish,* coming from Zebra Books in November 2000. Joy loves hearing from readers and you may write to her c/o Zebra Books. Please include a self-addressed, stamped envelope if you wish a reply.

BOOK YOUR PLACE ON OUR WEBSITE AND MAKE THE READING CONNECTION!

We've created a customized website just for our very special readers, where you can get the inside scoop on everything that's going on with Zebra, Pinnacle and Kensington books.

When you come online, you'll have the exciting opportunity to:

- View covers of upcoming books
- Read sample chapters
- Learn about our future publishing schedule (listed by publication month *and author*)
- Find out when your favorite authors will be visiting a city near you
- Search for and order backlist books from our online catalog
- Check out author bios and background information
- Send e-mail to your favorite authors
- Meet the Kensington staff online
- Join us in weekly chats with authors, readers and other guests
- Get writing guidelines
- AND MUCH MORE!

**Visit our website at
http://www.zebrabooks.com**

We're sure that you have enjoyed this BALLAD
romance novel and we hope that you are looking
forward to reading the other wonderful stories in this
series, as well as sampling many of the other exciting
BALLAD series.

As a matter of fact, we're so sure that you will love
BALLAD romances, that we are willing to guarantee
your reading pleasure. If you have not been satisfied,
we will refund the purchase price of this book to you.
Send in your proof-of-purchase (cash register receipt
with the item circled) along with the coupon below.
We will promptly send you a check.*